A SMALL WINDOW LET IN A SLIVER OF MOONLIGHT . . .

"Now we are totally alone," he said.

"You are a very determined man," she said.

"And you so beautiful, my lovely Rachel." His resonant voice was barely audible.

Warnings raced through Rachel's mind, something about lust was not love and Lord Abshire being a rakehell and having dishonorable intentions. But she could hardly remember with his lordship's warm breath against her cheek. She looked up into his solemn face.

"Don't kiss me," she ordered.

"Why not, Rachel? You want me to . . . I can tell."

"That's the prob—"

His lips smothered the rest of the word, and after that Rachel could not remember what she had wanted to say. Her lips quivered under his, and as the kiss deepened, a warmth began to wash over her. His wonderfully strong arms held her tighter still, and her own arm circled his neck and brought her to him to let her feel his desire.

She did not care about who she was or where she came from. She wanted the kiss to last forever.

A Touch of Merry

IRENE LOYD BLACK

ZEBRA BOOKS
KENSINGTON PUBLISHING CORP.

A Touch of Merry *is lovingly dedicated to my dear friend Jimmie Orene Moss, a Regency Lady of the Upper orders if I've ever known one. Thank you, Orene, for all your support in my writing, and for all the other nice things you have done for me over the past twenty five years. You are the greatest!*

ZEBRA BOOKS are published by

Kensington Publishing Corp.
850 Third Avenue
New York, NY 10022

First Printing: December, 1995

Printed in the United States of America

One

From the beginning, Rachel Storm's life had been shrouded in secrets. "Jumping lizards," she said one night when she was about ten to Mother Margaret, "If only someone would tell me I was left on the steps of this place, or under a pretty azalea bush, I would not question the exchanged looks between you and the other sisters every time I ask *how* come I'm at a home for abandoned children. I had to come from somewhere. Why all the secrecy? Who fathered me? I didn't hatch from an egg!" She raised an eyebrow. "Or did I?"

The good sister looked at Rachel pityingly and shook her head. "I've told you all I know, dear Rachel. You were brought to the Home during a raging storm. Sister Cecilia took you from a man in a black greatcoat, who put you into her arms, then turned quickly and dashed back out into the rain. She said you were wet and crying and looked to be no more than three days old."

The sister paused for a deep sigh. "As I've told you many times, that's all that Sister Cecilia told me. I was not allowed to ask questions. Mayhaps Mother Cecilia had made previous arrangements, but if that is so, I was never apprised of them. And she is gone now." She extinguished the taper and lay on her bed. "I suggest we go to sleep."

Sadness in Mother Margaret's voice stopped Rachel's interrogation. It was the same story she had been told since she was old enough to ask. Now, at seventeen and one half summers, she asked herself why she cared. But she did care. Very much. Soon she would be leaving the Home, with nothing more than Rachel Storm for a name; Storm because she'd been brought to the Home during a storm, Rachel because the good sisters had hoped she would grow up and be sweet, kind, and submissive, like the Biblical Rachel.

"At least you are kind," Mother Margaret had said, "but with your stubborn streak, you are anything but submissive."

Always a smile accompanied her words, as if she were proud of the way Rachel had developed under her strict guidance.

Rachel knew Mother Margaret had said all she would say. They were in the small bedchamber they shared, each in a narrow bed pushed against the wall. Moonlight cut a swath across the room, the only light. The raised window let in the cool October air and the night sounds: crickets rubbing their legs together, an owl's hooting, and the croaking of frogs.

Rachel stared through the gray darkness at the ceiling.

Most nights, after Mother Margaret's gentle snoring had begun, Rachel spent her time plotting a way to outwit the good sister and miss prayer time at the ungodly hour of five o'clock in the morning. This was a feat seldom accomplished.

But this night something more pressing than prayers was on Rachel Storm's mind. Christmas last she had vowed that by another Christmas she would have found her dear papa. Time was running out; Christmas 1819 was less than three months away.

No point in looking for her dear mama, Rachel reasoned, for surely she was dead and in heaven. No mama worth her salt would leave her child where prayers were said at first light.

Of course her papa would not have done this dreadful thing if he had had a choice. A man without a helpmeet simply could not bring up a daughter in the rightful way. And by no means would this virtuous man think of taking another wife, so grieved was he for his darling daughter's mother.

Such had been Rachel's thoughts and dreams for as long as she could remember,

Where did her dear papa live? Why had he chosen this particular orphanage? Did he reside nearby?

The Home was located at the northeastern edge of Bodwin Moor, near the hamlet of Bolventor. Once an abbey stood on this sacred ground, but it had been sacked by old King Henry VIII when he was having anything and everything destroyed that reeked of Papist. The present building had been built on the abbey's foundation, and the high wall, and of the same moorland granite, that surrounded the abbey still stood, closing the sinful world out. Never did a day go by that Mother Margaret did not quote from the Bible and set down another rule. Sin and temptation must needs be avoided at all costs.

Rachel turned to the wall. Sleep would not come. Sounds of Mother Margaret's snoring gurgled out into the room. Rachel raised herself onto her elbow and watched the tremble of the sainted woman's thin lips as she sucked in and then blew out big gulps of air. She covered her ears with her hands, which did no good, and then she flopped to her side, swore silently, and rolled onto the floor.

Very slowly and with great stealth she crawled toward Mother Margaret's black habit, which was draped across the foot of her bed. She only prayed when she desperately wanted something, and she desperately wanted the keys to Mother Margaret's office. This night she prayed the snoring would continue and smiled when her prayer was answered.

Lifting the habit with care, Rachel searched the pockets until at last her small fist closed tightly around the key chain that, during Mother Margaret's waking hours, was fastened to the waist of the black habit and could be heard jingling all the way down the long halls of the Home.

For a long moment, Rachel gripped the keys, sitting silently and feeling victorious. This was not the first time she had stolen the keys to search the office, but this time was the most important. This night she must find a name to attach to her dear papa.

In her pragmatic mind, Rachel knew blunt had been sent to

the Home by someone, for the sisters had been most generous with her, raising her apart from the other children and guarding her closely. That part was bad, for she was often lonely, but an excellent education had been provided: private tutors for lessons, a modiste to teach delicate sewing.

Rachel did not blame the sisters when she did not take to sewing. Patching was the best she could do. To sit a horse was more to her liking, and she liked taking dancing lessons from the caper merchant Mother Margaret had hired to come to the Home.

And always Rachel had slept in the room with Mother Margaret.

The other children at the orphanage thought her lucky. Rachel was not so sure. She had never been beyond the high stone wall without one of the sisters by her side, always cautioning her not to have sinful thoughts, not to look on things with envy, not to sin . . . not to sin. Which must be pretty wonderful, Rachel rationalized, else it would not occupy so much of the good sisters' thoughts.

Still holding the habit, Rachel listened as Mother Margaret let out a little moan, then sputtered as if a mosquito were buzzing her nose. Then, only seconds later, she turned to her other side and was soon snoring again.

Wearing only a thin nightdress, Rachel scooted on her bottom toward the door, which was always closed but never locked. Holding the keys tightly, she pushed herself up onto her knees and deftly turned the knob and pushed open the door just enough to squeeze her willow-slim body out into the dark hall. Only Mother Margaret's snoring invaded the quiet.

In anticipation of this night, Rachel had, the week before, secretly oiled the door hinges to keep them from creaking. And in anticipation of leaving the Home, she had put a few of her things in a cardboard box, tied it with twine, and slid it under her bed.

In the quietness, she now scrambled to her feet and began running as if the devil himself were after her, as soundlessly her bare feet hit the cobbled floor. The nightdress did little to shield her from the cold air that wafted through the hall.

Knowing every turn, she ran with lightning speed, stopping to catch her breath only when she was in the business wing of the building. Because she had been taught to do so, she crossed herself and thanked her Maker, though she was not sure that what she was doing was to her Maker's liking. For sure it would not meet with Mother Margaret's approval.

Rachel lit a candle and looked around the familiar, austere office. She had been here before, and the place was much the same as the last time she had visited: accounts of supplies brought in, accounts of supplies used.

A leather-bound book held names of priests who had visited the Home the past year, and following each name were glowing accolades of the good sisters' extraordinary devotion to caring for the precious abandoned children.

Rachel bristled at that. She was not a precious abandoned child. Without doubt her papa had planned to come for her, and since she was near grown and could look after herself, most likely that would be any day now.

But Rachel had no notion of waiting for his coming. Had she not been taught that God helped those who helped themselves? She slammed the ledger closed. She didn't care a fig about the priests' visits; she wanted the list of the donors. Holding the candle high, she searched for a door that would open to a hidden closet. It did not make sense to her that records of contributions were kept secret. Many times she had heard Mother Margaret and the other sisters talk of such contributions. And when the coffers were low, measures were taken, which meant supper consisted of bread and milk until things improved.

Religious symbols covered the walls, but there was no sign of a hidden door. Unless it was behind the one skinny cabinet that rested against the north wall. Placing the candle on the desk, she pushed against the cabinet with all her might. At first, nothing, and then it began to move, teetering and threatening to tumble to the floor. She settled it in time and almost let out a whoop. Behind it was a door available only by crawling on one's knees. Her pounding heart felt that it would burst as she sank to the floor. A huge lock dangled from a chain that held the door closed.

Rachel tried every key on Mother Margaret's chain with no luck. She started over again, this time steadying her hand by sheer determination. Finally the lock surrendered, and a loud click penetrated the silence. Pushing the door open, she stared into utter darkness.

There was nothing to it, she thought, and returned for the lighted taper and then carefully crawled through the small door. Inside the closet, she held the taper high. Her mouth flew open. It would take all night to go through all the ledgers stacked before her. Some were gray with mold

Her quick mind told her what to do. She would only go back seventeen and one-half years. That would be when contributions for her had begun. Chills raced up and down her spine. This was the closest she had come to putting a name to her dear papa, and she scolded herself for not thinking of it sooner. She knew what he looked like, and now she would have his name.

"Of course I took his features," she said aloud, "the same thick black hair and violet-blue eyes. But since he's a man, he won't have a widow's peak. The sisters had said her widow's peak added to her beauty, but Rachel had her doubts about that.

Most likely her dear papa would have an aquiline and aristocratic nose, she thought, and he would be exceptionally tall, and his complexion would be sun-browned from riding his black stallion on hunts and huge estates.

And he would be handsome beyond bearing.

Rachel's nose was small, her skin looked like warm milk, and she was only five feet three. But girls were supposed to be smaller, she reasoned.

It was so much fun to dream of her dear papa, but she must needs get back to the business at hand.

The first ledger she examined, dated 1801, her birth year, gave a clue she was so desperately seeking; one hundred pounds from a Lord Fox Talbert. Encouraged, she worked as fast as she could, not bothering to put the books back in the order in which they had been filed. Each ledger after the year of her birth had the same entry. Tears flooded her eyes as she held the last ledger to her heart and hugged it as if it could feel the pounding in her chest. Lord Fox Talbert was her dear papa; that was the whole of it.

Rachel had not been cognizant of the time passing so swiftly, and she was not aware she had company until she felt a presence. Looking up, she saw just inside the small opening a crouched figure wearing a black habit and a white sleeping cap.

"Mother Margaret," she exclaimed.

The old woman smiled. "Yes, Rachel, 'tis Mother Margaret, and I'm wondering what you are doing in this place, which I am sure you know is off limits to anyone except the sisters of the Home."

"Why so?" Rachel asked. It was not her intent to let the good sister know of her wonderful discovery.

"What are you looking for, Rachel? Why are the ledgers of such interest to you that you would disobey a rule laid down by those in authority?"

" 'Tis a stupid rule," countered Rachel. "Every human being has the right to know who his or her papa is."

"And did you think the ledgers would tell you?"

"I thought there might be a clue, that I might know his name should I see it. Or that mayhap the Higher Power would intervene and let me know when my gaze bore down on a certain name."

Mother Margaret laughed. "When did you start communing with a Higher Power. If I remember correctly, you've objected strenuously to saying your morning prayers . . . every day of your life."

"That's just it. Every day of my life I've been here, with no clue as to who I am. I don't see why you who are in authority have to be so secretive. I'm sure my lineage is nothing to be ashamed of. I'm sure my dear papa is an honorable man."

Mother Margaret looked at her charge of the past seventeen and one-half years, loving her more than anything, except the church, of course. Even in the dim lighting the young, innocent girl's eyes, rimmed with those extraordinary long black lashes, shone like a bottomless pool of violet-blue water, and the thin nightdress could not hide the brown nipples of her budding bosom.

She's nearing womanhood and I hadn't noticed.

Tears filled Mother Margaret's eyes. She said to herself, *How lucky I've been to have her. She's the only daughter I will ever know.* Taking a deep breath, she reached out a hand to Rachel. "Come, let's go back to bed. Five o'clock will come quickly."

Rachel refused to budge. "I notice in these ledgers the Prince Regent makes regular contributions to the Home, as do many Lords this and Lords that, even the Duke of Wellington. Is this a dumping ground for the upper-orders' bastards?"

Mother Margaret gasped audibly, and Rachel, even though she could not see clearly, thought her protector looked as if she might have a spell of the vapors.

"I'm totally shocked you even know such a word, Rachel. I've tried hard to bring you up to be a lady of the first water."

"I know. You've shielded me from the world, even had me sleep in the same room with you, but I do read, Mother Margaret, and I do use my mind. Now, that we've broached this subject, I have something else to ask you."

"I fear to grant permission, but I will. Pray, do not make it too worldly."

"Are you my mother?"

There was no doubt this time, even the dim lighting could

not hide the paleness of Mother Margaret's face as the blood drained downward. Her turkey gobble was as red as a cock's comb.

For a moment Rachel thought she had hit on the truth, and she was frightened. She did not want it to be so. Not that Mother Margaret would not be a wonderful mother, but she did not want to believe the good sister deceitful.

After waiting what seemed an interminably long time without an answer, Rachel asked, "Well, are you going to answer me?"

"I am in total shock, Rachel. You know I am a Bride of the Church. How could I be your mother?"

Rachel's resolve melted. She wouldn't hurt the old woman for anything. "I didn't really believe that, Mother Margaret. Sometimes these things just come out of my mouth. When I was small, I wondered why I did not sleep in the big room with the other children."

"Oh, that's an easy one to answer. You were so mischievous, and the other children followed your lead. It just seemed easier if I kept you with me."

Rachel laughed. "It hasn't been all bad. God's truth, Mother Margaret, it made me feel special. I guess my wont was to shock you with that stupid question. And I thought mayhap in that state you would tell me the whole of where I came from. Who left me in your care, never returning to visit?"

Rachel could not stop the sob that pushed up from her throat. It was the first time she had ever put into words the emptiness wrought by never having had a visitor. She did not want Mother Margaret to know; she did not want to think on it herself. Her fanciful dreams were much better.

Rachel looked at the ledger for a long moment before placing it back on the shelf, and then she said, "I'm ready to go back to bed. I beg your forgiveness for disturbing your sleep."

The old woman stood and opened her arms, and there in the dimly lit closet, for the first time ever, she hugged Rachel tightly, saying in a strained voice, "I wish I could tell you what you want to know, dearest Rachel, but I've told you all that was told to me."

Rachel believed her, and she knew what she had to do.

Together, they returned to their small bedchamber, and when the snoring began again, she slipped from her bed and went to a small table that held paper and quill, and in flowing script wrote:

Dear Mother Margaret:

I pray you do not think I am unappreciative of all you have done for me, but I cannot stand one minute longer not seeing my dear papa, who, I am sure, is in London.

Don't worry, Mother Margaret, I promise I will not sin, when and if I learn what sin is all about. But I will not promise to leave my bed every morning before first light to say prayers. I will leave that to you, for you are such a good person that I'm certain God hears every word you say. I'm not sure abut His listening to me. Most likely he would tell me to turn around and come back to the Home, and that I cannot do.

Love, Rachel Storm

Addition: I took fifty pounds from the poor box. Pray, do not consider it stealing, for no one is poorer than I, and I promise to repay tenfold when I find my dear papa."

Mother Margaret held the missive in her liver-spotted hands. Her shoulders shook and tears ran down her wrinkled cheeks and dripped off her chin. She must needs not cry, she told herself, for had she not seen this coming?

But I would not face the truth. I just went on pretending Rachel would always be with me.

The sister infinitely regretted not explaining to Rachel about procreation. The poor child out in this wicked world. What would happen to her?

"I intended to tell her, but I thought there was more time," she explained to the dreadfully silent room. She looked at Rachel's empty bed and tears, of their own volition, started again. She stopped them by sheer willpower, straightened her puckered face, and went to kneel before the altar in the corner of the room. Pray . . . that was what she would do. Her precious Rachel would need all the help the Lord could spare to survive in wicked London.

Two

Rachel could not believe how easy it had been for her to steal away from the orphanage. After writing the missive, she had simply pulled from under her bed the cardboard box in which she had packed her few belongings the day before, changed from her nightdress to her best day dress, a faded blue-sprigged muslin, and then donned her too-short coat and slipped away. She carried her half-boots until she was safe from waking Mother Margaret.

As she left the long hall through a side door and walked out into the night, the place was as quiet as death. The air was brisk. Her coat came halfway between her boot tops and her knees. Three years ago it had fit nicely. She wore a white bonnet that tied under her chin.

Only rarely did the children at the orphanage get new clothes, and even though she was the favored one, it was no different for her. Always her clothes were castoffs from people as far away as London. Rachel was thankful for the concerned people's kindness, and she was just as thankful that soon her dear papa would be buying her clothes, mayhap even have a modiste make them, if he was of the nobility.

His being of the nobility did not matter to Rachel, as long as he would reach out and draw her to his thick, broad chest and pat her hair and say how glad he was to at last see his darling daughter. This was her favorite dream.

By cutting across a field of freshly turned ground, made ready for planting come spring, she figured it would be two kilometers into Bolventor, where she would catch a public conveyance into London, two days travel away. The moon, a beautiful round orb in a blue velvet sky, poured its light onto the brown earth. She kicked a huge clod and laughed when she saw a rabbit skitter across the plowed ground. Night sounds pierced the thick quiet, and the country air was sweet and fresh. Smiling, she lifted her small chin and sucked in a deep breath. Never had she felt such freedom. She began to sing.

Since she had never heard a "worldly" song, she sang a church hymn, and in her mind's eye, she could see Mother Margaret's wrinkled face emoting the joy of saving grace when she knelt at the small altar in the corner of their bedchamber, in supplication to her Maker.

"After I find Papa, I shall write and ask Mother Margaret's forgiveness for being so wicked," Rachel said aloud. She looked up and marveled at the openness that surrounded her. Soon the sun would climb up over the distant hillock. She removed her bonnet and twirled it with her right hand, while singing another hymn. The sound seemed to echo from all the big, open world as she hopped and skipped and laughed. Only once did she look back toward the Home to see if she were being followed.

In Bolventor, she went straight away to Coverack Street, where she learned that the next public transport would be leaving shortly. She purchased her fare from the blunt she had taken from the poor box and sat down and leaned against the building to wait, stretching her legs out in front of her. A tattered little boy came by, begging. She gave him a shilling and savored his big smile, and then she watched as he went inside a sweetshop. When he emerged, he was wolfing down a large hunk of bread.

Realizing she was hungry, Rachel carried her cardboard box into the shop and bought a sweet tart for herself. She craved two but thought it unwise to spend the money.

Returning to wait for the coach, she sat in the same place she had left and ate slowly so the good taste of the sweet tart would remain in her mouth for a longer time. She watched as the small village began to come alive, people going into the places of business, carriages vying for space on the cobbled streets. Through framed windows, she could see flickering candles.

For a short while Rachel watched, and then, as time passed, she began to worry that someone from the orphanage would come and take her back, maybe accuse her of stealing from the poor box. At last a coach and four pulled to a stop and the driver on the box called for passengers.

With alacrity, she scrambled to her feet. No one let down the step, but a young man inside the coach extended his hand. Holding her cardboard box tightly, she climbed in to sit opposite him on a faded squab. "Thank you," she said, giving him a smile

"I'm going into Town to visit an aunt and mayhap find work while I'm there," he told her, his voice full of hope.

"I, too, am looking for something," Rachel said.

"You're a mighty pretty gel," he told her, and after that, when Rachel did not answer, he became silent and offered only an occasional smile.

Rachel thought him nice enough looking, most especially his smile, but Mother Margaret had repeatedly warned her against talking to strangers. She looked out the window at the countryside to discourage further conversation, and then the coach stopped for two more passengers. There was no chance to talk after that. She listened with interest as the new passengers discussed the Prince Regent's attempt to divorce his wife, Caroline of Brunswick, each having his own opinion on what Parliament should do about the disgraceful situation. Later, more passengers were taken, and everyone was talking at once.

Rachel dozed off and did not awaken until the coach came to an abrupt stop at a posting inn. "No more than ten minutes," the driver was saying.

Afraid she would lose her place, Rachel remained in her seat, and when passengers spilled out of the inn, some still chewing their food, she reckoned that she had made a wise decision. She had never seen the like, people shoving and scolding each other. A fat man gained the seat beside her, and after that, passengers began climbing atop the coach. Their feet dangled down over the windows.

The sound of the whip cracking the air over the horses' backs pierced the air, and immediately they were off to a fine gallop. Hearing squealing, Rachel asked the fat man how the passengers riding atop kept from falling off.

"There's straps to hold on to," he said, and then he placed a hairy hand on her knee.

As if Mother Margaret were speaking through her, she said, "I'll thank you to keep your hands to yourself." She knocked at his hand with a hefty swat and watched as his face turned red, and then purple.

"A man's got a right—"

"No, he hasn't," Rachel said before he could finish, and then she scolded, "You should be horsewhipped."

This brought laughter from the other passengers, but there were no more hairy hands on Rachel's knee. She listened to the conversation between the young man who had helped her into the coach and another passenger. The young man had returned from fighting in the Napoleonic war and was quite loquacious about his experiences, which Rachel found interesting.

A woman who had come aboard at the inn and was sitting on the opposite squab from Rachel leaned toward her and said, "My dear, how do you get your hair *that* black? It reminds me of wet coal. And pray, remove that dreadful white bonnet so that it can show."

Rachel answered quickly, without thinking, "I don't dye my hair, if that's what you mean. I got it from my dear papa. His hair is black like mine." She did not remove her bonnet.

The rouged woman laughed. "He must be one handsome Buck. Could I beg for an introduction?"

"He's taken," Rachel told her.

The woman gave another little laugh. "No man is taken forever, my dear. But of course you will learn that when you are older. How many summers have you seen? Twelve? That's entirely too young to be going to London alone."

Rachel felt herself bristle. "I'm seventeen and one half."

"You don't look it. Who is your father? He should be too smart to let you travel alone . . . at your age. Whatever it is. You appear to be a child."

" 'Tis plain you don't believe me," Rachel said, "but if you must needs know, my papa is Lord Fox Talbert."

Another laugh. "Yeah, and I'm going to see the Prince Regent. This night I'm to dine at Carlton House."

"I think that's wonderful," Rachel said, in a very conciliatory tone, not believing a word the woman was saying. They did not converse further.

What was the use, thought Rachel, and she resolved to be more discreet about her purpose in going into London. She would only tell someone she could trust wholeheartedly. She did ask the young man fresh from the war where he would go in Town if he wanted to see the most people. He smiled and said, "There's always a crowd at the Covent Gardens, miss. Good luck."

"Thank you," Rachel answered.

That night they stayed at a posting inn called The Golden Cow, Rachel slept on a pallet in a room with three older women, paying a shilling for her space. She slept well and felt rested when they left at first light the next morning.

The day seemed interminably long, the coach stopped for respites of no more than ten minutes, and then they were off again, arriving in London, at the Swan with Two Necks, late day.

Rachel did not tarry and immediately set out to find the Covent Pleasure Gardens, asking directions along the way. Before long, she became weary, and she suddenly felt lonely, and the cardboard box seemed to weigh mere than she did. People she met stared at her and smiled. She asked a gentleman in a top hat how far it was to the Covent Gardens.

"A great distance," he answered, then quickly moved on.

Rachel found a stoop and sat down to rest. She dozed off and was awakened by a woman screeching at her from an open window, "Get off my stoop, yer little tramp, and stay off."

Rachel did as she was told, clasping her box solidly to her side and walking as fast as she could. Soon she found herself in the midst of a crowd leaving a theater. Immediately she became alert and looked into every gentleman's face. She saw no one who favored the image her mind held of her dear papa. The women were dressed to the nines, bosoms showing disgracefully, mantles, some trimmed in fur, around their shoulders. Rachel became more aware of what she was wearing. *Her* dress buttoned to her neck. She removed her bonnet and let her thick black hair fall loose onto her shoulders. Then, turning away, she walked until she saw a sign that read, "Rooms for let."

"Twill be five shillings," the man behind a desk said when she asked how much it would cost to stay the night. That was far too much, weary though she was. She turned to leave.

" 'Tis late," the man said, "the room will just stay empty. Yer can have a cot in this small room for one shilling, though I never do such a thing. Yer look so mighty tired."

"I am, sir," said Rachel. "And I'll forever be grateful."

She paid the shilling and quickly entered the room and closed the door, securing it with a chain lock. There was a cot, as the man had said, and a spindle-legged table that held a chipped porcelain pan and an ewer of cold water.

A chamber pot, covered with a dingy cloth, was in plain sight. After using it, Rachel replaced the cloth and slid it under the cot. The room was so small she could barely turn around, but it seemed heavenly to her. She spent a moment or so on her knees, giving thanks. After which, still wearing her good dress and too-short coat and half-boots, she tumbled into bed, and hardly before her head touched the knotty pillow, she was asleep, dreaming dreams of dear Papa, handsome and smiling and loving.

A loud pounding on the door awakened Rachel. The voice was not from the kind man of last night. "Are yer going to sleep all day," he shouted. " 'Tis past noon. The charwoman wants to git the room ready fer tonight."

Rachel sat up like a bolt. The room was dimly dark, for there was no window to let in the day's light. "I'm sorry, sir," she called to the door pounder. "I'll be out shortly."

Quickly she poured water into the pan, stripped, and with a rag she supposed was to be used for washing, she scrubbed every inch of her body, using a bar of homemade soap she found with the rag.

Humming "Rock of Ages," she dried with a dingy towel, after which she pulled clean pantalettes over her slim hips and donned the same dress she had slept in, brushing away the wrinkles with her hands. She felt wonderful, and hungry. She would spend a shilling or two for hot tea and buttered bread and then be on her way to Covent Gardens. The night's rest had rejuvenated her, and once again she was charged with hope.

The room did not hold a looking glass, but she brushed her hair the usual one hundred strokes and tied it back with a riband, then pushed her white bonnet into her cardboard box.

Outside the room, Rachel smiled at the man who had shouted at her. "Thank you for waking me. I had no notion it was past noon. I must needs have been very tired."

He was a young man, and his eyes lit up when he saw Rachel was a girl, and a pretty one at that, so the look indicated. She did not like his smile.

"Usually thet room serves a man," he said. "Never seen yer kind here. Yer as purty as a June peach. Yer want breakfast? Porridge in the kitchen, if cook ain't poured it out. If yer ain't got the blunt—"

She cut his words short and crossed her fingers behind her back for the lie she was about to tell. "No, I'm not hungry."

Instinct told her it was time to leave, which she did, quickly, laboriously making her way up the cobbled street in the direction she had been walking when she had stopped at the inn. Her steps were quick and lively, and soon she came to a sweet-shop. She went in and ordered tea and bread, just as she had planned, savoring every bite before asking again how to find Covent Pleasure Gardens.

"No more than two kilometers," the woman who had served her said. She stared at Rachel, and Rachel could have sworn that pity spilled from the woman's eyes.

"Thank you," Rachel said.

With hurried steps, she was in no time at all, so it seemed, in a crowd of people darting about, some selling wares, others doing acrobatic stunts and looking anxiously to the audience for a shilling or so. Young girls pushed flower carts, and cheaply dressed girls, some only slightly older than the flower girls, brazenly rubbed against bleary-eyed men who looked as if they had been drinking blue ruin all night Not that Rachel knew about blue ruin, only what she'd overheard the sisters saying.

Papa wouldn't be in a place like this, thought Rachel, and it was all she could do to keep from crying. The young man on the coach had been right; there were people here, hordes of them, but no one who remotely resembled her papa. But not one to easily give up, she searched every face. Mayhap one would resemble hers. But after a while, she lost hope and darted into an alley and sat down. It was her only chance to sit and not be stepped on. She must needs think on what to do.

A man and a heavily rouged woman passed her, laughing and clinging to each other. After they had disappeared around a corner, an eerie quiet settled over the alley, and she held the cardboard box closer to her.

Rachel did not hear the footsteps; she only felt the box

jerked from her hands, and then she saw the culprit, a young lad running as if Satan were chasing him. She was instantly on her feet and running and screaming at the top of her lungs for someone, anyone, to stop him. No one did, as he slithered like a snake through the milling crowd.

Rachel did have a slight advantage, her hands were empty, and the boy's red hair shone like a beacon. So she gained on the thief, but it was a man wearing a black beaver and a black greatcoat came to her aid. He stepped in the fleeing boy's path, and he was repaid by a sting of swear words and a hefty kick on the shin.

Rachel dove for the attacker, taking him to the ground, and, after regaining her box, she sat on the screaming, squirming lad, while pedestrians walked around them. The man who had saved her box moved away with the crowd. She regretted this; she wanted to thank him.

"Let me up, you wench," the thief screamed at Rachel.

"Not until you say you are sorry you tried to steal the only thing in this world that belongs to me. Do you not know 'tis wrong to steal? That's one of the ten commandments of the Good Book."

"I ain't never read no good book," he retorted, "and if you don't let me up, I'm gonna pinch yer arse."

" 'Tis a good thing you are not at the Home. Mother Margaret would wash your mouth out with soap."

"Look, lady, I don' know nothin' about no Mother Margaret, or a good book, like I told yer. I just want up. I'm hungry. Is there food in yer box?"

Rachel looked at the pitiful, half-starved boy and tears flooded her eyes. His arms were the size of bird's legs, and his pale eyes were too large for their sunken sockets. Only his red hair, and his smile, looked alive. She knew, and she did not know how she knew, she could trust him. Nonetheless, she extracted a promise from him that he would not steal her box from her—it held only girl's clothes anyway—should she turn him loose.

"I have a little blunt hidden away on my person," she said, "I will buy you something to eat."

"Lady, do yer have windmills fer brains? You buy someone like me, a thief, food? Soon yer won't have food yerself."

Rachel relinquished her hold on the boy and stood, then helped him to his feet. "What you say is true, but I can't eat, knowing you are hungry. What's your name?"

"Napoleon," said the boy, grinning wryly.

"Oh, the little giant. You don't look much like a giant to me. You look as if you can stand several good meals."

"I'm telling you lady, it would be better fer yer if yer helped me steal. I don't want to take yer blunt, for I bet yer don't have enough to survive five days in this place."

"Oh, but I won't be here five days. I just came to London to look for my papa."

"When's the last time yer seen him?"

"Never. I've never seen him, and it was just recently that I learned his name."

Napoleon let out a low whistle: I knowed I wuz right, yer do have windmills fer brains."

They had moved away from the crowd, walking together, Rachel holding Napoleon's hand. She carried her cardboard box under her other arm, clasped tightly. Looking down at the little boy, she smiled. She wanted him to smile, to look alive.

He obliged, and for the first time since leaving the Home, Rachel did not feel lonely. They came to a vender peddling bread sticks and fried fish wrapped in newspaper. She bought three shillings worth, and then they ducked into another alley and sat down and ate. They spoke hardly at all until the last bite of the fish was gone and their fingers were licked clean of the fat.

And then Rachel told Napoleon her story.

"Do yer mean they named yer Storm because you wuz delivered to the Home when a storm was blowing." He laughed then, and it was a glorious sound to Rachel. She looked into his face again and thought how thin it was. His red freckles ran together across his small nose. "That's right, Napoleon, and I'm wondering where you got the name Napoleon."

"From my pap, but he's dead. Died of consumption. And I never knowed my mam."

"You poor little thing—"

"Oh, no. Don' yer go feeling sorry fer me. I got a good life. Most days I eat two times. Today, if yer'd not caught me, I'd done good. I'd sold yer clothes." He shot her his wry grin.

"Well, I made it up to you by sharing my fish and bread with you," Rachel said. "Where do you sleep?"

"I got a place . . . when I manage to git a shilling or two extra. And when I don't, I sleep in an alley like this, or someone's stoop. There be lots of places."

It was growing late. A gray dimness hovered over the alley. Rachel went to look out into the street; lamplighters were lighting the lamps, and Charlies, which she had read about, were leaving their boxes to call out the time, and the weather.

A saddened Rachel mused that it would be impossible to find Lord Fox Talbert in that crowd, no matter how hard she looked. She had begun to doubt she ever would, by just looking for someone with black hair and blue eyes who resembled her. Mayhap it had been a stupid dream.

"Oh, no," said Napoleon when she mentioned it to him. "No dream's stupid. " 'Tis when yer stop dreaming that yer stupid. What did yer say his name wuz? And he's of the nobility? Lady, mayhap you do have windmills fer brains."

"Lord Fox Talbert," Rachel answered, hardly able to stop the tears from starting. And Napoleon must needs have heard the tremor in her voice, she thought, for he quickly scrambled to his feet and told her that on the morrow they would go to the House of Lords and ask for the gentleman and tell him his long-lost daughter had come to see him.

"Yer'll see," he said, "as long as yer hope, yer'll be all right." He reached out and patted her hand.

Rachel did feel better, and she suddenly had an urgent feeling they should vacate the alley. "Let's get out of here, Napoleon, and find a place to sleep. I'm afraid someone will come in here and take my box."

"Mayhap they did teach yer something at that Home. I wuz thinkin' the same thing meself, only I wuz thinkin' they might take something more precious than yer box. Yer. Yer being so pretty and all."

Rachel took his small hands in hers. They left the alley and went to sleep where Napoleon slept . . . when he had had a good day . . . on a dirty quilt on a dirty floor with lots of other thieves, none older than Napoleon. She thought about the Home, and she thanked God for it. But that was not the last thing on Rachel Storm's mind when she at last fell asleep. She looked into the darkness and thought about how surprised her dear papa would be when she found him. Of course at first she would not identify herself; she would wait for him to recognize her . . .

Three

The next morning Rachel and her new friend set out to find the House of Lords. It seemed that the little ragamuffin knew everything about everything. As they walked, and not too fast, for he said it was a "fur distance," he told her about the madness that had overtaken King George III, so bad that he could not rule and they had made his son, George Augustus, Prince Regent. "And the Regent wants to make London beautiful, and he keeps spending the people's money on building. Like where he lives, Carlton House. A man by the name of Holland did that."

Rachel studied Napoleon's little face. When he spoke about building there was almost a reverence in his voice. She had read about the Prince Regent's interest in architecture, but how had Napoleon learned so much? "How do you know all this?" she asked. "Were you funning when you said you couldn't read?"

"Nah, I can't read. I listen . . . when I'm not stealing."

He talks about stealing as if it were a profession, thought Rachel, and then she told him, "Napoleon, I will teach you to read, if you will stay with me until I find Papa. I'll ask him to hire you."

Napoleon laughed his glorious laugh again. "Doing what? Stealing?"

"Of course not, peagoose. Stealing's not an honorable profession. I'm sure there's something you can do for his lordship."

"Well, we have to find this Lord Fox first. Are yer sure his name is Fox?"

"Absolutely. Every month Lord Fox Talbert made a donation

of one hundred pounds to the Home, starting seventeen and a half years ago. I'm seventeen and a half."

Napoleon shook his head, but did not argue with Rachel's reasoning. When walking past Carlton House, he gave minute details about the building, speaking of the Ionic screen that was added in 1809 by Henry Holland. He didn't stop talking about it even when they came to St. James's Park.

"You love buildings, don't you, Napoleon?" Rachel said conversationally.

"I do. I can't read, but I can draw, and if I had a piece of paper and a quill I would show you."

"Wait a minute," Rachel said. She put her box down on the grass, reached under her folded clothes, and pulled out a piece of thick wrapping paper and a small lump of black coal. " 'Tis all I have, but you can use it to draw."

The lad with flaming red hair, whose freckles bunched up across his nose, sat down on a grassy slope above the path.

Rachel joined him and was silent so as not to intrude upon his thoughts. Park visitors looked, and grinned. Some even laughed, and she knew they were laughing at the way she and Napoleon were dressed. A hot flash of anger sent blood boiling through her veins.

They, she and Napoleon, were wearing the best clothes they had. Her dress was faded from too many washings, and it was too tight across her developing bosom. But there was no help for it. What used to be round knobs were growing by leaps and bounds and pushing against every dress she owned, and all she could do was push and tug to make sure white flesh did not show. Mother Margaret had shown her how to tuck a handkerchief above the neckline, or better yet, she wore dresses that buttoned to the throat, like the one she was wearing now.

So what if Napoleon looks like a ragamuffin, she thought, giving him a warm smile he did not see. His attention was devoted entirely to his drawing.

Two Quality ladies stopped to stare at Rachel and Napoleon. They wore fresh, absolutely beautiful walking dresses, and, even though the trees along the paths afforded shade, they carried matching parasols. When Rachel gave them a friendly smile, they laughed behind pretty white hands.

At last Napoleon handed the drawing to Rachel. She gasped. It was an exact replica of the building they had passed minutes back. "Napoleon, this is wonderful," she exclaimed.

"Me pap said it wuz a gift," the little boy said with not a little pride in his voice.

"Well, we must needs do something about that. A talent like yours should not be wasted. I'll speak to my papa."

Napoleon squinted his eyes up at her. "Lady, don't go gittin' big notions about me studying with nobody. 'Tis bad enough for yer to believe Lord Fox . . . whatever his name is, is your pap."

"But Napoleon, you told me not to stop dreaming. What about you? Should you not have a dream?"

"Fustian! Yer must needs dream reasonable. That way yer ain't hert . . . like the way yer gonna be hert when yer learn Lord Fox Talbert ain't yer pap,"

Rachel was indignant. "Well, how do you know that? And I will tell you something, Napoleon, if I had not dreamed, I would've never left the Home. I want so much to know who I am, and Mother Margaret couldn't tell me."

Tears brimmed Rachel's eyes, and her voice broke. She turned her head away, so as not to make Napoleon sad. "I just want you to hope with me. I can't go through life with Storm for a name, especially knowing it's not my real name."

He reached to touch her arm with his thin little hand. "Ah, Rachel, I'll hope with yer. And we'd better be gettin' started if we're to find the House of Lords this day. This Lord Fox just might be there, and yer won't have to wait to see yer pap." His voice rose, then dropped to near whispering, "It jest might happen, Rachel."

"See there. You decided to hope with me, and already you are happier," Rachel told him, and they were off again, their steps lighter and faster.

When they were out of the park, Rachel kept her eye out for a pub. She could not stand to look at Napoleon's thin little limbs, and she was determined to feed him a square meal. That way she would he using the blunt from the poor box for exactly the same thing Mother Margaret would have used it, to feed the hungry.

They met a vendor, but he only offered bread and meat. That was not enough, Rachel decided. Napoleon needed vegetables, and mayhap a pudding. Surreptitiously she reached into her bosom and withdrew a sovereign and put it in her pocket. Of course it would not take the whole of it to feed them, but a good meal they would have.

It was not long before they came to a little hole in the wall from which the smell of hot food wafted into the street. Rachel stopped. "I'm hungry, and I know you are, Napoleon. I think we should eat."

Before he could answer, she took his hand and pushed the door open. Inside, men were sitting in little groups, their heads bent over platters of steaming food. Rachel's mouth began to water as she watched. They did not take notice of her and Napoleon until a grizzly-looking man, wearing a cook's cap, stormed out of the kitchen, yelling, "Git out! Git out! Beggars ain't allowed."

Rachel grabbed Napoleon just as he lunged at the man. "The demme jackanapes," the little boy said as he strained against Rachel's hold.

Rachel shushed him; then, straightening to her full five foot three, she raised her small chin and looked the grizzly man straight in the eye. "We are not beggars. I have money to pay."

She held out her hand with the sovereign in the palm but closed her hand quickly when the cook grabbed for the money. "I beg yer forgiveness." He gave a toothless grin. "Me name's Bradford, and we here will be happy to serve yer." Again, he reached out to take the sovereign.

"Not until we're served," Rachel said. She looked at a half-empty plate in front of a man who had stopped eating and was watching the exchange. "We want two plates of whatever you served him, and for the same price he paid you."

The cook grunted and left. Silence ensued, and Rachel could feel every eye in the room bearing down on her as she found a table in a corner and pushed Napoleon into a chair. When two platters of hot food were placed before them, laughter roiled up from the diners. One said, "Bested by a gel, eh, Bradford."

"I'll serve anyone who has money to pay," he retorted defensively.

Rachel had thought she would eat sparingly, letting Napoleon have the larger share, but when she saw him ladling boiled cabbage, stewed kidneys, and roast beef into his mouth, she began doing the same. Neither spoke until Napoleon belched, rather loudly, and Rachel stopped eating long enough to tell him he must learn good manners.

Pushing back from the table, he said, "We must needs get goin' if'n we can walk after stuffing our bellies."

Rachel laughed and called goodbye to Bradford, and then they left, their spirits high. The box even seemed lighter to Rachel, and she did not care a whit when Ladies of Quality—with their abigail following three steps behind them—looked down their noses and laughed when Rachel asked directions to the House of Lords. Tittering from behind her hand, one said, "You mean the House of Commons, do you not?"

"No, we are in need of seeing someone who is serving in the House of Lords, my dear papa," answered Rachel, and she and Napoleon walked on, leaving behind a gale of laughter.

At last a kind man they asked for directions pointed to a huddle of Gothic buildings. "The chamber you are looking for runs in a right angle to Westminster Hall."

Rachel thanked him, and they walked on. Signs led them to two huge double doors, on which Rachel pounded until a man in high livery opened up to them. "Yes?" he said. Looking through his quizzing glass, his gaze traversed the callers from head to toe.

Rachel, looking beyond him, saw an empty chamber lit by

candles in a chandelier hanging above a Speaker's chair and a green baize table bearing the Mace, all of which she had read about. Her heart sank to the pit of her stomach. She had so hoped to see Lord Talbert. "We have business with Lord Fox Talbert," she told the plainly astonished man. She assumed that he was a guard at this august establishment.

"I see. And what might that business be?"

" 'Tis personal," Rachel answered quickly. "But his lordship will be most happy to see me . . . us."

"I'm not so sure of that, but since you are of his constituency, I will tell you that his lordship left rather hurriedly this afternoon . . . it seems the nanny for their young son left without notice. So most likely you will find Lord Talbert at his home, although he did not say that he would be going there."

"Where's that?" Rachel asked.

"Near Blanchland, Northumberland, in northeast England. Talbert Hall is well known."

He closed the door before Rachel could ask how far this place was from London, but Napoleon told her there was nothing to it, they would simply ask the driver when they acquired public transport. He added, "Unless yer mean fer us to walk."

"But that's not the whole of it, Napoleon. I *know* we can get there, but what is my dear papa doing with a young son? He's supposed to still be in love with my dead mama."

The lad looked up at Rachel, and she saw pity in eyes that were too big for his thin, little face. After a long moment, he said, "Lady, just because yer git something one way in your head, that don't mean 'tis true."

Four

Talbert Hall, located north of the main road leading into Blanchland, Northumberland, sat at the end of a tree-lined winding road, atop a steep incline. The driver of the public coach stopped and deposited Rachel and Napoleon aside the road, pointed toward the stately manor house, then drove off with his other passengers.

Talbert Hall looked friendly and inviting to Rachel. Mayhap it was because she was inordinately weary. They had been traveling since first light, and now late evening sun lay shadows on brown-tipped grass and trees that swayed gently in the October wind. Void of most of their leaves, the trees were as tall as the four-story brown brick edifice thrusting upward into the dim glow of the sky.

Rachel and Napoleon laboriously trudged toward to the top of the hill, each taking turns carrying Rachel's box.

Before leaving London she had contemplated purchasing a new dress, even inquired about the cost, but had instead bought Napoleon new shoes and patches for his breeches. She smiled, remembering his hiding behind the posting inn's door while she sewed the patches to the tattered breeches.

The dress Rachel was wearing was quite plain and terribly wrinkled after being packed in the cardboard box. But there was no help for it, she told herself. She looked down at the little redhead, then looked again at the manor house in the distance.

Tall, narrow windows stretched across its broad width, and

smoke curled up from brick chimney pots. A warm feeling engulfed her. There, her dear papa lived. Her heart began to pound. Would she be hired as nanny to replace the nanny who had, according to the man at the House of Lords, just left Talbert Hall?

Although disappointed that her dear papa had remarried and had a child, Rachel knew she had to deal with this turn of events. When she discussed it with Napoleon, he had looked at her strangely, but it was he who had suggested that she apply for the position of nanny for young Lord Talbert. And no mention was to be made of her being Lord Talbert's long-lost daughter. Hopefully his lordship would recognize her and draw her into his arms and say how sorry he was not to have come to the Home to see her all these years.

She had spent five shillings to purchase lovely parchment on which she had written in flowing script her qualifications for the job. She had never even held a child and felt guilty for the false statements. But one did what one must needs do, she rationalized.

When Rachel mused aloud how, when the truth came out, her dear pap would apologize for having neglected her, Napoleon raised an eyebrow and said, "I believe yer the dumbest gel I've ever know'd."

Rachel had retorted, "Just how many girls have you known?"

A very staid butler, wearing a black coat with tails, and a pristine white shirt with high color points, opened the door to Rachel's vigorous knock with a brass knocker. He looked as if he might faint when he looked down his long nose at her, and then at Napoleon. Before he could call them beggars, as the man at the pub had done, Rachel handed him the folded parchment. "I've come for the position as nanny. As you can see there, I am well qualified."

"I will handle this, Charles." The masculine voice came from behind the butler.

"You are most welcome to it, m'lord," said the butler before bowing and starting to walk away.

"Don't take my resume," Rachel called to him.

Charles thrust the folded paper toward the tall figure that had materialized to fill the doorway.

Rachel's first thought was of his size; he was hugely tall, with broad shoulders and a slim waist, and he was handsomely dressed. She gave the rest of him a quick once-over, seeing a most pleasant smile, brown straight hair, and laughing brown eyes. Not deep blue, like hers. And he was much too young to be her dear papa.

She strongly willed the tears that pushed at her eyes not to spill onto her cheeks. She even bit down on the side of her jaw and thought of the pain instead of her disappointment. To come all this way and not find Lord Talbert was beyond the pale.

Letting a show of impatience mask her true feelings, Rachel lifted her small chin and asked, "Are you Lord Fox Talbert?"

"No, no, I'm not," the man said laconically. He stared at her untruthful resume, while, at the same time, he cast quick glances in her direction from out the corner of his left eye. There was a wry grin on his handsome face, and Rachel suspected he was actually smothering laughter.

"Then why are you reading my resume?" she asked. " 'Twas Lord Talbert we came to see for employment. Napoleon here also needs a job. He's good at mucking out stables." She squared her shoulders in a false show of dignity.

The man with light brown hair and laughing brown eyes laughed.

"What's so demme funny?" asked Napoleon. "The lady has come looking fer a job. There's ain't nothin' funny about thet. Yer ever been hungry?"

"I beg your forgiveness," the man said, his laughter dying to a smile that showed lovely white teeth. But he did not look to Rachel as if he were sorry. His gaze was not focused on Napoleon, but on her bosom where the top button would not button. Without thinking, she hid the white flesh with her hand, for she was certain the handsome rakehell was looking upon her with sin in his heart, the kind of sin Mother Margaret had warned her against. She glared at him unflinchingly. "I have good references."

"Which will not be necessary. Please do enter Talbert Hall. The position of nanny is yours."

He opened the door wider and stepped back, and with a peremptory flourish of his arm, invited them inside. Rachel's resume crackled with the action.

She didn't budge. "What about Napoleon? He needs a position, too. And I would like to be properly introduced. What's your name? Mine's Rachel Storm, and as I have said, this is Napoleon."

"And I am Lord Trenton Abshire. My sister, who is in need of a nanny for her young son, is Lady Talbert. Her husband is Lord Fox Talbert, the sixth earl of Bingston." He gave a wry grin. "Is that satisfactory, Miss Rachel Storm? And now, will you come in."

"Satisfactory," said Rachel.

Lord Abshire looked down at Napoleon, and again his lips curled into a half-smile. "Of course we can find chores for Napoleon to perform."

"Well, I guess that will have to do," Rachel said. To Napoleon, she half-whispered, "You should have told me your last name. 'Tis embarrassing when one is talking to Quality not to know someone's name."

"Yer didn't ask, but 'tis Napoleon Prigg. Me pa was George Prigg, but he said he wanted me to have a more important name than the one his pap gave him."

"Napoleon is just fine," said Rachel as she led her emaciated little companion through the door into a large foyer decorated with flowers and candles which put out a delicious smell, like day-old lilacs. "'Tis a grand place you have here," she said. The walls were crimson, and portraits of very important-looking people hung from long black cords with tassels. She looked up at the ceiling, which had flying golden cherubs flitting about. "My, my," she exclaimed, and when her half-boots sank into plush carpet, she said in wonderment, "I've never seen anything so grand, your lordship. But I just knew Lord Fox Talbert would live in a grand place."

She almost called him her dear papa, but caught herself in time.

Abshire was instantly alert. He looked at Rachel intently and asked, "Oh! Are you acquainted with Lord Talbert?" He paused into the silence, then added, "That's possible, I suppose, for his Lordship lives in town more than he lives here. Did you meet him in London? Did he send you here?"

"No, I've never met the gentleman. Not that I remember, but being such an important man, a member of Parliament, his name being mentioned in the newspapers, it would be quite normal for me to think of his having a grand place. Would it not?"

His lordship did not answer. Amazement showed on his face as he stared at Rachel, this time her face. For an instant their eyes met and held. She looked away but felt his gaze burning her flesh as she stood on one foot and then the other. Then suddenly he turned right, went through a wide opening, then entered into a large room as beautifully appointed as the huge foyer they had just left, the walls also covered with crimson silk. Elegant window coverings, tied back with thick gold cord, fell in great folds from the ceiling and puddled on the floor.

"This is the ballroom, which also doubles as a receiving room for important callers," he said. "I think a spot of tea is in order, and mayhap biscuits with jelly. After that, Miss Storm, I will have someone show you to your rooms. Napoleon you may join the grooms in the stables for now. But first, tea and biscuits."

Lord Abshire continued walking toward the far end, where a fire burned brightly in an enormous fireplace.

Napoleon lagged behind. Rachel felt him pull at her hand. She bent to ask, "What is it, Napoleon?"

"Yer had better watch this one," he said. "He'll teach yer about sin and then some."

Rachel whispered, "What do you mean, Napoleon? He's being very nice, inviting us in and hiring us both. Now offering us tea and biscuits. Isn't that what we want? That's my best chance of knowing Lord Talbert."

"I don't trust thet look he gave yer. So yer just be careful. I'm warning yer."

Rachel patted his red head. "I'm glad I have you to watch out for me, Napoleon, but I don't know what you are talking about."

"That's what worries me. As I said, yer the dumbest lady I've ever met. Didn't them sisters teach you nothin'?"

Rachel sighed. "Napoleon your grammar is atrocious. As soon as we are settled in, I shall begin your lessons, even if we have to meet after everyone has gone to sleep."

"What are you two whispering about?" inquired Lord Abshire, who had reached the fireplace and was now pulling the bell rope.

Rachel, terribly embarrassed, answered evasively, "Just talk between friends."

A comely maid, wearing black bombazine that rustled when she walked, appeared almost immediately, as if she had been hiding and listening. *Well, I quess we are a pretty sight,* Rachel thought.

The maid bobbed. "You rang, m'lord."

"Yes, I did, Adaline," Abshire said in a very kind voice. "Please bring tea and biscuits for Lord Frank's new nanny, Rachel Storm, and for Napoleon Prigg, who will be working in the stables."

The maid turned pale as her big eyes went from Rachel to Napoleon. "M'lord—"

"That will be all, Adaline. Please do as I requested, quickly, and make it a double order of biscuits and lots of jelly."

This time he spoke authoritatively, but still not unkind. Rachel liked that. It did not hurt to be kind to one's fellowman, a servant, or one of one's own peers. She sank into a plush winged-back chair.

Napoleon, intently watching, did the same.

His lordship sat on a white brocade sopha, crossed his long

legs, smiled wryly, locked his eyes with Rachel's, and waited silently for the maid to bring tea and biscuits. Nearby was a tea table covered with a white cloth and holding fine china cups and saucers.

The silence, and the locking of the eyes, continued for several uncomfortable moments. When Rachel could bear it no longer, she brazenly asked, "Your lordship, why are you staring at me like that? Do I remind you of someone? Mayhap Lord Talbert?"

He laughed, and the sound filled the room with a carefree ambiance, and it seemed to Rachel as if he were enjoying himself tremendously, which was a mystery to her.

"I like the color of your eyes," he said. "They are like violets at dusk, or at early dawn, almost deep purple."

It was Napoleon who spoke. "We'll have none of that, yer lordship. The color of Rachel's eyes has nothin' to do with her being some kid's nanny. And I have you know she's a lady through and through."

His lordship sobered and leaned forward in his chair. "Fustian, Napoleon, I meant no disrespect, and I beg your forgiveness. And yours, too, Miss Storm. I never meant to appear bold."

"Yer apology is accepted," said Napoleon, and when he leaned back in the chair, Rachel felt great relief. But what he said next made her want to drop through the floor. "Your lordship, Rachel here ain't never seen much of the world. I would've never come to Talbert Hall with her had I not been worried about thet. I had a job, but I left it to accompany her here, so that makes her my responsibility."

"What sort of job, Napoleon, and where—"

"In London," cut in Rachel. "Napoleon procured produce for one of the vendors in Covent Gardens."

That was not entirely a lie, thought Rachel; he stole and then took the produce to a fence.

"I see," his lordship said. He stroked his chin thoughtfully, while looking out the window.

The maid appeared with a silver tray and placed it on the tea table. His lordship thanked her, and she bobbed and left.

His attention turned to Rachel. "Miss Storm, would you pour?"

She thought that strange. Why would a nanny be expected to serve tea to guests? But she did as she was asked, glad that Mother Margaret had often invited her to serve as hostess and pour for the sisters at their Saturday afternoon tea, their weekly celebration.

Rachel was glad for the experience, for his lordship's gaze followed her every move as she poured and deftly handed out the precious cups. At least she was adept enough not to drop one. She could thank Mother Margaret for that, she told herself, while her hands trembled only slightly.

Smiling his approval, Abshire thanked her, then insisted that she take a second biscuit with jelly.

Napoleon had already eaten three, and as Rachel watched, he reached for a fourth.

She thought she had never tasted anything quite so good.

"Miss Storm, we are fortunate here at Talbert Hall to have had the new bathing tubs installed," said his lordship in an informative way. "I shall ask Adaline to show you to the nanny's room. After two days on the road, I am sure a bath will be welcome. One of my sister's gown's will be brought to you. I believe you are near her size."

You should know, thought Rachel, *if you can measure with your eyes.*

She said, "Thank you, your lordship, but I have a fresh dress I can wear, and I will gladly wash the ones I have worn and hang them out to dry."

"That will not be necessary."

That authoritative voice again. Rachel instinctively knew not to question his orders. But for someone who was only visiting his sister, he certainly seemed to be in charge. Lord Talbert should be telling her what to do.

She started again to inquire about him but before she could

do so, Lord Abshire was speaking to Napoleon, "There's no help for you about clothes, young man. We have no one your size. But I will have a groom see that you are properly bathed and deliced, and on the morrow I shall take you into Blanchland and purchase a new wardrobe."

He pushed his full length up from the chair and went to pull the bell rope.

"I don't need nobody to see that I'm properly washed. I can do it meself." Napoleon's words were muffled by his sleeve, on which he was wiping red jelly from the corners of his mouth.

"Napoleon, you have a napkin for that," Rachel said, but she gave him a warm smile. Hearing steps, she stood and turned, ready to leave with the maid who was to accompany her to her room. Instead, a lovely lady of not many more summers than Rachel was coming down the winding stairway, the hem of her royal blue gown trailing behind her. White bosom showed above the low décolletage, and brown curls framed her face and fell to touch her shoulders. She was frowning.

Chills marched up and down Rachel's spine. She smelled trouble. And things had been going so well.

"I'm glad you're here, Tessie," said his lordship. He went to stand at the foot of the stairs.

"And I am glad to be here, Trenton, if what Adaline tells me is true." When her gaze fell on Rachel and Napoleon, her hands flew up to cover her mouth.

Rachel thought she heard a small mew, like someone swallowing a scream.

His lordship was saying, "I'm anxious for you to meet Lord Frank's new nanny, and—"

"Frank's new nanny!" And then she fainted dead away and fell into her waiting brother's arms.

"Demme, she's having a spell of the vapors," he declared matter-of-factly, and then he shouted for Adaline to make haste and fetch the vinaigrette.

* * *

"How could you, Trenton?" asked his sister. "You must needs have windmills in your head. My little Frank deserves a trained nanny. I bound that gel has never held a baby." As she paced the floor, she flapped Rachel's resume in the air. "Did you read this? 'Tis beyond the pale. No one is that proficient in anything."

Abshire gave his disarming smile. "And this old house deserves some life. Of late, it has been as dull as an Irish bog in winter. Christmas is coming on, and I doubt that your husband will return in time for any kind of celebration."

"I don't care whether he returns or not. And the reason you are so bored is that you've been hiding out from Lady Cynthia. Instead of missing all the balls and soirees, why don't you tell her you're not the type to get leg shackled and have done with it. And be sure to confess to being a rakehell of the first water. In my opinion, 'twould do you good to take a wife and settle down. And Cynthia would be a good choice."

"A pox on Lady Cynthia. She's dim-witted, refuses to take no for an answer, and I have no notion of taking a wife, or of settling down, especially to a woman whom my brother, his grace, the high and mighty Duke of Welston, has chosen for me." He stretched out his long legs and sighed deeply in seemingly perfect contentment.

"His grace is only thinking of your own good."

"Sister, have done with the subject. Twenty and five is much too young for a man to become leg shackled for the rest of his natural life. I have plenty of time to produce an heir. Ain't that what marriage is all about?"

Lady Talbert did not answer, for that is what her arranged marriage had amounted to; she had produced the seventh earl of Bingston—when and if the sixth earl died. She was ready when the Lord was.

Lord Abshire sat for a long moment, pondering about something other than becoming leg shackled. He had been rather bored of late; the nights seemed long as a lifetime, each minute an hour, the dawn hopelessly out of reach. This, and this alone, accounted for his rash behavior in hiring Miss Storm for little Frank's nanny. His thoughts went rampant: *I've never peered into such eyes. A man could get lost in their watery depths. I wonder what the gel is all about? And where did she get that little ragamuffin? Most likely a thief from the slums of London . . .*

Adaline had, upon Lord Abshire's request, taken Rachel above stairs, with orders for a bath and clean clothes from his sister's closet. A footman had taken Napoleon to the stables, with orders to see that he was scrubbed and deliced.

Lord Abshire chuckled. The lad was a spunky one, didn't want to leave Rachel, afraid someone of the upper orders would not do right by her. A clock droned six times. Almost time for supper. He shook his head. His mind was in a whirl. So much had happened in the past hour, he felt that mayhap his life had changed forever.

Lady Talbert, still pacing, asked again, "Well, did you, or did you not read this obviously false resume?"

"I read: 'This is to introduce Rachel Storm, whose qualifications as a nanny are outstanding . . . ' " Lord Abshire laughed, then added, "One look at Miss Storm told me that she had never been a nanny."

"So you hired her to care for little Frank? Trenton, I don't know what to think of such irrational behavior. You don't appear drunk."

"I'm not. And I assure you the Talbert heir will be well cared for. Does he not have a wet nurse who guards him like a dog guarding a bone. Had she not been so possessive, your last two nannies would not have left. No doubt this Miss Storm can hold him and rock him, if the old crow will let her."

"When you talk, everything is plausible," said Lady Talbert. "That's the way you are. I think you are one of those people who can make anyone believe anything."

"Not Rachel Storm."

"What do you mean? She looks pretty innocent to me. Do you plan on doing wrong by her? I'm totally ashamed of you."

"To woo someone is not doing wrong—"

"In the way you are thinking, 'tis wrong, and I say again, I am totally ashamed of you."

She was looking at her brother fondly, and his lordship knew that she would never be ashamed of anything he did. Her marriage to Lord Fox Talbert had been a terrible disappointment to her, so she lived her life vicariously through her brother. He leaned back on the white brocade sopha, a thoughtful frown replacing his smile, and he remained thus for a time, until, at last he again addressed his sister: "Sister, I'm extremely curious as to why Rachel Storm has gone to such extremes, appearing here in disguise, to gain entry to Talbert Hall. When I purposely asked her to pour tea, she did it with the most grace, as if she were high born. She speaks well, and I believe she is well read." A pause, and then, "At least twice she inquired as to the whereabouts of Lord Talbert."

" 'Tis strange," Lady Talbert said, her brow drawn together quizzically.

Just then a footman came to say that supper was being served in the above-stairs dining room. "Will the visitors be dining as well?" he asked.

"Miss Storm will," said Lady Talbert. "Please send word that she is expected."

"Yes, m'lady." The footman bowed again before leaving.

Abshire looked at his sister. "Is it not customary for a nanny to dine alone in her quarters?"

"At Talbert Hall, we don't always do what is customary. You've whetted my curiosity, Brother. I, too, wonder why Rachel Storm is so interested in Lord Fox Talbert."

On the third floor, Rachel was trying in vain to cover *all* of her bosom with the dress Adaline had brought from Lady Talbert's chiffonnier. "Demme, they must have run out of cloth," she said to her.

The maid laughed. "M'lady, all fashionable gowns show plenty of bosom. 'Tis the thing."

"Well, 'tis not the thing with me. Where I worked as a nanny before, the women were totally covered, from head to toe, even their hair."

She stopped there, for she had almost forgotten and said the sisters instead of the women. The rest was true, except the part about her being a nanny. She sternly cautioned herself to be careful, and she decided that, to keep from slipping up and saying Mother Margaret, she would refer to the good sister as Mother M. Turning in front of the looking glass, she sucked in her breath. Outside of the indecency of the plunging neckline, it was a beautiful gown of blue silk, with a small bustle to accentuate her slim hips. Short, puffy sleeves barely covered her upper arms.

She turned again and again, not believing her eyes. She had been transformed into a woman of passable beauty. As Mother Margaret would say, she looked grown-up. She inquired of Adaline. "Is this one of Lady Talbert's castaways?"

"No, m'lady. It's from her personal wardrobe. I think 'tis new."

"Then I cannot wear it. It would not be proper."

"Don't you worry, m'lady, Lady Talbert has gowns she will never wear. Lord Talbert is deep in the pockets. Her ladyship passes her time ordering new clothes. And I don't know why. She never sees her husband, or hardly ever. She just stays here at Talbert Hall and takes care of things. Should her brother leave, I don't know what she'd do."

"Why would her husband not ever be home; he has a son, and Lady Talbert is stunningly beautiful."

"I know nothing about men," said Adaline.

"Nor do I . . . if you are sure it is all right for me to wear this gown . . . I want to appear presentable. Lady Talbert did not appear happy to see Napoleon and me. In truth, I suspect we caused her vapors."

"Don't you worry a whit," the maid said. "She minds her

brother as if he was her papa. Come and sit while I dress your beautiful hair."

"Dress my hair? Why, I can brush my own hair. And by the by, I'm not Quality, so don't call me m'lady. I'm not deserving."

"Stuff! You're a lady if ever I've seen one," retorted the maid, and then she was silent as she gave Rachel's thick, black hair a hundred strokes or more. After which she coiled it around her head, except for a few curls which she let fall onto her neck, and in front of each ear. "Makes you look older, and ever so uppity. I bet his lordship falls head over heels in love with you."

"I hope not," said Rachel, in all sincerity. She had not come to Talbert Hall to become involved with a nabob, no matter if he was extremely handsome, had a devastating smile, and was extremely sure of himself. And he seemed a gentleman, except when he was staring at her bosom.

At last the hair dressing was done, and Adaline insisted on what she called a tad of black on Rachel's brows, and just a tiny bit of rouge to make her cheeks glow. "Your lashes are so-o-o long," she said, making Rachel laugh.

And then Rachel said, "Adaline, I'm dressed to the nines, and no place to go, except to the nursery to see Frank." She stopped to giggle. "I bound that at six months he is too young to notice my gown."

Adaline shook her head. "You truly are thick in the head where men are concerned. His lordship will be sending for you to have supper with him and Lady Talbert." She grinned knowingly. "Watch my word. He'll be sending for you."

And that is exactly what happened. When the maid answered the scratch on the door, a footman bowed and said, "Miss Storm is expected below stairs to dine with his lordship and Lady Talbert."

Five

"Do you think I might see little Frank before I go down for supper?" asked Rachel of Adaline.

Rachel could not explain this sudden need to see the baby she had been hired to care for. Mayhap it was a ploy to delay seeing Lord Abshire, who stared at her bosom, and Lady Talbert, who obviously was appalled by her and Napoleon's appearance when they arrived at Talbert Hall. She could hardly blame her ladyship, Rachel thought. Stealing another quick glance in the looking glass, she wondered what Lady Talbert would think of the transformation.

Adaline did not answer right away, but at last she said, "I don't think they will mind waiting, but that woman Hannah may be a problem. She may not let you near him. That's why the other nannies left. She sleeps in his room, claiming that he might need her during the night. According to on-dits around the Hall, she never gave the other nannies a chance to care for him."

"Has he had more than one nanny? He's only six months old."

"There's been two, mayhap more. But two is all I know about."

"Well, she won't run me away," said Rachel with more bravado than she felt. "Will you wait for me? It will help to know you're close by."

"I must needs take you to the dining room. You'd get lost

in this big old house without someone to show you around. At least for a few days."

Luck was with Rachel. Hannah was dozing in a chair not far from Frank's crib. She was a big woman, with fine brown hair that stood out from her head. Rachel noted her big hands.

Rachel crept stealthily to Frank's crib. He was not asleep, and when she bent over him, a big smile greeted her, along with a gurgle that sent bubbles from his small mouth. She touched his flailing arm gingerly. She'd had a doll once, but it had not felt warm and soft like Frank's arm. A comforting thrill danced in Rachel's heart and filled it with pure joy. Mayhap it was because she and Frank had been sired by the same man. She wanted to hold him, hug him tightly, talk to him.

Knowing she would wake Hannah if she did not leave quickly, she bent closer and gave him a kiss on his rosy cheek and whispered, "I can see that we are going to be fast friends, your lordship. I'll come this night before repairing to bed to see you. I won't let her run me away."

Rachel slipped from the room. A giddiness rose up in her, and she was laughing when she returned to her own bedchamber where Adaline was waiting. The maid asked anxiously, "Did you see him?"

"Yes, and he's adorable. I felt such powerful love for him."

"Just be careful that you don't feel too much. That Hannah will have your hide."

Rachel giggled. "Lead the way to the dining room. I can't wait to see Lady Talbert's face when she sees my transformation."

" 'Tis his lordship, you must need be worried about," whispered Adaline when she left Rachel.

Standing unobtrusively in the doorway, Rachel observed the dining room, which was in shadows, warmed by a cozy fire in a black marble fireplace. Through the windows one could see a great expanse of sky, velvety blue sprinkled with sparkling stars. A golden moon furbished light. As Rachel watched, a bushy-tailed squirrel skittered down a brown tree trunk.

Upon espying Rachel, Lord Abshire jumped to his feet, an astonished look on his face. He was a very handsome man, she thought, and the winsome smile made him more so. The tiny lines that gathered around his soft brown eyes when he was smiling were very appealing. He came to seat her.

"You are extremely beautiful, Miss Storm," he said.

" 'Tis the gown. It belongs to your sister." She looked at Lady Talbert, who was staring at her and holding both hands over her mouth, clearly in shock. Rachel stood and curtsied, then said, "Thank you for lending me the gown, Lady Talbert. After tonight, I am sure I will be furnished a nanny's uniform."

"No, that is not true at all," said his lordship. "Nannies at Talbert Hall wear clothes from their own wardrobe, day dresses, walking dresses, carriage dresses, and they are not treated as servants. You will find that you are practically a member of the family here. Tessie . . . Lady Talbert will bear me out."

Rachel thought she heard a little moan from Lady Talbert before she said, "My brother is right, the dress is very becoming. The blue matches your eyes. I'm more than happy to share."

"Thank you, Lady Talbert, but tomorrow, I shall wash my own dresses, since I'm not required to wear a uniform."

Rachel was pleased on how well things were going. She would do almost anything to secure her position until she could meet face-to-face with Lord Fox Talbert. Well, most anything, she thought, very cognizant of the look coming from Lord Abshire. Mayhap while they ate, they would speak of Lord Talbert. She could not forget her purpose for being here. *Pray, let them talk of Lord Fox Talbert, my dear papa.*

Rachel, after regaining her chair, looked down the long table. Tall, lighted tapers cast yellow circles onto the white cloth, and fall flowers of brilliant colors spilled out of silver epergnes, running the table's length. Hanging from a gold-scrolled ceiling a chandelier, with lighted candles, cast shadows on the walls, and on the colorful rug that covered the wood floor.

She had never seen a room so handsomely appointed. Footmen stood beside a sideboard which held silver platters with domed covers. Delicious smells filled the room, and her mouth began to water. Skinny little Napoleon came quickly to mind. "Did Napoleon get settled in?"

"Indeed, he did," said Lord Abshire. "I've been assured that he has been washed and deliced. On the morrow, clothes will be purchased for him."

He smiled at Rachel, then let his gaze drop to her low décolletage. Her face burned with embarrassment. She spoke quickly, without thinking, "I would thank you not to look at me like that, your lordship. Mother M. warned me about men looking at me with longing."

Laughter spilled out into the room, and then Lady Talbert said, "I told you, Brother, that from this one you would get your comeuppance."

"I don't mean to be hateful," said Rachel, a little contrite. "But Mother M. told me many times that I should look the other way should a man look at me with longing. I suppose she meant when a man keeps staring at one place on one's body."

Another giggle, though not as forceful, from Lady Talbert. Her eyes cut to her brother, and Rachel thought that any moment the lovely woman would whoop with laughter.

" 'Tis a compliment for a man to desire a woman," said Lord Abshire. "There's nothing sinful about it . . . as long as he is a gentleman."

"Just you be sure you are a gentleman. Always," said Rachel. She rather liked him, she decided. He made her feel gay and happy. Lest she forget her purpose in being at Talbert Hall, she looked at Lady Talbert and asked, "When will your husband be home?"

"Most likely not until Christmas, which really is not so long away. He's a very busy man in London, being a member of Parliament and also having extensive business holdings."

Business holdings! silently scorned Lord Abshire. The thought was unpleasant, so he turned his thoughts to Miss Storm. He studied her countenance for a long while, looking deep into her blue eyes, while being very careful not to let his gaze drop lower. He smiled at the set-down she had issued. The girl had spunk. "Miss Storm," he began, "just who is this Mother M. you speak of? Did she have anything to do with your coming to Talbert Hall?"

"Oh, no. She doesn't know I'm here. She raised me, you might say, and then I ran away . . . to become a nanny."

Rachel felt a prick of guilt for the part lie. But not enough so that she would confess to her real reason for running away from the Home. Silence ensued, and the food was served. Rachel ate ravenously, with impeccable manners. She saw Lord Abshire and his sister exchange glances, and finally Lady Talbert said, "This Mother M. must have been Quality, for you certainly are well trained in your manners."

"Oh, she's Quality all right. If I did not use proper manners, she cracked my knuckles with her knife."

Lady Talbert gasped, and Lord Talbert, smothering laughter, again asked, this time more straightforward, "Did your mother M. send you to Talbert Hall on a mission? In disguise?"

Rachel took a bite of stewed kidney, chewed slowly, swallowed, and then said, "Oh, no. She didn't send me, not by any means of one's imagination. I told you I ran away. She knew nothing of my mission. And as for my being in disguise, I beg of you not to think that. The clothes I was wearing when I came here are the best that I have."

"Mission!" Lord Abshire and Lady Talbert said in unison, both looking startled.

Rachel wanted to die. Why had she mentioned her mission? Her next words were chosen with great care. "Yes, a mission to find a child to care for. And I think I've made an excellent choice. When I visited little Frank, I wanted to hug him to me." She gave a small chuckle. "He has the sweetest smile, and he blows bubbles when he coos."

Lord Abshire shook his head in disbelief. This gel must needs be from where fairies dwell, not real at all.

But she is real, he thought. One look at her in that dress told him she was the most real, the most intriguing, the most desirable, girl he'd ever met. The white flesh above the low neckline was driving him out of his mind with desire. He envisioned himself laying a moist kiss exactly between the two perfectly round mounds. *How can you think such a thing?* he asked himself, feeling passion roiling through his veins. Other things he would like to do to Miss Storm, like make love to her, entered his mind. It was sinning all right, unadulterated, delicious sin.

He jerked his gaze away and looked through the window. Anything for a distraction. Darkness had come. As he fought to gain his equanimity, he said in solemnity, "After we've finished eating, Miss Storm, I will accompany you to the stables to see Napoleon. He's such a small lad, he mayhap will be lonely and want to see you."

"Napoleon is eight, he thinks, but he's far advanced past leading strings. Given his life, I doubt that he wants to see me, but I want to see him. To be with him is far more real than my sitting here with Quality, eating this delicious food."

"Well, 'tis settled, then. Only a short walk will take us to him. There's a beautiful moon, and a sky full of stars."

Looking beyond the windows, Rachel was reminded of the night she had run away from Saint Cecilia's. "Would you like to accompany us?" she asked Lady Talbert, and her ladyship almost choked on the sip of tea she had just taken. Grabbing her serviette, she held it over her mouth.

"Did I say something wrong?" asked Rachel. She looked first at Lady Talbert, then at his lordship. Both were looking at her in a strange way.

"No," quickly answered Lord Abshire. " 'Tis just a little

thing between my sister and me. Sometimes she questions my motives when I offer kindness."

"Well, don't you worry, Lady Talbert. His lordship's motive had better be honorable, or I shall box his face."

"Did Mother M. teach you that?" asked Lord Abshire, his brow raised quizzically.

"That, and a lot of other things. She was a stickler for what was proper for a lady to do."

"What other things?"

"Not to sin."

Another giggle from Lady Talbert. "Your lordship, as I said, I think you have met your match. *This one* won't be falling at your feet." She looked at Rachel. "Thank you for inviting me to accompany you, but this night I shall pass. I believe you can take care of yourself."

Abshire scowled, and Rachel was ready to change the subject. Did they not know anything to talk about except her? She rose from her chair and said to Lord Abshire, "I'm through eating. If you are ready, I'd like to visit Napoleon."

"Oh, but the meal is not finished. A dessert and a fine liqueur will be served."

"I don't imbibe spirits," Rachel answered. "And I've eaten too much to care for dessert."

So they excused themselves from the table and left the manor house by descending the stairs and exiting through a side door. The air was cool to Rachel's face, and she wished she had not forgotten to wear her coat. She tried to conceal her discomfort from his lordship, but he was too smart for that, and right away she was wrapped in his coat. His arm lingered on her shoulders. "I would not have you cold, Miss Storm."

She shook his arm off. "Thanks for the coat, but that doesn't afford you privileges."

"Oh, I am ever so sorry, Miss Storm. 'Tis a habit I have, but can you blame me for wanting to embrace a very beautiful lady?"

"You may call me Rachel if you like. That, however, is as far as the familiarity goes. I'd appreciate your keeping your distance."

"But what if that is impossible, dear Rachel? I find you irresistible."

"And from Lady Talbert's words, I believe you find *every* girl irresistible."

"I don't take your meaning?"

"I think you do. She said that I would be one girl who would not fall at your feet, indicating that others have."

"But none have had violet eyes. From the moment I looked into your wonderful eyes, I've been lost in their depths. I think mayhap I'm falling in love."

It was true about her eyes, his lordship thought. From first sight they had mesmerized him, and he was more than intrigued by her demeanor, one moment a naive child, the next a woman. No doubt the woman part recognized the falseness of his wooing. He looked at her, smiled, and wondered if kissing her would be worth getting his face boxed. He decided that it would.

Rachel retorted, "Balderdash! Men don't fall in love with eyes."

"Did you swear in the presence of Mother M.?" his lordship asked.

"All the time, but under my breath."

This brought laughter, and it seemed to Rachel the night was filled with gaiety . . . and magic. Except on the night she had run away, she had never walked in the moonlight. She savored the quiet ambiance.

After passing through a copse, they came in sight of the stables, and Rachel stopped and stared. White buildings, almost as large as Talbert Hall glistened in the moonlight.

"Who takes care of Lord Talbert's estate?" she asked.

"There's an overseer, but I am the manager."

"You? You mean you live here? I thought you were visiting your sister?"

"I am. I have been since I returned from the war. She needs me. I am the second son of a duke; my earldom is only a courtesy title. I'm not needed at Worthington, where Lady Talbert and I grew up. His grace bought a commission for me, but the war is over." His voice dropped. "I feel needed here."

"Well, that explains a lot," Rachel said. "I mean that explains why *you* hired me and Napoleon, instead of Lord Talbert."

"'Tis true, and, as I told you, one look in those bottomless blue eyes and I was totally lost." He reached to take her hand.

She jerked it away. "You touch me, and I'll smack you good."

He laughed. "Or tell Napoleon that I'm not doing right with you?"

Rachel's steps became quicker. "Hurry, lets go see the little redhead. I promise I won't tell him about your forwardness."

"Pray, don't. He said he would break my leg. And then I could not take him into the village for new clothes. I've never seen anything quite like the way he was dressed."

"That's because you've never been poor."

When they reached the stables, the coachman, whom Lord Abshire called Burton, said Napoleon was in his quarters above the stables, wearing a blanket. "Mad as a wet hen," said Burton, " 'cause I wouldn't let him wear them filthy clothes. I've never seen the like of it."

"That's because you've never been poor," Lord Abshire said, smiling wryly. He gained the stairs two at a time. "Come on, slowpoke," he called over his shoulder to Rachel. "We don't have all night."

"My legs aren't as long as yours," Rachel countered.

On the landing at the top of the stairs, Lord Abshire waited for her. "This way to the quarters," he said, turning right when she was beside him. "I think you will approve. 'Tis quite nice. They even have a cook to prepare nourishing meals. I saw to that when I came."

"I'm sure Napoleon will be glad of that. He said the reason

he came along with me was to eat the food I bought for him, and to watch out for me. Poor little fellow. He has a good heart."

Lord Abshire knocked on the first door they came to. No answer. When his next knock settled into silence, he opened the door and stepped back for Rachel to enter.

Wearing a red-and-green horse blanket and the shoes Rachel had bought for him, a clearly angry Napoleon sat on the side of a narrow bed, his feet dangling over the side. His little eyes were drawn together in a frown.

Rachel refrained from laughing, or even smiling. "Hello, Napoleon." Quickly, her eyes traversed the room. "You have nice quarters here. Did they feed you well at supper?"

"After scrubbing me 'til my skin hurt. And then that demme Burton took my clothes and burned 'em, said he'd never seen the like. And they had new patches."

"Don't worry, Napoleon," Rachel consoled, "on the morrow Lord Abshire will be taking you to town for all *new* clothes."

"How kin I go with nothin' to wear but this horse blanket? I look like a Scotsman wearing one of them kilts which near shows a man's arse."

"Napoleon!" exclaimed Rachel. "Watch your tongue."

Lord Abshire noted the pleasant exchange between the nanny and, no doubt, little thief. "I have a capital idea, Napoleon. You can lie on the carriage squab, covered by the blanket. That way no one can see you while I purchase trousers and a shirt. I'll return and you can get dressed. Then you can accompany me to buy the rest of your wardrobe."

"The rest! One pair of breeches and one shirt is all any man needs. I got new shoes."

Rachel looked down. No stockings. The thinness of his legs brought tears to her eyes. "You'll need a change so that when you wash you won't have to wear a horse blanket."

"I don't plan on washing again, not with Burton scrubbing."

Rachel wanted to hug him, but she knew he would be embarrassed to death. She said instead, "Napoleon, I ate in the dining room with Lord Abshire and his sister, a grand meal, but I could not help but wonder if they had fed you well."

"I ate with Burton and the rest of the stable help, and now me belly is about to pop." He rubbed his stomach and at last gave a small smile, and this lightened Rachel's heart. Feeling satisfied, she turned her thoughts to Lord Abshire. She did so hope they could become friends.

But being friends was the last thing on his lordship's mind. He did not know where or when, but he would kiss this girl with the bottomless blue eyes if it was the last thing he ever did. It did not bear thinking on that he would fail. This night, he told himself, he could not afford to be too familiar. She might leave Talbert Hall. He decided to bide his time.

He chuckled, for he would wager that the gel did not know she had sensuous lips, the kind that begged a man to kiss them. How had she escaped this long, he wondered, and then he remembered her Mother M., that guardian angel. The good woman must have been kept her charge hidden under a basket.

Returning to the manor house, they walked in silence, and seemingly, to Abshire, in contentment. He strove to keep his desire under control, and only once, when an owl hooted not far from them, did Rachel reach an anxious hand to grasp his. He did not jerk his hand away, as she had done earlier, and when they had reached the second floor of the Hall, where his quarters were located, he reluctantly told her good night, keeping his voice calm. He watched as she climbed the stairs to the third floor.

She looked back once. "Good night again, your lordship."

She smiled that big, wonderful, innocent smile, and Lord Abshire swallowed a big gulp.

And then she was gone.

Rachel made her way to the nursery and quietly turned the knob on the door and pushed it open. It was dark, except for the moonlight through a window. Hannah was asleep in a cot pushed against the wall. Her gentle snoring reminded Rachel of Mother Margaret.

Frank, too, was asleep, looking like an angel in his long gown and white nightcap. She intended only to look, but a force within her heart would not settle for that. She had to hold him.

And should she do that, she reasoned, Hannah would surely awake.

The force won. Gingerly, Rachel picked up the child and laid him against her breast. He squirmed, but did not make a sound. What to do next? She could not stand there and take a chance on being found out.

"Oh, Frankie," she whispered, "you lie against me like a sack of potatoes, except you're warm and cuddly. You just continue to do that and I will rock you . . . and hold you to my heart's content." She took him to her bedchamber.

All nanny's rooms have rocking chairs, Rachel told herself. Or did they? There was one in the nursery, she distinctly remembered. But there was not one in her room, not that she could see with light only from dying embers in the fireplace and a narrow swatch of moonlight coming through the window.

There was nothing to it, she told herself; she could sit in any chair and rock him with the slow movement of her body, back and forth, his head resting on her shoulder. She hummed "Rock-a-Bye Baby."

Tears came to Rachel's eyes. She felt whole, a complete human being. She whispered to Frank, and to the silence in the room, "I'll wait here at Talbert Hall until our papa comes from London town. Then he will give me permission to stay forever. I'll have a real home, and you can be my little brother . . . half brother. But that's as good as whole . . . don't you think, Frankie? I wish that would hurry and happen. 'Tis against my upbringing to deceive . . ."

Rachel did not know how long she had been asleep when little Frank stirred and woke her. At first she was scared. What if she had let him slide from her arms? And then she realized that she was holding him too tightly, and that was why he was squirming. She slid him down onto her lap, thinking that she must needs return him to the nursery. No, she did not want to do that. Hannah might awaken and cause a ruckus.

The decision was made by Rachel's groggy mind; she would keep the baby during the night. After turning back the coverlet and placing him on the bed, she shed Lady Talbert's beautiful gown and donned the only nightdress she had brought with her, a homemade, well-worn white batiste, gathered high at the throat and trimmed with lace yellowed from age. Over the years, the lace had been used on more than one gown.

She then climbed up into the high bed and snuggled Frank to her. He smelled of soap and baby powder; he felt warm and good, and his breath tickled her neck.

Rachel's last thought before sleep again claimed her was that if the precious little boy became hungry in the night, she would take him to Hannah, and suffer the wet nurse's wrath for taking him from the nursery.

Six

The pounding jolted Lady Talbert awake. Loud sobs, sounding incredulously as if someone were swallowing loud large gulps of air, filled the room. She looked about. The room was dark, except for the light from the dying embers in the fireplace, which shrouded the walls with shades of darkness. She did not recognize the inaudible voice beyond the door, and thought at first she was having a nightmare. When the pounding stopped, she turned her throbbing head into the cool linen of her pillow.

And then the sounds began again, louder this time, muted only by the thick panels of the door. "Lady Talbert . . . Lady Talbert," a voice was saying, and then more hysterical sobbing, becoming a wail.

Bounding out of bed, her ladyship grabbed her dressing gown and draped it over her shoulders. She lit a taper before opening the door to find Hannah standing there, looking like a ghost in a long full white nightdress and a white sleeping cap.

"What is it Hannah?" Lady Talbert asked.

The answer came in the form of a wail. "Little Frank, little Frank, my baby, my baby, he's been kidnapped," and then she swooned.

"Oh, dear God," cried Lady Talbert. The house was silent with sleep. She told herself to be calm, but she had never been more frightened in her life. Lord Talbert had cautioned her against kidnappers. With his enormous wealth, it was a possibility, he had said.

Ignoring the woman on the floor, she screamed for someone to please come. But no one did. Stepping over Hannah's prone body, she ran to Lord Abshire's door and began pounding, not unlike Hannah. "Trenton, Trenton, wake up. That girl has kidnapped little Frank." Words spilled over words. "We don't have to wonder any longer why she came here, all dressed up like a street urchin. Oh, Trenton, please wake up and help me. We must needs send for the authorities."

The door opened. Wearing an emerald-green dressing gown, his brown hair tousled from sleep, Lord Abshire calmly reached out and took the candle from his sister. "Tessie, calm down. I can't understand a word you are saying." After a moment the sobbing subsided, and he said, "Now, tell me the whole of it."

The sobs did not cease, but somehow she managed to say, "Hannah fainted dead away in my doorway. She claims that Little Frank has been kidnapped. I bound I'll kill that impostor."

"I don't think that will be necessary. Rachel could not kidnap a child. She's only a child herself."

"I don't care about that. I just want my baby back."

His lordship guided his sister to a chair, set the candle aside, then pulled the bell rope for the butler, yanking it twice to show expediency. When Charles appeared, his white feet protruding from under a long-tailed black coat he was wearing over his nightshirt, he held his quizzing glass to his eye and said, "You rang at this ungodly hour, your lordship?"

A funny sight at another time, his lordship thought. "Summon a footman to check on Hannah, and then you stay with Lady Talbert while I look about."

"Send for authorities," said Lady Talbert, between sobs.

"A cup of tea might calm her," Abshire told the butler before leaving in a run.

Of course Rachel had not kidnapped little Frank. There must needs be an answer other than that. The thought of the child being gone was devastating, but that would not be the whole of it; little Frank would be found and brought back to Talbert Hall, but Rachel would be gone forever, to rot in Newgate, or on a prison ship, or be shipped off to Australia.

It did not bear thinking on, thought his lordship. With the long hall and the stairs behind him, he turned in the direction of the nursery. The door was open, the room empty. His heart sank. Mayhap the girl had taken the boy. Frank was heir to a large estate, as well as to his father's title. It happened in England all the time. Heirs held for ransom.

Shaking his head, Abshire turned and went to the door to the nanny's room. Nanny, indeed. He turned the knob and jerked the door open, his temper flaring. The possibility of Rachel taking Frank had begun to sink in, but his heart said that it could not be. What he saw made his heart sing.

The bed and Rachel, her head buried in a pillow, little Frank's head under her chin, both arms holding him to her, were barely visible. Lord Abshire stared in disbelief. Moonlight danced on Rachel Storm's peaceful countenance as her breath came in the perfect rhythm of deep sleep. Her long black hair was splayed out onto the white pillow, and her long lashes formed a crescent on her porcelainlike cheeks.

Relief such as he had never felt washed over his lordship. He recognized this, and thought that surely it was because the little boy was safe. Closing the door softly, he left and returned to his sister and the butler. "Frank is safe," he said, "the nanny has him in her bed. Both are sleeping peacefully."

"Taken him into her bed," exclaimed Lady Talbert. "Why . . . why, I've never heard of such a thing."

"Well, you have heard of it now, Tessie. I'm sure the girl meant no harm."

Abshire dismissed the butler, who left in a hurry, the long tails of his black coat flapping against his white nightshirt.

"I bound that 'twas unthoughtful of her, scaring the wits out of Hannah. And out of me as well," said Lady Talbert when she and her brother were alone. "I thought I would expire, and I might have, with my heart pounding so, had you not been so confident that it wasn't so." A pause and then, "Poor Hannah, screaming that her baby had been kidnapped."

"That may be a problem which you have not addressed, Tessie. It appears to me that the wet nurse thinks Frank is *her* baby. That is why every nanny that has been hired has run away. Had you thought of that? Is it not quite unnatural for a wet nurse to sleep in the same room as her charge? I thought wet nurses had babies of their own, with enough milk for two."

"She said her baby had died. I thought I told you that when she came."

"Mayhap you did; I don't recall." His lordship stood for a long moment, pondering, and then he said, "It is not my desire to alarm you, Tessie, but I quite expect Hannah to begin her campaign to rid Talbert Hall of Rachel, and I will not forebear that."

"Should we send Hannah packing?" asked her ladyship. "Would it upset Frank terribly should we find another wet nurse."

"Let's do nothing now. Let's wait and see how she reacts to Miss Storm after this."

Lady Talbert adored her brother, while at the same time knowing him for the rakehell he was. The years away in the war had changed him. He lived life to its fullest every moment of the day, always with a wry smile. The crisis over, she gave him a warm smile and asked, "Do you have seduction in mind?"

"Tessie! What a question. In proper society—"

"Don't give me that proper society stuff. Do you or do you not plan to work your charm on that naive little impostor? Of course I think she would be terribly lucky to have you for a lover, with or without marriage in mind."

"I assure you that marriage is not on my mind. Not for a long time. The war took a great chunk out of my life, and now I'm ready to enjoy my freedom. No, Tessie, don't count on Rachel for a sister-in-law."

"I think I shall warn her," Lady Talbert said, teasingly.

Just then Hannah and a bedraggled footman stood in the doorway. Hannah was crying. "Where's my baby . . . my baby—"

"He's safe," Abshire said. "I'm sorry I didn't come straight away and tell you, but Lady Talbert had to be calmed."

"Safe? Where? Did she bring him back?"

"Frank wasn't kidnapped. The new nanny took him to her bed, and both are sleeping peacefully. Now, I suggest you get some sleep yourself, Hannah. Frank will most likely wake early, hungry as a little bear."

"What right did that tramp have to take Frank to her bed. I will not forebear it. I'll see that she's gone in no time at all. Taking Frank in the night, while I slept."

His lordship's voice was firm. "You will *not* see that Miss Storm is gone. 'Tis not up to you to decide that." He turned to the footman. "Please repair her to the nursery, Wade, and see that she does not disturb the nanny and Frank. I'm certain that when the child is hungry, he will awaken Miss Storm and she will return him to Hannah for feeding. Now, have done with it; let the household return to normal."

"Yes, m'lord," the footman said, bowing first to his lordship, and then to her ladyship. Taking Hannah by the arm, he led her away.

Above stairs, Rachel awakened the minute little Frank squirmed and began nuzzling her bosom. "Are you hungry?" she asked in a sleepy voice.

Frank answered with a cry, which became louder, and louder. His small arms flailed, and his feet were going every which way. Rachel jumped out of bed, for she did not want to awaken the household. This crying had not been in her plan. What did one do with a baby when it cried?

The cries became increasingly louder, and more frantic. Rachel shushed him by kissing his cheek, for which she received a small fist in her face. There was nothing to it, he must needs be returned to the wet nurse. So she gathered him into her arms and made a dash for the nursery, where she found candles burning and Hannah sitting in a high-back rocking chair, looking as if any moment she would spring like a tiger onto Rachel.

Rachel held the baby out. "Here, Hannah, he sounds as if he's terribly hungry."

"Why don't yer feed him?" was Hannah's angry retort. She leaned back and placed her arms across her ample bosom.

Rachel felt her temper rising. She wanted to slap the obstinate woman. "Because I don't have anything to feed him with," she said, not too kindly. Frank let out another squeal. "I suggest you feed him, or shall I go for Lord Abshire?"

Hannah visibly paled, but she was not through. "Yer had no right to take my baby in the night. I was scared half out of me wits. And Lady Talbert, too, I'll be bound."

"I'm sorry about that. I was not aware. . . . balderdash, what does that matter now, with little Frankie so hungry? Here, feed him. Now."

Hannah at last took the baby and opened her breast to him, and the cries were instantly replaced with contented sucking. Rachel watched in amazement. She had never seen a baby nurse. Smiling, she reached to rub the tousled hair on Frank's head.

Hannah slapped Rachel's hand away. "Keep yer hands off me baby." And then she laughed, cynically. "Yer can change him when he's through eating. Dripping wet, he is. No wonder he was wailing loud enough to wake the dead."

"Change him?"

"Yes, change him." She gave Rachel a long look. "Thet's jest what I thought. Yer ain't no nanny. You've never changed a baby in yer life. Who are you? Up to no good, I would wager my last shilling."

"I am a nanny. Did I not sleep with little Frankie last night, and hold him. He was happy as could be, until he wanted to nurse. Nannies don't wet nurse, too."

Another cynical laugh from Hannah. "How old are yer? Five

and ten summers? And what is it yer want from Talbert Hall? Yer ain't lower quality as yer claim. Yer don't speak broad, like me. Quality, yer are, like Lady Talbert and his lordship."

"I'm seventeen and a half, and I'm not highborn, not that I know of." Rachel had to fight to keep her voice from breaking. She could not tell this wet nurse who she was, for she did not know. Low quality, high quality, she did not care, if only she could belong to somebody. Why did things have to be so hard? When she was writing her resume, she had thought only of getting inside of Talbert Hall, without much thought as to how to change a baby. Now she supposed Hannah would ask her if she could wash and dress little Frankie. Well, she could do that. She had dressed her doll.

As if she could read Rachel's thoughts, Hannah said, "I suppose yer know how to wash and dress a baby." The look on her face was clearly a smirk.

"Of course I do. I'll go to my room now, and when it's time for Frankie to be dressed, just knock on my door. I'll wash and dress him."

Without waiting for an answer, Rachel was out of the room like a flash. She would pray. Mayhap Mother M. would tell her what to do.

Back in her own room, she lit a candle and then started looking for a book on how to be a nanny. She crossed herself and silently thanked Mother Margaret, now Mother M., for teaching her to read. "And I would thank you more if only you had taught me a few other things about the way the world works."

Just then Rachel spied a book on a shelf: *Duties of a Good Nanny.* The print was in Latin.

Rachel grabbed the book and jumped up onto the high bed. Her legs crossed Indian-fashion, she placed the book in her lap. Through the window, she saw that first light was settling over the leafless trees. The light drifted in through the window.

The room was cold, but she did not notice as first she looked for pictures in the book, and she laughed aloud when she espied a picture of a nanny changing a baby's diaper. The cloth was folded with three corners.

Rachel devoured the book, and for the first time she was thankful that Mother M. had forced Latin upon her. Almost giddily she remembered the good sister refusing to answer her unless she asked in Latin. She studied the picture of a very sedate lady bathing a baby, in a small tub placed on a table. "I won't do that. Little Frankie and the tub might spill to the floor," she mused aloud.

Feeling quite smug, Rachel hid the book under the feather mattress and went to the dressing room, where she washed and dressed, and brushed her hair. She braided it into two braids, and then tied them with two white rags she had brought in her box.

"Come, Miss Storm," Hannah said. "Show me if'n yer can wash a baby. I'd like for her ladyship to see this. Next time she will be more careful about who she hires to care for the Talbert heir. It don't bear thinking on. Yer no more than a baby yerself."

"I told you that I'm seventeen and a half, soon to be eighteen."

"When?"

"Near Christmas. I shan't tell you the exact date."

"That's a farrago. No one, except Christ, wuz born on Christmas day."

"Hannah, I didn't say I was born on Christmas day, and I don't have time to argue with you about when I was born."

And pray, don't ask me where.

Rachel pulled the bell rope, and then she picked up Frank, who was smiling his sweet, wonderful smile. She placed him on her hip and laughed when he reached up to touch her face with his small hand. "You're still wet—"

"Of course he is. I wuz waitin' fer yer to change him, if'n yer know how."

"I know how, but I will bathe him first." With her free hand she moved the small bathing tub onto the floor. Sitting on the floor herself, she removed Frank's nightgown and his wet diaper. His private parts were no surprise to her. Although she had never seen a naked boy, she had seen the statue of Biblical David when Mother M. had taken her on the Grand Tour. She remembered that Mother M. had spoken to her about how God had made Eve from Adam's rib, and that they were supposed to replenish the world with their offspring, adding, "That takes a man and a woman, because they are made differently. With his private handle, the man plants the seed in a woman, and then she carries the baby for nine months." And she was quick to say that Eve covered herself with a fig leaf.

Adaline rustled in in her black bombazine. Rachel greeted her, "I'm glad to see you, Adaline. I need warm water for Frank's bath, and then will you stand by and hand to me what I need?"

"Yes, m'lady," said the maid. She left and shortly returned. After pouring water into the small tub, she handed Rachel a bar of soap and a washcloth from the bathing table.

Hannah sat in her chair, watching, a knowing smile, more like a smirk, Rachel thought, on her face. But the smile vanished when Rachel, with the expertise of a professional nanny, bathed, dried, powdered, and dressed little Frank in a fresh frock that came below his knees. He gurgled and kicked, smiled and cooed. Rachel handed him up to Adaline.

"Help don't handle Quality," Hannah said in a quarrelsome tone.

Rachel pushed herself up onto her feet. "Why not? Frank likes Adaline. Don't you sweet little darling?" She nuzzled Frank, and he repaid her with laughter.

A thunderous look came over Hannah's countenance, and she practically tumbled out of her chair when Rachel announced that she would be taking him below stairs when she went for breakfast.

"'Tis not done, yer young whelp. Yer can't take my baby away from me."

Rachel looked at her for a long moment, seeing the devastation in her eyes, the loneliness, the sadness. Or was it something else, mayhap greed, possessiveness? Either way, it was frightening. Rachel addressed the wet nurse in a kind voice, "Hannah, I will bring him back. You can't keep him here in this room, not ever letting him see the other part of this wonderful house he will someday inherit."

"He visits his mama every day fer an hour. That's the way 'tis done with the upper orders."

"I think that's terrible. As his nanny, I shall see that he sees every nook and cranny of this house, and mayhap we'll visit the stables."

Hannah looked as if she might faint dead away.

Rachel took the baby and straddled him on her hip.

"Adaline, will you come with me? You can hold Frankie while I eat breakfast. I'm starved."

"I beg of yer," said Hannah, "don't do this thing."

"Don't do what?"

"Take my baby below stairs in them drafty rooms, or to the stables for the horses to kill. Yer don't know what them beasts might do to the poor little thing."

Rachel straightened the skirt of her dress. "Oh, all right, Hannah, I promise I won't take him to the stables, but a walk in the fresh air will be good for him. I'd like Napoleon to see him."

"Who's Napoleon? Someone up to no good. Most likely someone waitin' to assist in Lord Frank's kidnapping. I beg of yer, Miss Storm—"

"Balderdash! Napoleon wouldn't kidnap Frank. Napoleon's only eight . . . he thinks." She waved Frank's hand. "Say goodbye to Hannah."

Hannah refused to say goodbye, or anything. She just stood there wringing her hands, tears streaming down onto her plump, rosy cheeks.

Rachel genuinely felt sorry for the woman, but that was not reason enough to allow her to possess little Frank. Rachel knew little about children, having lived separately from the other children at the Home, but she knew enough to know that isolationism was not healthy. When would the child learn to talk if he heard no one speak except Hannah, and his mama for an hour each day.

Quitting the nursery, Rachel, followed by Adaline, went below stairs and to the dining room. Smells of hot food emanated from the sideboard, where a liveried footman waited to do the serving. She did not feel right, eating with the family this way. But his lordship had said it was the right thing to do. She turned and handed little Frank to the maid. "Here, you hold Frank while I eat, and then I'll hold him while you eat. Be careful, don't let him pull on the tablecloth. The china and crystal, I imagine, is quite valuable."

"Oh, Miss Storm. That here ain't the thing. I'm not to eat at the table with Quality. My dining is done in the basement, with the other servants."

"Stuff! I'm not Quality, and his lordship told me I was *expected* to eat with the family, and they are most certainly Quality. I just think here in the country they are not so particular."

The footman, obviously listening, cleared his throat and covered the smile on his face with his hand. Rachel gave him a smile and asked for porridge.

Adaline held the baby, but she did not sit.

Rachel ate her porridge hurriedly, so anxious was she to take the baby out into the fresh air. And she wanted to see Napoleon before he left with his lordship to go into the village. She almost laughed aloud when she thought of the little boy lying naked on a carriage seat, covered with a horse blanket, while a man of the nobility went inside the store to purchase clothes for him. She took another huge bite, and just as she had scraped the last bit of porridge from the bowl, Lady Talbert entered the dining room, followed by Lord Abshire.

They were conversing, and Rachel heard her ladyship say, "I failed to sleep after that terrible interruption of thinking Frank had been kidnapped. I can't imagine that girl taking him to her bed."

"That was last night. Let us not dwell on the past," said Abshire.

Lady Talbert laughed. "Oh, Brother, you are the greatest hedonist in all of England. Live for today, that's your motto."

Then they both stopped in their tracks, their eyes turned to the table.

Rachel wiped her mouth with her serviette, then smiled at them. She looked at Adaline, who looked as if she might bolt and run, or worse yet, drop the baby.

Lady Talbert gasped. His lordship quickly put his arm around her shoulders. "Steady, Tessie. I'm sure there's an explanation."

Rachel jumped to her feet and gave a half-decent curtsy, at least she thought so. "Good morning, your lordship, your ladyship."

Lord Abshire said, "Good morning, Miss Storm. Mayhap you can explain why Frank is here, and a servant—"

" 'Tis simple," said Rachel. "I feel that Frank should not be holed up in the nursery, hearing no one talk except Hannah. At least that is the way the wet nurse wants it. He'll never learn to talk that way. As his nanny, and that is what you hired me to be, I felt it incumbent upon myself to take him from the nursery. We'll be going to see Napoleon. That will give him fresh air, which every child needs, and then we'll begin getting acquainted with the house he will someday inherit—"

Laughter from his lordship interrupted Rachel, and she was glad, for she was near out of breath. She would not tell his lordship, or Lady Talbert, that, while exploring the manor house, she hoped to find a portrait of Lord Fox Talbert, her dear papa.

Lady Talbert spoke: "Miss Storm, I'm sure you have your notions on how to raise a child, but to bring him here where adults are eating breakfast is hardly the thing."

"I see no harm in it," his lordship said. "Frank seems perfectly content to me." His eyes cut to Rachel, who was standing beside the chair she had just vacated, wearing an awful dress that was not only wrinkled but struck her six inches above her half-boots. An ingenuous idea, so he thought, came to him, and when silence quivered between the occupants of the room, he said, "Miss Storm, the gown you are wearing is entirely unsuitable. As I told you earlier, at Talbert Hall, you will not be expected to wear black uniforms, for you are not considered one of the staff. More suitable gowns, at least gowns which fit, will be expected. Since you don't seem to want to wear Lady Talbert's gowns, if you can tear yourself away from Frank, I suggest you accompany Napoleon and me when we go into the village. I'm certain a modiste of some sort can be found, and there just might be suitable gowns already made up in a draper's shop. I've never had occasion to shop there."

"I think that's a capital idea, your lordship," Rachel quickly answered, "but I see no reason why I should tear myself away from Frank. Most likely he will enjoy the ride in the carriage."

A low groan escaped his lordship.

Seven

"No! 'Tis impossible," Lord Abshire said in a firm tone, "the baby will be a nuisance. How can you shop for gowns with a babe in your arms?"

"You could hold him while I try on—"

"No," he said again. "I shall do the shopping by myself." He walked over to Rachel, took baby Frank, and handed him to his mother. He then measured Rachel's tiny waist with his big hands. "Two hands, exactly."

Rachel jumped back as if suddenly she had been touched by a flaming torch. "Don't touch me like that. Mother M. said—"

"I know. Mother M. said it was sinning." Abshire gave his wry grin. His eyes were alight with laughter.

It seemed to Rachel that he was constantly bordering on laughter, that everything was funny in a mordant self-deprecating way, and she was again struck by his handsomeness. *All the more reason I should not let him touch me.* "I'm not sure I want you to choose my gowns . . . if I must have new ones. I see nothing wrong with the gown I'm wearing. 'Tis perfectly all right for a nanny."

For a long moment Abshire did not speak. He just stood there, his gaze fixed on Rachel while he shook his head. Rachel looked at his sister, who was obviously hiding a smile.

Rachel failed to see the levity. "If you choose my gowns, your lordship, they will show half my bosom, and, as I told you last evening, I'm not fond of your staring at me the way you do."

He bowed from the waist. "I beg your forgiveness, Miss Rachel, but if you do not wish for a man to stare at you, then you should not be so beautiful."

"A bosom is a bosom," she said with alacrity. "I assume they are all alike."

Lady Talbert could not contain her laughter. When she could speak, she said, "I have a capital idea, if I may interject my thoughts into this argument. We shall all go to the village, and I will hold little Frank while Rachel is measured for gowns." She looked at Rachel. "I agree with my brother, you do need clothes that fit. What you are wearing is lovely, but several years too short." *And it's faded and worn from years of wear.*

Lady Talbert, being a kindhearted person, did not wish to hurt Rachel's feelings. The gel was an enigma, but very much human, her ladyship thought, studying Rachel's pretty face, her deep blue eyes, cradled in so much hurt. *Mayhap someday she will tell me the whole of it.* She turned her attention to the conversation that was taking place.

Lord Abshire was saying, "'Tis settled then. I will gather Napoleon while you two ladies get yourself and little Frank ready. He will need a coat, or a blanket. Morning chill is still in the air."

He left, and Rachel watched him go, his tall, muscular body moving with graceful ease. Deep in thought, she felt a hand on her arm. Her first inclination was to demand to be unhanded. Touching was something she was not used to. Realizing it was Lady Talbert, she turned to her and smiled.

First, her ladyship dismissed the maid, and then she said to Rachel, "Dear, we must needs talk."

"About what? Have I done something wrong?"

"No. You've done nothing wrong. I love the way you are watching over Frank, even though it is a little unconventional. No, 'tis about something altogether different."

Rachel stared at her. "Well, pray tell me. It must be something awful. Does it have to do with your husband?"

"My husband? Oh, my no. He seldom crosses my mind." As if she had said more than she intended, Lady Talbert's pretty face was suddenly flushed.

"No need to feel embarrassed with me, your ladyship," Rachel said. "I just thought you wanted to speak about something personal between you and your husband, something between two females that men shouldn't hear."

" 'Tis something between two girls," Lady Talbert said, "and I do not wish to hurt your feelings. I only mean to be helpful."

"About what? Lady Talbert, I appreciate your interest. Don't be afraid of hurting me."

Lady Talbert heaved a deep sigh. "Rachel, my dear, one does not mention bosoms in polite society. It is against propriety."

Rachel reached for Frank, for she was sure the woman was going to drop him. How could a mother not know how to hold her own baby? "Then, tell your brother to stop staring at me. I was so ashamed when I was wearing your beautiful gown."

" 'Tis nothing to be ashamed of, having a well-formed figure. A man likes to look. Especially Trenton. I think you are right to draw the line to his touching you, though I doubt that he means harm. But let him look. It should make you feel flattered to be desired."

"His lordship doesn't look, he stares. And I don't know about this desiring part."

"Rachel, where did you come from? Where did you get your schooling? Obviously you are well read."

"But not books about bosoms, or anything like that. Mother M. never mentioned desiring."

A frown creased Lady Talbert's brow. "Have you never felt that you would like to be kissed by a man?"

"God's truth, I never thought about it. Except I would have

liked for my dear papa to kiss me on the cheek, and mayhap hug me in a fatherly way. But he never did."

"I'm not talking about *that* kind of feeling. Rachel, you need help. I'll lend you my book, if you will read it in the privacy of your room. I'm bound that it will titillate you. You are seventeen and a half, much too old to be in the dark about such things. Why, most gels are married before seventeen summers. Anyway, you should know what is happening should these feelings come over you."

"What book?"

"Lord Byron's *Childe Harold's Pilgrimage.* It caused quite a stir in the *ton* when it was first published. I hear the gentlemen of the upper orders even joked about it, and that the ladies took it to bed and held it under the covers to read a few lines before they fell asleep."

Rachel was curious. She did not like being ignorant about anything. "Thank you, Lady Talbert. I promise to read it, but I won't promise to become titillated. Mayhap there's something lacking in me."

"I doubt that," Lady Talbert answered with a little laugh.

Walking side by side, with Rachel carrying Frank, they had quit the dining room and were making their way to the stairway, where Rachel and Frank would ascend to the third floor. "Wait here, and I will get the book for you," said Lady Talbert. "Of course you will have to wait to read it. Any minute we will hear my brother's voice booming up from below, saying 'tis time we left for the village and wanting to know what we are doing." She was laughing when she left.

Rachel suddenly felt happy and warm inside. Little Frank was asleep, his head on her shoulder. It felt wonderfully good. Obviously Lady Talbert wanted to be her friend, and that was a joyous feeling. Rachel wondered why Lord Talbert stayed away from such a lovely person. And did he not care about little Frank? Parliament was not in session now, and still he stayed in London. And Lady Talbert had said that she seldom thought of him. It all seemed so strange.

Lady Talbert's return with Lord Byron's book interrupted Rachel's musing. "Hide this when you get to your room, and pray hurry. I'm excited about shopping for new gowns for you, though I don't see why you refuse to wear mine. I have so many."

"I told you I don't like my bosom showing," Rachel said. Turning, she ascended the stairs. Halfway up, she called to Lady Talbert, "I promise to hurry."

By the time Rachel reached her room, she had decided it would not be fair to Frank to take him into town. He was fast asleep, and he would not see one thing along the way. And, too, she remembered his crying and flailing when he was hungry. What if he became hungry while they were away from his wet nurse? She could imagine Lord Abshire's ire, for he had been against taking him and had only acquiesced when Lady Talbert had agreed that most likely Frank would enjoy it. Now, he was asleep and seemed to be enjoying that very much. She gave him a light hug before placing him in his crib.

"Yer wore him out, yer did," quarreled Hannah. "Look at the poor little thing, so fast asleep. He's even frowning, so tired is he."

"Hannah, Frank is not frowning, and he had a perfectly good time, watching me eat breakfast."

"Yer didn't feed him anything?"

"No. But I was tempted to give him porridge. He's six months old."

"My milk is all my babe needs, and yer hear me, I'd better not catch yer feeding him from the table. He might choke."

Rachel did not have time to argue with the woman, nor did she wish to do so. When she returned she would read the nanny book. Surely it would tell at what age a child should have something other than breast milk. She would go by the book, not by what Hannah said. "I'm leaving now, Hannah, going into the Village to purchase new gowns. When I return, I shall take little Frank for a walk in the fresh air."

The woman half-rose from her chair, the look of pure fright

on her face as she said, "Little Frankie is too young . . . there's germs out there."

"Balderdash! The fresh air will be good for him." Feeling sorry for Hannah, Rachel promised. "You can go for a walk with us, if you would like, Hannah. I know you are concerned about Frank, but please believe me, I would do nothing to harm him."

"Yer too young to know, to understand," said Hannah, starting to cry.

"Goodbye, Hannah. Frank will most likely be starved when he wakes. I know you will take good care of him."

With that, Rachel left.

Below stairs, as Lady Talbert had predicted, Lord Abshire was shouting that the girls should get a hurry on, that Napoleon would not like to be kept waiting. Rachel smiled, and just then Lady Talbert, wearing a lovely gown of pale green, and a mantle of the same color, appeared. Rachel explained briefly why she had not brought along little Frankie.

"A wise decision," said Lady Talbert. Looking below, she said loud enough for Lord Abshire to hear, "I told you he would be roaring like a lion, but don't let his lordship frighten you. He's a sweet lamb."

"Tessie," scolded Abshire, "don't you be misrepresenting me to Nanny Rachel. I'm not a sweet lamb." His voice was stern, but he was laughing. "Where's the baby?"

"He was sleeping so peacefully that I decided not to take him," Rachel said, her happiness bubbling over into laughter. She could hardly believe that Lord Abshire had called her Nanny Rachel, but she much preferred that over being called Miss Storm. Nanny Rachel gave her a place in which to fit into the household. Until her dear papa claimed her, she could not be family.

Lord Talbert's claiming her for his child was never far from Rachel's thoughts, but until it happened, Nanny Rachel would do quite nicely, she told herself. She joined Lady Talbert and together they went out of the house to the carriage and his lordship handed them up. Rachel sucked in her breath.

The handsome carriage was midnight black trimmed with gold inlay. The interior was royal blue velvet. Gingerly, she rubbed a hand over the soft fabric.

Napoleon sat crouched as far in the corner of the carriage as he could possibly get. Rachel looked with pity at his skinny little legs protruding from under the red-and-black horse blanket. He wore the high-top shoes she had purchased for him in London. He was scowling ferociously.

"I don't see why yer gels need to go. How can I get dressed with yer around? I ain't showing my nakedness to nobody."

Rachel gave him a soft little laugh. "We promise to repair into a store while his lordship gets you all fixed up in new clothes. They seem to think I need new gowns to wear while I'm tending Frank."

Napoleon's intense gaze went from Lady Talbert to Rachel, both sitting on the opposite squab. "I would say they be right."

Lord Abshire spoke candidly. " 'Tis all right for you and Lady Talbert to browse in the shops, Rachel, but I must needs be present when you purchase new gowns. I'm thinking a pre-Christmas Ball is in order at Talbert Hall, and a modiste will be summoned to make a gown for that."

"Who ever heard of a nanny going to a ball?" Rachel asked as she sat slightly forward on the squab." I think you have windmills in your head, your lordship."

"Why not a costume ball, with everyone wearing a mask?" asked Lady Talbert. "With Rachel as our mystery guest. When it is over, we shall unmask her and introduce her as Frank's new nanny."

"A capital idea," answered Lord Abshire. "And since she is so secretive about where she comes from, we shall invent a very exciting background for her. Mayhap an impoverished Russian countess who came to England looking for work."

Rachel found herself caught up in the excitement. It would be her first ball, and from what she had read, they were excellent fun. She was ever so glad that Mother M. had had a dance instructor come to the Home to teach her the basic steps. He had said she had natural talent and would have no trouble dancing with the gentlemen. And Mother M. had cautioned her that under no circumstances did bodies of the lady and gentleman touch when dancing.

She told Lord Abshire, "I will choose my own gown."

"No! I will not have you looking dowdy," his lordship said rather sternly, and Rachel responded with, "What are you, your lordship, a control freak?"

She had no idea where such a statement had come from. Unless it was her gut feeling and she simply expressed it without thinking. But if his lordship chose gowns with low necklines, she would not wear them, she determined, then shut her mouth in a stubborn line. No need to say more. She would wait until the gowns were being ordered.

"I can see this shopping spree will be delightful," said Lady Talbert in her good-natured way. "I'm enjoying myself already."

When they reached Blanchland, the driver was ordered to stop at Madame deMoss's draper's shop. Rachel and Lady Talbert alighted, with the help of his lordship. "Remember, no blunt exchanged until I am there," he said. "The gowns must needs be pleasing to one's eye."

"We'll remember," said Rachel, wondering how she could exchange blunt when she didn't have any, except what she had left of the money she had taken from the poor box. She told Napoleon goodbye and watched as the carriage tooled down the cobbled street before she entered the shop.

"I can hardly wait to get started," Lady Talbert said, grabbing Rachel's hand and pulling her toward the draper shop.

It was not unlike shops Rachel had been in with Mother M. Draped everywhere were beautiful silks, thin muslin, sarcenets, cotton twills, stuffs, and satins in rich colors. But this was different. They had come to buy.

"They have dresses and pelisse already made up and hanging from racks, Lady Talbert said. "Many folk from the country do not use modistes."

"I would like to look at those already made before his lordship returns." Rachel rubbed the sprigged muslin with small blue flowers between her fingers. "'Tis lovely," she said.

Madame deMoss came to greet them and asked what she could do for them. She spoke with a definite French accent, and Rachel told her in French that she would like to see the dresses from the racks.

The shop owner looked Rachel up and down, clearly taken back that the poorly dressed girl could speak French. And Lady Talbert looked at her askance, as well. But neither asked, and Rachel did not volunteer to tell them that at the Home she had been forced to learn the language of other countries.

"The racks are at the back of the shop, so if you will follow me." Madame deMoss began walking in that direction.

"Mayhap we should wait until Trenton returns," said Lady Talbert.

"Stuff! His lordship is entirely too bossy. It was his idea that I have new gowns, but I never did say that he could choose them. He said it, and I just went silent, for he's a terrible person to argue with."

Lady Talbert laughed softly and followed behind Rachel, who was following behind the shop owner. When they at last came to the racks, Madame deMoss measured Rachel with her eyes. "You are quite small, but with a beautiful bosom."

Rachel looked down. The dress she wore was stretched to the bursting point. "Never mind my bosom. It only looks full because my dress is two years too small."

Madame deMoss pulled from the rack a gown of blue sarcenet. Lace trimmed the tiny sleeves and the layers of fabric that constituted the skirt. "This is lovely; it matches your blue eyes."

"It will never do," Rachel said with alacrity. She stepped forward. "If you don't mind, Madame, I will look through the dresses, for I know *exactly* what I want."

In no time at all, as the shop owner and Lady Talbert looked on, Rachel had found two gowns that suited her perfectly, a blue muslin and a cotton twill, both with high necklines and very plainly made. From a riband tied high under her breast, the unadorned skirts fell straight to her boot tops. When she held one in front of her, she did not miss Lady Talbert's groan, or Madame deMoss' look of disapproval.

"These two will do," said Rachel. To her the gowns were absolutely beautiful. As she looked at them her heart pounded in her chest and her eyes filled with tears. Not that she felt sorry for herself for not ever having the opportunity to purchase a new gown, but that she was so happy that fate—she was sure it was Mother M.'s prayers—had brought her to Talbert Hall. How could she ever thank these wonderful people? She buried her face in the gowns and smelled the newness.

"His lordship will not let you buy those gowns," Lady Talbert said in a quiet voice. "They are entirely too plain."

"Too plain? I'll be taking care of little Frank, not going for rides in a crested carriage."

"Just you wait and see. His lordship will be in here shortly, roaring like a lion."

"Yes, but you said yourself that he's a sweet kitten, regardless of his being bossy, and roaring like a lion. Well, I'm getting these two gowns, else I will tend little Frank in what I have on."

"Should you not have more than two?" asked Madame deMoss, disappointment of such a small sale showing in her composure.

"Two will be plenty. I shall wash them out at night, alternating and wearing a fresh gown every day. Of course I will press them. And as far as the gown for the before Christmas ball, I will leave that up to you, Lady Talbert, and to Lord Abshire. I know nothing about what a ballgown looks like."

Lord Abshire most certainly did roar like a lion when he saw the gowns Rachel had chosen. Rachel let him roar, but he did not change her mind. Two gowns were enough, and the ones she had chosen were perfectly all right to tend little Frank. And she had plenty of the unmentionables, as long as she laundered them every night. To spend money foolishly was a sin.

"I know. Mother M. said so," Lord Abshire retorted. But he could not help but smile. It was impossible to be angry with her. No doubt she was sincere, and the way she looked and held the new gowns, ugly though they were, one could believe she had never had anything new before.

He asked of his sister, "Tessie, would you take Rachel and Napoleon—he's out front in the carriage—to the sweetshop while I confer with Madame deMoss about the gown for the costume ball?"

"A capital idea," Lady Talbert answered, and she quickly left the shop with Rachel, who was reverently carrying the bag that held her new gowns.

"I can't wait to wear these," she said, as soon as they were out of Lord Abshire's hearing. She was disappointed that he did not approve of the gowns, but she was sure it was because they did not have a low neckline. His lordship must needs have a fixation with bosoms, she decided.

The carriage and four was parked directly in front of the shop, and Napoleon looked lost sitting alone on the blue velvet squab. "I look like a swell," he said when Rachel opened the door to ask him to go for a sweet.

"But you look handsome," she told him, a lump swelling up in her throat. He wore yellow breeches, white stockings, and a coat of deep green, his shirt a pristine white. He did look like a swell, Rachel thought, smiling, for he looked positively wonderful. And she could tell that he was as proud as a peacock.

"Come, let's go get a sweet," she coaxed.

"Rachel, do you think we have died and gone to heaven. I ain't never had new clothes before."

"Nor I. No, I don't think we've died and gone to heaven, Napoleon, but I do think that Mother M. is watching over us."

"Yer can believe that stuff if yer want to, but I call eatin' and wearing new clothes heaven." He then whispered, "What about yer dear papa. When's he coming home?"

"Christmas, they say. Seems a long time, but I can't afford to pry more than I have. Waiting won't be so bad; I love tending little Frank. And there's to be a pre-Christmas ball, which I'm to attend as a Russian countess. Won't that be simply grand? Lord Abshire is inside the store now, selecting my costume."

Napoleon's voice rose an octave. "Yer going to a ball?"

"Shhh . . . Lady Talbert will hear you."

Rachel took his hand and they joined her ladyship, who waited near the storefront. At the sweetshop, they enjoyed a sweet, and then another.

In the draper's shop, Madame deMoss was asking of Lord Abshire, "How can I do all this without her standing for measurements? 'Tis impossible."

"I'm telling you that she is two hands around the waist, and she touches my chin when we stand facing each other."

The store owner raised a quizzical brow. "Oh, I see . . . 'tis like that, is it?"

Her meaning was obvious. Abshire's voice was strident. "No, 'tis not like that. I want the young lady to have decent clothes if she is to stay at Talbert Hall. You saw what she was wearing, and those gowns she selected are for little old dried-up dowagers."

"Without a bosom to show off," added Madame deMoss.

Lord Abshire selected five plates from *La Belle Assemblée* and *The Lady's Magazine,* all plates very Parisienne, the gowns with very low décolletages. In his mind's eye, he could see

Rachel wearing the fabulous creations. *When she sees how beautiful she is in them, she cannot refuse to wear them.*

He smiled as the thoughts raced through his mind, and being a red-blooded man, other thoughts sent the red blood rampaging through his veins.

He then selected the plate for the costume ball. That was not difficult, for any draper shop owner, especially if she was the shop's modiste as well, knew what a Russian countess wore. Had not the wife of the Russian Ambassador, Countess Lieven, taken the *ton* by storm, with her gorgeous clothes, and with her affinity for the waltz, which, until she appeared on the scene, was considered quite scandalous.

"I think a rich gold satin," said Lord Abshire. "And shoes made to match. Her feet are about this long." He held up both hands, with space between.

Madame deMoss shook her head. "What if none of this fits? Will she be coming in for a fitting?"

His lordship thought for a moment. "She seemed agreeable to going to the ball . . . yes, yes, I'm sure she will agree to a fitting for the ball gown. That's a capital idea. Then you can use those measurements for the other gowns as well. I'll go to the sweetshop and fetch her back here. But remember, not a word about the other gowns you are to make. And I'll leave it to your opinion on the mantles and pelisses she will be needing. Some with fur lining, and of the latest style."

The look of pure joy washed over the shop owner's face. Her grin was as wide as a barn, thought Abshire. "I'll take care of everything, in record time," she said. "I have helpers who are excellent at fancy stitching."

"While you are measuring, I shall get Lady Talbert to shop for the unmentionables, secretly of course. Miss Storm thinks nothing of washing clothes at night and putting them back on the next morning. She's very thriftwise."

His lordship turned to leave, but turned back when Madame deMoss asked, "Pray, forgive my forwardness, your lordship, but who is this Rachel Storm? Should I know her? Where did she come from?"

"She's very secretive about her background; however, I believe that she's an impoverished Russian countess who has, out of necessity, come to Talbert Hall to tend my sister's child."

He left, and Madame deMoss went to the window and watched as he disappeared out of sight, in the direction of the sweetshop. A gentleman of the first stare, she thought, and how strange that a man of the nobility should take such an interest in such a strange girl. Russian countess, indeed! But he had given a good order, and if he wanted to pretend it was for a Russian countess, so be it. She was smiling as she turned from the window and began gathering up fabric.

Eight

The following days were days of organization for Rachel. She found them wonderfully exciting, and for short periods she even forgot her reason for being at Talbert Hall. Lady Talbert on several occasions had sought her out to go riding, insisting that she wear one of her lovely green riding habits, and she chose a sprightly bay mare for Rachel to ride. Rachel often thought that even though so far she had failed to find her dear papa, she had found a warm and loving household. Lord Abshire was away much of the time, taking care of estate business, but when he was home, he asked Rachel to walk with him in the moonlight. She felt comfortable in doing this, for seemingly he had stopped ogling her bosom, or at least he was not so obvious about it.

She began Napoleon's lessons and was amazed how quickly he grasped the alphabet and how skillfully he used the pen. "Soon we will begin sums," she told him, and he gave her his big smile, which came often now. He had filled out and no longer looked like a walking skeleton.

Lord Abshire had suggested that Rachel use the library for the lessons, and what a grand library it was, leather-bound books from floor to ceiling, ancestral portraits smiling down on a desk of the finest mahogany with gold inlay, with lions' heads on the gold-encrusted legs. Napoleon said the desk was much too grand for him to use, but after Rachel insisted, in truth, was adamant about it, he came every day dressed in yellow pantaloons, dark coat, white cravat, his red hair pomaded close to his head.

For two hours each day, Rachel did this labor of love. Lord Abshire made special trips into Blanchland for supplies, often taking Napoleon with him.

"I haven't seen my brother this content in a long while," said Lady Talbert one day to Rachel. "He's taken such an interest in Napoleon, and he thinks you've brought life to Talbert Hall."

"Mayhap he is learning that happiness is found in helping someone less fortunate than himself," Rachel said. "I can't see where his wild escapades at parties and soirees I hear the servants talking about could bring much satisfaction to anyone."

Lady Talbert laughed. "The servants do like to prose on about Trenton. He keeps their lives titillated. Half of which is true, the other half not."

"There's that word again, your ladyship. I've read Lord Byron's *Childe Harold's Pilgrimage,* and it did not titillate me one whit. God's truth, I didn't know what it was talking about."

"You will. Just wait until Trenton kisses you."

"Kisses me! I will not forebear such a thing happening. Why, I won't even allow him to touch me. 'Tis disturbing."

Lady Talbert smiled to herself. The girl did not know that being disturbed by a man's touch was the forerunner to being titillated by his kiss. She had watched her brother's gentle pursuit of Frank's nanny, and his patience had astounded her. Patience was not his long suit, especially with the ladies. But of course he had never pursued a girl before; the girls had pursued him.

Having grown quite fond of Rachel, Lady Talbert had several times contemplated warning the innocent girl about her brother's intent. Upon observation, however, she had decided that Rachel could very well take care of herself. She had yet to wear the gowns his lordship had ordered made for her. Once, when he had insisted that she wear a beautiful purple gown when they were having supper alone, Rachel had done his bidding, but she had sown a white lace handkerchief onto the neckline, covering the naked flesh above her bosom.

This had immensely delighted the servants, and they had spoken of it where she, Lady Talbert, could hear. When questioned about how they had learned of this, it was readily admitted that "someone" had listened at the door. Who that someone was Lady Talbert never learned.

Behind a hand it was whispered loudly, "His lordship must've reached fer the handkerchief, fer a slap was heard, as if she wuz slapping his hand away, and then he groaned and asked her why she had sewed the thing. 'Because I knew you would try to remove it," the young gel said." And then more laughter from the servants.

Rachel was not unaware of the flying on-dits. Adaline had repeated to her every word, and they had laughed together, Rachel not admitting, nor denying, the truth of it.

October slipped quietly into November. Still, there was no sign of Lord Fox Talbert. At night, in the quietness of her room, Rachel thought about her dear papa, and she would count the days until Christmas. Try as she might, she could not pry information from Lady Talbert. Just that he spent most of his time in London, and that was satisfactory with her. *Be patient,* Rachel scolded, and then hot tears dampened her pillow.

Over and over she read the book on how to be a good nanny, and she learned that little Frank could indeed have thin gruel made from finely ground wheat. Despite Hannah's objections, Rachel made the gruel herself and brought it to the nursery and spooned it into his mouth. She laughed when it ran from the corners of his mouth and dripped off his little chin.

"You're killing me baby," said Hannah, and Rachel would gently remind her that Frank was not her baby.

"Besides, anyone who knows about raising children certainly knows that at seven months a child should have something more than milk. As Frankie's nanny, 'tis my responsibility to know these things."

This usually ended Hannah's arguments, but not her pouting, and when Rachel took him for long walks in the winter sunshine the wet nurse bundled him in enough blankets, which he kicked himself free of before they were down the stairs, to keep three babies warm.

On several occasions Rachel and Frank went exploring inside Talbert Hall, under the pretext of her showing the young heir the beautiful manor house he would someday inherit. From room to room, and there were many of them, they prowled, through beautiful bedroom suites, above stairs withdrawing rooms, all beautifully appointed, and many done in the crimson that one saw when first entering the manor house. There was a second library, with more family portraits.

Rachel studied the portraits, thinking she had never seen such ugly men. None resembled the mental picture she held of her strong, handsome papa. Oh, how she longed for a glimpse of his face. The portraits showed only solemn expressions, or angry ones, and many of the men held swords, as if they were ready for battle. Not a smile in the lot of them, Rachel thought. Her dear papa would be smiling. Strength, and also kindness, would show in his countenance.

Rachel even employed subterfuge. One day she knocked on Lady Talbert's door and asked if she and Frank could visit, thinking surely she would see a picture of Lord Talbert in his wife's quarters.

"I would love to have you visit," said Lady Talbert, reaching for her son, laughter gurgling up from his throat as he practically jumped into her arms. "My sweet baby." She kissed him on both cheeks.

Rachel's eyes traversed the room. Surely over the black marble fireplace there would be a portrait of Lord Fox Talbert. But there was not. Instead there was a painting of a strutting peacock, its wings encrusted with brilliant emeralds and shimmering blue lapis. Its eyes were red.

No doubt rubies, Rachel mused to herself.

Nowhere in the room of gold and white tables and deep

white sophas and handsome chairs could she see a portrait of any kind. Oil paintings by Claude and Poussin, which she instantly recognized, adorned the walls covered in blue silk. Blue, gold, and white, a beautiful room, but no portraits. Rachel was immensely disappointed. She turned her attention back to Lady Talbert and Frank. Her ladyship was saying, "Rachel, it was God's blessing that you came to Talbert Hall. I so love spending time with Frank, but I had been told by my husband that 'twas not the thing, that properly reared children did not spend more than an hour a day with the mother."

"A pox on the thing," declared Rachel. "Any mother worth her salt wants to hold her child."

"Why, Lord Talbert even told me that some upper orders sent their children to another household to be reared."

"That may be so . . . in proper society, but I know how much a child craves to be held and touched by his or her mother, even by the father. So, 'tis my opinion that proper society is wrong."

With Frank's head on her shoulder, Lady Talbert sat in a chair near the fireplace, where a lively fire burned, Frank sucking contentedly the thumb of his left hand. She held him with one arm and patted his back with the other. Rachel could not help but smile. When she had first come to Talbert Hall her ladyship held Frank as though she might let him slide through her arms onto the floor.

"Please sit, Rachel." Lady Talbert inclined her head to the chair opposite her. "I say again that I am delighted to have you here. A coze with you is very informative."

Rachel sat, and before speaking, she carefully measured her words. "It appears to me that your husband is very inconsiderate. Please don't think I am forward, but aren't you terribly lonely? He is not here with you, and he does not want you to form an attachment with your child?"

Rachel wanted Lady Talbert to say that Lord Talbert was far from being inconsiderate, that he was the most loving, understanding man in all of England.

"You must needs understand, Rachel, my marriage to Lord Talbert was arranged by my brother, the Duke of Winston. Being young, I quite naturally expected love. But it was understood from the beginning that my duty was to produce an heir to the earldom. I hoped for more, but it did not happen."

"After the heir is produced, then what? Are you to live like this the rest of your life? I think 'tis a terrible injustice to you. And why would he not want to be here with you? You are so beautiful."

Lady Talbert laughed. "He finds life in London more exciting, and after I recovered from my shock of a loveless marriage, I prefer he stay in London. He has given me permission to take a lover."

Rachel jumped to her feet. "Take a lover! That's against God's law. Mother M. would faint dead away should she hear of such goings-on."

"Calm down, dear. It is not my intent to indulge in such, but believe me, 'tis done all the time with the upper orders. As far as myself, I am perfectly content with my duties here at Talbert Hall. I take care of the tenants' needs; I manage the household, and I am learning to be a mother." Smiling at Rachel, she added, "Thanks to you."

Rachel took a deep breath before asking the very crucial question, "Lord Abshire mentioned that your husband is much older than you. Had he been married before, and were there children by that union?"

A lump formed in Rachel's throat, and she clasped her hands tightly together so that Lady Talbert could not see them trembling. She was sorry that she had asked. What if he were only ten years older, making him thirty? Then he could not possibly be her papa.

"Lord Talbert is twice my age plus ten summers," answered her ladyship.

Rachel sighed with relief. The first hurdle had passed.

"That would make him near forty and ten . . . fifty years old. . . . w-what about children? Mayhap a girl? I know there wasn't a son, else you would not be calling little Frank Lord Talbert's heir." To hide her nervousness, Rachel smiled at Frank, whose long lashes were closed against his cherub cheeks as he relished his thumb.

Lady Talbert looked at Rachel quizzically.

Rachel shifted in her chair and felt her face flush hot with embarrassment. Oh, why had she asked? It was bad manners, or, as the *ton* would say, *'Tis not the thing.* She gave an embarrassed laugh. "I hope you don't find my curiosity annoying, Lady Talbert. I'm just made that way. Mother M. said my curiosity would kill a cat someday."

"Lord Talbert's first wife died in childbirth, and I understand the baby also expired. He never mentions that part of his life, and I am not curious enough to ask."

Oh, but the baby did not die. I'm here, at his fabulous estate, waiting for him, and 'tis just as I thought; he placed me, his daughter, in Saint Cecilia's Home for abandoned children. Except he didn't abandon me. He sent money every month to assure my good care. That means he cares about me.

Rachel almost blurted out the truth of her coming to Talbert Hall, but caution warned her not to be hasty. She must needs confront Lord Talbert first. She mused aloud, "Christmas seems so far away. 'Tis only November."

"I think it is coming entirely too fast," declared Lady Talbert. Only yesterday I addressed invitations to our costume party. That will usher in the season, and from then on, it will be one yuletide festivity after another. Just because we are two days out of London doesn't mean that we country folk don't celebrate the yuletide the same as they do.

"And there's Christmas baskets to be made for the Talbert tenants, and, of course, baskets for the poor. I'll engage you to help with those, if you don't mind."

"I would love to help." Rachel laughed. "You make it sound very exciting. I've never been to a Christmas ball."

Lady Talbert looked at Rachel incredulously, again wondering where the poor girl had been. "I promise that you will have a lovely time at our costume party. Lord Abshire has great plans, won't even tell me who he will be impersonating."

Rachel rose to go. "Will your husband come home for the party?"

"I doubt that he will. I will send an invitation, but I won't hold my breath if he doesn't come. For certain he will be here for Christmas. His constituency expects it."

Rachel did not miss the questioning look and said quickly, "I must needs go. Frank is asleep on your shoulder. I should put him to bed." Giving a small smile, she added, "That will please Hannah, to have *her* baby back in her care."

"Oh, that possessive woman! At least she has not run you away, as she did the two nannies before you. And I'm glad, Rachel. You are a great comfort to me. You speak well, and you are well-read. 'Tis nice to have someone to talk with, especially when Trenton is absent from the Hall."

"When will his lordship be returning?" asked Rachel.

"On the morrow. He's gone to Worthington, our ancestral home, to confer with our brother. Though they don't rub well together, they still have business to discuss. His grace will most likely have some wealthy heiress for Trenton to wed."

"I find myself missing our evening walks."

Lady Talbert's countenance became solemn. "Don't miss them too much, Rachel. My brother has left a trail of broken hearts in his path. I should not like to see you hurt."

"Oh, I don't think of him with my heart. He's a good friend, nothing more. God's truth, Lady Talbert, I must needs get my life straightened out before I give my heart permission to care about a man."

She took Frank from his mother, and Lady Talbert stood and embraced them both. "Just remember, Rachel, guard your heart where my brother is concerned."

Rachel did not answer. She bade her ladyship goodbye and quit the room, going quickly to leave Frank with Hannah, and then to her room, where she could assimilate the wonderful news about Lord Fox Talbert. She wished she could talk with someone, but only Napoleon knew her reason for being at Talbert Hall, and his lesson was over for this day. Tomorrow she would tell him.

Rachel decided to write to Mother Margaret and tell her that she was at Talbert Hall. The good sister had been very kind to her, and, in her way, had loved her. It was not fair, Rachel mused, not to keep the woman apprised of what was happening to her. In less than a month Rachel would be eighteen, and the Home would no longer have a hold on her. So on parchment she had purchased to write her résumé, using a feathered quill, she wrote:

"Dear Mother Margaret:

I am now at Talbert Hall, near Blanchland, Northumberland, employed as a nanny for Lord Fox Talbert's son and heir. Thank you for forcing me to learn Latin, for it was from a book written in Latin that I learned how to care for a baby.

I am enclosing the money left over from that which I took from the poor box. I now draw fifteen pounds per month for my work. I thought that far too much, but Lord Abshire insisted that it was a fair amount. I miss his lordship when he is away from Talbert Hall. We take moonlight walks together, and I must needs tell you that your teachings about sin have stood me in good stead. When he touches me, I slap his hand, and he has kissed me only once, and that was on my cheek, in a brotherly way. He did not at all show desire to kiss me on the lips. Which I would not allow anyway, even though Lady Talbert says that such a kiss would be titillating, whatever that means.

I trust all is well with you and the others at the Home. I miss you, but I confess that I do not miss the five o'clock morning prayers. I do pray, though, from habit I guess. In truth, I feel that 'tis your spirit watching over me, and I thank you for it.

I am growing to love little Frank. I hold him close, and the most wonderful feeling comes over me.

Mother Margaret, please do not write to me here. Most especially until after Christmas. After that, the truth will have come out, and I would love to receive a letter from you."

Rachel signed and sealed the missive. She would be forced to slip away and take it to the post office the next time she went into the village. She longed for the time when she could be open about everything she did. Best though for now, she told herself, to keep her mission to herself, except for Napoleon. Hiding the letter in her pocket, she left the manor house and went to the stables. She could not wait until tomorrow to tell him what she had this day learned about Lord Talbert.

Napoleon was mucking out the stables, and when he saw Rachel a big smile spread across his face. "This ain't no place fer a lady, I mean no place for a lady."

Rachel laughed. "Napoleon, I must needs talk with you. Do you suppose we can go for a walk. I would not want anyone to hear what I am about to tell you."

"Must be something real special like." He leaned the shovel against the side of the stall, and they walked into the thicket of trees which had been stripped of their leaves by a killing frost. "Nobody can hear us now," Napoleon said.

Rachel began. "Well, I was talking with Lady Talbert, and she told me that Lord Talbert, her husband, is near fifty summers, and that his first wife died in childbirth."

"So, what does that have to do with him being your pap?"

"Oh, Napoleon, don't be so skeptical. You just don't believe anything good can happen. But I know better. What that means is that he is the right age to have fathered me. Lady Talbert said the baby died with its mother, but don't you see, Napoleon, the baby didn't die. Because it was a girl, his lordship couldn't see his way clear to raising her properly so he left me at Saint Cecilia's. It makes perfectly good sense to me. He married Lady Talbert so that she could produce an heir. They don't love each other at all, and I had that figured also. He was too much in love with my mama to ever really love another woman. But marriage was necessary . . . to produce an heir."

Napoleon looked up at Rachel. Tears clouded his eyes. The poor girl so desperately wanted to find her papa that she would grasp at any straw. Why could she not let it go? he asked himself. And then he remembered when his own pap died and how lost he had felt. He reached to pat Rachel's hand. "I hope you find your pap, miss, but the way I see it is that yer . . . you are letting that stand in your way of appreciating our good fortune of being employed at Talbert Hall. Your cheeks are all filled out and rosy, and I know for sure I've never had so much good food in my life."

"I know food is important to you, and to me, too, Napoleon, but I so want to know my birth parents, to belong to somebody. I just know in my heart that my mama is dead; she would not have left me in a home for abandoned children. Mothers just don't do that."

They sat in a bed of dead leaves and leaned against a tree trunk, Rachel wearing her too short coat over her new "nanny" dress, her long, black hair falling to her shoulders. She put an arm around Napoleon's shoulder, and he did not pull away. She told him, "I'm glad you tried to steal my box, Napoleon. I can't tell anyone else about these feelings. Not yet. I wrote to Mother Margaret, but I couldn't even tell her what's in my heart. I wanted to tell her that I am all right, and I sent back what I had left from the money I took from the poor box. I'll send what I owe later, when I get it."

"You have a good heart, Rachel," said Napoleon, moving closer to her, but stopping short of putting his head on her shoulder. He patted her hand again. "Like my pap."

When Mother Margaret received Rachel's letter, she blubbered like a baby. At least that was the opinion Sister Alice

Marie expressed. "You've stewed and stewed, and now when you hear that the girl is all right, here you are, crying your eyes out."

"I know. I'm a silly old woman, but I do love her so very much." She sniffed again, then blew her nose into a white handkerchief she took from the sleeve of her black habit. As if she were talking to herself, she mused aloud, "I will need a new dress."

"Whatever for?" asked Sister Alice Marie. "I haven't seen you in a dress more than twice since I came here ten years ago. Why would you be needing a new one?"

They were in the Home's austere business office, and Mother Margaret rose to leave. "I'm going to Talbert Hall, and I must needs make plans. Would you take my duties while I'm gone?"

"Of course I will, but this is quite unusual."

"Unusual but not unheard of," said Mother Margaret as she left. She went to her room. It was lonely without Rachel. Noticing that she had crumpled the missive in her hand, she smoothed the wrinkles and read it again. How in the world did Rachel end up at Lord Fox Talbert's country home?

"I must needs tell her all the things I neglected to tell her, the things a mother would have by instinct known to say to her daughter," Mother Margaret said to the silent room. From her drawer she took a map and found Blanchland, Northumberland, and whistled through her teeth. A four-day journey, mayhap five by public transportation. It would require a night's stay in London. But she was going, she determined, then laughed. As if anything could stop her. There had been no doubt in her mind from the moment she received the letter, which she read again.

The sister drove the trap herself into the village and went directly to a shop that sold dresses from a rack. She selected a plain black and white wool day dress with a white collar and white cuffs on the long sleeves. She then went to a millinery shop and selected a black hat with a wide brim, and a long, black plume in its band. She turned and turned before the looking glass, smiling at her new image. Her black fur-lined pelisse would keep her warm. Although it was twenty years old, it was still in excellent shape. The fur that trimmed the neck and hem showed only a little wear. How could it show wear when it had hung in the chiffonnier all these years?

Her mind went back to the letter. Why did Rachel ask that she not write to her until after Christmas?

Mother Margaret took the crumpled letter from her reticule and read it again, and for a long while she stood deathly still, pondering before saying, "That Regency Buck is up to no good, and that woman speaking of being titillated . . ."

Mother Margaret's mind went back twenty years. She remembered other brotherly kisses, and then the truth and the heartbreak that had brought her to Saint Cecilia's. Quickly she paid the lady who had been patiently waiting for the few shillings the hat cost. Outside, it was growing late and people were leaving the shops to go home. She joined them, going to her equipage and black horse tethered to a post in front of the shop. Her steps were hurried, as if she were leaving this moment to go to Blanchland, she thought. She would leave on the morrow. She owed it to Rachel. She blinked back tears and fought blubbering again as, in a choked voice, she murmured, "I so much want to see my Rachel again."

Nine

Lord Abshire sat in his brother's handsome library and contemplated the world beyond the wide windows. Snow blanketed the undulating hillocks, and branches on the tall trees hung heavily downward with it.

A lively fire warmed Lord Abshire, and words from his grace bored him. He had heard it all before, but not in such strident tones.

"You must needs settle down, Trenton," his grace said, his voice authoritative. " 'Tis not the thing for a man of twenty and five summers to race carriages at breakneck speed over country roads. Your youthful escapades are the talk of the *ton.*"

"Where else would one race a carriage? Certainly not down Oxford in good old London Town, though I believe it has been done," replied Abshire laconically. "And as far as my actions being the talk of the *ton.* I frankly don't give a demme."

"That's just it, you don't give a demme about anything. You should be here . . . on the family estate, helping me take care of business."

"You mean being your errand boy, do you not? No, thanks, Benford. I prefer watching over our sister whom you married off to that scoundrel Fox Talbert."

"That's one of the best marriages of the upper ten thousand. He's titled, a member of Parliament, and she has unlimited blunt. What more could a woman ask for?"

"Love."

Sarcastic laughter was his grace's answer. "You just refuse to accept *ton* ways, Trenton. Love is seldom found inside a marriage of convenience."

Lord Abshire rose from his red leather chair and went to stand by the window. It had started to snow again. He hated these confrontations. The duke was fifteen years his senior, born of a different mother. Their overbearing father had put two women in their graves. And his oldest son Benford had inherited the same controlling traits.

His lordship turned back into the room and looked at the duke, who had also inherited their father's good looks: midnight black hair, the same broad shoulders and handsome build, his deep blue eyes, from behind which burned an intense sharpness. Benford's hands moved in a threatening way, just as their father's had, right up until death claimed him. This mannerism used to scare his lordship, but now it was a relief to sit under the overpowering voice and feel nothing but calmness. He studied his grace, whose dress this day, as always, was of the first stare. The best tailor, the best bootmaker in all of London.

Lord Abshire spoke in a nonchalant tone, "Benford, did you summon me here for a dressing-down over a carriage race?" He gave his wry grin. "I won ten pounds. That should speak to your heart."

"Don't be obstinate, Trenton. You do not need to risk your neck for ten pounds." His grace paused for a moment before saying, "With your recklessness, I do not see you living to inherit my title. So it is imperative that you marry and produce an heir. I demand it. And I do control the family wealth. I can discontinue your allowance."

"Marry!" exploded Lord Abshire. He caught himself before he spoke his mind about the leg-shackled state. Always best not to let Benford know his thinking on anything.

"Yes, marry. There must needs be an heir to the Dukedom, and to the entailed lands that make us rich beyond measure. Would you like to see those lands returned to the Crown? As far as I know, there is not even a distant cousin to inherit."

"Why do you not grasp the honors? The duchess looks as if she were meant to bear many heirs."

Lord Abshire thought his brother's wife horribly ugly, broad in build, a large nose, and he could understand why no children had been born to the union. *'Twould be impossible, unless someone sacked the poor woman's head.* The thought brought laughter to his lordship's throat, but he did not release it.

He also knew that was not the reason there were no children. His brother, because of an unmentionable disease during his salad years, had been rendered sterile. This was not known until several years into the marriage. By then Hortense had taken a lover, the duke a permanent mistress.

"There will be no heir unless you produce one," said his grace, his countenance downcast. "I was foolish when I was a young man. I'm trying to keep you from the same fate. Since you refused Lady Cynthia, I have recently spoken with Sir Charles Stuart about the possibility of a match between his sister, Lady Aileen, and yourself. He promises a considerable dowry."

"She's out of the question."

"Why, pray—"

"I don't like her. She is not suitable."

"How do you know she is not suitable, or that you don't like her, when you haven't had the pleasure of meeting her?"

No answer came from Lord Abshire, just a sardonic smile, and his grace heaved a deep sigh. Lord Abshire was now back in his red leather chair. His brother was standing, leaning against the mantel and looking worried. "Her brother tells me that she is agreeable to your paying your addresses."

This argument could go on all day, Lord Abshire thought. He said quickly, and without thinking, "Which I do not intend to do. I have already selected my helpmeet when I decide to take the plunge."

"You've already decided! Without consulting me?"

Lord Abshire laughed. This was too ridiculous for words. Whatever made his grace think he could choose his lifemeet?

Oh, because he had inherited their father's title, not that he was filled with wisdom. Because, by a quirk of fate, he had appeared on this earth as the first son? An idea came to his lordship, and without equivocation, he blurted it out. "I plan to marry the new nanny at Talbert Hall."

It appeared that his grace would jump out of his skin. "A nanny?" he shouted. He flailed his fist in the air, and for a moment Lord Abshire thought his grace would strike him. But he settled himself and, raising his glass, he glared incredulously at Abshire. His voice was strangled. "Are you daft?" Dropping his quizzing glass, he turned and slammed his fist against the mantel.

This is getting better by the minute, thought Lord Abshire. He chuckled to himself. "I may be daft, Your Grace, but this nanny has the most incredible blue eyes I have ever seen. From the time she appeared at Talbert Hall, looking to take care of little Frank, when she did not know one thing about caring for a child, I've been lost . . . totally, totally lost."

His grace left the mantel and began pacing. He stroked his whiskers, until finally he found enough voice to ask, "What are her credentials? Her family background?" And then, "Trenton, you must needs be funning. 'Tis unheard of. A son of a duke marrying a nanny. A bit of muslin, no doubt." He shook his head. "Too disgraceful to think upon."

"Well, feel yourself disgraced, for Rachel Storm will be my wife before year's end."

Gaining the chair he had previously left, his grace buried his face in his hands. "Pray, tell me about her."

"There isn't much to tell, except I fell in love at first sight." With tongue in cheek, Lord Abshire went on, "She stood at the door of Talbert Hall, holding a cardboard box, which I was to learn held her earthly possessions. She wore the most unflattering gown I had ever seen, two years too small if a day, buttoned high at the neck, not a speck of flesh showing, and the hem of the skirt struck her halfway between her knees and her half-boots, which were scuffed and near worn out.

"And that wasn't all that caught my attention. Standing beside her was a boy of about eight who looked for the world like a child thief of which London's East End abounds. I hired him to muck out the stables."

"And what will Lord Talbert think of your brazen miscarriage of judgment. The boy could steal him blind, and no doubt the girl came looking for a soft skull such as yourself. Well aware of her beauty, she's most likely preyed on every rich nabob she's met. How many summers? Most like thirty or more, on the shelf, but still carries that innocent look. I know the type."

"You should, your grace, with your experience with mistresses. But you are wrong about Rachel. If she had made a conquest such as you mention, she would have had at least one decent gown. Why, it was necessary for me to buy her a whole new wardrobe. She's seventeen and a half, and she slaps my hand away when I attempt to touch her. But I'm sure we shall produce a gaggle of heirs . . . after I tame her."

"Oh, that touch-me-not is the oldest trick in the world," his grace said sarcastically. "Just as I said, carries that innocent look. No doubt a well-trained cyprian, and you've foolishly fallen for her. What would the late duke say?"

"He's dead. He can't say anything, except through you. If I closed my eyes, I would swear your voice is his voice, and I've had enough of it for one day. Pray, when you summon me again, have something interesting to talk about."

His grace glared at him.

Giving his wry grin, Lord Abshire stood and bowed from the waist. "Your grace. I'll see that you receive an invitation to the wedding." He retrieved his greatcoat, which he had tossed onto the back of a chair, and turned to leave. Knowing his stay would not be long, he had asked the groom to keep his equipage out front. Nothing would convince him that he should spend the night under the same roof with this paragon of virtue. "Good day, Brother. I will let myself out," he said, as he left.

Abshire was still chuckling when he reached his handsome Stanhope tilbury. He took the ribbons from the groom and thanked him, then gave the horses office to go at a breakneck speed. It was a day's journey back to Talbert Hall, and it was late day. A coaching inn was a few kilometers down the road; he would stay there.

Anything, anywhere to absent himself from his brother, thought his lordship as he settled back in the seat and let the horse have its head. The heavy body of the tilbury, supported by excellent springs, made for a very pleasurable ride. The snow was still falling, although very lightly, and he thought that he had never seen the countryside more beautiful. It was cold, but not overly. His greatcoat kept him comfortable.

It was not until Lord Abshire was cozily ensconced in his room at the coaching inn—they had given him the room reserved for the nobility—that he again thought of Rachel Storm. A fire burned in the grate. He stretched his feet toward the flames, and her startling blue eyes were staring back at him in the most unusual way, causing his heart to quicken. He thought of what he had told his brother and smiled, and then he surprisingly found himself wishing it were true.

"How ridiculous," he said aloud.

But it wasn't ridiculous at all, his heart told him. And it would set his grace's world to spinning out of control. For a long while he pondered this sudden desire to become leg shackled. It was near the eleventh hour into the night before he gained his bed. There, his body had its say about Rachel Storm, in flaming fashion. He had never desired a woman so much in his life, not even when in battle for long periods of time and away from all pleasurable sport. He tossed and turned, and swore, and the next morning his eyes were red from lack of sleep. Otherwise, he felt wonderful. His step was light, his smile wider than usual, and he took considerable time with his dress.

After the tenth try, reminding himself of the dandy Beau Brummel, the folds in his cravat were as he wanted them. He gave his brown hair extra swipes with the brush, then turned in front of the looking glass to see if his fawn-colored breeches stretched over his muscled thighs satisfactorily, and if his boots shone like a looking glass.

"Am I becoming vain?" he asked himself, laughing in the silent room, for he knew that was not so. He was acting as a man in love. But that could not be, his logical mind argued. He only wanted to bed the girl with the haunting blue eyes. And that was what they were, haunting. The night past, every time he had closed his eyes, those blue eyes were there, staring innocently into his face, her lovely mouth smiling at him. How many times during the night had he undressed her, felt her naked in his arms, kissed her until she no longer wanted to cover her bosom?

And how many times had he smiled to himself when he thought of his brother's reaction to his announcement of his intent to wed the nanny. Could that be the reason for this sudden change of heart about becoming leg shackled?

Did he wish to wed the girl to spite his brother? A chuckle formed deep in his throat, and when he let it go, it was a very satisfactory feeling.

With these thoughts trampling his mind, things which he would in time sort out, Lord Abshire breakfasted hurriedly in the inn's dining room and was soon on his way to Talbert Hall. He would kiss Rachel Storm as soon as he arrived. Somehow he would manage a private moment with her, and mayhap that moment would turn into hours. First the kiss, and then . . .

Time passed quickly as the Stanhope tooled quickly over the road. The snow had abated during the night, leaving the hills banked, the corries full, trees heavy. Now, the yellow sun battled white floating clouds for a place in the winter sky, and the sound of hooves hitting the road resounded into the morning quiet.

Lord Abshire whistled and cracked the whip. Upon meeting a carriage and four, the coachman on the box wearing a many-layered coat, his lordship waved in a friendly fashion. Never had his heart felt so light, and when he arrived at Talbert Hall, he went first to his quarters and asked his valet to choose clean garments while he bathed. He had decided against seeking out the nanny just yet. A shave was in order, and the valet arranged it with immediacy.

"You're mighty chipper," Lawrence, the valet, said. Then, as was his custom, he waited for a full explanation for his lordship's good mood.

Lord Abshire hedged with, " 'Tis a relief to be away from my brother and his infernal matchmaking."

The valet whooped with laughter. "Who this time? Last time it was Lady Cynthia. But always 'tis some hoity-toity who can bring plenty of blunt to the marriage?"

"His grace gave the girl's name, but God's truth, I've forgotten it already. I told him that, even though I had never met the lady in question, I did not like her, and that was that."

"You'll be the death of your big brother yet. What else did you tell him? Knowing you, you goaded him to despair."

"That I did. I informed him that I planned to marry Frank's new nanny. He appeared to be on the edge of the vapors, turned pale as a sheet and snorted the most outrageous threats, like cutting my allowance, which would not worry me a whit."

The valet raised a questioning brow. "How so, your lordship?"

"I have income from my deceased mother which his grace has no say over, and I manage the Talbert estates on a profit-sharing basis."

"But surely you're not serious about marrying little Frank's nanny."

"I'm thinking on it. If she will have me, and no doubt she will. Marriage is the best route for a miss in Regency England. There's no future in being a nanny."

"And what future would she have in marrying you? She might look on carriage racing and boxing bouts with disfavor."

A small chuckle from Lord Abshire. "Most likely she would call it sinning, but I would not do those things should I have a helpmeet." And then his lordship surprised himself with, "Fustian, Lawrence, I just might be in love with Rachel Storm."

"In lust, more likely," replied the valet, who knew his lordship too well to believe that he could be in love.

"Mind your tongue," said Lord Abshire, still in good humor. He hurried from the room before his valet could advise caution. He was not looking for approval for his rash actions; he just wanted his heart to settle down and stop jumping up into his throat every time he thought of the girl. This was his second day not to have seen her, and it seemed more like a month.

His lordship went directly to his library, and, before summoning a servant to fetch Rachel, he stood before the looking glass and admired the clothes the valet had chosen, a blue superfine coat of the new style, nipped at the waist and made to wear on informal occasions, a ruffled white shirt, open at the neck and showing brown chest hair, skin-tight doeskin pantaloons that stretched over his muscled thighs. All above Hoby tall-boots made of black leather and finished at the knee with a buff leather turned-down top. He felt all the crack and could not wait for Rachel to tell him so.

"You look like a dandy," Rachel said when she entered the room. The footman who had come to fetch her carried a huge box. Bending over, he sat it on the floor. "Thank you," she said to the footman, giving him a smile, and when he was gone, she turned back to smile at Lord Abshire. "Did you have a pleasant journey?" she asked.

"The journey was pleasant enough, but no meeting with my brother has ever been pleasant." He came to take her hand. "I would rather not think of his grace, or what he had on his mind. I have more important things to speak with you about. Come, let's sit before the fire."

"What important things do you have on your mind?" She

pulled her hand from his. "I don't want to sit. I have something to show you. After you've spoken."

For the first time in his life, Lord Abshire was at a loss for words with a damsel. He had not planned on telling her his plans to marry her until he had at least kissed her in the way a man kisses a woman to whom he's about to break such news. But there was nothing to it; he would say the words and then kiss her. And so he did ask her, after heaving a big sigh. "Nanny Rachel, it is my intent to make you my wife."

Rachel laughed, merry laughter that rang out into the staid room. "Lord Abshire, it is not my wont to make you my husband. Even though you have been most generous with me. That's what I'm waiting to tell you. You must needs return these beautiful mantles and pelisses in this box. I will try them on, and you can choose two or three which you think speaks most favorably for my needs. Thirteen wraps, even for the upper orders, is quite ridiculous. There are orphans in this world who don't have one decent coat."

I didn't buy wraps for orphans, thought Lord Abshire, going to sit on a short sopha near a window. He felt rebuffed, which, indeed, he was, he told himself. With Rachel one never got what one expected. He watched as she took the first garment from the box and slipped into it, a fur-lined pelisse in heavy Carmine wool, with Russian sable around the hem and neck.

The bright red shade of wool, in his lordship's opinion, contrasted beautifully with Rachel's long black hair and made her blue eyes speak with animation. "Keep that one," he said, and Rachel smiled and said, " 'Tis my very favorite, Lord Abshire, so I'm pleased you like it. And the fur muff is absolutely the most divine thing I've ever seen.

"In truth, your lordship, I had never seen a fur muff before, except in pictures." And then, looking straight at him, she said, "Even though we both favor this garment, it is much too elaborate for a nanny to wear. I'm sure the on-dits would fly."

"Let them fly. As my wife, you will be appropriately dressed."

"I told you it was not my intent to take you for my husband."

"Well, it is my intent to make you my wife. I've already informed my brother, and before repairing to bed this night, I shall so inform Tessie."

"I wish you had not done that, m'lord, for you will now have to uninform your brother. I am Frank's nanny, nothing more. I am not in a position to marry anyone."

Lord Abshire rose from the sopha and took Rachel's arm. His voice was kind when he asked, "What do you mean, you are not in a position to marry?" His eyes probed hers, and he felt that drowning sensation again. Her warm flesh under his hand sent his blood to boiling. How could a girl so innocent exude such appeal and arouse him so?

"I can't tell you the reason I can't marry you," Rachel said. She did not pull her arm from his lordship's grasp. It felt good there, and, for a moment, she was overcome with a strange sensation she did not recognize. Cautiously, she stepped back, to put distance between them.

This did little good, for in the next instant the distance had been closed and she was in his arms, and his lips were on hers, and, from that moment on, she knew little else. A strange warmth invaded her body as she let him pull her closer to his length. She felt a hardness she did not understand. He kissed her eyes, her cheeks, and her tiny ears, before returning to once again claim her lips with his own. His tongue probed until her lips opened, plunging her deeper and deeper into the vortex of strange desire.

It was not until she felt a big hand close over her throbbing breast that Rachel came to her senses. She pulled herself free and delivered a good sound box to his lordship's jaw.

Instead of being angry as Rachel expected, Lord Abshire grinned wryly and told her, "It was worth getting my jaw boxed just to feel your response to my kiss."

"That's sinning for sure," Rachel spat out angrily. "I shall tell Mother M. when I see her again, and this night I shall say my prayers twice. Now, if you will keep your distance, I would like you to help me decide on these wraps."

Removing the red pelisse, she flung it onto a chair. She was glad she was wearing her "nanny" dress, the blue sprigged muslin that hid her bosom, else his lordship would have been kissing her there.

And I might not have forced myself to stop him.

The next wrap was a mantle, in Devonshire brown—rich brown with a reddish tint—no ornaments and untrimmed with fur. Rachel thought she might keep it, if his lordship agreed. It was more practical, a large rectangular piece of fabric gathered at the neck and reaching to her half-boots. There was a round hood, which she pulled over her head, framing her face. He had regained the short sopha, and she turned to face him.

"I think this most practical, your lordship. 'Tis heavy enough to guard against the coldest of weather."

Lord Abshire sucked in his breath. Even in a garment that hid her well-formed figure, she was beautiful. Her eyes were like a beacon in his dull life. It is strange, he thought, until she came, I thought my life exciting and full. Now he was utterly speechless with delight.

"Don't just stare at me, your lordship. Do you or do you not think I should keep this mantle?"

"Yes, yes, keep it. You are beautiful in it, and the Kashmir is exceptionally warm, which you need in this kind of weather."

"Kashmir! That's expensive, is it not? I'll put it aside."

And so it went, garment following garment, each so elegant that Rachel felt like a princess just trying them on. Of the thirteen, she chose two, the Kashmir mantle, which, in Rachel's opinion, was too expensive. Her second choice was a cottage cloak made of heavy wool. She put the mantle and cloak aside and began placing the others in the box in which they had been delivered.

Lord Abshire watched until the third wrap had been meticulously placed inside the box before pushing himself up from the sopha and going to pull the bell rope. He said nothing, and Rachel kept packing. When a maid came to his summons, bobbing and asking his wont, his lordship asked her to take the wraps and hang them in Miss Storm's chiffonnier, all of them.

Rachel glared at him until the maid left with the box, and then she exploded: "Why did you let me parade in front of you in all thirteen wraps when you had no notion of living up to our agreement?"

"It was your idea to keep only two wraps. I never said—"

"But you smiled when I said it."

"I smile every time I look at you. No, Nanny Rachel, I will not return the wraps. They are yours to enjoy. As my wife, you will be expected to dress well. Besides, the wraps will keep you warm when I'm not there to hold you."

Rachel looked at him openmouthed. "I told you—"

"I know that you said you were not in the position to marry any man. Would you explain what you meant by that? Mayhap I can correct whatever is wrong."

"There's nothing anyone can do."

He came and held both her arms with his big hands. Looking deep into her eyes, seeing the hurt, he said, "Tell me Rachel, what is wrong? You came to Talbert Hall looking for something or somebody. Can you tell me—"

"No."

A rush of tenderness rose and clutched his throat so that he could hardly speak. A long pause, and then, "Rachel, pray tell me why you can't marry me. Incredulously, I find myself hopelessly in love with you. From the moment we met I had these very strong feelings, for which I made excuses to myself. At first you were a conquest, I intended to seduce you, a notion of which I'm now very much ashamed. And then it was my intent to marry you in defiance of my overbearing brother. Fortunately, on this journey I faced the whole of it: I truly do love you . . . with all my heart."

Rachel could not believe what she was hearing. It simply

could not be so. She was by no means ready for a husband. That had not been in her plan, and she told herself the reason her heart pounded when his lordship kissed her was because she was inexperienced with men. Or mayhap it was fright. Aloud she said, "I can't marry you, your lordship, until I know who I am. Mayhap when Christmas is past, I will know, and then I can think about whether or not I'm in love with you. Should I marry, that is what it must needs be, love. None of this *mariage de convenance* for me."

That night, in bed, Rachel relived the strange time in the library. She tried to recall exactly how Lord Abshire had looked when he declared his love for her. Could he have been funning? How did she feel when this declaration was made? In truth, she admitted as she sat by the window looking out at the snow-covered night, she was so upset over the kiss that she could not recall how she felt. She knew now what Lady Talbert had meant when she said a kiss would titillate.

She remembered the warmth that invaded her body, and she remembered also that it was his lordship's touching her throbbing bosom that brought her to her senses. Crossing herself, she told the Higher Power, or Mother Margaret, whichever was higher, that she was sorry she had sinned. And then in the same breath, she admitted that she had never felt so alive, so deliciously wonderful, as she had when his lordship was kissing her. She touched her lips with the tips of her fingers, rubbing them to see if they were still warm, and she longed for Lord Abshire to kiss her again . . . and again.

Sleep would come late this night, she thought. In her thin nightdress, she went to stand by the window, to look out and think. His lordship had pleaded with her to go for a walk in the snow, promising to keep her warm, but, not trusting herself, she had refused. Before they parted, he had vowed again they would marry, she just as adamant that they would not.

"Who am I?" she now asked the silent room, not expecting, nor getting, an answer. "When I know that, I will be free to marry," she said, again addressing the silence. Tears threatened, and she willed them away. She longed to talk with Mother Margaret and admonished herself for the longing. No longer was she a child of the Home. She must needs keep her own counsel, make her own decisions.

Should a thrilling kiss make a girl want to wed? She thought not, especially a rakehell such as Lord Abshire. Should she not wait until Lord Talbert returned to Talbert Hall and acknowledged her as his daughter before worrying about the momentous decision of matrimony? He might even offer guidance. Counting the days until Christmas, she thought it a long, long time, when in reality, compared to all the years she had waited to know her dear papa, it was not. And, she reasoned further, he might even come to Talbert Hall *before* Christmas.

She returned to bed and snuggled under a down-filled quilt, enjoying its warmth, and at last she slept. Her last thoughts were not of the man whose kisses thrilled her until she hardly knew her name, but of her dear papa, a handsome, tall, broad-shouldered man with black hair and deep blue eyes. In the fuzzy state between half awake and half asleep, she envisioned his smile when he saw her, felt his arms around her, heard his kind voice calling her his daughter. Oh, this was going to be the best Christmas ever.

Ten

It was near midday when Lord Fox Talbert's valet entered the elaborate bedchamber. He walked apprehensively to the bed where his lordship was sleeping with his head resting on a plump down pillow covered in the finest linen. The valet pulled the red velvet bed hangings back and stood for a moment, listening to his lordship's snoring and watching his lips tremble as he exhaled each breath.

"M'lord, someone awaits you below stairs," said the valet. "The butler has ordered the young girl to leave, but she keeps pounding with the brass knocker. 'Tis an awful disturbance, m'lord."

Lord Talbert opened one eye and then the other. Overcome by the need for sleep, for he had not gained his bed until after first light, he hardly apprehended what his valet was saying. A young girl at the door? Impossible, his foggy mind told him. His address in Grosvenor Square was a well-kept secret from that *other* world. And then he remembered that he was a member of Parliament. Surely this was one of his constituents. "What does she look like, George?" he asked.

"Very young and very pretty, m'lord."

His lordship sat up and swung his long legs over the side of the high bed. His long nightshirt was twisted around his knees. He was exceptionally tall, two inches over six feet, and his feet almost touched the floor. Groaning his discomfort, he slid his body until they did so, and, as if his valet had never seen his legs before, he pulled at his nightshirt to cover them.

"Demmet, George, London is full of very young, and very pretty girls."

"This one has hair between blond and brown, m'lord, and dirty-looking. She is fashionably dressed, though a little daring for day, I would say. And as I said, she's very pretty. She seems frightened."

"And well she should be," snorted Lord Talbert, mumbling under his breath. *How dare she come here.* He pushed himself up to his full height and glanced at his image in the gilt-framed mirror that hung from ceiling to floor on the wall. He was very proud of his physique. Even though he had seen fifty summers, and he had indulged in his share of debauchery, his stomach was as flat as a twenty-year-old's. This day his handsome broad face was worse for wear, his blue eyes red rimmed from too much drink, and his sideburns in need of trimming. His valet would take care of that when he did his toilette. A shave would come first.

"Go at once and tell the girl to return two hours hence. Then please return to help me with my dress. I will not hear her complaint until I'm properly attired. And properly fed. Have the butler bring a loaded tray, with lots of hot coffee."

Forcing a false smile, the valet bowed from the waist and departed. He did not like his employer but found it best to hide his feelings.

Left alone, Lord Talbert swore out into the quiet room. The girl was Opal, yesterday's courtesan. But how did she learn his address? Well, never mind, he told himself, when she returned he would be long gone to his club, where he would mix and mingle with gentlemen of the upper orders. He would have a go at the gaming tables, eat a sumptuous supper, and then depart for his other world, a dark world which had held his fascination since his days in leading strings. Ruby would be waiting. The thought sent his blood boiling.

She was fresh and new. He smiled and marveled at the years he had managed to fool his peers in Parliament. What Lady Talbert thought was of no consequence; she had fulfilled her duty by affording him an heir, and he fulfilled his duty to her by keeping her well endowed with blunt. He hated the country and went there only as it was necessary to keep his constituents happy. He was relieved Lady Talbert's brother looked after the estates.

How boring Lord Abshire's life must be, Lord Talbert thought as he quit his bedchamber and went into his dressing room. There, for some inexplicable reason, his lordship's thoughts turned to Christmas, not far in the future, and he swore aloud at the prospect of having to go to Talbert Hall for the festivities. If it were not necessary, he would somehow escape that horrible fate.

His lordship was still contemplating this thought when his valet returned. He held in his hand a silver salver on which an ivory envelope made of fine paper rested. Taking the missive and ripping it open, his lordship recognized his wife's flowing script. He asked if the girl had left the premises. "No, m'lord," answered the valet, "she's sitting on the steps."

Anger snapped Lord Talbert's dark eyebrows together. "I thought I told you to have the butler get rid of her."

"He tried, your lordship, but she won't budge. Do you want him to physically remove her?"

"No, no. That won't be necessary. I'll simply leave by the back way. She can't stay there all night."

"I would not count on that, your lordship. She looks to have a fighting spirit."

His lordship went to his desk and fastly scribbled a message on a piece of parchment. The feathered quill made him sneeze, and he swore from that, and from his anger. He reached for the bell rope and pulled it heartily, and when a footman answered the summons, he handed him the sealed missive and asked that it be taken to his man of business. The footman bowed and left.

Lord Talbert, chuckling, said, "George, money can cure any ill, most especially where a woman is concerned." He crossed himself. "I thank my Maker there's no shortage of Talbert blunt."

The valet did not answer, but busied himself with stropping the razor and making suds in the soap mug. There was no shortage of hot water in the elegant town house, the finest in Grosvenor Square. After lathering his lordship's face, the valet slapped a steaming towel on and prayed that it would permanently scar him. No matter what the young girl was, she deserved better treatment than she was getting from Lord Fox Talbert.

Jerking the towel from his face, Lord Talbert swore at his valet and called him a slowtop. Later, studying the valet's reflection in the mirror, he said, "You're very quiet, George. Something wrong?"

"I was thinking on the young girl, m'lord. She seemed so frightened."

Lord Talbert scoffed. "My man of business will take care of her fright. As I said, there's no limit to Talbert blunt."

They were quiet after that. Cleanly shaven and powdered, Lord Talbert donned an impeccably tailored, dark-blue coat that showed off his trim figure, a ruffled white shirt, buckskin breeches and top boots. Later he would add his glossy black top hat with its high crown, making him the best-dressed gentlemen of the upper orders. He ate the breakfast brought to him on a huge silver tray and then left by a side door and went to the stables, where his Town Coach and four waited. A well-decked-out coachman was perched on the box, a tiger on the tongue, and a highly liveried footman on the boot.

He was not only vain of his appearance; he was also very, very proud of the crested equipage in which he traveled, and of his sleek horses, the best Tattersall's had to offer.

The November air was brisk and slightly damp. But the early fog had lifted, and it made for a pleasant ride from Grosvenor Square to White's in Saint James's Street.

White's was foremost among the Gentlemen's Clubs, the oldest and most splendid. For that reason Lord Talbert held membership there when he much preferred Brooks's or Boodle's. He leaned back languorously against the squab, leaning forward only when, as they passed through Green Park, they met a young lady dressed handsomely in a morning dress and carrying a matching parasol, her abigail walking three steps behind her. He would then lean forward, smile broadly, and tip his handsome hat.

He tried in vain to keep his mind from the letter from Lady Talbert, in which she advised that he would be expected to come to Talbert Hall for a delightful costume ball opening the Christmas season. She had made it clear that his presence was required only for appearance sake. Of course he would have to go, he mused, hating the very thought of it.

At White's, a footman bowed very low and then took Lord Talbert's top hat. He seldom wore a greatcoat, unless it was extremely cold, and that was not the case this day.

His shoulders squared, he strolled nonchalantly into the reading room, where he encountered Lords Argyle and Scott. Engaging them in a lively conversation on the Prince Regent's futile effort to divorce his wife Caroline, he held forth with great knowledge on the subject about which he did not care a whit. But one must needs talk with these boring men of the upper orders on something so they would later remark to others that they had visited at length with the great Lord Fox Talbert on this or that subject, and that he certainly was a well-read gentleman of the first water.

Having finished that part of his daily ritual, Lord Talbert went to the gaming room where he joined in a game of whist. He was only mildly successful. He was restless this day, and he blamed it on the girl who had shown up at his Grosvenor square town house. He kept telling himself that he should not worry, that his man of business was paid to take care of such matters.

But worry he did, and when his lordship lost two large bets in a row, he decided to depart early and go to his own place, normally called a Hell because the gaming for the riffraff of

London was located underground. He also kept bits of muslin for hire in the hole, a very lucrative business.

His partner in whist had been Sir Dominic Walters. After begging Walters forgiveness for his early departure, Lord Talbert took his leave and went to his traveling equipage.

"To the Covent Gardens," he told his driver as he sprightly leaped up to settle himself into the plush squabs. His thoughts went to his new bit of muslin. Mayhap his anxiety at the whist table had been caused by his eagerness to go to her. He called to the driver to put the horses to their bits.

Back at White's, at the whist table, Sir Dominic Walters laughingly remarked, "The fox has gone underground. A little early for him. Don't you think, eh?" And the others laughed with him.

Eleven

At Talbert Hall, Lord Abshire raised his quizzing glass and bent forward to stare through the window. Coming up the tree-lined lane that led from the main road to the manor house was a woman wearing a long fur-trimmed cloak and a black hat, and carrying a small bag. He continued to watch intently. As she drew nearer he determined that he had never seen the woman before. It was late day, an odd time for a caller.

When the expected knock came, a very loud and determined banging by the brass knocker, he immediately opened the big door and greeted the visitor. A comely woman, except for a big nose, he thought, and although she was much past her prime, she seemed ageless.

"I'm Trenton Abshire," he said pleasantly. "May I inquire as to your business at Trenton Hall?"

The woman bobbed, a gesture which told a great deal. She knew he was Lord Trenton Abshire, and her next words confirmed that knowledge. "I'm Margaret Teasch, and you are the young buck I'm looking for, your lordship."

There was something about the way she spoke, as if she were speaking to a child, that made Lord Abshire smile. "In that case, I invite you to enter my domain." He stepped back and, half bowing, waved her into the crimson foyer. "You are most welcome, Margaret Teasch. Is it Mrs. or Miss?"

"Neither. Just call me Margaret," she answered as she stepped inside. A look of wonder came over her face. As if

Abshire were not there, her quick eyes surveyed the large foyer. Without embarrassment, as far as his lordship could tell.

Holding her bag in one hand and a small reticule in the other, she turned completely around, her gaze traversing the scrolled ceiling, the colorful carpet, then coming back to give her host a lingering, thoughtful once-over.

"My Rachel said you were handsome enough," she said, "but that's not what I'm interested in. Beauty is as beauty does. What do you do? Other than dress up like a dandy and act as butler when a strange woman comes calling?"

His lordship gave his wry smile. "You must be the Mother M. of whom Rachel speaks so often, the lady who taught her about sinning."

"I didn't teach her about sinning; I taught her *not* to sin, but from the sound of her missive, I'm afraid I didn't teach her well enough. She wrote about titillation, of all things. Are you responsible for that?"

Again her gaze surveyed him, causing him to chuckle. "I've asked her to become my bride."

"She didn't tell me that, and I would not have believed her should she have. Oh, I would have believed you had suggested such a thing, but I would have known it was a farrago of nonsense. A man of the nobility does not marry a nanny. Unless he has some ulterior motive, like to spite his family."

Lord Abshire was taken aback. Had he not first announced to his brother, whom he loathed, that soon he would be marrying little Frank's nanny? And then the idea of marrying Rachel had grown inside of him until it became genuine desire. But was it love? He must needs measure his words with this woman, he quickly decided. He could feel her strength, and the determined look emanating from her eyes would make the strongest of men quake in his Wellingtons.

"I beg your forgiveness," he said. "I'm afraid I've been remiss, Mother M. That is what I shall call you. I'm not comfortable with just Margaret, seems disrespectful."

"How have you been remiss?" she asked.

"By not inviting you to come sit with me a spell. My sister, Lady Talbert, and Miss Storm are away, making social calls."

"Why would a nanny be making social calls?

"I asked Lady Talbert to take Frank's nanny under her wing and train her in social amenities so that when we are married she will feel comfortable." He reached for Mother M.'s bag, only to hear her say, "I can carry my own bag."

She did, however, walk beside him as they entered the large receiving room. Lord Abshire thought to lead her to the small receiving room to the right of where they were, but somehow he felt that he was on safer ground with space around him. They walked the room's length, coming to the huge fireplace where he had taken Rachel and little Napoleon when they had arrived at Trenton Hall.

Maybe I can learn from this woman why Rachel came to Trenton Hall, thought Lord Abshire.

He recalled the awful dress, much too small for her bosom, her too-short coat, and her incredible blue eyes. A shiver of wanting raced through him. In the presence of this woman so against sinning, he was ashamed.

Motioning for Mother M. to sit, which she did, his lordship then gained a matching chair opposite her. The fire in the grate popped and sparked and threw out its warmth. He watched as she reached out to warm her hands against the flickering flames. Her right glove had a hole in its palm.

So as not to embarrass her, he pretended not to notice. "When you are warm enough, I will summon a maid to take your coat and hat, and your bag. If you will release it. I'm sure Miss Storm will expect you to stay the night."

She sat straight back, the bag on her lap. "It won't be necessary to summon a maid. Could be that Rachel won't be asking me to stay the night. I realize this visit is much too impulsive. I should have done what she asked."

"And what was that?" his lordship eagerly asked.

"Wait until after Christmas to answer her missive." She wrinkled her brow, and her eyes filled with tears. "I couldn't wait. I had to come. A letter would not have sufficed. I can see that."

Lord Abshire leaned forward. "You can see what?"

"That I will need several days to teach Rachel the things I should have taught her before she went out on her own to work as a nanny. I must needs warn her about men who are out to take advantage." A gloved hand went to her mouth, and her face flushed red.

Smiling, he said, "Are you going to teach her to stay clear of bucks who dress like dandies?"

She smiled in a shy way and answered, "Yes."

"At least you are honest. But God's truth, you have nothing to worry about. Your Rachel is as pure as a white dove. More than once she has slapped my hand when I attempted to touch her, accusing me of sinning. She adamantly refuses to discuss becoming leg-shackled. Says she has to get her life in order."

When silence became obtrusive, he studied the strange woman's stoic face. "Do you know what she meant by that?" he asked.

The expected answer did not come. The strange woman just sat there with her thin lips pursed, her hands clasping the handle on her bag. One would think she held her fortune in it. Peeking out from underneath her fur-trimmed cloak, her long, narrow feet stretched toward the fire. She wore black half-boots, recently polished but still registering lots of wear.

He asked again, "Do you know what she meant about getting her life in order? 'Twould help me a lot to know why she rejected me so emphatically. I don't know whether to keep my pursuit or just give up."

That was a lie. He had no notion of giving up on the girl with the captivating blue eyes, now that he had made up his mind to take the plunge.

"Yes, I know," said Mother M., "but if Rachel wants you to know, she will tell you. I'm here to see her, not to tell what she doesn't want told."

Lord Abshire groaned inwardly. It was certainly plain where

Rachel learned her stubbornness. Even so, this Margaret Teasch had as much as admitted that not only Rachel, but she as well, was hiding something. But it couldn't be bad, he thought, for there was something in each demeanor that exuded honesty. He studied her countenance. Clearly she was at peace with herself. She had come to Talbert Hall looking for Rachel, who had come to Talbert Hall looking for something, or somebody. And neither was going to confide in him.

His brow drawn into a frown, his lordship stared out the window. He wished the ladies would return, and he found himself wanting very much to see Rachel. It seemed that he was only happy in her presence. Rising from his chair, he went to pull the bell rope, saying to the visitor, "I must needs beg your forgiveness, Mother M. I should have offered you a repast. No doubt your journey has left you hungry. Public coaches are notorious for their short stops at posting inns."

He then went to stand by the window and look out. When she did not answer, he asked over his shoulder, "Did you travel far?"

"Four days," she said succinctly, and after that nothing.

Lord Abshire turned to stare at her and found her thin lips closed in a tight line. As if to say, *Pry all you want, but I will not tell you what you want to know. Let Rachel do that. When she is ready.*

A maid appeared, rustling in her bombazine. She bobbed. "You rang, your lordship?"

"Yes. Please bring tea and biscuits, and jam as well, for our visitor."

"For two, or just for the lady?"

"Bring tea for me," he answered, going to sit again, swearing under his breath. Demmet, he wanted Rachel to come home. The maid bobbed again before leaving, and soon thereafter she returned with a huge silver tray. Steam curled up from the teapot's spout, and tea biscuits formed a large mound on a fine china plate. There were several pots of jam.

"Thank you," his lordship said to the maid, who left quickly.

He poured, then handed the steaming cup out to Rachel's Mother M. "I fear you must release your bag. Or can you manage with it on your lap?" He was smiling.

The bag went to the floor. "I appreciate your kindness, your lordship. I find that I am indeed famished."

Lord Talbert sipped his tea as he watched her drink and eat as if it were her last meal. Never in his life had he been hungry, not even in battle, and he felt great pity for anyone who suffered such fate. He grimaced when he remembered how terribly thin the boy Napoleon had been upon his arrival at Talbert Hall, and he smiled at how he had filled out since.

And what a worker the boy had turned out to be, thought his lordship. But his mind did not linger long on Napoleon, for his thoughts consistently turned to Rachel Storm. More than ever he wanted to know the purpose of her coming to Talbert Hall. But for sure this woman was not going to tell him. And where did *she* come from?

Over the large room a gentle quietness settled, broken only by cup meeting saucer after Margaret Teasch had taken a great gulp of tea. She smiled at him, and he liked that. At last she broke the silence with, "Did Rachel and Lady Talbert take the child with them? A nanny should not leave her charge untended."

"Oh, little Frank is not left untended," his lordship said defensively. "He has a very doting wet nurse." He laughed and then told about how Hannah had managed to drive other nannies away from Talbert Hall, but not Rachel. And he told about Rachel taking little Frank to her bed, and the wet nurse, thinking her baby had been kidnapped, had had a spell of the vapors.

His lordship's voice grew soft when he said, "When I went to Rachel's room, she looked like an angel, her black hair a halo on the white pillow, her arms curled around little Frank. I could not help but envy the child."

Lord Abshire was aware of the studied, almost harsh, look from Margaret Teasch. Her hand, holding a biscuit and jam, stopped halfway to her mouth as she said, "One would think that you are in love with her."

"I am. Desperately so."

"Pshaw! More like lust. The Bible says—"

"That 'tis a sin," his lordship finished, laughing.

Margaret Teasch also laughed. "I can see that I was right in coming. No gel would be safe around your charm."

"Only Rachel. Much to my regret."

Soon after that, his lordship heard laughter. When he looked around, he saw Rachel and Lady Talbert entering the room. He called to them. Both turned to his voice, and Rachel's mouth flew open and disbelief covered her countenance. She screamed, "Mother M.," and began running, her arms open to embrace Talbert Hall's newest guest. "When did you get here? Why . . . it must have been a tiring journey. You should not have come . . . not until after Christmas."

"I knew you would scold me," Margaret Teasch replied as she hugged Rachel back. Rather awkwardly, thought Lord Abshire, as if hugging was not something she frequently did.

A lump formed in his throat, and he did not know why. Except that something was amiss. He heard Rachel introducing Lady Talbert to Margaret Teasch, calling her Mother M.

"But she's not my mother," Rachel quickly added, almost defensively.

He looked at Rachel longingly. If she would put her arms around him, he would hold her tightly and tell her he loved her. Going to her, he took her hand and said, "Rachel, don't scold Mother M. for coming to see you. She's welcome at Talbert Hall for as long as she wants to stay." He looked at Lady Talbert, who was shaking her head affirmatively.

"You are a kind man," said Margaret Teasch, and then she asked, "May I share Rachel's room?"

"Of course you may," Lady Talbert said. "I'll ring for a maid to take your bag. And pray do take off your cloak and hat. Are you not too warm?"

"I'm comfortable, thank you. And I don't need a maid to

carry my bag. But I am terribly tired. Rachel, if you don't mind, I'd like to go with you to your room." Turning, she thanked his lordship for the tea and biscuits, and then she and Rachel left.

"Let me carry your bag," said Rachel as they left, only to be refused.

Lord Abshire watched as they climbed the stairs, side by side, neither addressing the other. What he would give, he mused, to be a mouse and listen in on the word exchange between his darling Rachel and her Mother M. He prayed the young girl would not scold too harshly the old woman, who had obviously made the long journey to Talbert Hall out of love.

"Why did you come, Mother M.?" Rachel asked when they had reached the third floor and were well out of hearing distance of those below. Her voice was firm but not unkind. "I asked you to wait until after Christmas before answering my missive. I don't understand—"

"I knew you wouldn't," cut in the old woman. "But I had to come. When your missive arrived by post I was overwhelmed by my failure to talk with you about the facts of life, as any good mother would have done. Embarrassment kept me from it, dear Rachel."

"There's nothing embarrassing about love, Mother M."

"But I never told you the difference between lust and love. And I feared you were approaching trouble, here in this household working as a nanny. I felt danger. And I should have explained what transpires between man and wife on their wedding night."

Rachel opened the door to her room and stepped back. "There's plenty of time for that, Mother M. I'm not anyway near getting married. When I do, my husband can explain. So stop your worrying."

As if Rachel hadn't spoken, Mother M., upon entering the room, went to sit in a chair. Placing her bag on the floor beside her, she continued with obvious determination, "It was clear to me that this man of nobility . . . this Lord Abshire, was out to have his way with you, and I knew only too well that you were not prepared . . . I had to come before it was too late."

"He has asked me to marry him."

"A man will do that, Rachel. That's the first step, making a tender girl believe his intentions are honorable, and then he leaves her for someone of the upper orders . . ."

Rachel heard the break in Mother Margaret's voice and was suddenly aware that the dear lady was speaking from the heart. "Did that happen to you, Mother M.? Did a man leave you?"

"Yes. It was then that I went to the Home to offer my services, and to accept the church as my bridegroom. I never told anyone . . . except God."

"You didn't tell me because you thought I was too young to understand," said Rachel, "but now that I'm nearing eighteen summers, we can talk as adults, can we not?"

"I . . . I guess that is why I came. I knew I should wait until after Christmas, as you asked, but I just couldn't. I hope you can forgive me." Reaching up, she removed her black hat with a purple plume and placed it atop her bag.

"Stuff! There's nothing to forgive," said Rachel.

"I was very careful not to tell Lord Abshire that you came to Talbert Hall from the Home. He certainly did try to pry." A pause, and then, "Why did you come to Talbert Hall, Rachel?"

Rachel sat on the side of the bed and for a long moment did not speak, and then the words came, the secret she had shared with no one except Napoleon: "I believe that Lord Talbert is my papa, and he will not return to Talbert Hall until Christmas."

"Why do you believe this, Rachel? There's no proof."

Rachel told her then about learning that each month since the year she was born Lord Talbert had sent a stipend to the Home. "I know that my mama is dead. She would have never left me. And I am sure that Lord Talbert would have kept me if it had been possible. But a man alone can't rear a child in the right way. I'm positive that he knew I was in good hands at the Home. He couldn't know how I longed to belong to someone." She went to place a hand on Mother M.'s trembling shoulder "You were the next best thing to a parent, but I was not of your blood."

"And what if he does not claim you, even if you truly are his daughter."

"That's not possible. When he sees me, he will know I am his, and he will hug me to him. Why else would he have sent the money all these years if he had not cared about me?"

And why did he not visit you all these years? thought Margaret Teasch. There was so much wishfulness in Rachel's voice that the old woman found that she was near crying. She wished she could tell Rachel who she was, where she came from, who fathered her. Mother Cecilia, in charge of the Home when baby Rachel arrived, had taken the secret of Rachel's origin with her to her grave. Now, Rachel had set herself up for a terrible hurt. *Word has it that Lord Talbert is not an honorable man.*

Mother Margaret decided she would bide her time; mayhap she would caution Rachel on the pitfalls of her fantasy when the time was right. Her real purpose in being here was to see that Lord Abshire did not teach Rachel the meaning of titillate. She smiled and said to herself, *I know he's a rakehell, but a charming one, and I must needs warn Rachel.*

Aloud she said, "Rachel, Lord Abshire assured me he intends to marry you. What are your feelings? Are you in love with his lordship?"

"I don't know anything about *that* kind of love, and I don't wish to know, not until I know who I am. That may seem silly to someone else, but 'tis very important to me. Besides, I think he is exaggerating his feelings. Most likely, I am the first woman who has not fallen at his feet. His sister warned me of his bent."

After that they talked for a long while, both sharing true feelings with the other. Time passed swiftly. It was decided that Mother Margaret would stay until after the costume ball opening the Christmas Season. Mayhap Lord Talbert would come. She said, "I would like to be here when you learn the truth, Rachel. If you are hurt, I want to be near." After a long pause, she continued, "I wish I could convince you to leave. In truth, I don't want you to be Lord Talbert's daughter."

Rachel smiled. "You need not be jealous, Mother M. I could never forget what you've been to me all these years."

" 'Tis not that I'm jealous, dear Rachel. That would be selfish of me, but Lord Talbert could be the kind of man you would not want as a father." She stopped, for she was coming dangerously close to telling Rachel that she'd heard Lord Talbert was a scoundrel.

"I don't care what he is. I know he's not a good father to little Frank, his heir. I just want to know where I came from. I want him to tell me about my mama. Then I can get on with my life."

It felt good to be talking with this wonderful woman, Rachel mused. She was glad Mother Margaret had come. Jumping up from the bed, Rachel said to her, "Come, you must see little Frank, and then we will visit Napoleon. You'll like him. He told Lord Abshire that if his intentions toward me were not honorable that he would break his lordship's leg."

They laughed together as they left the room. The old woman warned again, "Believe me, seduction is on Lord Abshire's mind, not marriage. I can't say it often enough, dear Rachel—gentlemen of the upper orders tend to marry ladies of the upper orders. Ladies of Quality I believe they are called. I traveled four days to warn you of that. And it makes little difference if the lady he chooses for his wife is ugly, as long as she will give him a heir with pure blood."

Of course she would never think of marrying his lordship, Rachel told herself, and seduction was out of the question. Just before she opened the door to the nursery, smiling mischievously, she said, "I told Lord Abshire that when he stopped glaring at my bosom I would wear the new gowns the modiste made for me. I think I shall wear a very daring one when we dine this night. He wouldn't dare goggle my bosom with you present . . ."

Twelve

Lord Abshire rejected the third cravat which his valet creased around his neck. "Demmet, Lawrence, can't you do anything right?" he asked in an exasperated tone.

"My, my, you are testy this night," declared the valet. "What has brought on this rare mood of wanting to be perfectly dressed? Are you competing with the Beau? Or is it the new visitor at Talbert Hall? Isn't she a mite old for you?" Chuckling, the valet tried yet another cravat.

"You know demme well 'tis not the new visitor. She's the Mother M. Rachel speaks of, the woman who taught her so much about sinning, rather *not* sinning."

Lawrence's laughter filled the dressing room. "So you fear the old woman will thwart your plans to have your way with the pretty Rachel?"

"No such thing. I told you that I plan to marry Miss Storm."

"After you've seduced her."

"Seduction was my plan at first, but I've since changed my mind. I plan to take the plunge—"

"To spite your brother?" The valet pressed the last crease in the last cravat, exactly the same size of the other creases and looking the same as the three discarded cravats. He stepped back to admire his work. "So, when is the big day? Have the banns been read?"

"You know the banns haven't been read. She won't have me."

"But why? Because you've given up on getting her into

your bed without matrimony? If that be the case, I'm disappointed in you."

"Don't be obstinate. Is it beyond the pale to believe that I'm in love with the girl? She has the most incredible blue eyes."

"I know. You've spoken of those before, but one does not marry because of eyes."

His lordship scowled ferociously. "You are lacking in sensitivity, Lawrence. You know nothing of how a man can ache with love." He turned before the gilt-framed looking glass to admire his superbly tailored coat and his waistcoat embroidered with butterflies and humming birds. Above his Hessian boots, with a tassel dangling from the V-shaped front, he wore tan trousers that clung to his masculine physique and muscular thighs as if they were a second skin. "What do you think? Do I look all the crack?"

"Well enough for Almack's or a Gentleman's Club in London, overdressed for dinner at Talbert Hall. Did the latest visitor, the old woman, scold you for your dress?"

Lord Abshire laughed. "She did accuse me of emulating the dandy Beau Brummell. But 'tis Rachel I wish to impress."

The valet looked Abshire up and down, then cocking an eyebrow, said, "Well, if it can be done, you will set her blood to boiling this night, for your wearables leave nothing to one's imagination."

"Wish me luck, Lawrence. By Christmas I shall be legshackled to the prettiest nanny in the whole of England."

"I'd like a wager on that," Lawrence called after him, still laughing.

The challenge was ignored, and Lord Abshire stepped lively as he descended the stairs to the dining room. He had ordered roast beef, a special pudding, and champagne in honor of their latest guest. In truth, he admitted to himself, he had been thinking of Rachel, not Mother M., when he gave Cook the order. What in the demme hell did she mean by "getting her life in order?"

It even entered his lordship's mind to put a man on the case who could report back to him where these two mysterious women had come from and why they had come to Talbert Hall. He dismissed the thought rather quickly, for he knew that should Rachel learn of his doing such an underhanded thing she would be lost to him forever.

But things were moving entirely too slowly. He must needs kiss Rachel in the way a man in love kisses a woman. Mayhap that would take things out of her control. *If I could make her feel a little of what I feel.* He was not used to a girl being hard to get. Nonetheless, this was the night. Somehow he would arrange for them to be alone.

In the dining room, Lady Talbert was already seated at the table, lighted with tall tapers that cast circles of light on the pristine white tablecloth. Fresh flowers, hurriedly sent from a flower shop in Blanchland, spilled from epergnes placed the table's length. Tall crystal flutes awaited the chilled champagne, and the best silver had been placed beside fine china bearing the Talbert crest. Rachel, his lordship mused, would sit across the table from him, so that he could look into those incredible blue eyes.

"One would think we were having a banquet for Prinny," said Lady Talbert, and his lordship laughed. "I wanted this night to be special for Rachel's guest."

Lady Talbert gave a knowing smile. "Brother, you did this for Rachel, not her Mother M. But 'tis a capital idea. I enjoy dining in style, and I am sure Rachel feels the same, although I doubt you will achieve your goal. That girl has a mind of her own."

Lord Abshire took a chair beside his sister. "Tessie, do you have any idea what she means about getting her life in order before she can think about love? Seems a farrago of nonsense to me."

"That's because your life has always been in order. Being the son of a duke, even though the dukedom went to your older brother, you gained the privilege of a courtesy title, and you have income from the estate. Unlike Rachel, providence set your destiny, opened doors for you. Rachel has had to forge her own way.

"I know not what she means about getting her life in order," Lady Talbert continued. "She has not confided in me, and I have the feeling that you will know only when she is ready to tell. Is it still your bent to marry the girl?"

"More than ever. I tried to pry information from this Margaret Teasch, but she's as tight-lipped as Rachel."

"You'll know in due time. Be patient, Trenton."

"Patience is not my long suit. I just wish—"

Just then Rachel and Sister Margaret entered the dining room, and Lord Abshire felt his eyes almost pop out of his head. Half of Rachel's bosom was showing. For the first time in his life he was tongue-tied. Jumping up to seat them, he stumbled over his feet. God's truth, she was the prettiest thing he had ever seen!

The scent of lavender water assaulted his lordship's nostrils; his head swam. He seated the older woman, then took Rachel's arm and steered her to the chair directly across the table from him. He could not forebear sitting at one end of a long table with his love at the other end. Whoever invented that custom anyway? In a low voice he said to Rachel, "You are lovely tonight, lovelier than I have ever seen you."

Rachel smiled and nodded her thanks.

She is too lovely to be true, Lord Abshire thought, as he made his way back to his own chair, looking at Rachel out of the corner of his eye. Her gown, with a small bustle, was of blue-lavender silk, the exact color of her iridescent eyes, and light from the tapers danced on her shiny ebony hair. He sucked in his breath and desire attacked him, so that he sat quickly, lest it show. A kiss, a real kiss, not just a peck, this night, he silently vowed.

But he must needs think of a way to be alone with Rachel, away from the old woman who was watching him like a hawk measured a chicken. He looked through the window, studied the stars and round moon in a cobalt sky. "Would you walk with me after we've eaten?" he asked, looking at Rachel.

"I think that is a capital idea," said Mother M., "but she must needs wear a warm cloak."

"She has a fur-lined pelisse."

"And I have the warmest of coats," said Mother M. "I felt the cold hardly at all on my journey here. And I have a wool bonnet that I knitted myself. I shall be happy to act as chaperon."

Lord Abshire gave a dry chuckle. " 'Tis not necessary. Things are done differently in the country than in Town.

"Temptation is temptation, your lordship, whether one is in town or in the country."

Demmet, why does it have to be so difficult? He tried another approach, addressing Rachel, "Mayhap you would prefer spending time in the music room. I could instruct you on some of the most recent dance steps, the waltz for instance. It would be helpful for you to be adept at dancing at the Costume Ball, which is only a fortnight away."

"Why, Rachel has been instructed by a dance master. I'm sure she will be proficient at dancing at the ball," said the older woman.

Lady Talbert looked at her brother, laughter hidden in her smile. He met the look with a frown which dared her to let the laughter loose. He knew too well what she was thinking; that he could not win with this Mother M. Well, he would.

"I would love to practice the dance steps with you, your lordship," Rachel said. Then, turning to Mother M., "Would you care to join us?"

"Oh, it has been years since I danced. Most likely I would fall all over Lord Abshire's Hessians."

"I'll take the chance," Lord Abshire said, a plan forming. He would tire out the old woman and she would repair to bed, leaving him alone with Rachel. "What about you, Lady Talbert? Would you care to join us?"

"Thank you, no. I shall visit Frankie before he is put down

for the night. I so enjoy rocking him in the evening." She turned to Mother M., "Until Rachel came to Talbert Hall, I believed, because I had been told, that it was harmful for a mother to rock and cuddle her child. Rachel told me that rules were meant to be broken, that all children needed to be touched and loved. And I so enjoy it."

A quivering silence settled over the elegant dining room. Mother M. looked at her plate for a long moment at last saying, "Rachel did not receive that sort of attention. I, too, had been told it was not healthy to cuddle a child. Even though I was not her mother, she was my charge." Her voice broke. "I know now she needed loving she never got, but I loved her so much."

"I know, Mother M.," Rachel said.

"Well, 'tis settled then," chimed in Lord Abshire. "To the music room after we have stuffed ourselves on roast beef and have drunk our fill of champagne."

Rachel smiled her agreement. She had never tasted spirits, but this night she would. She was very hungry by the time the two footmen served the meal. She found herself eating as if she were starved.

It had been an exciting day, in the morning taking care of little Frank, and then, over Hannah's protest, taking him for a short walk, laughing with him when his cherub cheeks turned red from the brisk air.

The calls she'd made with Lady Talbert had been most enjoyable; never had she seen such country homes; ladies serving tea and holding their silk fans just a certain way. Then to come home and find Sister Margaret talking with Lord Abshire. Mother M. had fallen in love with little Frank, and later with Napoleon, who told Mother M. that he would always have Rachel's interest at heart. It was like a dream, a happy dream. She looked across at his lordship and wondered what he was thinking. For sure he had wanted to take her for a walk without a chaperon. This brought a giggle, thinking on how Mother M. had thwarted his plans. Rachel knew her concern, but the good sister really had nothing to worry about. Rachel might allow a small kiss only; that is, if he did not start ogling her bosom.

To test his lordship, Rachel stole a glance over the rim of her champagne glass and saw that he was, out of the corner of his eye, looking at her low neckline. She frowned at him and when he noticed her watching him, he jerked his gaze away.

During the rest of the meal, Rachel quietly listened to the exchange of words between Lord Abshire and Mother M., with Lady Talbert occasionally joining in.

The exchange was lively, mostly about old King George's latest spell of madness, and then about the coming Christmas Season. It would be a busy time, Rachel thought, with all the routs and balls in the country homes. She listened intently for mention of Lord Talbert's return to Talbert Hall, only to be disappointed.

Rachel had to smile when Lord Abshire skillfully questioned Mother M. about her background. He learned nothing, not even that for years she had been known only as Sister Margaret. The delicious pudding was served and devoured, and then they, with the exception of Lady Talbert, repaired to the music room, where Mother M. sat at the pianoforte and played while Rachel and Lord Abshire danced.

At first it went well, both gliding over the floor with fluid steps. Rachel felt gloriously happy and gay, and she smiled often at her partner. He teased her about flirting with him; she denied that it was so.

"I want to be alone with you, Rachel," his lordship told her when they again came together.

His hand was on her arm, burning into her flesh. With great effort, obvious to Rachel, he kept his gaze from her bosom. "Why is it necessary for us to be alone, your lordship?" she asked. "We can hardly dance without music."

"Do you play? If so, I shall dance with your Mother M. until she is so tired she will repair to bed and leave us alone."

Grinning, he asked Mother M. to dance and she surprised him with her agility. He tired, but she didn't.

"We've been dancing for quite some time," he said. "Are you not tired?"

"No," she answered. "But I'll relinquish you to Rachel."

Giving a grand curtsy, she returned to the pianoforte and began playing.

"I'm tired, and she has many summers on me," his lordship complained to Rachel.

Rachel laughed. "She may tire, but she will not leave us alone."

His lordship guided Rachel near the pianoforte. "Mother M., do you wish to rest awhile? If it is your wont to act as chaperon, may I suggest that you sit before the fire in an easy chair, while Rachel and I enjoy each other's company on the small sopha. We'll be in plain sight."

"I suppose that would be permissible," said Mother M. She rose and went to sit in a large chair near the fire. Rachel noted that her steps were considerably slower than when they had walked to the stables to see Napoleon, and it was not long before her sharp chin rested on her chest and gentle snoring, so familiar to Rachel, was fluttering her thin lips.

The small sopha was at the far end of the huge room, and at first chance Rachel whispered, "What a scoundrel you are, your lordship."

Laughing, he accused, "You are as guilty as I am. You knew she would go to sleep."

He took Rachel's hand, squeezed it lovingly, then brought it to his lips and kissed the palm. "I wanted so much to be alone with you, Rachel. Is there harm in that?"

Suddenly Lord Abshire was engulfed with the feeling that he had found the part of him that had been missing, and, until now, did not know was missing.

"We are hardly alone," Rachel said. "Her eyes can pop open any moment, and she has excellent hearing."

"Then I shall whisper. I love you. I want to marry you as soon as possible."

"Mother M. says that nobility does not marry into the lower orders."

"That doesn't bother me a whit," he answered unequivocally.

Releasing her hand, he placed his arm around her small waist, standing and pulling her up onto her feet. Gently and quietly he guided her to an alcove, out of sight of Mother M., should she suddenly awaken. A small window let in a sliver of moonlight. "Now we are totally alone," he said.

"You are a very determined man."

"And you are so beautiful, my lovely Rachel." His resonant voice was barely audible.

Mother M.'s and Lady Talbert's warnings raced through Rachel's thoughts, something about lust was not love and Lord Abshire being a rakehell and having dishonorable intentions. But she could hardly remember with his lordship's warm breath against her cheek. She knew only that she hungered for love, yearned to belong to somebody, so when Lord Abshire's arms went around her, holding her as if he would never let her go, his heart pounding against her throbbing chest, she did not pull away. What she felt was stronger than she was. She looked up into his solemn face. Why did he not give her his wry grin?

Dear God, he's going to kiss me.

"Don't kiss me," she ordered.

"Why not, Rachel. You want me to . . . I can tell."

"That's the prob—"

Lord Abshire's warm lips smothered the rest of the word, and after that Rachel could not remember what she had wanted to say.

Her lips quivered under his, and as the kiss deepened, a warmth began to wash over her until she felt as one with this man of the nobility. His wonderfully strong arms held her tighter still, and her own arms, of their own volition, circled his neck, as one of his hands moved down her back to bring her to him, to let her feel his desire. Between kisses he whispered against her lips, "Say you will marry me, dear Rachel, and put my aching heart at ease. I love you."

"I love you, too," Rachel said, now knowing it was true.

"Will you marry me," his lordship urged.

"Yes, yes," she whispered.

At the moment, who she was, where she came from, even that his lordship was a rakehell, or that his intentions were dishonorable, or that he was nobility and she a commoner, did not matter a whit to Rachel. She wanted the kiss to last forever.

Thirteen

Dowager Countess Marcella Longworth
Grammacy Chase

Above stairs at Grammacy Chase, in an elegantly appointed drawing room, Dowager Countess Marcella Longworth stood by a window and stared out, not at the manicured shrubbery, or at the winter-killed grass, but at the far distance, seeing nothing. A servant had just delivered on a silver salver two missives, one an invitation to a costume ball at Talbert Hall, the other from Castle Mackinaw, which belonged to the Duke of Marcel, her father. As yet she had not opened that one. It was not in her father's handwriting. Mayhaps he was dead.

She prayed that it was so. Hatred for the man who had sired her, then broke her heart so completely, boiled up inside her. For years she had sought to exorcise the hatred from her heart, but it had been impossible. Bury it in its deepest corner had been the best she could do.

Turning from the window, she walked toward the fireplace, thinking to burn the missive. She bent, her hand holding the missive outstretched. And then something stopped her. She straightened, and with trembling hands, ripped at the crested seal.

The dowager countess was a comely woman, small in stature, straight as an iron rod, squared narrow shoulders, as if in defiance of something. At thirty-six her round face was still unlined, but her long, straight hair, which she wore in a neatly twisted bun at her nape, had turned white, and troubled years had taken the light from her once sparkling gray eyes. Only when she was angry did they spark with life. She did not have to consult a looking glass to know that her eyes were now the color of molten steel, fired by that unyielding anger, the shield that had kept her alive when she had wanted so badly to die.

"Your ladyship," she read aloud, "please come to Castle Mackinaw. The duke is dying and wishes to see you."

It had been written and signed by Bexford, the Duke of Marcel's valet, a man who was only a little younger than the duke himself. The Countess couldn't remember when Bexford had not been in his grace's service, the valet having come to Castle Mackinaw soon after he had graduated from leading strings. The Duke of Marcel had never lifted a finger for himself, not even when he was a child, and as he grew older, he demanded complete servitude from those who worked for him. None, except Bexford stayed for any length of time. She remembered the valet as a small man, stooped even those years ago, with kind eyes.

She sat in a chair near the fire, her mind not looking forward, nor backward. She was in shock. She looked around her. The room had always been her favorite, red velvet drapes, deep sophas and chairs in white silk, and deeply scrolled gold leaf on the high ceiling. Warmth from a lively fire in the marble fireplace warmed her, and for a moment she soaked in the warmth and sought comfort in not thinking. "I can't sit here idle forever," she at last murmured. Her thoughts returned to the missive she held crumpled in her hand.

Of course she would not go to Castle Mackinaw. She had not been there for many years, and only when the duke came to Grammacy Chase had she seen him. At those times she had managed to keep a civil tongue in her head, and then her husband, the sixth earl of Bennington, Melvin Longworth, whom her father had forced her to marry, had died. As mistress of her own home, she had bitterly asked the duke not to come again.

She rose from her chair and went to pull the bell rope. She would order tea to settle her nerves and ask Nora to come sit with her. When the dowager countess was newly married to the late earl, Nora had come to her as an abigail, but had since become her companion and confidante. The countess smiled. Nora referred to herself as the lady in waiting to the queen of Grammacy Chase.

She knows all my secrets, the countess thought, *all except one.* Only the Duke of Marcel, and mayhap his valet, knew that one, and soon his grace would take it to his grave with him.

This thought brought the countess upright. She breathed deeply. It did not bear thinking on.

What a time for the old duke to be dying. Below stairs, in the great hall, Christmas boxes were in place, decorated with red and white paper by the servants. Each box held a gift for her. Later she would add her gifts to them, a box with money in it for each. And then there were the special gifts. As yet she had not bought them. Soon she would go into Town and spend a day doing just that. After Christmas they would be placed in the attic with gifts from previous years. Excruciating pain pulled at her heartstrings. Each Christmas she hoped the pain would lessen; each year it grew more severe.

The missive from Castle Mackinaw lay on the floor beside the dowager's chair, having fallen there without her notice. Hearing a noise, she turned and saw Nora coming into the room. Nora stopped and curtsied. Her gray-streaked brown hair was braided neatly around her head. Tiny wrinkles crinkled the skin around her brown eyes. This day, her day dress was of blue chambray.

Nora's loyalty to the countess was boundless, and her ladyship loved her as a sister.

"Did you wish to see me, your ladyship?" Nora asked. It was something she always asked when she had been sent for. She made her way across the room to the chair that flanked the other side of the fireplace. Something like a ritual, she thought, giving the countess a warm smile.

But this day there was no smile forthcoming from the countess. Deep hurt showed on her face. Nora went at once to kneel by her chair and take her hands in hers. "What is wrong, your ladyship?"

Tears clouded the countess's gray eyes. "He's dying."

"Who's dying." Spying the crumpled white paper on the floor beside the countess's chair, Nora picked it up but did not attempt to read the message scrawled on it. That would be against propriety.

"Read it," the countess said, and Nora did. A quizzical brow shot up. "But, m'lady you've always claimed hatred for the duke. Why the sadness now?"

Unleashed words poured from the depth of the countess's soul. "Because I had always prayed he would come to me and tell me what happened all those years ago. In my heart I knew he would not do such a kind thing, but hope dies hard."

Nora rose and went to sit in *her* chair. This kind of talk worried her. Countess Longworth was the kindest woman she had ever known; she cared for her servants, visited her tenants, saw that the ill were tended by a physician. She seldom spoke of the estrangement between her and the Duke of Marcel. Nora looked at her now and felt great pity swell in her heart. What could have been so hurtful that a woman as kind as the countess could hold a grudge for so many years? And why had the valet, who surely knew about the feud, sent a missive asking that she come? Had the old duke's heart softened toward his only child?

Nora asked, "Are you going to Castle Mackinaw, your ladyship?"

The countess squared her shoulders, and her gray eyes sparked fire as she said, "Yes, and I would very much enjoy your company, Nora. 'Tis only a day's journey. We shall not be gone from here for a long time. Knowing the old gaffer, he will take his time in dying. I shall not stay for that." She paused, and her words were barely above a whisper as she continued, "I only want to ask his grace one question before he departs this earth to dwell in hell."

Nora sucked in a sharp breath. She had never heard the dowager countess blaspheme.

A maid with the tea arrived, ending the conversation. She placed the huge silver tray on a white-clothed table, then bobbed. "Terribly sorry to be so long, m'lady, but Cook had trouble getting the coal to blaze under the water. I brought biscuits as well, though they did not say you wanted them, and I brought a cup for Miss Nora."

The dowager countess gave a wan smile. "Your timing was perfect, Melba, and the biscuits were a capital idea. It seems ages since I had breakfast. Thank you for being so thoughtful."

Smiling from the praise, the maid bobbed again, then left, and Nora shook her head. That was the dowager countess's way; no matter the depth of her hurt, she was always kind.

"When do we leave for the castle?" Nora asked.

There was not an immediate answer. Her ladyship poured tea in one of the cups, added a lump of sugar, then handed it to Nora before pouring tea for herself. She did not want a biscuit, but she would eat one, for she knew Melba would check when she came to retrieve the tray.

At last she said, "We'll leave immediately, but first help me eat these biscuits. We would not have Melba's feelings hurt."

"But, m'lady, if 'tis a day's drive and it's now mid-morning, that means we will be forced to stay in a posting inn."

"The Flying Horse. When I was young, Papa often went to the inn and occasionally, when he was in good humor, I accompanied him. One hears strange tales from those places.

"When we have finished with this tremendous repast, I'll send word of our impending departure to Shaw at the stables and ask that he send a man ahead and apprise the proprietor of the inn that we wish rooms this night. If you will, Nora, have Cook prepare a food basket for us to share on the way."

"Of course," Nora answered.

Suddenly filled with hope, the dowager countess felt a great weight leave her shoulders, and now that she had decided to go to Castle Mackinaw, was anxious. "We must needs hurry," she said to Nora.

Placing her cup back on the silver tray, Nora rose to leave. "I'll ask that the carriage be brought round, and I'll see that a stable hand is sent to The Flying Horse to tell them of your arrival."

"I'm sure we'll be late, so tell them that," said the countess.

"And I'll send Mary to you, your ladyship," Nora said as she was leaving, and the dowager countess smiled, thankful that Nora knew without being told what needed to be done.

Soon the countess left her chair. It was time to prepare to leave.

Her chambers were on the same floor as the withdrawing room. On the way there, she pondered telling Nora the whole of it about the feud between her and the duke. But she thought better of it. Partly because she could not bring herself to put the things buried deep in her heart into words. She decided to reply to the invitation to the Talbert's costume party before Mary came, and she had just gotten seated at her writing desk when she heard a scratch on the door.

"Enter, Mary," the countess called without looking round. She heard the door open and close, then soft footsteps. "I'll be finished directly. Would you please lay out a traveling dress for me? I think the red one."

"Yes, m'lady."

The countess knew without looking that the maid curtsied; her servants always did. And she would not deny them that. Many times servants had said to her that working for the nobility made them feel very important.

She sealed the letter and went to put it on the salver on a table near the door. The Talbert Ball was over a week away, and she only planned to be gone to Castle Mackinaw three days, two for traveling, and a partial day to confront the duke.

The dowager countess had another problem which she also kept to herself. When her late husband had died, he had left her Grammacy Chase—it was not entailed—and a small amount of blunt. In truth, he had left his mistress more ready cash than he had left her. The countess was well aware that she had spent hers foolishly, at least, the people, should they know, would call it so. She had done it secretly, and without the results she had hoped for. But she would not change a thing. And she would most likely spend her inheritance from the duke in the same way. Castle Mackinaw was not entailed and would be sold immediately. The enormously wealthy Duke of Marcel was bitter because he had not had a son to inherit. Nor a grandson. She shrugged her shoulders, saying aloud, "Oh, well, they will find a distant cousin somewhere, male of course, to inherit the entailed part of his grace's estate."

"What did you say, m'lady?" asked Mary, who had laid on the bed the scarlet dress and a matching bonnet.

"I was talking to myself, Mary," confessed the countess. "Did Nora tell you that I am going away for three days?"

"Oh, no, m'lady. You will need me, I'm sure."

The countess's small laugh was without mirth. *No, I must needs leave you here. I would not have you, or any of the servants, know why I'm going to Castle Mackinaw.*

"Nora and I will manage just fine," she said to Mary. "While we're gone, you take the time off and go see your mother. She would like that, I know."

"She would, indeed, but if you need me, my place be with you. And by the by, I've poured warm water for your toilette."

The countess patted the young girl's cheek and thanked her, and then disappeared into the dressing room. Mary had not been with her long. Her mother was cook at Tadsworth Manor, not far from Grammacy Chase. She called to the maid, "If I had a daughter I would want her to visit me, so you just take yourself over to Tadsworth Manor and see your mama."

"Thank you, m'lady," Mary said. She stood back, her arms crossed in front of her, and waited. Soon the dowager countess reappeared, wearing a clean chemise and long drawers. Mary dressed her white hair, twisting it into a bun on her nape, and then she helped her with the dress, buttoning the tiny buttons that closed the bodice. The hem covered red half-boots.

"You have the figure of a young girl," the maid said.

The dowager countess thanked her for the compliment, draped a red fur-trimmed mantle around her petite body, and placed her red bonnet on her head. The cloak covered her feet and swept the floor as she walked. Without so much as a glance in the looking glass, she said to Mary, "Please put three days of clothes in a satchel and see that it is in the boot of the carriage before we leave. Nothing fancy, because I don't feel very fancy."

With that, the dowager countess quit the room and went to the small chapel to pray.

As the carriage—with Shaw, who was wearing a many-layered coat and a tripod, on the box, the countess and Nora as the only passengers—pulled away from Grammacy Chase, the countess looked back. The unpretentious brown brick manor house was surrounded by hillocks which were vibrantly green in spring and summer, and often covered by snow in winter. This day, last week's snow filled the crevices and made heavy the winter-naked limbs on the trees. But it was not oppressively cold. For this, the countess was thankful. Hot bricks were at her feet, and she was comfortable. From the roof of Grammacy Chase, gray smoke curled up from the chimney pots to meld with the blue sky. Winter sun glinted off the mullioned windows.

When the manor house faded in the distance, the countess leaned back against the squab and smiled across at Nora. "Who would have ever thought the old duke would pick the Christmas Season to die." She paused, and then, "But why not Christmas? He never believed the Christmas story anyway. After mama died Christmas was never observed at Castle Mackinaw."

"And you were only eight," replied Nora, looking pityingly

at the countess and clucking with her tongue. "Children so love the season."

"Well, I managed. Nanny Richards and I secretly celebrated. His grace never came to the nursery. Nanny would purchase a doll for me, and other things, and I would buy her a lace handkerchief. And on Christmas morning, we made a game of serving each other hot chocolate and cookies. I felt sorry for the servants . . ." Her ladyship's voice died away, and she gave a little laugh. "His grace never did outsmart me . . . except about one thing."

They talked about other things then, and there were long periods of silence. The countess mused that that was what brought Nora close to her; neither felt chatter was necessary. While they were eating from the basket of food, Nora asked, "Have you ever regretted not having children by your late husband, your ladyship?"

"No," came the quick, succinct answer. "I did not love the man, and because he married me only to produce an heir to his title and entailed estate, I refused to be a participant. And then there was the old duke. He wanted a grandson to tie the two estates together. I vowed I would never give him anything he wanted, so I refused to consummate the marriage."

"You didn't!"

Before Nora could ask how she had managed to do this, the countess told her, "I was devastated when the duke forced the marriage on me. I was in love with someone else, a man without a title. I told Lord Longworth about this love and that I did not want to marry him. But he went along with the duke. I had seen nineteen summers and was not exactly a child. So the night before the wedding, which was a sight to behold and held at Castle Mackinaw, I made my plan."

The countess bit into the chicken leg she held in her hand and then chewed slowly. Nora stared at her and waited, holding her own chicken leg halfway to her mouth. "Your ladyship, pray don't just sit there and chew when I'm about to fall off

Allow us to proposition you
in a most provocative way.
GET 4 REGENCY
ROMANCE NOVELS
FREE
An
$18.49
Value
RENATO
NO OBLIGATION TO
BUY ANYTHING, EVER.

Say Yes to 4 Free Books!

COMPLETE AND RETURN THE ORDER CARD TO RECEIVE THIS $18.49 VALUE **ABSOLUTELY FREE.**

(If the certificate is missing below, write to: Zebra Home Subscription Service, Inc., 120 Brighton Road, P.O. Box 5214, Clifton, New Jersey 07015-5214

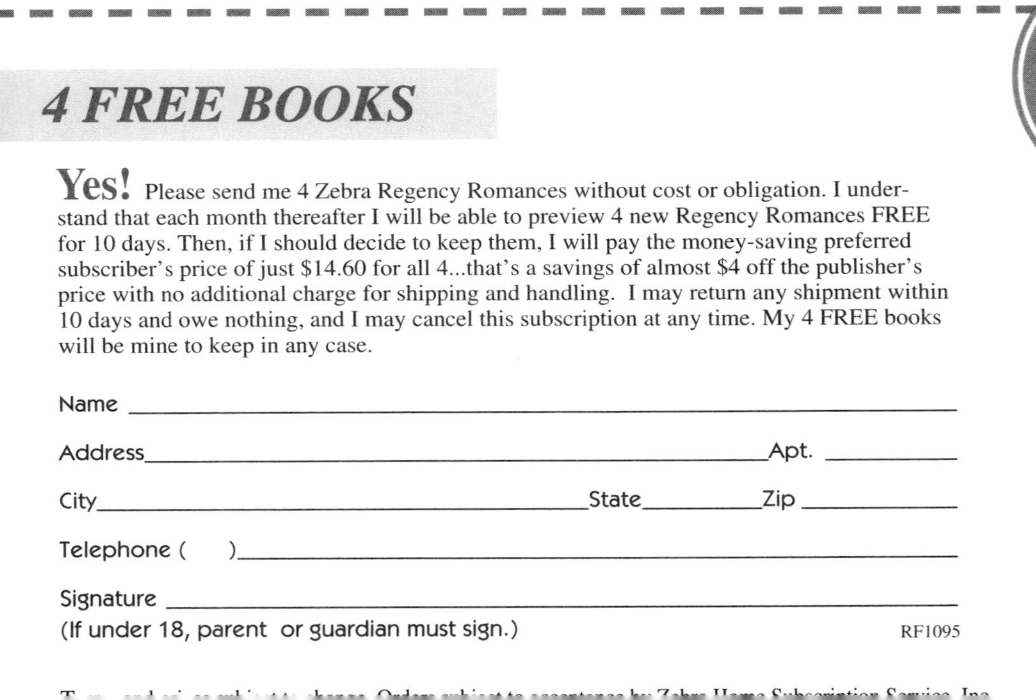

4 FREE BOOKS

Yes! Please send me 4 Zebra Regency Romances without cost or obligation. I understand that each month thereafter I will be able to preview 4 new Regency Romances FREE for 10 days. Then, if I should decide to keep them, I will pay the money-saving preferred subscriber's price of just $14.60 for all 4...that's a savings of almost $4 off the publisher's price with no additional charge for shipping and handling. I may return any shipment within 10 days and owe nothing, and I may cancel this subscription at any time. My 4 FREE books will be mine to keep in any case.

Name ____________________

Address ____________________ Apt. ________

City ____________________ State ________ Zip ________

Telephone (   ) ____________________

Signature ____________________

(If under 18, parent or guardian must sign.)

RF1095

this squab, so curious am I. I've never heard of such a thing. I thought a man took what he wanted."

Hollow laughter rolled from the dowager's throat. "It was not funny at the time, and it took me several nights of wondering what to do before the answer magically came to me. Even then I didn't know whether or not it would work, but I certainly didn't have anything to lose." Her ladyship took another bite of chicken, hiding a grin.

"It turned out to be quite simple. Cook kept a string of red peppers hanging beside the fireplace where she cooked. As a little girl, I thought they were so pretty that they must needs be delicious. I bit into one, and my mouth burned for a week."

"How did you get the earl to eat a dried red pepper? Surely he knew better."

"Don't be a peagoose, Nora. I didn't try to get him to eat a red pepper."

"Well, I don't get your meaning." Nora was still holding her chicken leg in midair. She had never married and most certainly she had never had a conversation such as this.

Hiding a mischievous grin, her ladyship explained. "I insisted that we spend our first night of wedded bliss at Castle Mackinaw, and I was prepared. A week before I had ground the red peppers into a fine powder and sat it on a ledge beside the bed. Behind a curtain, of course. On our wedding night, after we had repaired to my bedchamber, I insisted that he drink more champagne . . . and more champagne. I almost pushed it too far. I remember well that there were no preliminaries before he claimed his marital rights, not even a kiss. The room was dark, and I pretended to sneeze, and in finding a handkerchief to wipe my nose I managed to dip my fingers into the ground red pepper . . . now I think you can imagine the rest—"

"No, I can't."

"Well, first I moved my body so that he could not get the job done—that wasn't hard with his being heavy with champagne—then I pretended to help him, and in doing so I rubbed the red pepper on the end of his tool, and he thought it had come from the inside of me. He ran from the room screaming."

Nora laughed until tears streamed down her face. When she gained a modicum of composure, she said, "Surely the earl didn't give up on one try."

"No, but the memory of that one incident rendered him unable to perform, so he returned to his mistress and left me alone. I suppose he would have divorced me had he not been so embarrassed. He certainly had grounds."

In the lightened mood, they returned their attention to their basket of food, enjoying it immensely. The countess noted that the smile never left Nora's face, even when she was chewing the chicken. It surprised her that she had spoken of such a delicate matter to anyone. It was something that was not addressed in polite society. But the countess did not now, nor did she long ago, always follow society's rules of propriety.

The six horses at the tongue stepped lively, and the winter countryside passed in a blur to the countess. The sun moved lower and lower, until it was a red and orange blob in the west sky.

At last Nora asked, "Your ladyship, why had you not told me about your wedding night before?"

The countess waited a long moment before answering. Finally, sucking in a deep breath, she began. "It was such a painful time in my life that I would not allow my thoughts to torture me. Only now, it occurred to me that I wanted to share it with you. It has always seemed a shameful, unfair measure that I had taken to protect something, which was myself, that could never belong to his lordship. I had not wanted to marry him . . . I belonged to someone else . . ." Her voice dropped to an inaudible whisper.

Nora leaned forward on the squab. "Why did you not run away? To France, anywhere, to the colonies?"

"How could I? I had been the old duke's prisoner for . . ." The words died, and she began to cry, softly. She wiped her eyes with a white handkerchief she took from her bosom. And Nora cried with her.

"Now that you have voiced your feelings, mayhap your heart can heal," Nora said after awhile.

"There's only one thing that will heal my heart. That is why I'm going to Castle Mackinaw."

Nora did not pry. In the dowager countess's own good time she would share with her the whole of it. But not this day, Nora was sure. The depth of the countess's pain was on her face, and in her faded eyes. Nora had always known there was something in her ladyship's past about which she did not wish to speak, but she had always kept a pleasant, if not entirely happy, composure.

Nora had never seen the countess like this.

"I shall always be here to listen, your ladyship, should you wish to confide in me, and my lips will be sealed forever if you ask me not to tell."

"I know that, Nora. You are a jewel of the first water, and I don't know what I would have done all these years had you not come to me when my former lady's maid died. God can take away, but He can also give. I think He knew my need for a friend and sent you to Grammacy Chase at the right time."

"I'm thankful to Him," said Nora. Reaching across, she took the countess's small hand and gently squeezed it, saying, "I feel your pain."

"Thank you, Nora. But I doubt that anyone could know of my tortured soul, all due to the old duke. And I'm going to see him. 'Tis ironic, and if it were not for that one thing, I would ask Shaw to turn this carriage round and take me straight home."

The dowager did not say more, and Nora sat quietly. Soon the countess's head began to nod, and her eyelids closed over her eyes, her long, dark lashes forming a crescent on her porcelainlike cheek.

Nora crossed herself, saying in a soft whisper, "Give her a peaceful sleep, Lord, pray, give her peaceful sleep, and let her learn from the old duke what she so desperately wants to know, whatever that is."

After that, the hum of the carriage wheels on the hard road, an occasional crack of the whip, and an owl hooting in the distance, was all that broke the night's silence. The countess slept, sitting, her back straight, her head nodding. It was well past nine o'clock when the carriage surged to a quick halt in the gravel drive in front of The Flying Horse and woke her.

She jerked her head upright and smoothed the skirt of her red traveling dress and then bent to look out the carriage window.

Every window in the inn framed lighted candles, and boisterous laughter flooded the stillness when a young man opened the door, coming immediately to let down the step and help the countess from the carriage. She looked up and saw on the slate roof the statue of the white horse, wings outstretched, long white mane swept back, four legs reaching back under its belly, as if he truly was flying. A lighted lantern hung around the horse's neck.

As she had done when she was a child and had come here with the duke, the countess imagined the horse snorting and blowing his breath into the still night.

"Welcome, your ladyship," said the young man. "I am Ted Simpson, proprietor of the Flying Horse, and 'tis my goal to make you as comfortable as possible. His grace the Duke of Marcel would expect such treatment for his daughter."

"Thank you." The countess waited for him to assist Nora from the carriage.

After the bags were taken from the boot of the carriage, Shaw tipped his hat to the countess. As the two women followed the proprietor, he said to the countess, "I'm so grieved to hear of the duke's impending demise. I met him only once, but the men you will see here tonight know him well. They are holding sort of a wake. I did not tell them the duke's daughter was expected, and, if you like, I will not tell them you have arrived."

"I would appreciate that very much," said the countess.

"Your rooms have been made ready. I would advise having your supper served there."

"No," the countess quickly answered. She had come here to listen to the patrons of the inn talk; she wanted to hear the latest about the old duke. "May we sit at the small table near the window?"

"Of course," Ted Simpson answered, bowing from the waist. He led the way to the table and seated them with the utmost graciousness. It was obvious to the countess that nobility did not often frequent the place, and that the young proprietor was overwhelmed by her presence. She thanked him again before he departed saying he would send a waiter.

The stench of spirits and food assaulted the countess's nostrils. She was not hungry, but she must order something for herself and Nora so they could sit in proximity to the other patrons. Her eyes traversed the room, not a woman among them.

A black-clad waiter came to take their order. The countess ordered tea and fried fish. She could sip the tea and move the fried fish around on her plate. Nora ordered the same, but she admitted to having every intention of eating the fish.

It seemed to the countess that the boisterous camaraderie had died down since she and Nora entered the inn. And then, as if they were not there, "Did yer hear about the old duke?" one asked a newcomer.

"Yea. I herd he got some terrible disease and was about to pass over, and I'd say 'tis about time." The man lifted his glass. "I'll drink to that all night."

"And why do you say, me lad, thet 'tis about time this fine man of the nobility kicked the bucket?" The man speaking with an Irish brogue had fiery red hair.

A roar of laughter went up, and the countess knew the question had been asked tongue-in-cheek.

"The tyrant has bought up all the land hereabouts, and if yer want to work, yer have to work for him. He demands his overseer flog men who don't do enough to please him," the first man answered. "And I hear tell that him and old King George is just like that." He held up two fingers, one twisted around the other. "If'n the old duke wants a man sent to prison 'tis the same as done."

Another spoke up. "He works children 'til their backs bow, and when he feeds 'em, he only allows half enough."

The countess was appalled. Why had she never heard these things before? Because, she told herself, when she had come to the Flying Horse the old duke had been with her, and no one would dare say a disparaging word about his grace in his august presence. His weight and height were enormous, at least six feet four, and nearing two hundred seventy-five pounds.

The drinking and talking continued. In the circuslike atmosphere it seemed a contest to see which one could say the very worst about the old duke. Wagers were laid on how long the rich old tyrant would last. The countess began to regret stopping. What if he died before she reached the castle?

The food was brought. Her ladyship sipped her tea. "What were you hoping to learn here, your ladyship?" Nora asked. "I believe you already know the things you are hearing."

"I did not know that he was so mean to his help, or that he could get a man sent to prison. He must have gotten worse since I left." She rose from her chair and made ready to leave. "You are right, Nora. I've been foolish. I'm learning nothing that will help me. Let's repair to our rooms. Suddenly I'm terribly tired."

"Will we be leaving at first light?" Nora asked.

"Yes. I want to make it to Castle Mackinaw before the old duke expires."

Fourteen

Sprawling Castle Mackinaw sat atop a steep hillock, towering above winter-stripped trees and reaching upward to the blue winter sky. As the carriage tooled over the narrow road that snaked through the valley below, morning sun glinted off the castle's crenelated roof and the many small slitlike windows. Only remnants of the brick wall that had once enclosed the keep, remained; the gatehouse stood empty and silent.

To someone else, the countess thought, the castle would appear impressive, and beautiful, but it could never appear so to her. It was the home of her heartache. She was here to do what she had to do. She wore the same traveling dress she had worn yesterday, and the same red bonnet.

Acknowledging that she was scared half out of her wits of the granatum duke, who had always towered over her, her ladyship prayed that the flaming red gown and bonnet would give her an edge. Her steps were quick when she alighted the carriage without assistance and ran up the steps to bang the brass knocker. The door opened immediately.

Bexford bowed from the waist. "Welcome, your ladyship. I'm happy that you have at last returned to Castle Mackinaw."

"'Tis good to see you, Bexford," the countess said, praying the lie would not send her to hell. She introduced Nora as soon as they were inside the great foyer, then immediately asked, "Where is the duke?"

"He's in his chambers, your ladyship, in bed. I fear he's

quite angry at the good doctor. He told his grace he was not long for this world and advised he get his accounts in order."

'Tis time he set his account with me in order, thought the dowager countess. "Do you know why he wanted to see me, Bexford?" she asked.

"I pray that he's had a change of heart. Death sometimes does that."

"I pray so, too, Bexford," said the countess, and then something struck her as strange about the castle; where were the servants? Why had her father's valet opened the door? The great foyer was dark, cold, and lonely. An eerie quietness floated down from the high ceiling, and the walls seemed to be listening.

"Where are the servants? Is there not a butler?"

"No, your ladyship. His grace has closed most of the rooms. A housekeeper tends the few rooms in use, Cook prepares the meals, and I take care of his grace, as well as he will let me. He's been sick for nigh on a year."

"That is strange, indeed, that his grace would not have servants. There used to be two for every room it seemed."

"One servant after the other left, most soon after they came; his temper was short. His grace refused to replace them."

Oh, dear, thought the countess, *I fear impending death hasn't changed him. Most likely my journey has been made in vain.*

She said to Bexford, "If you, or somebody, will show Miss Nora to the rooms we will occupy, I shall pay the duke a visit."

"Yes, your ladyship. I helped the housekeeper air the rooms yesterday. I knew you would come." The valet picked up the two bags by their handles and walked from the room, Nora following him.

When the countess found herself alone, she took a deep breath and closed her eyes and prayed silently. She was terrified. So much depended on the old duke. But had that not always been so?

"This is it," she said aloud, at last opening her eyes. She

crossed herself. Quitting the foyer, she went out into a long hallway, and then into the great hall. There were two huge fireplaces, one on each side. At the far end, a great sweeping staircase curved upward to the second floor.

But the countess turned in another direction, to a side door that opened to narrow and steep stone stairs. The castle had been built before the Norman invasion, and the stone stairs had been left intact. Early childhood memories surfaced; her mama had been so dear; it was after her death that her papa had turned so mean.

The countess pushed nostalgia from her thoughts. She reached the top of the stone stairs and found herself in yet another hallway, but not an unfamiliar one. Her steps slowed as she neared the gigantic double doors that would momentarily open into the old duke's bedchamber. Her heart pounded against her ribcage, and her breath came as if she had been running.

Her steps slowed, to let the hope last. It had been so long since she had felt the wonderful emotion. At the doors, she gingerly turned a knob and pushed hard.

The old duke was sitting up in bed, even though the countess could not imagine where he got his strength. His white nightshirt looked as if it were draped over a stack of bones. When he was young, she had thought he looked like a huge, roaring pirate. Now, folds of yellow skin hung over his once strong chin, and from under thick white spiky eyebrows, the eyes that stared back at her were like two burned holes in a blanket. His white hair hung in long, unkempt strands around his bloodless face.

The countess closed the big doors behind her and went to stand at the foot of the duke's bed. Regret and pity washed over her, pity that he had not found happiness in his irascible self. The smell of death permeated the room, lighted only by the fire that burned crisply in the fireplace. The heavy red window coverings were drawn, closing out the world beyond.

"How are you, Papa?" she asked. She had not called him papa since she was twelve years old.

"That's a demme foolish question. Can't you see I'm dying? At least that's what old medicine man says I'm doing. Told me to get my accounts in order." He stopped and gasped for breath.

The countess did not speak. Her hands squeezed tightly the reticule she held as she stared at him. Then, at last, between spasms of coughing, he went on, "I sent for you because I'm a wealthy man . . . unfortunate enough to have a daughter to inherit that's not entailed. I'm doing this even though you never gave me a grandson." He eyed her through slits, "I suppose you can't wait to get your hands on my blunt." Coughing cut off his words. Still, the countess did not speak. "You're to do exactly as I have directed you to do in my will. Castle Mackinaw is yours. You're to live here . . ."

The countess swallowed the lump in her throat, and her heart sank to the pit of her stomach, resting there like a stone. His grace's dying thoughts were how to rule from his grave. She no longer had to wonder if he'd had a change of heart, or if impending death had made him kind.

The pity the countess had felt upon seeing his grace's emaciated body left her, and the anger of years past returned. A sudden trembling took over her body as the duke fell back on the huge pillows behind his back. Taking a deep breath to steady her voice, she forced calmness. "Your grace, I did not answer your summons to discuss your wealth."

"Then leave," he gasped.

"I have no notion of leaving until you tell me what you did with my baby, my precious little baby."

Rage filled the old man's pale face and brought fire to his dark eyes. For a moment, the countess thought he would rise up and levitate toward the ceiling. He swore the most foul words. Then, sputtering, he glared at her. "What baby?" he finally shouted in a loud, raspy whisper. "There was no baby."

The countess wanted to cry, to expel the tears banked in her eyes, in her heart, the tears that were choking off her words. But she had cried so much then, and it had done no good. The old duke's heart was flint-hard. Tears would never soften it. "There was a baby, mine and Ramey's baby, which you took from me in the cruelest manner, not letting me know whether it was a boy or girl. All these years I've had to wonder, and all these years I've lived with the memory of that first cry, a newborn's first tiny wail." The countess's voice broke, then became pleading. "And Mr. Ramey, what did you do to him? I know he would not have left without a word."

"That nobody! How could you disgrace me so? And me a duke. I pray to God he's dead."

"Did you kill him? Or have him killed?"

The countess, without thinking, was suddenly on the bed with the old duke. Pulling her red dress and cloak up over her knees, she straddled his skeletal body, took his bony shoulders in her small hands, and shook him until his head bounced around on his neck, and his shaggy white hair flew out in every direction. She screamed wildly, "Tell me, tell me what you did with my baby . . . please, before you die. Oh, dear God, make him tell me." She stopped the shaking and let her head drop to his bony chest.

"There was no . . . baby . . ."

She raised her head and stared straight into his eyes. "You are lying. My baby is somewhere, and I want to know where. I've spent all the blunt I could lay my hands on looking for him . . . or her, and for Mr. Ramey. And I'll spend every dime you leave me . . . my baby is somewhere."

"I'll disinherit you. I'll make a gift of that which is rightfully yours to the Crown." He tried to dislodge the countess and push himself up. "Bexford, send for my solicitor."

Those eyes that reminded the dowager countess of two burned holes in a blanket bore into her face as he sputtered, "You won't get a pound, not even what your mother left."

Hysterical laughter escaped the countess's throat, filled the room, and when she could laugh no more, she, because she could not control her voice, said loudly. "There'll be no solicitor. For the first time in my life, Your Grace, it is I, not you, who is in control. No solicitor will be allowed near you, for I will stand guard over you until you are dead."

Calmly then, she unstraddled the sick old man, pushed her skirt and cloak down over her legs, and slipped to the floor. She still wore her red bonnet.

Behind her, the big doors opened. It was Bexford. "I heard abnormal laughter, and a loud voice. Am I needed?"

"So-solicitor," mumbled the old duke.

"No, you are not needed, Bexford." She pulled a chair near the bed and sat down. "Since you are here, there is something you might do. Would you have someone bring a repast? A cup of soup for his grace. If he awakens, I shall feed him."

It was not her wont to hasten his grace's demise, neither was it her wont to see him leave what was rightfully hers through her dead mother to the Crown. She could just see Prinny licking his lips, while calling yet another architect to remodel Carlton House for the third or fourth time.

The valet was not to be easily put off. "Did his grace not just now call for his solicitor?"

"He may have, Bexford, but he's out of his head. And should the solicitor just happen to call to inquire of his grace's health, he is not to be invited to stay. I'm here now. I will see that his grace's needs are taken care of."

The valet left, a puzzled look on his face, and the countess went to get a book from a shelf. She lighted a half-burned candle that was on a table beside his grace's bed and then sat down to read Shelley's poems. Noticing her reticule on the floor, she picked it up and put it in her lap.

The room lapsed into silence, with the exception of the old duke's labored breathing. When the fire popped, it sounded as if a shell had exploded beside her.

Time passed interminably.

The housekeeper appeared with a tray, and the countess attempted to awaken his grace. Failing, she said, "Oh, dear, my coming has put him into a coma. Don't you think the doctor should be sent for?" the countess asked the housekeeper who had said her name was Bessie Beasley.

"The doctor can do no good," the housekeeper said. "He's said so. His grace is suffering from failure of the heart, failure of the lungs, failure of the kidneys, and anything else he has to fail. He won't take his medicine unless we pry his mouth open and pour it down his throat. Says we're trying to poison him. A card, he is, and no one can stop his dying. I think he would have gone months ago if he could have taken his blunt with him." She put her hands on her ample hips. "Did you know that he didn't hire servants when the others left because it was not his wont to pay them. I went two months without pay. And him as rich as crocus."

"No, I didn't know," said the countess, suddenly feeling drained. She looked at the haunch of beef and plate of biscuits and wondered why in the world she had ordered them. She poured herself a cup of tea and sent the rest away with Bessie Beasley.

Tears of failure streamed from the countess's eyes. His grace had been her last hope. *My baby is no longer a baby.* And Albert Ramey, her beloved Ramey. She could still feel his arms around her, his lips hungry for hers. The curtain swung back, and long-ago yesterdays entered, and her dear Ramey took possession of her, in all dimensions, and there, in the circle of light from the half-burned candle, warmth spread over her, and she felt engulfed in his precious love.

The countess was barely cognizant of his grace's shallow breathing. Because he was her father, she reached and touched his bony hand and then turned away to escape back to that other life, the time when she was surrounded with Albert Ramey's love.

They were dancing, she and Ramey. They had only met . . .

"Why don't we quit this awful party and go for a ride in the moonlight," he said, his brilliant blue eyes twinkling with mischievousness.

"My father would kill me," she answered. "This is my come-out, in case you've forgotten."

"A total waste of time. Husband-snatching is what the London Season is all about, and you've no need for that. You are going to marry me. I saw it in the cards."

"What cards?" she asked, looking up at him, feeling happier than she had ever felt in her life. When he touched her, which he managed to do often— "demme propriety," he said—flesh burned flesh, and chills danced up and down her spine.

"The Tarot cards," he answered. "I consulted them last evening, in anticipation of meeting you this night. I'd been told of your beauty. Now I know for myself. The light dances on your soft brown hair— "

"Ramey, you are crazy," she quickly countered, laughing.

He was tall, with a nice set of shoulders, and he moved gracefully, like the limbs of a willow tree caught in a gentle wind. A grown boy waiting to be a man. But she had only seen seventeen summers and had a lot of filling out to do herself. She could not take her eyes from his face, so full of life, speaking volumes. His blue, intense eyes, when he looked at her, held desire, and that awakened desire in her, a feeling so foreign to anything she had ever felt, but oh, so beautiful. She wanted to stay with him; let the others go home, or to their clubs, or back to their mistresses. Intuitively she knew he was not like the others.

Amazement filled her. Among all these titled men with whom she had this night danced, gentlemen of the first water, the pinks of the ton, *she had chosen for her lifemate a man without a title. If only they could dance the dance of love forever.*

"I'll tell you a secret if you will promise not to tell," he had said, and she promised with alacrity.

"I'm an impostor. My name is Albert Ramey. My cousin, Lord Malvey, found that he could not attend the most elaborate affair of the Season, and he offered his invitation to me. I purposely arrived late, so that when I was announced the guests would be too busy to note that I was not Lord Malvey.

Nonetheless, the old butler examined me good through his quizzing glass, before letting me in."

She laughed with him. "His grace will have your hide should he find out."

"Oh, but he'll never know. You won't tell, will you?"

"No, I won't tell," she answered, her voice soft. It was as if someone other than herself was dancing with this man. Mayhap she was having an out-of-body experience. At that moment, she looked into his bottomless blue eyes and gave herself to him. She would always love this man who could take her out of herself, into a world where people laughed, where happiness was not about blunt and titles and heirs.

Just then his grace, the Duke of Marcel, cut in, and, in a mean, grumbling voice, stated that he would finish the dance with his daughter. Which he did. "Who is that jackanapes monopolizing your time?" he thundered. "Three dances he has stood for. I will not have you acting as if he were the only gentleman here. This come-out ball cost plenty of blunt, and I expect you to find a husband."

"The jackanapes is Albert Ramey, and I think I love him. I would like to dance every dance with him. In truth, I wish all these other people would go home, and then we could dance all over this huge ballroom."

The old duke exploded. "Stop the prattle-tattle! Are you out of your mind? Lord Longworth has asked to pay his addresses, and I have consented. He will be calling on the morrow."

"Your grace, he's so old."

"Forty summers is not old. I've only seen forty-five myself."

"Well, I don't want to see him—"

His grace cut off her words. "You will do as you are told. Longworth is enormously deep in the pockets. He needs an heir. I expect you to have a son to inherit not only Longworth's estate, but mine as well. You would have come by that had you been a boy."

"I will tell you now that I will not have a son by Longworth. I don't plan to marry him. I shall marry for love."

Through gritted teeth, the duke again told her, "Demmet, you will do as I say. You've seen only seventeen summers."

His grace left her then, going straight to Albert Ramey. She watched as words were exchanged, and then she was whisked away by yet another titled man. Her heart ached for Ramey. Knowing the old duke, she could imagine what he had said to him, most likely frightening him within an inch of his life.

But moments later Albert Ramey came to dance with her, and he didn't seem frightened at all. His blue eyes twinkling, he whispered loud enough for anyone in proximity to hear, "I've been asked to leave. On the morrow at two o'clock meet me in Green Park, by the angels, and when the pinks of the ton *make their morning calls, to loll at your feet and say pretty things, pray remember that I am the only one who offers his heart."*

"I'll be there," she whispered back to him, and then he left her. At the door, showing his white teeth in the most wonderful smile, he looked back at her and blew a kiss, and she, laughing, reached up into the air as if to catch it . . .

Now, sitting there by the dying duke, it was difficult for the countess to remember what she had looked like then, those eighteen plus years ago, but she could remember how Ramey had made her feel, the spring he put in her steps, the laughter in her heart.

He had loved her; she had loved him.

And I still do.

The old duke moaned and mumbled. She leaned toward him to hear. She would get anything for him except the solicitor. He had taken away from her, now he would give back to her the means to find what he had taken away. "Do you want something, your grace?" she asked and received no answer.

The room became quiet again, the quietness broken only by his grace's shallow breathing and the fire that occasionally sparked and popped through dancing flames.

The countess stared at Shelley's book, seeing nothing, except with her mind's eye. Again the windows of memory opened and the curtain, of its own volition, opened her heart, and she saw Ramey clearly. She had arrived first in Green Park that day, handling the ribbons herself, in her own tilbury. Stealing away from the town house had been easy. As soon as the morning callers had dispersed, the duke had left for his club, taking Lord Longworth with him. The servants never enquired as to where she was going . . .

This day Cook clucked her tongue and cautioned that a lady of Quality did not go out unchaperoned, and she, Lady Marcella, laughing, had said, "Mayhap I'm not a lady of Quality. Besides, rules are made to be broken."

"Don't you let his grace hear you say that," replied Cook, a big cackle spilling out into the room. She swatted Marcella's backside. "Get on out of here, I've never seen you so happy."

The sound of racing hoofbeats caught her attention, and a big smile spread across her face when a white stallion came into view, Ramey in the saddle. He sat the horse as gracefully as he had, the night before, danced the minuet. His black hair glistened in the sunlight.

"I rented him at Tattersall's, hoping to impress you," he said, as he alighted. "I wanted to be the knight on a white horse when I saw you . . . your knight." He dropped the reins and went straight to Marcella and touched her cheek. "When I awoke at first light I told myself that I had windmills in my head, that no girl could be as pretty as the picture that kept flashing before my eyes. I could hardly wait to come here and see. The morning was a year long."

"And what is the verdict?" Marcella asked, her heart in her throat.

"You're even prettier," he said.

They talked about themselves, as if there was only one day, one meeting, in which to get to know each other. Ramey managed the estate of Lord Malvey, his cousin, the one who had given Ramey his invitation to Marcella's come-out ball. He told Marcella that when he had been orphaned young an uncle had seen that he was educated at Eton, and then at Oxford. He thought to become a man of law, but the love of land had pulled him in another direction.

His cousin, Ramey explained, was the fifth earl of Morventor, having come by the title upon the death of a distant cousin he had not met. "Lord Malvey's more like a brother than a cousin. We rub well together," Ramey had said.

When she began to tell him about herself, he already knew all there was to know. This amused and frightened her. "When I first heard your name a chill washed over me," he said, his eyes now serious. "I knew that you would be very special in my life, as if a psychic power had ruled it to be so. It was then that I started my inquiry."

"Did you like what you learned?" she asked.

"Everything." A long pause and then, "Except that you are the daughter of the most powerful duke in all of England, unless it would be the Prince of Wales, and the most ruthless." He stopped abruptly. "Pray, forgive me. I did not mean to hurt you. But it does not bode well for us."

She said in a low voice. "My father is a tyrant. He wants to rule everything and everybody. He owned my mother, as if she were chattel, and only last evening he promised me to Lord Longworth, a man of forty years."

"Surely that is not so."

"I told his grace that I would marry for love, not to join two estates."

Ramey looked at her for a long moment, and then asked, "Will you marry me? Dear Marcella, as I've told you, I loved you even before we met. I believe now that I will die if I cannot have you. Look at my hand, 'tis trembling, and I'm afraid to touch you . . . Lady Marcella, if I were only titled, mayhap your father would give his consent."

"I will ask him."

* * *

That had been a terrible time, the dowager countess mused as she sat beside the old duke's death bed. His grace had threatened to lock her in her room at Castle Mackinaw if she mentioned Ramey's name again. Pretending to accept her fate, she bargained: If his grace would allow her a few months before announcing her engagement, she would marry the man he had chosen for her, Lord Longworth.

The duke had acquiesced, and every afternoon she met Ramey in the park, where they would disappear into a copse and he would kiss her and tell her how much he loved her, and she kissed him and told him how much she loved him.

It couldn't go on, they both knew; their hunger for each other was too great. There was a desperateness about their love. When they kissed, she felt herself quiver, felt her heart beat in the back of her throat, in her stomach, and in her thighs, where they angled toward her private self. So they began to make plans.

"Every one runs away to Gretna Green to be married," Ramey said. "That's the first place your grace would look."

"After we are married, he can't take me away. I'll belong to you then."

"You belong to me now, my love. Our hearts are intertwined, and nothing will ever change that."

So the plan was made: They would travel north to Lord Malvey's seat and be married there. Lord Malvey would ask for a special license that did not require reading of the banns.

It should be simple, they both had said.

And luck seemed to be with them. An emergency called his grace back to Castle Mackinaw. He would be gone a week, and on the wake of his shirttail leaving London, the lovers fled to Lincolnshire, to be wed by a vicar who knew nothing of the circumstances. Had he known, he would not have performed the ceremony. No vicar in England would have, for everyone knew of the Duke of Marcel's far-reaching power.

The wedding and the three days that followed, before the old duke found them, were the most wonderful of the countess's life. Always, when she let her mind dwell on that time, it brought a smile, along with the pain. She had worn a flowing white gown that had belonged to Ramey's mother, and he wore black tails, and a white shirt with high collar points. The ring he put on her finger had been a simple band of gold. Now, she looked down at it fondly, feeling as she did then, filled with love. The Good Book had been wrong. What God had brought together man could put asunder. But not really, she mused, for she and Ramey had never been apart; their hearts were inextricably joined. The old duke's power could never destroy that.

She remembered their wedding night. There had been no sense of urgency, the house was theirs, having been vacated by all wedding guests, and the sweet darkness belonged to them. Now, in this room of death, her heart struggled to recapture the happiness she had felt, the giving and taking of love when Ramey had entered her. The spiral of the love dance had gone on and on, taking her out of herself, out of her loneliness, and making her one with him. She had wondered about his endurance, but had not wanted him to stop . . .

Oh God, I love him so, she thought, but did not say it, and she noted that her thoughts had been in the present tense. She could never think of their love as something that had been. It was ongoing, always would be. She could hear him whispering, "I will love you forever," and she hugged herself, holding the words to her heart.

"Do you, Ramey? 'Tis forever. Where are you? Do you still love me? I love you, my darling," she whispered as she sat alone in the death room. But she would choose heartbreak over stone-cold death inside, she told herself. No, no, she would not stop loving him, even if she could. She welcomed the heartbreak, the unfulfilled longing in her body. Ramey was the heaven, and the stars, the light of daybreak, the dusk in the evening, the stillness of a lovely night, the depth of joyous laughter.

She missed the laughter.

Fifteen

When the dowager countess awakened, she immediately knew the old duke had died. She looked down and saw that their hands were entwined. Who had taken whose hand she did not know, but when death had come they were reaching out to each other. And that is how it should be, she thought, at last allowing her eyes to look on his restful face.

In death, his tyrannical countenance had softened, and he appeared years younger than his sixty-three years. Taking two coins from her reticule, she closed his eyes and placed the coins on them, and then she pulled the sheet up over his shaggy white head. She knelt beside the bed and prayed for his soul, and when she was again standing, the hatred was gone, leaving only the anger and the heartache for the unjust thing the old duke had done. Only when she found her child, and her dear Ramey, would the anger leave her. She needed that to keep her going.

Going out into the hall, she encountered Bexford and Nora, both looking at her anxiously. "He's gone," she announced and then she said to Bexford, "Please go into town and send someone to prepare his body for burial. Place a notice in the square that the funeral will be this day at sundown, in the family graveyard here at Mackinaw. Ask the vicar to come if he would like. If he doesn't, then I will read over him and lead the mourners, if there are any, in song. He will have a decent burial."

The stooped valet bowed from the waist. "Your ladyship,

may I express my condolences. I do pray that the unfinished business between the two of you was taken care of before he passed over."

"It wasn't."

"I'm sorry to hear that, your ladyship. After the burial, mayhap I can fill you in on a part of it."

The dowager countess's mouth fell open. Many times she had asked Bexford what he knew about the night her baby was born. He had been in the duke's service long before that. Bexford had denied any knowledge of what had happened. Now he was willing to talk.

"Tell me now, Bexford." She strained to keep from grabbing the lapels of his long frock coat and pleading. She looked into his face and saw that the customary tight, frightened look was no longer there, and she knew that fear had heretofore sealed his lips.

"After the burial," Bexford promised. "It would not seem fitting now, so soon after he passed."

He does know something. It seemed ironic that it should come on the wake of the old duke's death. Tears flooded her eyes. "I can wait, Bexford, I've waited such a long time."

Nora was looking on in puzzlement, but she did not speak until the dowager turned to her and said, "Thank you, Nora, for being here during this awful time."

"What can I do to help, your ladyship?" Nora asked.

The countess thought for a moment. "Go with Bexford into the village, to the employment office, and hire servants, at least twenty, all good workers who can dust and sweep. It will take at least ten to pull window coverings back and let in light. The castle must needs be brought back to its former glory so that it will sell quickly. And fetch the solicitor."

"Your ladyship," Bexford said. "The solicitor is waiting below stairs in the receiving room. I begged him to leave, but he insisted that his grace might need him."

A pang of guilt washed over the countess. But she had done

what she had had to do. All that she wanted from the estate was blunt to pay for her search. She would change things if she could, would make the old duke a kind man, a loving father, but that she could not do. She smiled sardonically at her own naivete. On her way from Grammacy Chase, she had hoped he had changed from his irascible self, becoming kind and thoughtful of his fellowman as death neared.

"Be off," she told the valet and Nora. We shall need at least two cooks, and plenty of groceries. After the funeral, food will be served. I will go below stairs and talk with the solicitor. His name, Bexford?"

"Ryan," your ladyship, Howard Ryan."

The countess did not immediately go to the receiving room. Instead, she stepped out into the fresh air and breathed deeply. She suddenly became cognizant of her dress; scarlet gown, covered with a scarlet velvet cloak. Reaching up, she found the matching bonnet crooked on her head, and, looking down, she saw the wrinkled mess her clothes had become.

She removed the bonnet and loosened her hair from the bun resting on her nape. There was a mist in the air, and it felt good to her face. To the east, the sun was rising above the mountain that held Castle Mackinaw; below, in the valley, lay miles and miles of fertile land, now dormant and waiting for spring. The countess looked at the winding road that split the valley and led upward to the castle. Had she traveled that road only yesterday?

She waited until her heartbeat slowed and returned to normal, took another deep breath, and turned to go inside. Finding the solicitor asleep on a deep burgundy sopha, she sat in a matching chair.

He was a small man and wore his long hair tied at the nape with a string of brown cloth. His face was lined and brown. Clasped under an arm was a small portmanteau that was closed with a small lock. No doubt it held her father's will, the countess mused, now anxious to get on with the business of the estate. It occurred to her that mayhap the old duke had changed his will in his last years. At last Ryan stirred, and, seeing the countess, sat immediately up. And then he was on his feet and bowing and saying, "I beg your forgiveness, your ladyship, but the night was quite long."

"Have you been here all night?" the countess asked.

"Thought his grace might need me. I understood that he was on his last breaths. Did he say . . . did he ask for me?"

"Yes, he did, Mr. Ryan. He wanted to disinherit me, but I sat by his side all night to prevent that from happening. He was going to give what came from my mother to the Crown. I knew Mama would not like that. And neither would I."

"You know that Castle Mackinaw was from your mother's family and is not entailed."

"Yes, and I'll have it prepared to sell immediately. I've sent for workers to start the cleaning."

"'Tis yours to do with what you want. There's two thousand acres attached." He gained a seat on the sopha he had slept on, and, taking a key from his waistcoat pocket, opened the lock on the portmanteau saying, "His grace was a very wealthy man, your ladyship, and there are immense assets other than the castle and the attached land. There will be no need to sell . . . unless you just want to rid yourself of the responsibility of ownership. 'Tis a shame he does not have an heir for the dukedom."

The countess thought to say that if the old duke had let her live her own life with Albert Ramey, his grace might have had several grandsons in line to inherit his title. Not knowing the solicitor, she kept the thought to herself and received the Last Will and Statement of his grace, the Duke of Marcel, the solicitor was proffering. She looked at it briefly, then lay it aside. "Did his grace ever speak to you about our estrangement? As you must surely know, we had not spoken in ten years?"

"He talked to me about it, but he never told me the details."

"Did he mention Albert Ramey?"

"No. Never heard that name before. He just said you had

failed him by not having a son by Lord Longworth, and that there had been some hard words."

"Is that all? Are you sure? Did he mention a baby?"

"Whose baby? No, he never talked to me about a baby."

The countess gave up. She rose languorously from her chair and went to the door, where she turned back and said, "The services for his grace will be at sundown, here, in the family graveyard. If you wish to come."

"What about his will? Don't you care?"

"Only that he didn't disinherit me. There'll be plenty to do what I want to do. We can tend to that later. I will send the housekeeper with a repast for you. If you've been here all night, you must be very tired."

He thanked her and she left and went first to the housekeeper and then to her quarters. They were not her old rooms, and she wondered why the valet had not put her there. She looked about. Before a lively fire was a copper tub and tankards of hot water. She smiled. Someone, most likely Nora had known how much she would need a bath after the ordeal was over. She closed the door and lifted the smallest tankard, filling the tub half-full.

From a huge gilt-framed looking glass her reflection stared back at her, showing the wrinkled dress and cloak, the weariness in her oval face. She rubbed the tip of a finger over her right cheek. Just as Ramey used to do. "Oh, Ramey," she said, "please just be alive, and I will find you. I love you so much my darling."

Slowly, as she shrugged out of her clothes, then sank into the hot water, the import that his grace's passing would have on her life sank in, and she felt a moment of pure happiness. No longer would those who knew be afraid to talk with her about her beloved Ramey.

When she was no longer being held prisoner by his grace, indeed was married to Lord Longworth, she had gone to Lord Malvey, whose estate Ramey had managed, and inquired as to Ramey's whereabouts, receiving only a fearful look from downcast eyes and a slow negative nod of his head. She would go again, or send someone. No, she would go herself, and she would make Lord Malvey tell her what he knew. She would hire Scotland Yard to search for Ramey, or she would engage the Bow Street Runners. Now that she would have blunt to offer, all kinds of opportunities would open up.

Not once did the countess think that Ramey had married, and she would have never married had she not been forced to do so. She remembered with pain the dark room where she was held, in a keep on one of her father's estates. There had been daily lashes with a razor strop. So she had married Lord Longworth, but she had never been his.

"Your grace, I'm glad you're dead," she murmured, lifting her chin and scrubbing her delicate flesh until it showed red in the looking glass. A pitcher of warm water sat by the tub. Standing, she rinsed her white hair until it squeaked, letting the water trickle over her naked body and run back into the copper tub. She stood straight and stared at her reflection. Her breasts were round and firm, the nipples taut, and she still had the youthful body she had given to Ramey all those years ago.

"I'm glad you're dead, your grace," she murmured a second time. This was truly so, but she grieved for the papa she had known when she was a child, before her mama had died, and before he became mean and cruel, before money and possessions had become his God. *I'm surprised he didn't find a way to take it with him,* she thought, almost smiling.

The fire warmed her skin, and her eyelids suddenly became heavy. She had slept precious little as she sat beside the deathbed. After brushing the tangles from her hair, she donned a chemise and drawers, then lay on the feather bed and was asleep almost before her head hit the pillow. Albert Ramey danced through her dreams, and a child, first a little boy, looking like Ramey, then a little girl who looked like her. It was Christmas, and they were opening presents.

The sound of wheels turning on hard earth and of harness jingling awoke the dowager countess. She looked at the ormolu clock on the mantel and found that she had been asleep for two hours. Watching through the window, she saw the tilbury carrying the valet and Nora, with three wagons loaded with workers and a pine box following. No man of the cloth was among them. The undertaker rode alongside the wagons on a black stallion.

The countess, feeling refreshed, dressed quickly, choosing a day dress of blue sarcenet trimmed in delicate lace. She had no notion of wearing mourning black.

Within an hour after the workers had set to work on the many rooms of the castle, the countess could smell polishing wax and soap. She went out front and looked up, watching the stone facade change as the heavy coverings were pulled back from the windows. It began to look like the Castle Mackinaw she once loved. It should sell quickly, she thought, going back inside.

Five-thirty came rather quickly for the countess. Several times she looked down the winding road, hoping the vicar would have a change of heart and come to pray over his grace. When she realized that this was not going to happen, she squared her shoulders and climbed the small hillock that swept away from the castle. She went alone, with her own thoughts, as the dying sun distributed its gentle splendor on the canvas of the evening stillness. Her words were few and very kind as she stood under the huge cedar tree, under which the wooden casket rested, and spoke to the small circle of people, mostly the newly hired workers. A few had come from the village. She asked that those who had known his grace remember the good, and not to judge.

"Things are clear to God, the final judge, which are not clear to us," she said.

After she had read from the Twenty-third Psalm, the small crowd said in unison the Lord's Prayer, and sang "Rock of Ages," a song all of them knew and sent forth over the hillock in soft, reverent voices.

And then it was over. The sun was gone, and dusk had

captured the hillock. An owl hooted, and lightning bugs flitted here and there, their orange tails shining.

The countess turned and walked slowly back to the castle. Earlier, she had asked Bexford to join her after the service in an upstairs drawing room. To her surprise, the valet was already there when she arrived. He jumped to his feet and bowed from the waist. "It was a nice service, your ladyship," he said, and then to the countess's amazement, he added, "Due to the wrong he did to you, I thought you were most kind."

"What do you know about that wrong, Bexford?" the countess asked, still standing.

"That his grace had your Mr. Ramey sent to prison in Australia. But he did not stay long. He escaped and went to America. Through Lord Malvey, we have kept in touch, and I wrote to him that his grace was dying."

For a moment the countess could not speak. The words he spoke were a lifeline to her starving soul. "What do you mean you wrote to him?"

"He was afraid to return to England, knowing the old duke's power. I knew Albert Ramey when he was in leading strings, from another household where I had worked. I knew he had done nothing to be sent to prison for." After a pause. "Loving you was not a crime, except in his grace's mind."

The countess found a chair and sank into it, for her knees trembled until she feared she would fall. She had never had a spell of the vapors in her life. "Pray, tell me the whole of it, Bexford. When did you write?"

"Six months back, when the doctor said there was no more he could do for his grace. My missive had to pass through Lord Malvey. I couldn't take a chance on his grace learning about Ramey's whereabouts."

"Oh, thank you, thank you, Bexford," the countess whispered, and then she struggled to ask, "What did the old duke do with my baby?"

For a long moment the valet stood on first one foot and then the other. The sadness in his face answered the question for the countess before the words came from his mouth. At last, he said in a low, hurting voice, "I asked his grace that, and he swore to me that she had died two hours after she was born."

Sixteen

At Talbert Hall, Rachel hugged little Frank to her bosom and whispered close to his ear. "Please go to sleep. You'll wake Mother M. and she needs her sleep."

Frank gurgled with laughter.

"I sure do need my sleep," the good sister said. She pulled herself up in the bed and looked over at Rachel and the wiggling baby. "What are you doing with that child in bed with you? Don't you know that Hannah will be sounding the alarm that someone has stolen her baby?"

"She knows," Rachel answered. "I heard him fretting and I went in to see about him. He was wet. I tried to change his napkin without waking her, but she woke anyway. He didn't seem inclined to sleeping, not even when I rocked him. So when Hannah started fussing I brought him in here. Hopefully, she's back to sleep."

" 'Tis better to keep me awake, I suppose."

Rachel laughed. "I'd rather hear you fuss."

"You're spoiling that baby. I'm sure you know that," said Mother M., chuckling.

"I see no harm in making him feel loved. Besides, it was cold in the nursery and every time I put the blankets over him, he kicked them off. When he reached his little arms up to me, smiling his big smile, I couldn't help myself. I think he'll go to sleep in a minute. I'm sorry to be bothering you."

"Stuff! You're not bothering me. 'Tis time for prayers anyway."

Rachel groaned, and Mother Margaret slid out of bed and went to the window and looked at her watch. The room was dark except for the moonlight the window allowed. "Just as I thought, five o'clock. Get up, Miss Rachel, and pray with me."

"Mother M., when I left the Home, I swore I would never again say prayers at five o'clock in the morning. 'Tis against my religion."

"You should never say you won't do anything, young lady, for you most likely will do that which you are saying you won't do."

There was good humor in Sister Margaret's voice, and Rachel knew she didn't mean to be scolding. "I'll say my prayers at five o'clock this afternoon."

Rachel watched as the good sister, wearing her long white nightdress, lit a taper and placed it on the table beside the fireplace. She bent by the hearth and added chunks of coal to the banked embers and then struck a lucifer to it, and soon red and orange dancing flames made the room bright and cheery and warm. Rachel yawned and stretched, feeling happy with her life. She thought about Lord Abshire and imagined that someday she would go to the nursery and bring their baby to their bed, and most likely his lordship would fuss. Not meaning it, just like Mother M. He would then start the fire, and he would suggest that the baby be returned to the nursery, and after a while she would do as he asked. When the door had closed the world out and they were totally alone, he would make love to her, while whispering sweet, endearing words for her ears only. The light from the fire would shine on his face, and she could see his wry grin when she said, "No, not again," but not meaning it.

Rachel felt her face. It was hot to her hands. Out of the corner of her eye, she looked at Mother M. and prayed that she could not read her thoughts. Since Lord Abshire had taken her into the alcove and kissed her and stirred her up like a burning house, so against propriety for a gentleman to do, she had spent a lot of her time daydreaming about their future.

She loved him, and had told him so that night, and of course they would be married. Then, the next day, when he wasn't kissing her and she could think straight, she had made it plain that marriage would have to wait until after Christmas.

"Why after Christmas?" he had asked, not a little irritated. "What can possibly happen between now and Christmas?"

Lord Talbert will be home and then everything will be out in the open, thought Rachel.

"After Christmas is not too long to wait," she had told him. "We don't want the festivities of the Holiday Season to take away from our wedding."

Just thinking of marrying Lord Abshire made blood rush to Rachel's skull, like waves splashing the shore. It was so wonderful to be loved . . . and to love. A wonderful warmth crept over her body. She was beginning to believe that she loved Lord Abshire to distraction. He was on her mind all the time!

By now, Frank was sitting up in bed and clapping his fat little hands together. Rachel took a handkerchief and wiped the drool from his mouth. "You should go to sleep, you little scamp," she scolded, kissing him on the cheek and bringing more laughter. She hugged him fiercely, then rocked back and forth and hummed a tune to him, and the room became quiet. Orange flames danced in the grate, and light from the taper cast shadows onto the walls.

Mother Margaret watched Rachel and the baby. Why had she never rocked Rachel? She regretted this infinitely. She should not have listened to those who said, "Spare the rod and spoil the child." How foolish she had been to believe that non-sense. And to think that many women of the upper orders sent their children away for someone else to rear, to avoid a deep attachment! She closed her eyes and said her prayers, adding a special one for Rachel's future.

So worried was Mother M. about Rachel that she pondered

on staying at Talbert Hall until after Christmas. If Rachel was doomed for heartbreak when Lord Talbert came home, then she must needs to be near. There was something very strange about this Lord Talbert. What kind of father would stay away from a sweet baby like Frank? And a pretty wife such as Lady Talbert?

And Rachel thinks this man is her dear papa.

There was something else bearing heavily on Mother M.'s mind, and she had stewed about it long enough, she decided. She would talk with Lady Talbert about her brother. If anyone knew whether or not his intentions toward Rachel were honorable, it would be his lordship's sister.

"I think he's asleep," said Rachel as she scooted off the high bed, holding little Frank close to her breast. "I'll take him back to his bed. He might fall off this high one should I let him sleep here."

"I'm certain Hannah will be happy to have him back," Mother M. said, smiling.

"Be back in a second," Rachel said in a low voice, and as quietly and as quickly as she could she deposited the sleeping baby in his crib, then returned.

"'Tis so early, I think I'll visit Napoleon. I have something I want to ask him, and he's always so full of news."

"Do you want to wake him up, too?" Sister Margaret asked teasingly.

"He rises at first light. Would you like a walk in the cold air? Might wake us both up."

"And make us hungry."

They dressed hurriedly, taking turns in the dressing room, and then they stole down the stairs and out a side door and hurried toward the stables. The morning air was crisp and cold to Rachel's face. She pulled the heavy head scarf forward to cover her cheeks. Thick gloves kept her hands warm. "Are you cold?" she asked Mother M., who was bundled up in her fur-trimmed pelisse and wearing a woolen bonnet.

"No, not particularly, but I'm glad 'tis not far to the stables."

In the quarters above the stables, Napoleon sat at a small square table, half bent over an enormous plate of food.

"Come in, ladies," he said, smiling when they appeared in the doorway. Rachel wanted to hug him, but feared he would be embarrassed and push her away. His red hair, uncombed, stood in spikes, and light from a candle made shadows on his freckled face. Rachel immediately knew he was bursting with news, and, as soon as he had chewed and swallowed, he informed her that Lord Abshire had enrolled him at Eton.

"Thanks to you, Rachel," he said, "for showing my drawings to his lordship. I promise not to let you down." His smile grew wider. "If the mad old king ever dies and Prinny becomes his majesty, he will be calling on me to remodel Windsor Castle."

"I'm so happy for you, Napoleon." Tears filled her eyes, and she said, "And I have something I want to ask you."

"Shoot away, but first let me ask you ladies to sit." He stood and motioned toward the chairs around the table. Rachel noted the sparsely furnished room was neat and clean, the beds made and everything picked up. And Napoleon had not been expecting company. She was pleased.

"Now, what do you want to ask, Miss Rachel?"

"I think it a capital idea if you move into the manor house and live with the rest of us. I take it that you are not leaving for Eton until after the holidays."

Napoleon raised an eyebrow. "That's right, but what would his lordship say about that? He hired me to muck our stables."

"I haven't asked him yet," replied Rachel "I wanted to know if you would like to live in Talbert Hall before I suggested it to him. Would you, Napoleon? I'll tell his lordship you can help tend little Frank."

Mother M., quiet until now, let out a cackle of laughter.

"Just what the little boy needs, someone else to spoil him." She looked at Napoleon. "I think you should do it. 'Twould make you more comfortable with the boys at Eton. You can say truthfully that you lived at Talbert Hall.

"I guess so," he said. "I sure want to do well at the school. My pap said I had the gift to be a fine architect."

Rachel couldn't help herself. She went to him and gave him a big hug. Before he could object, she teased, "Don't you dare push me away, Napoleon. I do love you so very much."

He accepted the embrace, but his freckled face turned as red as his hair. Rachel said to him, "Now, I have something else to tell you . . . if you'll promise not to tell."

"Cross my heart." He crossed himself. "But wait until I've served you ladies tea. I'll get the cups. I would offer breakfast, but Cook has already taken himself off for his morning ride. On-dits have it that he's courtin' one of the tenant's sisters."

The cups turned out to be mugs, one with a big chip out of its rim, the tea was hot and it tasted good to Rachel. Back in her chair, she took a sip of tea and then blurted out, "Napoleon, I have promised to marry Lord Abshire."

Napoleon looked at her quizzically. "When?"

"Well, no date has been set, so it isn't official yet. As you know, I have something that must needs be settled before I can become any man's wife."

"That's balderdash, Rachel Storm. Best you let him get a special license and you marry him first thing on the morrow. Not often that a girl of the under orders gets to marry a man of the upper orders—not that you ain't worthy of two upper orders—but that's just the way it is. That other stuff about finding your papa don't signify. Every *ton* lady in all of England would envy you should you marry Lord Abshire."

Rachel was quiet for a long moment before saying, "I just can't, not until I know who I am. Lord Abshire . . . any man . . . deserves better than that. I don't mind the Rachel—"

"I think Storm is a beautiful name," said Napoleon before Rachel could continue.

Mother M. was quietly drinking her tea. She winked at Napoleon and in a teasing voice said, "She was named after the Biblical Rachel in hopes she would be like the good woman in the Bible. You know, complacent and never stubborn. Well, as you can see, Napoleon, it didn't work."

Napoleon drained his mug. "I hope you're not still thinking Lord Talbert is your pap. From what's been passed to me, he's a scoundrel of the first water. Not that Lord Abshire said that, but I've been making inquiries among the others round here. You may not want him for your papa, Rachel."

"But don't you see, Napoleon, if someone is your papa, you must needs accept him and not be judgmental. Belonging to someone is what counts. And having a real name."

"You should marry Lord Abshire, Rachel. I'm telling you a chance like that don't come along but once in a lifetime. 'Tis plain you're in love with him. When you say his name you can hardly breathe. That makes it better still to be in love."

"You misused 'don't', Napoleon. Say it over to yourself. Does a chance like that 'do not come by but once in a life time' sound right? 'Doesn't' is the right contraction."

Napoleon threw up his hands. "We're talking about your future and you worry about my grammar."

"I do so want you to do well at Eton, Napoleon. Your future is important, too."

"I believe God brought you both to Talbert Hall," interceded Sister Margaret. With love pouring from her faded eyes, she looked long at Rachel. "I prayed so hard for you, dear Rachel. Just think what could have happened to you."

Napoleon smiled. "I'm glad I stole her box. God must have wanted me to watch out for her. If she'd just get this silly notion about Lord Talbert being her pap out of her head."

"Shhh," Rachel cautioned. "Someone might hear."

The big room became quiet, and then—Mother M. said, "Rachel, I've decided to stay at Talbert Hall until Lord Talbert comes home. If you should need me I want to be near."

"I want you to stay, but I promise I won't need you. Things will be settled at Christmastime."

"I feel it in here, Rachel. She put her hand over her heart. "The Lord is telling me to stay."

Seventeen

When Rachel and Sister Margaret returned to the manor house Rachel changed to a fresh gown, a blue morning dress of delicate lawn imprinted with tiny roses. Flesh showed above the neckline, and a rose-colored ribbon held the fabric tightly under her bosom. She brushed her black hair, letting it fall around her shoulders, added a smidgen of rouge to her cheeks, and then asked Mother M. if she were ready for breakfast.

" 'Tis early, and I doubt that anyone else will be there, but I am starving."

"I will be down directly. I must needs notify the Home that my vacation will extend beyond the Christmas holidays."

Rachel knew there was no point in arguing. If Mother M. believed the Lord was telling her to stay at Talbert Hall, she would stay.

"I'll wager a new habit for you that I will not need you. Lord Talbert will come, I will confront him about his monthly stipends to Saint Cecilia's for the past eighteen years, and he will admit that the money was for the benefit of his daughter, which, of course will be me."

Mother M. looked pityingly at Rachel. "I don't gamble, but should you win, what would I owe you?"

"Just your blessings, no matter what kind of man his lordship turns out to be."

"From what Napoleon said, and from what I've observed since coming to Talbert Hall, it might be difficult for me to give my blessings."

Rachel's countenance became somber. She turned then and quit the room. She did not understand why the good sister and Napoleon were so negative. Did they not know that *any* papa was better than no papa at all?

What a wonderful Christmas gift it would be to at last have a papa, she thought, as she ran down the stairs.

Lord Abshire was already at the table when Rachel arrived. His eyes were on the door, and when he saw her, out of breath from running, he smiled broadly.

"I've been waiting for you. I sent a footman to say that I wished for you to come down early, but no one answered his knock."

"Mother M. and I went to the stables to visit with Napoleon."

He took her hand, holding it lovingly for a moment, and then he kissed the palm. "A night away from you is torture, dear Rachel." He looked into her blue eyes and felt a big lump lodge in his throat.

She gave a little laugh. "You were in my dreams, your lordship, so I feel that I spent the night with you."

Abshire doubted that Rachel had ever been told about what happened on a girl's wedding night, and he knew she was too innocent to even think such thoughts as he was having. But he could not help himself. Since he had decided to give up his suit to seduce her—which she let him know 'twould be impossible—he had come to love her with all his heart. And that love would only come to fruition when he held her and made love to her, making them one.

To his lordship's surprise, he found his eyes moist. He drew her into his arms and held her, feeling that at last he had found the part of him that had been missing. "I sent the servants away. I will serve you for the rest of our lives."

Uncomfortable with the depth of his reaction to her presence, Rachel gave a little laugh. "Pray do not make rash promises. I might hold you to them."

He laughed with her, and then drew her to the table to sit beside him.

"Should you ring for a footman to bring our food?" she asked, glad for the change of ambiance in the room.

"I'm supposed to serve you, and I forgot. Shall I choose, or do you wish to order?"

Just then Lady Talbert and Mother M. entered the dining room, talking and laughing together. Rachel whispered to his lordship, "Saved by the bell. Now, you will have to ring for a footman, unless you want to serve all of us."

"I'd rather do that when we are alone." He rang the silver bell that rested by his plate.

"What are you two whispering about?" asked Lady Talbert.

"About how I plan to serve Rachel's breakfast in bed after we are married," said Abshire, giving his wry grin.

Two footman, in full livery, came to take their orders and serve them, moving about the dining room stealthily, their steps a whisper against the plush rug. Rachel ordered scrambled eggs, ham, biscuits, jelly, and hot coffee. It seemed her heart, beating fiercely only moments earlier when she was in Lord Abshire's arms, had ceased to beat at all. Her head felt dizzy, and her palms were damp, her mouth dry. She wanted to marry him as much as he professed to wanting to marry her. Why could she not forget Lord Talbert and say yes to him?

She shook her head, imperceptible she hoped. As much as she wanted to acquiesce to Lord Abshire, she just could not. And Christmas was not long to wait, she told herself.

Rachel realized that the others were talking, and all had been served. Loading her fork with scrambled eggs, she pushed them into her mouth and then she smiled inwardly. No doubt every girl who had been in love had acted as she was acting. She heard Lady Talbert saying, "I plan to call on Countess Marcella Longworth at Grammacy Chase today."

"That's two hours away," objected Lord Abshire. "And she

has accepted our invitation to the costume ball. 'Tis only five nights away. So why the call?"

"I take it that you haven't heard that her father, his grace, the Duke of Marcel, died just recently, and I'm certain she will be in mourning and will not attend the ball. I feel it incumbent upon myself to pay my respects. Will you go with me, Trenton? And you, too, Rachel, if you would like. 'Twould be one more country neighbor you would know when you and Trenton are married."

Abshire spoke quickly. "I have already made plans to go into Blanchland and purchase Napoleon's Eton wardrobe, and I was hoping Rachel would assist."

"I shall be happy to help, your lordship, but before we make plans for the day, I have a request to make of you, Lady Talbert, and of your lordship, of course. I beg your forgiveness if I appear forward, but do you not think it appropriate for Napoleon to move into the manor house and live with the rest of us in preparation of his going to Eton? 'Twould be terrible for him to be ostracized by other students, and he surely would be should they learn he came straight from mucking out stables."

Lord Abshire grinned. "Most likely Napoleon will tell them, and about his being a thief before coming to Talbert Hall as well."

"I'll instruct him not to," said Rachel in a firm tone. "He needs only to say that he's from Talbert Hall. I've already asked him if he would like to make the move."

"Of course, he may," said Lady Talbert. "Trenton and I should have thought of it without your prompting. We know the cruelty of society when one is not of them."

His lordship placed his big hand over Rachel's small one. "Move him today, and I shall help . . . if afterward you will go into town with me. I need your company."

"I will have Napoleon's lessons early, then mayhap he will watch Frank while I go into town with you. Or should he go, since it is his wardrobe we will be selecting?"

"I remember the last time when he was so adamant about not wearing this and not wearing that," said Lord Abshire. "We'll take his measurements with us, and if he takes a disgust for what we purchase, we'll tell him that it's the last stare at Eton."

They all laughed, and the subject came back to Lady Talbert's planned sojourn to Grammacy Chase. Until now, Mother M. had been quiet, but not missing anything. Her gaze went from Rachel to Lord Abshire, and then back to Rachel. They looked as if they were in love, but she did not entirely trust his lordship. In a flash, her mind was made up. She would do this day what she had been planning on doing. If her ladyship turned a deaf ear and refused to discuss her brother, then that would suggest the falsity of his pursuit of Rachel.

"May I accompany you, Lady Talbert?" she asked. "A drive through the country sounds delightful, even though it is quite cold."

"Oh, I'd adore it if you would come, Mother M. I never dreamed of your wanting to, and I beg your forgiveness for not asking."

"Stuff! There's nothing to forgive. 'Tis all settled then; Rachel and Lord Abshire will help Napoleon move into the Hall, then after lessons, they will go into town, while Napoleon watches over little Frank. Rachel, are you sure he knows how to take care of a baby?"

"Hannah will be near," Rachel answered.

Lady Talbert spoke quickly. "I am such a peagoose. I forgot to tell you the latest about Hannah. She is enceinte. You know she had given birth before coming to Talbert Hall, and her baby died. Well, she's expecting again, and she plans on leaving us soon after Christmas."

"Oh, I'm so happy for her," spoke up Rachel. "But when could it have happened? I didn't know she ever left the Hall."

Lady Talbert laughed. "She must have left sometime, when no one knew. I'm really happy for her. Her attachment to Frank concerned me more than I wanted to admit. And the timing is perfect. By the time she leaves, little Frank will be taking solid food and drinking milk from a cup. With Rachel becoming Lady Abshire, I will engage another nanny." Her ladyship paused for a moment, "Thank goodness nothing has to be done until after Christmas."

His lordship turned to Rachel and smiled. "It seems that nothing can happen around here until after Christmas."

To the others he said, "I have tried and failed to talk Rachel into getting leg-shackled as soon as possible. A pox on Christmas."

"Don't say that," scolded Lady Talbert, "tis a very special time of the year for all those of the Christian faith. Besides, little brother, there are three women here who believe the bride should set the wedding date. I'm afraid you are outnumbered."

"When Napoleon moves in, mayhap he will be on my side," Lord Abshire said teasingly.

"He already is," Rachel said. "Only this morning he lectured me, saying I should marry you as soon as a special license can be obtained."

"See, great minds move in tandem," retorted Lord Abshire.

And so the conviviality went, until, now stuffed with the delectable breakfast, they were ready to quit the dining room, each to carry out his or her own plan.

An inexplicable shiver passed over Rachel, and her thoughts went back to Napoleon's insistence that she marry Lord Abshire as quickly as possible. Did the little boy know something she did not know? Or could he see into the future, seeing something that would keep her from marrying Lord Abshire?

Eighteen

Lady Talbert was pleased that Mother M. was going with her to Grammacy Chase. Having taken notice of the old woman's protectiveness of Frank's nanny and the inquisitive looks she had cast at Trenton, her ladyship was certain there would be questions.

And I have a question of my own, she thought. *Why did Rachel Storm come to Talbert Hall?*

Of late, Lady Talbert had spent considerable time pondering this question, without a clue, and she had intensely observed Trenton's pursuit of Rachel, an innocent young lady if she had ever known one. Not many women stayed innocent in Lord Abshire's path, she mused. But she believed that Rachel had managed rather well, and Mother M. was there to help her. Lady Talbert smiled, and the feeling of joy rose like a geyser in her throat. Trenton deserved a break in life, having been raised under the authoritative arm of his older brother. His grace had tried to break Trenton's will, but now, the most amazing development had been that Trenton had mellowed; the harshness, even the bitterness, had seemed to dissolve and slide from his countenance in one big swoop . . . after Rachel's arrival at Talbert Hall.

Upon excusing herself from the table, Lady Talbert asked a footman to order a carriage brought around, and then she went to the nursery, where she bathed Frank and dressed him in short breeches, a white blouse, and long white silk hose. "We'll save the rocking for tonight, Frankie," she told him, and he gave her a huge smile that turned into gurgling laughter. She hugged and kissed him before turning him over to Hannah. Quitting the room, she went below stairs, where she encountered Mother M.

The old woman was dressed in the clothes she was wearing when she came to Talbert Hall, black-and-white woolen dress, draped over this was her fur-trimmed pelisse, definitely not new. Perched on top of her head, covering most of her gray-streaked hair, was the black hat with a purple plume.

"I'm so happy you will be accompanying me," Lady Talbert told her. "I expect a lovely journey, and you will like the dowager countess. She's plain-spoken and has a smile at the ready at any given time. I'm really sorry about the loss of her father. He was a powerful duke, right in the old King's pocket."

"I thank you for letting me come along," Mother M. said. "I'm sure I will enjoy meeting the dowager countess, but 'tis you I wish to talk with. I thought this would be an excellent time."

Lady Talbert's clear, soft laughter interrupted Mother M.'s confession. "I thought you might be wanting to speak with me about Rachel and my brother."

"Indeed I do, but that can wait until we are settled in the carriage. Did his lordship not say it was a two-hour journey?"

"About that. I've only called on the dowager a small number of times, considering the distance. When she comes to Talbert Hall, she is invited to stay the night. And that would have been the case had she had not lost her father, thus preventing her from attending our pre-Christmas Ball."

Lady Talbert heard a horse snort and knew the carriage was coming. Stepping out into the cold, she pulled her fur-lined cloak around her slender body. Already her bonnet strings were tied beneath her small chin. She wore black leather gloves to keep her hands warm.

Mother M., watching out of the corner of her eye, thought her ladyship one of the most beautiful women she had ever seen, even comparable to Rachel. Lady Talbert's eyes were brown and expressive; her complexion like warm milk. But nothing about her was as appealing as her kind nature and her soft laugh. A feeling of love engulfed the old woman. It almost seemed that she belonged to this strange household.

A footman let the step of the crested carriage down and helped the ladies in to sit on plush blue velvet squabs. "Shall I ride the boot, your ladyship?" he asked, while moving the wrapped, warmed bricks in proximity to their feet.

"For heaven's sake, no," answered Lady Talbert. "Twould be too cold, and totally unnecessary. The coachman is used to the cold, and his coat is layered for warmth."

The footman bowed and closed the door before the carriage rolled away from the house and down the tree-lined road that led to the main road. The winter sun was warm against the carriage windows. Lifting a tiny gold watch, hanging from her shoulder on a gold chain, Lady Talbert raised her quizzing glass and looked at the time. "We should be there before eleven. I pray the countess is home, and I'm sure she will be, since it's against propriety to go out so soon after a death. Not even into the village."

"Most likely we will have to wait in line to see her," added Mother M., becoming quiet and thoughtful, and for a short while quietness settled over the inside of the elegant carriage.

Lady Talbert watched as the countryside passed in its winter splendor. Snow crowned the hill's peaks, and lay in their crevices and corries. At last she spoke, repeating what she had said earlier, "I'm so pleased you could come along, Mother M. I would have loved for Rachel to come also, but Trenton is so jealous of her time. He wants to be with her every waking minute. Have you noticed?" She laughed then. "He reminds me of a lovesick puppy."

"More like a wolfhound," said Mother M., smiling. "God's truth, that is why I wanted to come along today. When I saw Rachel's intent was to take care of Napoleon, and to stay near his lordship, I seized the opportunity to be alone with you. I have so many questions."

"I shall enlighten you if I can."

"You know I'm concerned about Rachel. She is so much in love with Lord Abshire. I wish you would tell the whole of it if you know. Why would a member of the nobility be so taken with a girl of the lower orders, who has never even gone to public school? She knows nothing of the world."

"And that is why you followed her to Talbert Hall, because you were afraid for her?"

Mother M. gave a positive nod of her head. "Rachel became my responsibility when she was but a babe, and I fear I failed in her upbringing. I never told her anything. I never warned her about how some men can be, all the grand promises they can make, knowing they don't mean to keep them." As if she had said too much, she stopped and drew herself up.

Lady Talbert looked steadily at the old woman across from her, feeling her concern and the outpouring of love she felt for Rachel. She reached to pat Mother M.'s bony hand. "I think you are worrying needlessly. I believe Trenton is genuinely in love with Rachel; I believe he is sincere in wanting to marry her as quickly as possible."

"But his lordship is quite the man of the *ton,* or he could be if he should so choose. He can have any girl he wants, pretty, ugly, rich, or poor. I've heard the servants talk. So why my Rachel?"

"That's true, but none has made his eyes light up like leaping flames, nor has one turned his wry grin into a wonderful smile the way Rachel has. I think on it as a miracle. Not just occasionally, but every time he sees her. I have watched, for I, too, care about this match. Trenton needs a love match, not one of convenience."

Deep frown lines formed on Mother M.'s brow. "You still have not explained *why* she makes his eyes light up, except to say she is innocent. Aren't all unmarried girls innocent, that is unless some disreputable man gains a hold on her? Why does he need a love match, when most men of the upper orders prefer to keep mistresses?" And then the good sister added, thoughtfully, as if talking to herself, "I could understand more clearly if Rachel were of the upper orders."

Sucking in a deep breath, Lady Talbert leaned back against the squab. "I can see you have considered all angles, and you have a right to know. When Rachel first came to Talbert Hall it was Trenton's full intent to have his way with her. Knowing his pattern, I observed very closely. I can tell you it was a delight to see her thwart his every move. Not knowing that one did not speak of bosoms in polite society, she castigated him fiercely, and more than once, for ogling her bosom. She refused to wear the low-cut gowns he purchased for her, even after he told her all nannies dressed like that.

"Still, I did not see a noticeable change in his lordship. It was when he was summoned home by our brother that upon his return, I noticed something was very different. He made clear his intent to marry Rachel.

"I spoke with him, and he told me he had been ordered to become leg-shackled to a lady of Quality and produce an heir. His grace had one picked out. Trenton would die before he would let our older brother tell him what to do. So he announced then and there he was going to marry Frank's nanny.

"I don't believe marriage had entered his head until then. But once the words were out of his mouth, he realized he was in love with Rachel, and had been since she appeared at Talbert Hall waving a fictitious resume in his face. He says one look into her violet blue eyes and he was lost forever to bachelorhood. He claims up until then he could not picture himself as a married man, but now he wants it more than anything. That's why I said he reminded me of a lovesick puppy."

Lady Talbert's answers satisfied Mother M. There was nothing to do but wait and see what the future held. "I appreciate your being candid with me," the old woman said, and then she was quiet.

The carriage tooled along at a healthy pace. It was Lady Talbert who broke the silence. "Why did Rachel come to Talbert Hall, Mother M.? And what is this business of her not wanting to marry Trenton until her life is in order? I'm concerned about Trenton, just as you are about Rachel. So 'tis only fair that you tell me."

The carriage hit a hole in the road, jarring Mother M. sideways. She grabbed the holding strap and held it tightly until things settled. Lady Talbert was staring at her expectantly, but she, Mother M., did not know what to do. How could she betray Rachel's confidence? She thought of Lady Talbert's many kindnesses to her, and to Rachel, who was still very young. Mayhap Rachel did not know what was best for her. Then, as was her custom, the good sister silently asked for God's guidance, and immediately the feeling came over her that Lady Talbert would not hinder Rachel's cause, but would be an ally.

"Only if you promise you will not tell Lord Abshire," Mother M. finally said, then added, "He and Rachel must needs work out their problems. When she is ready to confide in him, she will."

"I promise," said Lady Talbert. "You know that I've grown fond of your Rachel, and anything I can do to help, I will do it. As long as Trenton is not hurt by what I do."

"That's understandable," Mother M. said, and she began: "Rachel was reared in Saint Cecilia's Home for Abandoned Children."

A soft laugh came from Lady Talbert, filling the carriage. "That much I have already discerned, that she had come from some kind of home, and that she was in your care. But the rest, the more I think about it, the deeper the mystery becomes. I think it starts with *why* Rachel came to Talbert Hall. And where did Napoleon come from? Was he at the Home?"

"Oh, no. He was a thief in Covent Gardens. When Rachel left the Home, she went into London. Napoleon stole her box of clothes, and she ran him down."

Mother M. told Lady Talbert why Rachel was named Rachel Storm, the whole of it, all except the part about Rachel thinking Lord Talbert was her dear papa. "Rachel is desperate to know who fathered her. She says she cannot marry until she knows her real name. I've advised her to give it up, but she is adamant . . . she thinks she knows who her father is."

It was a long while before Lady Talbert asked the question Mother M. knew was coming. She braced herself accordingly, and Lady Talbert's gaze did not waver when she said, "Rachel has reason to believe that my husband is her father, does she not? Is that why she came to Talbert Hall, on the pretense of being a trained nanny?"

Nineteen

As many of the manor houses of England sat atop steep inclines, hillocks, or mountains, striking a grand view and sparkling like jeweled crowns, it seemed oddly strange to Lady Talbert that Grammacy Chase sat grandly in flat land surrounded by undulating hills that spanned the horizon. This day, fingers of pink clouds brushed the blue winter sky hovering over the manor, and from the chimney pots, gray smoke swirled upward to flirt with scudding clouds.

As the carriage descended into the flat land, Lady Talbert thought about the few times she had visited the dowager. She had liked her immensely, even though there was something mysterious about her, as if she was fighting some inward unhappiness. But she was always smiling, always, and her lovely unlined face looked the work of a famous sculptor who refused to quit until his work was perfect. She could still pass as a very young woman; only her silver hair showed she had gained hard years. Losing Lord Longworth when she was so young most likely contributed to that.

And she was always very proper. Of course, Lady Talbert mused, the dowager had been brought up by one of the mightiest dukes of the kingdom, and no doubt he had insisted she adhere to every stricture of the *ton.*

The immediacy of their arrival stopped Lady Talbert's ruminations. She looked for black crepe on the huge entry doors.

There was none.

In the absence of a footman riding the boot, the coachman

quickly climbed from the box and rushed to let down the step, only to be usurped by a highly liveried footman who had rushed out of the manor house, practically, in his haste, falling down the front steps. Standing in the doorway was a straight and tall butler, just as finely liveried.

"My goodness, what a welcome," said Nora.

"Isn't it so," Lady Talbert answered. Then she thanked the footman and asked, "Is her ladyship receiving? We don't mean to intrude upon her grief."

The footman looked askance. "What grief? Her ladyship is anticipating Christmas as I've never seen her. Wait 'till you smell the house. Everything's been waxed and polished at least ten times, and mistletoe hangs all over the place." He gave a little laugh. "As if she's 'specting a lot of kissing to be going on."

Lady Talbert did not say more to the footman, though she wanted to. Propriety was such a bore. He handed her over to the butler, giving a deep bow.

"Welcome to Grammacy Chase, Lady Talbert," the butler said, bowing as deeply as the footman.

"How did you know who we were?" asked Mother M., and the butler smiled. "The Talbert crest shows splendidly, even as far away as the top of the hill."

Lady Talbert gave her sunny laugh. Wafting up to assault her nostrils was the smell of beeswax and lemon oil. They were in a handsome foyer, with walls covered in coral Chinese silk imprinted with tiny bluebirds, with spread wings. The same beautiful fabric covered the walls of the large central room they soon entered. Window coverings, the color of the bluebirds hung from the high ceiling to puddle on the dark floor.

In the center of the room, a round marble-topped table held a huge epergne of tall and overflowing flowers of every color in the rainbow. Gold candelabra, with outstretched arms, held burning candles.

"It appears she's ready for a party," said Lady Talbert in a low voice. Lady Talbert answered with a raised brow. She sucked in deeply the smell of the crackling fire and felt its warmth.

"The Countess Longworth will be most happy to see you," the butler said. "Yesterday and the day before there were many callers, paying their condolences, but today, you are the first." He took their coats and headwear. "I will announce to Countess Longworth you are here."

Lady Talbert thanked him. She then looked at Mother M., who had a half smile on her face, as if to dispute the earlier words of the dowager countess's mourning. "I know," Lady Talbert whispered, "she's probably glad the old gaffer is dead."

The old woman laughed.

Looking up, Lady Talbert saw descending the curving stairs the dowager countess. She wore a dazzling gown of bright pink, bustled, and the skirt longer behind, sweeping away her footsteps. Her silver hair was parted in the middle and tied back at the nape with a pink ribbon. She was smiling.

An act, to hide her grief, thought Lady Talbert.

"I'm so happy to see you, Lady Talbert. I knew you would come when you heard of his grace's death." She came and took Lady Talbert's outstretched hand.

Mother M. curtsied, not too gracefully, but acceptable, Lady Talbert thought, hiding a smile. She introduced Mother M. as Margaret Teasch, and then said, "Countess Marcella, I was so sorry to hear of your father's death. Knowing of your propensity to the dreadful rules on mourning, I knew you would not attend the Talbert Costume Party. I'm sorry about that, too. I came today to pay my respects. I was fortunate that Miss Teasch could accompany me."

"I have every intention of attending your party." The dowager countess smiled and directed them to chairs and sophas grouped around the huge marble fireplace. She sat on a small sopha of pale blue silk.

A perfect setting for her exquisite pink gown, mused Lady Talbert, as she waited for an explanation of the dowager's intent of attending a party so soon after a death she should be mourning.

"I shall order tea, and then we will talk," the dowager countess said. "I'm afraid I have some explaining to do."

Rising gracefully from the sopha, she went to pull the bell rope, and when a maid appeared quickly and almost noiselessly, she asked that tea and scones be brought.

" 'Tis lovely weather for Christmastime," she said in way of conversation when the maid had left.

Lady Talbert agreed, and the conversation about the weather and other such nonimportant things continued until the tea was served. The dowager countess did this grandly, pouring a cup for Lady Talbert, and then one for Margaret Teasch.

Lady Talbert's curiosity was whetted tremendously. Why was the house draped in mistletoe instead of mourning black? Christmas boxes and Christmas angels were on a table covered with a red-and-green cloth.

Lady Talbert looked at Mother M., whose countenance appeared as if she was just about to ask the dowager countess if her father really had died, or if they had acted on a rumor by coming here. The ambiance of the room was strange indeed.

"I'm not in mourning," Countess Longworth said as she poured her own cup of tea. "I had not seen his grace, nor did I care to, for the past ten years. He did a terrible injustice to me, and to those whom I loved, and still love, more than life, and I'm not hypocritical enough to mourn for him. A pox on the *ton*'s expectations. In truth, I plan a wonderful Christmas. Grammacy Hall will be filled with a little of the merry for the first time in a very long time."

Although she tried not to show her surprise, Lady Talbert's mouth fell open, and she knew she was staring incredulously at the countess. It was Mother M. who sputtered, "You're not mourning your father?"

"I mourn for his life. I shall always do that. He was a very unhappy man; one always is when one lives only for oneself.

And he cared only for himself. My happiness meant nothing to him."

"I don't take your meaning," said Lady Talbert, and then she was sorry she had said such a thing. It was the countess's business if she wished not to mourn, and it was not her, Lady Talbert's, place to be judgmental. A strange thought struck her—if Lord Talbert should die, she might grieve outwardly, but not inwardly. He, too, lived only for his own pleasure.

The dowager countess sipped her tea and looked over the rim of the cup at her guests. How could she tell a part of her story without telling the whole of it? After only a moment of contemplation, she decided that the truth would come out when Albert Ramey arrived at Grammacy Chase. Then the world would know he was her legal husband, and the *ton,* and everyone else would have something to gossip about. The old duke had had all records of her marriage destroyed, but no one could destroy the memory of her standing beside her beloved and promising to love, cherish, and obey him until death parted them . . . So why not let Lady Talbert be the first to know? And her companion, this Margaret Teasch.

Feeling such a rush of happiness that her breath seemed to have lodged in her throat, and feeling warmth and gaiety flowing over her, the dowager countess said, "I'm expecting my husband home for Christmas." Tears filled her eyes, then spilled over to make opaque silver trails on her cheeks.

Lady Talbert was glad of Mother M.'s silence, rendered speechless no doubt, Lady Talbert thought, and in her own mewling voice, she managed to say, "Did not Lord Longworth die several years ago?"

The dowager countess gave a joyful little laugh and said, "Pray, do not think I'm ready for Bedlam. 'Tis just that I don't know how to explain . . . there's so much." She placed her cup on the white-clothed tea table and leaned back into the blue sopha.

"I apologize if I appear taken aback, your ladyship," said

Lady Talbert, "but 'tis inconceivable to me that your late husband can come back from the dead."

"Lord Longworth was never my husband."

"Never your husband!" said Mother M., her eyes wide and ready to pop out of her head. Looking apologetically at Lady Talbert, she placed her hand over her mouth. "I'm sorry. I have no right to speak up." She turned to the dowager. "I beg your forgiveness, but Lady Talbert has told me about your being left alone, and so young."

" 'Tis puzzling, I know." After a long pause, she said in a low voice, "I had seen only eighteen summers when I was left alone, really alone, and I think I would like to tell you the whole of it. It was my father, his grace, the mighty Duke of Marcel, who rendered the unforgivable deed. I was in love with a young man who was untitled. His grace forbade my seeing him; in truth, he promised me to Lord Longworth over my stringent protests, and after I'd told him of my love for this untitled man. Even Lord Longworth knew that I was in love with someone else.

"His name is Albert Ramey. We ran away and married, not at Gretna Green, but at his cousin's seat in Lincolnshire, and we spent three gloriously wonderful days together before the old duke and his retinue of Bow Street Runners found us and snatched me away. He had my beloved Ramey sent to prison in Australia on some trumped-up charge, and he kept me prisoner, with daily lashes, until I consented to marry Lord Longworth. But the marriage was never consummated. How could I? With me so much in love with someone else. And, too, the marriage to Longworth was not legal. I was already married."

She stopped then, for she was openly crying, wiping her tears with a lace-trimmed handkerchief she had taken from her bosom. Lady Talbert was crying, too, as was Mother M.

"We're a sorry sight," Lady Talbert at last said, laughing without mirth. "Marcella, I never dreamed anything like this."

"No one did. I kept smiling, and I never gave up hope that

I would someday be reunited with my Ramey. And now it is going to happen."

"How's that?" blurted out Mother M.

"After the old duke's death, I learned that after two years Ramey somehow managed to leave Australia. He went to America and waited for the old duke to die. Only his cousin and the old duke's valet knew he was alive. When his grace became terminally ill, Bexford, the valet, informed him of the imminent death. That was long enough ago for the letter to reach Ramey, and for him to sail across the Atlantic. I know he will come. I pray in time for Christmas. But whatever time he arrives, it will be a glorious celebration. We will kill the fatted calf to welcome him home."

Mother M.'s skeptical nature about men came to the fore. "If he doesn't come, pray don't despair."

"I know he will come," the dowager countess said obdurately. "Why would you say that?"

Mother M.'s face flushed red. "I beg your forgiveness . . . I didn't mean . . . it's just that it would be so terrible should you be disappointed. You haven't heard from him in all these years."

The dowager countess settled back on the sopha. "I won't be disappointed. My Ramey will come."

There was something ethereal, spiritual, about the countess, Lady Talbert thought. As if a Higher Power had visited and told her what would happen, and nothing would deter that belief.

Lady Talbert stood. "I'm afraid we have overstayed the appropriate calling time, your ladyship, but I'm so glad we came. I'm happy you are not in grief. I admire your tenacity, your belief in the future, and I do so hope that your dream comes true."

The dowager countess rose from the sopha and the two women embraced each other. Lady Talbert felt a kindred bonding with this woman who had lost her life but, out of knowing she was loved totally, and out of loving totally herself, had found it.

I would like to know that kind of love, Lady Talbert thought, feeling tears mist her eyes.

"I will pray for your happiness," promised Mother M., "and I'll ask for God's comfort if it doesn't happen."

Countess Longworth thanked her, and rang for the butler to bring their wraps.

The callers left, with the dowager countess assuring them she would be at the grand party at Talbert Hall. "May I bring my Ramey if he arrives in time?" she asked, and Lady Talbert answered, "Of course you may bring him."

Dowager Countess Marcella Longworth sat for a long time after her callers left, puzzled at what she had done. After all these years she had finally told about her marriage to Albert Ramey. *When he comes home, I want him to come home as my husband. I care not that he isn't titled. I will renounce my title as countess . . . and together we will find our daughter . . . using the old duke's vast wealth. I'm glad I did not get carried away and tell Lady Talbert that Ramey and I have a daughter. I'll save that wonderful news for him.* She recalled that Bexford had said he had not told anyone there was a baby, not even Lord Malvey, Ramey's cousin.

She left the sopha and went to look out the window, as she had done with regularity since returning from burying the old duke, looking for Ramey. And she had all the servants watching for a stranger's arrival. A footman had come running to her when the Talbert crested carriage was atop the hill. She was glad they had come. Lady Talbert was a lovely woman.

The dowager countess only had one thing of Ramey's, a linen handkerchief, now yellow with age. She had snatched it from the floor, where it had dropped when they were dragging him away. She had hid it on her person, lest the old duke take it away. Always when she could no longer bear the pain, or when doubt began to seep into her belief that he was the one true love of her life, and that he felt the same way about her, and that someday they would be reunited, she retrieved the handkerchief and held it to her breast, smelled it, kissed it, spoke to it as if it were her Ramey. She would do that now. Like a girl of eighteen summers, in love for the first time.

As she ascended the stairs, the hem of her bright pink gown trailing behind her, she reminded herself that she had seen thirty-six summers, and rationality shrieked at her. How did she know that Ramey would come? According to Bexford, he was waiting until his grace, the Duke of Marcel, died to return to England. But did that mean he was coming to her? Mayhap he had a wife; it had been such a long time. No, she would not believe that.

Giving a little laugh, she stopped still for a moment, letting the joy of anticipation wash over her. Ramey was not coming home to England, he was coming home to her. She would not let Margaret Teasch's skepticism, which was more in the tone of her voice than in the questions she asked, put her into the desponds.

In the receiving room of her suite of rooms, done in pale peach and soft green, she took from a secret drawer of her chiffonnier the yellowed handkerchief and held it to her flushed cheek. Slowly, once again the curtain opened onto the past.

At first she heard his laughter, that wonderful laugh, so full of life, and then she looked into his blue eyes that burned with fire and passion. She remembered when and where they had met, at her come-out ball; he had told her they would marry, and he had blown her a kiss, and she had caught it, both laughing, both believing.

While they were dancing, at every chance, he had held her to him. She could smell him, the smell of a wild thing, sensual, perhaps a tiger, or a lion, and the smell had entered her, gone into her bloodstream, and when he had said they would marry, she had believed him, for she suddenly knew that anything and everything was possible. Reality was far away, in the sky, in the wind, far away from where she was dancing with her love.

And then the old duke had come and ordered him to leave.

Even then Ramey had smiled, and after that he had blown her the kiss, and the next day they had met in the park, where they touched and talked. The following day, they had kissed, and he held her, until dark came and the night sounds began. "I can't leave you," he said, and she believed him, for inside of her, an inferno of longing and wanting kept her awake long after the night was old and dawn was breaking. There was no way she could have sublimated those feelings. She loved him with all her young heart, with all her soul.

"We'll go to Lincolnshire, to my cousin's place, and be married," he said after their fifth meeting. "He can't take you away when you are my wife."

"He'll find us before the banns can be read," she said.

"Lord Malvey will get a special license. We'll be married immediately."

They left the old duke's town house in disguise, she dressed as a maid in black bombazine, he wearing a tricorn and a coat of many layers, like those of a coachmen, and they traveled by night in a rented chaise . . .

Thinking back on it now, the dowager countess smiled. What a wonderfully romantic thing they did. Fear of the old duke could not dampen their excitement as they sped through the night, the horses to their bits. When an owl hooted in the distance, they said it was calling to its mate, and the sound of hoofbeats reverberated through the still night, and the moon smiled down on them, as if giving its blessing for this wild thing they were doing.

"The gown is too big," she had said of Ramey's dead mother's white wedding gown that was trimmed with the most elegant lace. Quickly, a seamstress stitched the gown to fit, and Ramey said she was the most beautiful bride in all of England.

And then the vicar had asked, "Will you take this man to be your lawful wedded husband, to have, and to hold . . ."

"I will," she said, loud and clear, while whispering under her breath, *forever and ever . . . and a day after that, even in eternity I will belong to him.*

And when they were alone, in the gatekeeper's cottage a good mile from the big house, and deep in the woods, she gave herself to him completely, letting him take possession of her, in all her dimensions, mind, body, soul. "Oh, Ramey," she said when she felt as if she would melt and be one with him, "my husband, my beloved husband."

"I love you," he had said over and over, and when he began the love dance again, they were silent, each knowing the completeness of belonging to the other, spiraling upward, and upward, until she was full of him and he of her. And when he climaxed, he called out her name, the sound filling the room. And when her own climax came, she was wrought with surprise and intense joy. She had not been told that a woman took pleasure from lovemaking the same as a man, and she rode the same wind, made the same unintelligible sounds, and arched her body to meet his rhythmic thrusts. For three days and three nights.

When their strength waned and their knees became wobbly when they stood, they laughed and went for strolls through the woods, ate by candlelight, and drank champagne in the gatekeeper's small parlor, with moonlight cutting across their bodies, tethered together with an unbreakable cord.

"Nothing, no one can take you from me," Ramey said, and then he whispered in his low, resonant voice, "Our love transcends forever, my dear, dear Marcella. It was meant to be, even before we met. God made you from my rib."

Those were the words the dowager countess remembered so vividly as she now went to stand by the window and look out, and a great rush of joy washed over her in the remembering.

"Our love transcends forever," she whispered to the silent room, and she willed her mind to stop there, not to remember the awfulness of the day the old duke came for her. But come back it did, assaulting her mind like waves thrashing a shore.

The fourth day of her honeymoon, quite early in the day, they were dressed for a leisurely walk through the woods, feeling relieved that the old duke had not come for his daughter . . . "Mayhap it's because he knows I would refuse to leave you," she said, and, believing this, they made plans for their future.

They would live with Lord Malvey and Ramey would continue managing the estate. His lordship, nearing his dotage, traveled on the continent and spent much of his time in the south of France.

"We'll have six children," Ramey had said, laughing and nuzzling her neck, and she, recognizing the prelude to lovemaking, said, "Not again," and he said, "Yes. Unless you object." Of course she hadn't objected, and when they were through, he said for certain they had started the first of the six babies they planned to have. "Soon you will be heavy with child and too big to sit on my lap," he teased.

They heard the cold, deadening voice first, the voice of the old duke. "Marcella, open this door or it will be broken in. How dare you disgrace me so. And Albert Ramey, you will rue the day you disobeyed the Duke of Marcel." Pounding on the door continued. At first she was too frightened to move, and then, seeing Ramey dressing with alacrity, she followed his lead, barely getting her walking dress over her head when the door came crashing down and the old duke stood there, very much like a gargantuan pirate ready to take the spoils of a ship. She ran to him. "I love him, Papa. I will not leave him. He's my husband."

"There was no marriage," countered the old duke. His arm reached out to cast her aside in a hurtful way, but Ramey's strong hand stayed him. "Don't touch my wife."

"Your wife!" the old duke spewed bitterly, and then he shouted, "Come in boys and do your duty."

The Bow Street Runners rushed the gatekeeper's cottage and dragged Ramey away. He fought with all his considerable strength, but was no match for four strong men. He was openly crying as he screamed to the great outdoors, "Marcella is my wife. I love her. You can't take her from me. You can't."

And then he damned the old duke to hell.

She stood lifeless, frozen in place, holding his handkerchief that had dropped on the floor of the gatekeeper's cottage. She felt her life had ended, and so it had until she learned that she was enceinte and would have his child. She would always have a part of him.

And then the child had been taken away.

Still holding the handkerchief in her hand, the dowager countess turned from the window. Soon the Christian world would be celebrating Christ's birthday. A joyous, wondrous time that filled the world with hope. From far off, she heard the wail of a newborn baby, a girl, she had just recently learned. Each Christmas she had prayed that by another year, she would have found her child. Still, she hadn't, and still she hoped. She would never believe the baby had died at birth.

Feeling as if she had been on a long journey and was fatigued from it, she gained a chair in front of the fire and stretched out her feet to its warmth. A knock on the door cut into the silence.

"Enter," she said, not looking around. Behind her, the door creaked opened, and Nora's voice was saying, "Your ladyship, you have a visitor. A gentleman."

Twenty

Lady Talbert could not forget what the dowager countess had told them. Love had hugged every word she said about her Ramey. In truth, Lady Talbert mused, she envied the woman who had suffered so much, who loved so much, and suddenly she was cognizant of what a deep vacuum her own life had become. Was there not more to life than producing an heir and running a huge household? She certainly could not say she had a marriage.

For the first time ever, her ladyship thought of ending her marriage to Lord Talbert. "I will speak to Trenton."

"About what?" Mother M. said.

Lady Talbert gave a small laugh. She had not realized she was speaking aloud. "About ending my marriage to Lord Talbert. I don't think his lordship will mind. He has another life he prefers."

"Don't believe it, my dear. A man wants to have his cake and eat it, too. You are the respectable side of his lordship. What are you going to say? By the by, I've decided to petition Parliament for a divorce.

"Yes, I know. As I said, I shall speak to Trenton first. He will advise me."

What Lady Talbert did not tell Mother M., nor would she, was that Lord Abshire had confided in her about the life Lord Talbert lived in London, his other life. She had been appalled, and had, after that time, refused Lord Talbert his marital rights, and she felt justified in doing so.

Mother M. asked in a low voice, "What if Lord Talbert truly is Rachel's father?"

"I pray he is not. The girl deserves better than that. I'm sorry I put that burden on little Frankie. But I was so innocent when the marriage took place, and I thought Benford, because he was the first son and had inherited the family title, had the right to arrange my marriage. Dowager Countess Longworth taught me a great lesson today. A woman's wonts have a place in this world."

"I pray that her Ramey returns to her. I couldn't help it; I just had to warn her that dreams don't always come true. I had no right to speak up like that."

"Albert Ramey will prove your doubts unfounded, I am sure," said Lady Talbert.

The subject was not discussed further. Mother M. told her ladyship about the Home, where Rachel had grown up. They stopped at a posting inn for a leisurely repast, and then her ladyship found herself all at once anxious to return to Talbert Hall. A sudden chill danced up and down her spine. Something untoward was happening.

A soft rain began to fall, turning quickly to snow, dancing in the air and blanketing the hillocks. Lady Talbert stared through the window, deep in thought, while Mother M. snored gently from her corner of the carriage that was moving with great speed.

Lady Talbert could not get the dowager countess out of her mind, the love she spoke of, the three wondrous days she had spent with her Ramey. Love was the core, the center of life. Her life was without either. She felt heat in her face and chest and down low in the pit of her stomach. She had not yet seen twenty-one summers; she was too young to live without love. She thought of her brother Trenton, the love that shone from his eyes when he looked at Rachel, a girl who did not know who she was or where she came from. A severe yearning came over her she could not squelch. She wanted to be loved as

Trenton loved Rachel, as the dowager countess loved her Ramey.

As the carriage turned off the main road onto the lane that wound its way up the hill toward Talbert Hall, Lady Talbert leaned forward and stared. Ahead was a carriage, and as the road curved, she could see through the snow, which had abated somewhat, that it bore the Talbert crest and was pulled by six horses with gold trappings. A tiger rode the tongue, and a powdered footman, dressed in gorgeous livery, rode the boot.

Inside the elegant carriage, the profile of Lord Fox Talbert was visible. He was wearing his black, high-crowned beaver, and sitting tall and straight. Across from him, on the opposite squab, was a man whom she presumed was his valet.

Lord Talbert was coming for the Christmas party, to be seen by, and to mingle with, his constituents.

This was not what she wanted, for his lordship to appear before she had had time to talk with Trenton. And then she quickly decided she was no longer a tender young girl, but a woman, capable of making her own decisions. She would handle this on her own, and quickly.

When the carriage halted in front of Talbert Hall, Lord Talbert and his valet had already alighted from his lordship's ostentatious carriage and disappeared into the house. Lady Talbert was glad. She would go directly to her quarters and wait for him to come knocking on her door. When he was at Talbert Hall, he was the perfect *ton* gentleman. He would even make a call at the nursery to see his son.

A footman came to let down the step and the butler greeted Lady Talbert and Mother M. with a bow. "His lordship has arrived home," he said.

"Yes, I know," Lady Talbert replied. "I saw his carriage in front of us as we came up the lane."

"Shall I advise him that you are now home? He asked of your whereabouts."

"No, thank you," Lady Talbert said quickly. Turning away, she made her way across the great hall and up the winding stairs. So much was happening at once, she thought. Preparations for the upcoming party were in full swing, wonderful smells emanating from the kitchen, polishing, dusting, the hanging of holly and mistletoe. But that was far removed from his lordship's sudden appearance, and from what she was feeling. As she walked down the hall to her rooms, the air around her shivered, and the chill came over her again.

Inside her rooms, she quickly went to look in the tall looking glass, to see if her inward change showed. She saw determination in the reflection. After removing her hat and cloak, she summoned a maid and asked that a bath be prepared. "And lay out my latest gown from London, the red silk with a train."

The maid, grinning, bobbed. "I understand, m'lady. Lord Talbert is home, and you want to look your best."

Lady Talbert did not answer. To herself, she mused, "I want him to see what he is losing."

When the maid had gone, her ladyship went to the sideboard and poured a glass of brandy and sat in front of the fire and sipped until her bath was ready. Not that she needed spirits to bolster her resolve, she told herself. That was firmly in place. She was celebrating her new life. No longer would she acquiesce to being the prim and proper *ton* lady. She would demand and get the right to live a life with meaning.

In the nursery, Rachel put little Frankie down for his nap and then returned to her own room to find that Mother M. had returned from calling on the dowager countess of Grammacy Chase.

"Did you enjoy your journey?" she asked.

"Yes, very much. The dowager countess is a lovely person, and very spunky. Not at all what I expected. Said she isn't mourning her father, and she plans to come to the Christmas party at Talbert Hall."

"I can't imagine not mourning one's father, if one is fortunate enough to have one." There was a wistfulness in Rachel voice.

Mother M. looked at her pityingly, and said, "In her case, she would have been better off not to have had a father. When she was your age she fell in love with an untitled man and married him. The old duke, her father, tore them apart, had him sent to prison in Australia, and then made her his prisoner, with daily lashes, until she agreed to marry Lord Longworth."

"How terrible," Rachel said.

"Yes, 'tis that, and she, poor dear, believes that Albert Ramey, that's the untitled man she married, is coming home to her at just any time. I warned her not to get her hopes up too high. Mayhap I shouldn't have done that, but after what happened to me, 'tis difficult for me to trust."

Rachel was sitting on the side of the high bed, her feet dangling over its side. "All men aren't bad, Mother M. Mayhap her husband will return as she hopes."

"Oh, I do hope so. Now, I have some news for you. Lord Talbert is at Talbert Hall."

Rachel jumped to her feet, looking to Mother M. as if she might faint, or cry, or both. "How do you know? Did you see him? What does he look like? Did you see a resemblance?"

There was such hope in Rachel's voice that Mother M. wanted to cry. She was glad she had stayed on at Talbert Hall, just for this moment. "I didn't see him. His carriage arrived at Talbert Hall only moments before Lady Talbert and I arrived."

"I want to see him. I've waited so long, and now he's here."

"You must needs bide your time, dear. I suppose he's with his wife now, and surely he will visit his son in the nursery." She waited a long moment before asking, "Will you marry his lordship, even if Lord Talbert turns out *not* to be who you think he is?"

"Oh, but I know he is. In truth, I'm so sure of it that Lord Abshire and I this day set the date for our wedding. 'Tis Christmas day. Isn't that just the most wonderful time to be marrying? We talked for a long while after we returned from Blanchland. And, oh, Mother M., we bought Napoleon wonderful clothes to wear to school. Of course, he will be in uniform there, but he will certainly arrive and leave in fashion. You should have seen him. He almost popped with pride. I can't believe how wonderful everything is working out."

Mother M. rose from the rocking chair and went to hug Rachel. It was better late than never, to show affection, she told herself, and the girl needed it now. Her heart was going to be broken. Even if Lord Talbert should be the dear papa she had been searching for, he was a scoundrel. Such things the servants said about him!

"I wonder if Lady Talbert knows the kind of man her husband is?" the old woman said. She did not think it prudent that she tell Rachel of Lady Talbert's talk of divorce.

"What do you mean? He can't be all bad, if he sent money to the Home for me. It seems to me you should be grateful."

Mother M. returned to her chair and began rocking. Her heart felt as if it would break inside her breast. "Well, I just don't want you hurt. I feel that I should warn you."

Rachel spoke with alacrity, and firmly. "I don't want to know. Any kind of papa is better than no papa at all. If he will love me, I will love him."

They grew silent after that, and the rocking of Mother M.'s chair gained in rapidity. Rachel looked at her, sensing her concern. And it seemed so uncalled for. Had she, Rachel, not been waiting for this moment? Was this not why she had come to Talbert Hall? Her black hair was in braids, wound around her head like a crown. She began taking it down, combing it with her fingers.

"What are you doing?" asked Mother M.

"I'm going to wash, and then I'm going to put on the prettiest gown I have. I want his lordship to be proud to claim me for his daughter."

Mother M. turned her face away, so that Rachel could not see her crying.

* * *

Lord Fox Talbert sat in front of the blazing fire, smoking a long cheroot, his booted feet stretched out in front of him. The gray light through the window fell in stripes across his long, angular length. The feeling of great importance washed over him. He blew the smoke upward, smiled, then spoke laconically to his valet. "George 'tis not all bad being at Talbert Hall. Here, I am the king, the tyrant, whatever I want to be. And no young mendicant is hanging on the doorstop asking to see me."

"What happened to the young girl?"' the valet asked.

"She said she was with child. I had my man of business see to it. I think she was placed in a home . . . somewhere. The child will be placed with a family. She refused to let a doctor take care of her unfortunate condition."

"Does this not bother you, to have a child you will never see?"

"Why should it? That's the girl's problem. She will be well-compensated. As I told you, there is no shortage to Talbert blunt."

When George did not answer, but stood by the window and looked out, Lord Talbert asked, "You do not approve of me, do you, George?"

"How could a man not want to see his child?"

Lord Talbert did not respond to the question. He was more interested in his valet's reason for working for a man of whom he did not approve. "Why do you work for me?"

"Because I need the job, your lordship. I have a mother to support, and a sister. They need my help."

Lord Talbert laughed, loudly. "You're too sentimental for your own good, George. You'll never get anywhere in life."

The valet was quiet. Should he anger the old earl, he would be out of a job, without references.

Lord Talbert took a big draw on his cheroot, then he looked around the huge room that held large, masculine chairs and sophas, the kind in which a man could relax. His quarters were not as elegant as those in his town house in Grosvenor Square. Here, one could feel a woman's touch, Lady Talbert's.

This started him to thinking about his wife, something he seldom did. But lately she had come to mind a little more than usual, and he remembered when they had married. She had cared enough for him to take an interest in his rooms. Special meals had been prepared for him. A warm feeling came over him, starting in his loins, and his grin widened. Since he had to make this appearance at Talbert Hall, he would make it worthwhile by impregnating his wife. Mayhap it would behoove him to have two heirs, in case something happened to the first one. Turning to his valet, he said, "Would you have a servant summon Lady Talbert, and then please leave us alone."

Twenty-one

Lord Abshire watched the gently falling snow and swore under his breath. The Christmas costume party was only two days away, and he had so hoped it would be a great gathering to hear about his coming marriage to Rachel. And he would tell them she was Frank's nanny, not a Russian countess as first planned. Their life would be built on truth. A smile curved his lips. He could almost hear the gasp that would go up from the bejeweled women, mothers and daughters alike, for he was not unaware of their hopes of snaring him into their matrimonial web. "The son of a duke marrying his nephew's nanny," they would say. And no doubt one or two of the *ton* gentlemen would be crude enough to ask why he would marry a woman he most likely could have as his mistress.

The smile turned into a chuckle. His answer would be that one would have to know Rachel to realize what a ridiculous assumption that was. He had loved her from their first meeting, but his recalcitrant heart had fought against such foolhardy emotion. Men of the *ton* did not fall in love with the woman they wed to bear their children.

Only today Rachel had told him they would marry on Christmas day, and it was still strange to him. In truth, incredulous. Why had she abandoned her resolve to get her life in order before committing herself to marriage?

Because she's in love with you, slowtop, a little voice said, and this brought even greater joy to him. To love her was wonderful, but to have her love him back was more than his heart could comprehend. Before Rachel, he had been crippled by callowness, and he had actually thought his rough and rowdy life was fulfilling.

Tomorrow he would petition for the banns to be read.

A niggling thought marred this perfect happiness. His lordship tried to deny that it mattered, but it made him uneasy. What had Rachel meant about getting her life in order? Why had she refused to tell him when he had pressed for an answer?

"You will know soon enough," she had said, smiling her winning smile and planting a soft kiss on his cheek. He liked that, her kissing him. Just as no one had told her that one did not speak of bosoms in proper society, she had not been told that a proper *ton* lady did not allow anything more than a chaste kiss before marriage. He was glad no one had enlightened her, for their kisses had been anything but chaste.

No longer watching the snow, or the day's dying sigh into twilight, he turned back into the room. He was restless, and he wondered what was going on in the rest of the household. Rachel had said she would spend time with little Frank and wait for Mother M.'s return from calling on the Dowager Countess Longworth. Hopefully she would find time to rest before supper, he mused. The day had been so filled with excitement, purchasing clothes for Napoleon, and then their long talk about when they would marry. She had appeared tired when they parted.

He decided to venture out and seek companionship from his sister. She should be told of his plan to announce his and Rachel's engagement at the upcoming party.

But out in the long hall a palatable charged atmosphere took hold of his lordship, as if something or someone were pushing the walls back, and at any moment an explosion would occur and Talbert Hall, as he had known it, would be no more. He felt the hair on the back of his neck tighten and prickle, the reason becoming clear when he neared his sister's rooms. Loud voices emanated from behind the slightly ajar door. Lord and Lady Talbert were arguing. He had not known Lord Talbert had arrived at Talbert Hall. As he turned to leave, his sister's words stopped him in his tracks.

"I plan to have the family solicitor petition Parliament for a divorce." Her voice was as calm as if she were announcing she would be going into the village to shop.

Lord Abshire was not fooled by the calmness. He could visualize her small chin raised, and he could visualize Lord Talbert's dark eyes flashing at her, his prow of a chin jutting forward as his words spewed loudly out into the room, "You are going to divorce me? Is that why you refused to answer my summons, and I had to come to you, like some sniveling boy?"

Silence from Lady Talbert.

Lord Talbert's raucous laughter spilled out into the hallway where Lord Abshire was standing. Lord Abshire's first thought was that he should not be intruding on a family argument, but then he reconsidered. He could not leave Tessie to the mercy of this man of the world, an ugly world at that. He wondered why and when she had concluded that a divorce was in order. Did she not know a divorced woman was cut by society?

"I have every intention of placing in your belly another son," Lord Talbert was saying. "What if something should happen to my heir? 'Tis foolish to have only one to inherit such an estate as I own. I need two, mayhap three sons for insurance. So come now, your ladyship, and do your duty. I promise a pleasurable experience. You're fetching in that flaming gown. Red is an excellent color for you." He gave out a playful laugh.

With the toe of his boot, Lord Abshire pushed the door open and stood obscurely where he could view the room. What he saw jolted him to the point of alarm.

Tessie was holding a long-barreled pistol and saying, "Don't come near me, you scoundrel. Do you think I'm blind to your secret life? The sad little waifs you pick off the street and place in service of lowlife men such as you? The babies you father and cast aside?"

Lord Abshire stood transfixed. There was not a quiver in

Tessie's voice, nor were her hands shaking as she held the pistol firmly, stretched out in front of her, her eyes locked with those of her husband's.

Lord Talbert, now scowling furiously, took one step, only one, and the gun exploded, and sparks followed the deadly boom, and the smell of burned powder filled the room. A huge hole appeared in the scrolled ceiling.

"You chit . . . you'll never get away with this," said Lord Talbert. "I'll take my son . . ." His voice was strangled with uncontrollable anger.

Lady Talbert laughed hollowly. "You wouldn't know your son should you see him on the street, nor he you. Little Frankie stays with me. Unless you want your peers to know about your double life. Now leave, and don't darken my door again. I'm perfectly capable of taking another shot at you, and next time I won't miss."

Lord Abshire stepped aside, lest he be knocked to the floor by the scurrying Lord Talbert, who swore and snorted until he was out of sight. If it were not so serious, it would be funny, thought Abshire, going to his sister and taking the pistol from her hands. "Is this my innocent little sister whose laughter can light up a room pointing a gun at her husband?" He tried for levity. "That's quite a hole in the ceiling, Tessie."

"I . . . I would have shot him . . . if he'd . . ."

And then her ladyship sank ungraciously to the floor.

Lord Abshire picked her up and carried her into the bedchamber and placed her on the bed. Little mews and unintelligible words were coming from her throat. He did not summon help; instead, he fanned her with his hand and slapped her cheeks gently. "Tessie . . . Tessie, 'tis all right. He's gone, and I don't think he'll be coming back."

At last she opened her eyes and looked up at him. "Oh, Trenton, why did you not help me?"

He grinned his wry grin. "Fustian, Tessie, I didn't think you needed help. But I am at a quandary as to why you decided to propose a divorce from Lord Talbert."

She struggled to sit up. Wrapping her arms around her bent knees, she spoke slowly. "I just decided today, and the time of the year, the holiday season, had nothing to do with my decision. I didn't even think about that."

"Then what did make you decide? If I remember correctly, I apprised you of your husband's other life soon after little Frank was born. I felt it my duty to tell you, so that you could protect yourself from disease, and from having another child."

"I did take those precautions," she said, looking up at him. "If you'll sit, Trenton, I will tell you about what transpired today at Grammacy Chase. 'Tis a story you'll find hard to believe. Had I not seen the dowager's countenance and heard the pain and joy in her words, I would not believe it myself."

Giving a huge sigh and still hugging her knees with her arms, she settled herself against the tall headboard. The velvet trappings were tied back with thick gold cording. Lord Abshire sat in a plush chair not far from the side of the high bed. For a long moment, he studied her face. He had never seen his sister like this, her brown eyes strangely alight in a deathly pale face. His curiosity was whetted.

"How can one feel pain and joy at the same time?" he asked.

"First, there was extreme joy, and then the pain came, caused by her tyrannical father, his grace, the Duke of Marcel. Now, she is joyous again. The man who brought her such joy, and who loved her so much, is returning to her, as least that is what she believes. Oh, Trenton, there was such love and happiness in the dowager's eyes, and in her voice."

Lord Abshire wondered for a moment if Lady Talbert had not lost her senses. She was talking in circles. "I fear you will have to start at the beginning. Mayhap I'm a little dense where affairs of the heart are concerned."

"No, you're not dense. You were smart enough to recognize that you loved Rachel."

"Not at first," his lordship hastily countered. "But what does the countess have to do with your wanting to divorce Lord Talbert? You know that a woman is seldom granted a divorce, and when her husband divorces her the consequences are traumatic."

"Not any more traumatic than my living with the scoundrel I married." Lady Talbert told him the full story she had heard earlier. At the end, she heaved a deep sigh and said, "Don't you see, Trenton, I want to know love like that, and like what you feel for Rachel. It was such an eye-opening experience to hear the dowager speak of this man whom she loved so many years ago, and how that love still fills her heart. 'Tis not enough for me to be the mother of an heir, and to run this huge household for Lord Talbert. I want to love and be loved, as you and the dowager feel it. I can only hope that this man, Albert Ramey, truly will return to the dowager, and that Rachel feels the same for you as you feel for her."

Lord Abshire's response came quickly. Grinning hugely, he said, "She does. In truth, we have set our wedding date. Twill be Christmas day. She said her life would be in order then, and there would be no reason to wait."

"Do you know what she meant by her life being in order by Christmas?"

The look in Lady Talbert's eyes told his lordship that something was of deep concern to her. He waited, dreading her answer when he at last asked, "Do you know, Tessie? Rachel continues to be so secretive. I've racked my brain."

Lady Talbert's words were low and filled with caring. "Yes, I know, Trenton. Mother M. and I had a long discussion today, and I learned a lot."

"Can you tell me?"

"I can see no reason why you should not know since you will learn soon enough."

"Gadd, Tessie, don't keep me on tenterhooks. Is it something that will keep us from being married?"

"Depends on how you look at it. Rachel believes Lord Talbert to be her father."

Lord Abshire jumped to his feet. "I don't take your meaning."

Lady Talbert recounted the tale and when she paused for breath, her brother, who had been pacing the length of the room, asked how Lord Talbert entered the picture.

"Rachel learned he made a monthly contribution to the Home, starting about the time she, Rachel, was delivered there. So she came here, pretending to be an experienced nanny. Pretty ingenious of her, I would say. She plans to confront him."

His lordship went to lean an elbow on the mantel. He felt his trembling knees would at any moment fail his weight and let him crumple to the floor. His dear, dear Rachel, living through so much pain. It didn't bear thinking on. "Could it be true, Tessie? Could Lord Talbert have sired such a lovely person as Rachel?"

" 'Tis possible, Trenton. The number of children he has sired then cast aside is most likely unknown, even to him."

Twenty-two

Rachel paced the floor of her bedchamber and waited for Lord Talbert's footsteps in the hall. When he came to visit his son, the moment the nursery door closed behind him, she would introduce herself as Frank's nanny. She would watch his eyes closely for recognition of her. Oh, and she must needs not forget to curtsy.

To avoid getting nervous as she waited, she chattered incessantly to Mother M, stopping occasionally to stare at her reflection in the looking glass. "I think I'll change to the blue sprigged muslin with flowers embroidered on the sleeves and hem," she said, turning once again in front of the looking glass.

Another plan began to take shape. She would dress little Frankie in his long stockings and new sailor dress and take him to Lord Talbert's quarters. "How lacking in the head of me," she mused. "Nobility has their children brought to them. Most likely Lord Talbert had never seen the nursery. After quickly changing her dress and once again brushing her black hair until it shone like wet coal, and letting it fall to her shoulders, she said goodbye to Mother M. and went to the nursery.

Frankie was still sleeping. "Come on, little sweetheart, wake up," she said. "We're going to see your papa."

"Hannah was standing with her feet apart, her hands on her ample hips, and with her sparking eyes fixed on Rachel. "Are you addle-brained? You can't wake the child from a dead sleep. He ain't seen his papa in many moons, so why wake him up?

Rachel was busily changing the baby's clothes. "Oh, Hannah, stop glowering. Little Frankie needs to see his papa before the bell rings for supper and he becomes otherwise occupied."

"Harumph! If you ask me, he's otherwise occupied all the time. I don't see how her ladyship can claim to have a husband."

"That's for her ladyship to be concerned about. 'Tis my duty to see that Frankie sees his papa." Taking Frank up into her arms, she kissed him on his forehead. "You do want to see your papa, don't you, sweet baby?"

She then quit the room as fast as she possibly could and sped down the hall, holding Frankie tightly to her breast. At the top of the stairs, she stopped abruptly. She did not know the whereabouts of Lord Talbert's quarters. "What a farrago," she exclaimed, and Frankie gurgled with laughter.

"'Tis funny to you only because you don't realize I'm lost in this big house."

But Rachel did not let the setback deter her. She would find a servant and ask. Looking around, she soon realized there was not a servant in sight, not even on the second floor when she had descended the stairs. A voice caught her attention. It was Napoleon. "Rachel, I was on my way to your rooms. Where are you going?"

"I'm looking for Lord Talbert's quarters. I want to take Frankie to see him."

He leveled a questioning gaze on her. "Is that true, Rachel? Or could you not wait to see him yourself? That is why I was coming to see you. I want to be there when you confront him. The jackanapes had better not talk mean to you."

"Oh, Napoleon, you are just like Mother M., thinking the worst. Do you know where his quarters are?"

"I'll show you. I ain't seen him yet, nor would I want to if'n it weren't for your bent on seeing him."

"Please, no lecture, Napoleon. 'Tis something I have to do." Her heart was pounding in her throat, and a part of her wanted to turn and run, but she knew she could not do that. She must needs get this meeting over with so that she could be happy when she married Lord Abshire on Christmas day. "I don't want to be married as Rachel Storm," she said sotto voce. "Please, God, give me a real name." She felt tears on her cheeks, and she did not dare speak, lest Napoleon know she was crying and would scold her more.

" 'Tis around this corner," Napoleon said. He was walking in front of Rachel, as if he would stand between her and trouble, should trouble come. When he looked back, Rachel noticed his brow was drawn together in a worried frown.

It was Napoleon who rapped loudly on a deeply carved door with a brass plate above it, with Lord Fox Talbert, in swirling script, embedded into the brass.

"Napoleon, do you think I should do this?" Rachel asked in a quavering voice.

"No, but since I've alerted the occupants that someone is out here wanting admittance, I don't think you should turn and run. Might as well get it over with. You've waited a long time, I guess."

"I have, Napoleon, and I know things will turn out right."

"Right may not be the way you want it, Rachel," Napoleon said, looking up at her, his frown deepening. Deep concern visible in his eight-year-old countenance. With a small hand he reached out and patted her arm.

The door opened.

"His lordship is not available," said a man in a blue coat and gray breeches. He wore white silk stockings above highly polished half-boots.

"And who are you?" asked Napoleon.

"I'm Lord Talbert's valet, and he asked that I tell you he is indisposed."

"Do you mean he does not want to see his son?" asked Rachel, her voice shaking uncontrollably.

Just then a loud voice boomed out into the hallway. "Who is it, George? If it's Lady Talbert, tell her that she will be crawling on her knees before I receive her. The audacity of the woman. She doesn't know her good fortune to be married to a man of my wealth, and of the nobility. She'll rue the day she threatened me."

" 'Tis not Lady Talbert, m'lord," said the valet. " 'Tis a young girl holding a little boy. I presume your son."

"Tell her to go away. If I wish to see my son, I will ask that he be brought to me. At the moment, I am busy getting drunk as a wheelbarrow. Get rid of the callers. That's what you are paid for."

Rachel wanted the floor to open up and swallow her.

Napoleon began pulling on her skirt. "Come on, Rachel. A drunk man is never easy to deal with."

The valet said, "I'm sorry, but his lordship is in the depths of desponds."

"Will he come to supper?" Rachel asked. She had to see him. What if he left Talbert Hall without allowing her so much as a glance at him, or he a glimpse of her. Obviously, he and Lady Talbert had had a tiff. Oh, it was so complicated. She let Napoleon lead her away, and behind her the door to Lord Talbert's quarters closed with a sharp click.

Napoleon went with her to the nursery, where Rachel handed Frank over to Hannah, who asked, "Well, what did the scoundrel think of his little son? I wager he didn't even know him."

"His lordship was not expecting us and was indisposed. He'll ask for Frankie later, he said." That was only a partial lie, Rachel thought as she hurried from the room before the wet nurse could needle her further. Now she must needs face Mother M. and listen to her lecture. But the old woman rose from her rocking chair and came to embrace Rachel. "I don't have to ask. I can see the disappointment on your face."

"I didn't get to see him," Rachel said. Turning from Mother M., she went into the dressing room. There, she splashed cold water on her burning face and washed the tears from her eyes. She wanted to see Lord Abshire. When she was with him, everything seemed all right when it wasn't.

"Napoleon, will you find Lord Abshire and tell him I'm in need of seeing him. Supper will be shortly, and I wish to spend some time with him before then. I'll come to his quarters if he wishes."

"Rachel," scolded Mother M., and Rachel managed a little smile.

"Nothing will happen, Mother M."

"I know that, but 'tis against propriety."

"Lots of things are against propriety," countered Rachel.

Napoleon left and returned in the span of a few minutes. "He's not in his quarters, Rachel, and no one seems to know where he is. I'll go watch for him and fetch him as soon as he appears. Or I'll go to the stables looking for him. I'll do whatever you want me to do."

Rachel, who was still standing near the fireplace, rubbed Napoleon's red hair. "I know you will, Napoleon, and I thank you for it. I'm fortunate to have such wonderful friends as you and Mother M. But I'll just wait until supper. I'd like his advice before seeing Lord Talbert, but most likely Lord Talbert will take his meal in his room. Since he and Lady Talbert are at odds."

Lord Talbert, dressed to the nines, was sitting at the head of the long table when Rachel entered the dining room. At the opposite end was Lady Talbert, and halfway between sat Lord Abshire. He jumped to his feet when he saw Rachel, coming to her and kissing her on the cheek. "Your face is hot," he whispered. "Is something wrong?"

"No . . . not now that I'm near you," she said in a low voice, and this brought a huge smile to Lord Abshire's face. He assured her, "If I had my way, I would never be far from your side."

"What are you two whispering about?" asked Lord Talbert in a grumbling voice.

Rachel turned to look at him, and their eyes locked. It seemed to her that he momentarily lifted himself up from his chair and then settled quickly. Definitely there was recognition in his gaze, and relief washed over her like a tidal wave. She had not been wrong; he did know her. This was her dear papa.

From far off, she could hear Lord Abshire saying, "Lord Talbert, may I present Rachel Storm, little Frank's nanny. Miss Storm and I will be married on Christmas day. The banns are being read."

"The devil take me," swore Lord Talbert. He jumped to his feet, then quickly sat back down. His face was pale.

As if he'd seen a ghost, thought Rachel.

She remembered to curtsy before going to sit beside her future husband. His nearness gave her strength. Just then Mother M. and Napoleon joined them at the table, and Lord Abshire presented them to Lord Talbert.

Mother M. did not curtsy, nor did Napoleon bow. In truth, a mumbled acknowledgment of the introduction was all they offered, and they hardly looked at Lord Talbert.

Lady Talbert was keenly observing the happenings, Rachel noted, and she was certain that she, Rachel, was the only one who was happy to see Lord Talbert. The others looked as if they were facing doomsday.

White-gloved footmen came to serve the meal of stewed kidneys, roast beef, small green cabbages, and hot bread. Rachel watched Lord Talbert shovel the food into his mouth. Occasionally, he let out a big belch and broke the oppressive silence. And then he would laugh. Several times she caught him watching her out of the corner of his eye.

"Lord Talbert, your manners are atrocious," scolded Lady Talbert. "You would not act this way in front of your peers."

"But I'm not with my peers, my dear. You are a possession, and 'tis my duty to entertain you. You have become very bored, isolated in the country. I'm thinking of having you accompany me when I return to Town in a fortnight. The shops in Oxford Street can be your playground."

"I have no interest in going into London with you," said Lady Talbert.

Her voice sounded strange to Rachel. Her demeanor was a

set jaw, and anger showed in her brown eyes. Dismissing the exchanged words as a tiff between husband and wife, which most likely would be resolved when they were together later, Rachel wondered when she would have a chance to speak with Lord Talbert. He had mentioned being at Talbert Hall a fortnight, plenty of time for the opportunity to present itself. And now that she knew he had recognized her, she did not need to frantically search him out. She just wished everyone could be as happy as she was at the moment. Looking at Lord Talbert, she gave him her happiest smile.

He returned the smile, but the worried look on his face did not disappear. The footmen served the dessert, which was eaten in silence, while long tapers down the long length of the handsome table flickered into the charged atmosphere. The hovering silence grew longer and louder. Lady Talbert at last rose from her chair and left, without a word.

Rachel watched Lord Talbert's gaze follow his wife until the door closed behind her. He then turned to address Lord Abshire: "I would very much like a conference with you, Abshire. Over a glass of port in my quarters, if you can spare the time away from the beautiful Miss Storm."

Twenty-three

"I'll come to your chamber later," Lord Abshire said, "but I will not drink port with you."

Before Lord Talbert could answer, Lord Abshire, taking Rachel by the arm, escorted her from the room and to the door of her quarters, where he gave her a long, lingering kiss. He then returned to his own quarters, glad to find Lawrence, his valet, available to drink port with him.

His lordship sat in front of the fire and stretched out his booted feet. He had been glad to escape the dreary room. Here, soft lights cast dancing shadows and the windows let in slivers of moonlight. It would be perfect if Rachel were here with him, he mused. He smiled at how she had clung to him when he kissed her good night and told her to sleep well. In her innocence, she did not know what that did to a man.

"Before long I will not have to leave you like this," he had said, and she had answered that Christmas seemed so far away.

"Not much more than a fortnight," he had promised.

Now, sitting before the fire, seeing her face in the flames, Christmas seemed centuries away for him. Not only did he long to make love to his future bride, that was a constant with him, he wanted her by his side forever and a day. She was his soulmeet. He felt only half a man here by himself.

"Your port, your lordship," said Lawrence as he stood in front of Lord Abshire, offering the drink in a sparkling crystal glass.

Lord Abshire sat upright. "I was deep in thought, Lawrence. I beg your forgiveness."

"I could see that something was on your mind, so I was slow about pouring the drink."

"You're a good man, Lawrence. I don't know what I would do without you."

The valet laughed. "We've been through a lot together, the war, some near misses there, as well as in your salad days, but I've never seen you in love before."

Lord Abshire, holding the port in his hand, sniffed the bouquet, then sipped slowly, savoring the warmth it brought to his throat. " 'Tis a wonderful feeling. And to think I almost missed it. I think you were the first to tell me that I was in love. I thought desire was keeping me awake at night, making me act foolishly."

"You'd been in desire before, but this time you were different, the tender way you spoke her name, the way you raved about her blue eyes, the way you called her name in your sleep, as if she were far off and you were beckoning her to come to you. Only a man in love could say a name with such feeling."

"The devil take me. I didn't talk in my sleep?"

"Only her name. I could hear you from the next room."

The valet stood in proximity to his lordship; he would never sit unless asked to do so, and Lord Abshire knew this well. This night, his lordship wanted company. "Lawrence, pour yourself a drink and sit for a coze. I've been summoned to Lord Talbert's quarters, but I'm in no hurry. With luck, by the time I get there, he will be passed out, drunk as a wheelbarrow."

But Lord Talbert was not passed out when Lord Abshire arrived. He was pacing the floor, expelling expletives as if there were no tomorrow. "I want you to stop this foolishness of your sister's," he said upon Lord Abshire's entry into his quarters. Lord Talbert was still dressed, but his cravat was askew, and if Lord Abshire was not mistaken, port had been spilled into the once immaculate folds.

"It is not my wont to stop my sister from divorcing you. The marriage was a mistake, and I see no reason why she should live with it the rest of her life. Our brother had no right to give his consent to such a union."

"Give . . . give his consent? He was anxious for the marriage. He knew of my wealth." Lord Talbert stopped to spew out a cynical laugh. "His greed got the better of him, and I needed an heir. 'Twas as simple as that."

"I fear it will not be so simple to undo the union. However, I believe Lady Talbert has the resolve to bring it about. I've never seen her so determined, and she knows I will support her effort. She has summoned our solicitor."

"Won't you sit?" said Lord Talbert. "There's lots to discuss. For one, what do you think will become of you if your sister throws me over? I've furnished you employment—"

"I've lived here only for my sister. I have adequate income to live anywhere I choose. Tessie needed me, in the absence of a husband."

Lord Talbert's voice was suddenly cajoling. "Demmet, Abshire, sit down. Let's talk, one friend to another."

"I prefer to stand, and you are mistaken. We are not friends. As I've just told you, I've stayed at Talbert Hall to protect my sister."

Lord Talbert sat in a chair that flanked the fireplace.

Abshire, because he wanted to look Lord Talbert in the eye as they talked, went to lean an arm on the mantle. The fire warmed his backside, and he was surprised at how relaxed he felt. Only his anger stirred him. "It would behoove you, your lordship, not to fight my sister on the divorce; I've never seen her so determined."

"Insane is a better word," said Lord Talbert. "Imagine the chit taking a shot at me."

"I believe she shot the ceiling on purpose, but if I were

you, I would not give her cause to take a second shot. She's a fair markswoman."

"I don't know what's come over her."

"She wants to be loved. Of course you can't understand that."

"Love! A waste of one's time. Besides, that's for the common folk, the lower orders. I'll happily give her permission to take a lover. After she's given me another heir. Demmet, Abshire, that's the thing with the *ton*. Did not Lady Melbourne on her deathbed admonish her daughter to be true to her lover, without a mention of how she was to treat her husband?"

"That is not Tessie's way."

"Well, she'll never gain a divorce. I'll see to that. And when I'm through, there won't be a man in England who'll have her."

Lord Abshire gave out a mirthless laugh. "You overestimate your power. I suggest you not contest the divorce, less you wish to see your secret life exposed on the front pages of every newspaper in England. You'll be cut by your own peers and you'll no longer be welcome in the House of Lords. I'm sure White's would be the first to take action. Many a scoundrel goes there, I am sure, but none who deal in white slavery. The balladeers and lampooners will have a field day."

Lord Abshire was pleased to see the blood drain from his brother-in-law's face. "I have no secret life. I'm a respectable gentleman of the *ton*. I serve my constituents well."

"You do have a secret life, a hell in Covent Gardens. I have photographs to prove it."

Lord Talbert left his chair and, for a moment, Abshire thought he would lunge for him, and he made ready by spreading his feet and raising his fists to battle position. It had not been too long since he'd had a go with Gentleman Jackson, the exchampion pugilist of England.

Lord Talbert stopped after only two steps and shook his balled fist in the air and swore, using words Lord Abshire had never heard. And then he said, "So you're the one who tittle-tattled to your sister. After I've given you a place here." He pulled himself up to his full height, squared his shoulders, and bellowed like a bull. "Meet me on the field of honor."

Lord Abshire laughed, enjoying himself immensely. "Duels are illegal. Besides, you wouldn't know a field of honor should you stumble onto it. In truth, you are not worth my time." He turned to leave.

"Not so fast," said Lord Talbert. "Did I understand that you're marrying that bacon-brained hoyden who someone was rattlebrained enough to hire for my heir's nanny?"

"I do indeed plan to marry Rachel Storm."

Lord Talbert's laughter filled the room. "What a fool you are. She's straight out of Covent Garden. I saw her there myself. No one could forget those blue eyes. And that little thief was with her, most likely her man of business."

He did not get to finish, for Lord Abshire hit him square in the mouth, knocking him to the floor, where he lay supine, out cold. Nothing ever felt so good, thought Lord Abshire as he slammed the door behind him.

Twenty-four

"Your lordship, is the house on fire?" he asked. "The way you're putting yourself together."

"Demmet, Lawrence, I overslept."

Lawrence knelt to help slip on his employer's boots, which he had polished while Lord Abshire slept. "What's the big hurry. 'Tis still snowing. Not much you can do outside."

"I want to get to Rachel before great harm is done."

"Harm done to Rachel? I don't take your meaning."

"I don't have time to explain. Shave me quickly, and I'll be on my way. I'm certain she's already been down for breakfast, and he may have been there."

Last night, before a fitful sleep finally claimed him, and that was quite late, Lord Abshire had concluded that he would not allow Rachel to talk with Lord Talbert. He would tell her he knew she had been thinking Lord Talbert her lost papa, that she had come to Talbert Hall looking for him. He would also tell her should she ask the depraved man, he would deny it. And, in truth, he most likely would not know if he had sired her.

Lord Abshire certainly did not want Lord Talbert saying to Rachel what he had said to him, that she was light skirt from the underground of Covent Garden. He left the valet looking askance and hurried to the dining room. With the exception of one white-gloved footman, it was empty. The footman bowed from the waist. "Are you ready to be served, your lordship?"

"No. I'm looking for Miss Storm. Has she been down this morning?"

"Oh, yes, much earlier. As was Lady Talbert and the older woman and young boy."

Lord Abshire's breath lodged in his throat. "Lord Talbert? Was he not present?"

"Oh, no, your lordship. He was seen leaving at first light. They said his carriage will most likely crash before it reaches London. No one knows his hurry to leave."

"By no one, you mean the other servants?"

"Yes, your lordship. It was not mentioned around the breakfast table, and the others . . . the other servants . . . said most likely everyone was asleep when the high-sprung carriage tore off down that narrow lane like the devil himself was after it."

"The devil was in the carriage," Lord Abshire said under his breath as he quit the dining room and headed for the third floor. Had Rachel sought out Lord Talbert and asked if he were her father, making him angry and giving him reason for leaving Talbert Hall at first light?" It did not bear thinking on.

Mother M. answered Lord Abshire's frantic knock. "Where's Rachel?" he asked without preliminaries. He saw instantly the old woman had been crying.

"Napoleon is looking for her. When we returned from breakfast, Adaline came to help with Rachel's toilette. The maid could not stop her tongue, and before she was through, she was saying that Lord Talbert had left without saying a word to anybody, and in such a hurry he was. Of course the foolish gel had no way of knowing what this meant to Rachel."

"I'm terribly concerned about Rachel, Sister. I fear we've handled this all wrong. I should have warned her against that unscrupulous man."

"I did warn her, but it did no good. She so much wants to be married with her real name, said it would not be fair to you otherwise."

"I know. Now can you tell me where I can find her. I must needs comfort her,"

Mother M. looked beseeching up at him. "Napoleon is looking for her. I told him she had dashed out of here at great speed when the maid told her Lord Talbert was gone. The little fellow swore, something I had never heard him do before. He feared she'd gone to the stables and rode off after the carriage."

His lordship left quickly. Outside, he bent his head to snow that was falling in sheets. He needed his greatcoat. "Did you saddle a horse for Miss Storm?" he asked the groom who was polishing Lady Talbert's carriage.

"No, your lordship. She wuz plainly distraught, and I did'n think it right she be riding in this weather. I hope I said the right thing, your lordship. That little boy, Napoleon, come, and they went upstairs to where he used to stay."

"You said the right thing," Lord Abshire said. "Rachel, Rachel," he murmured as he climbed the stairs two at a time and hurried to the coachman's apartment. The door was ajar, and he could see Napoleon near the fireplace, pouring coffee from a black kettle into a cup. A lone candle flickered in the dimness.

Rachel was lying on the bed, her face buried in a pillow. The sound of muffled sobs filled the room. "Here, Rachel," Napoleon was saying as he walked to the bed. "This will make you feel better. I can't stand your crying like this. The jackanapes ain't worth it. Storm is a nice name, and Rachel, you know that comes straight from the Bible. A name can't be much nicer than that."

When Rachel did not respond, the little boy sat the cup on the bedside table that held the candle and knelt beside the bed. Reaching out, he patted her heaving shoulder with his little hand. With a balled hand, he swiped at the tears that were rolling down his pink cheeks and off his quivering chin.

Lord Abshire found that his eyes were damp with his own tears. Clearing has throat, he walked into the room. "I'm glad to find you with Rachel, Napoleon. May I speak with her?"

Napoleon jumped to his feet, as if he were embarrassed by

his emotions. "I tried to give her coffee. I hope you can get the windmills out of her head."

"I'll try, Napoleon, and thank you for taking care of her. I was frightened when I learned she had left her rooms. I felt exceedingly better upon learning that you'd gone after her." He wanted to hug the little street-smart boy but knew it would not do. Napoleon was trying so hard to be the little man he envisioned himself to be.

Napoleon bowed from the waist. "I'll take my leave."

"Would you go to Mother M. and tell her Rachel is all right, that she is with me?"

"I will. She loves Rachel very much."

"As I do. And as you do, Napoleon. Thank you for that."

"She saved my life, your lordship. I would give mine for her."

"Let's hope that won't be necessary," said Lord Abshire. He turned to pick Rachel up and hold her in his arms. Behind him, the door closed on Napoleon.

Rachel's sobbing had stopped. Her eyes were red, and as Lord Abshire looked into their blue depths, he saw the pain she felt, and he felt it with her. He kissed her on the forehead, then placed his cheek against her damp one, holding her tightly for a long moment.

"I'm sorry," she said in a low voice. "I'm ashamed of my outburst."

"Shhh," his lordship whispered, and then he tried for levity by saying, "I don't know what to do with you. I can't hold you like this all day."

Rachel gave a small smile. "You might try putting me down. I believe I can stand."

He carried her to the fireplace, in front of which lay a worn rug. Coal burned in the grate, emitting warmth. "We'll sit in front of the fire. We must needs talk."

They sat cross-legged, facing each other. Holding her small hands in his, he began. "Rachel, Lady Talbert confided in me your thinking that Lord Talbert is your father. I should have come to you right away and told you what I know about the man. And I would have had I not felt I would be betraying my sister. Lord Talbert is, after all, her husband."

"What do you mean, Trenton?"

"He is a scoundrel, I pray he did not sire you. I can hardly say father you, for that is not what the man does. He uses a young girl for his pleasure and then casts her aside, leaving his man of business to pay the damages, if the young girl presses. So you see, Rachel, the money coming to the Home from Lord Talbert could be for any girl there."

"But the money started coming on the month I was born."

"That could be a coincidence. Believe me, my sweet Rachel, if you are the man's child, 'tis better you don't know."

Lord Abshire then told her Lady Talbert would soon be petitioning Parliament for a divorce. "When I came home from the war, I heard rumors," he told her. "I went to his place in Covent Garden, a disreputable place called a hell. I have evidence enough that I believe Lord Talbert will consent to the divorce. He doesn't want that part of his life known."

"I so wanted my real name before we married," Rachel said. "And I was so sure he recognized me."

"He did remember seeing you and Napoleon in Covent Garden . . . when Napoleon stole your box. He tried to tell me you were in a place where young girls pleasure men."

"Oh, Trenton, what did you say? You didn't believe him, did you?"

Lord Abshire allowed the wry grin to soften his face. "I hit him in the mouth. Most likely he left at first light so no one could see his busted lip."

She laughed lightly, with only a touch of sadness. "I guess I don't want him for my papa after all."

"Oh, sweet Rachel, as Napoleon told you, Storm is a beautiful name. It reminds me of you. Those incredible blue eyes can become quite stormy when you are angry, or when you are anxious, and then, as if the wind were a whisper, they can be as calm as the sea when there is no wind, as blue and as bottomless. On Christmas day, I shall marry Rachel Storm, and no man could be prouder."

The sky was overcast and dreary. Yesterday's snow clung to the limbs of the trees lining the lane that led to the main road. A crested carriage was approaching at breakneck speed, and in only moments stopped in front of Talbert Hall. Benford, Lord Abshire's brother, alighted with alacrity. Taking up his cane, he strode toward the house, leaving his wife, Hortense, to fend for herself.

Lord Abshire watched from a window, his brow holding a deep frown. Could Benford be arriving early for the party? His lordship quickly discounted the theory; his grace's hurried stride as he left his carriage indicated anger.

Lord Abshire did not dread a confrontation with the duke, but an instant protectiveness for Tessie grasped him. He would not allow their older brother to badger her about the pending divorce from Lord Talbert.

The crested carriage disappeared from sight, as did Hortense. Lord Abshire stroked his chin thoughtfully. How could his grace know about Tessie's wont to divorce her husband? Only a day had passed since she had announced her intention. Knowing anything was possible, he quit the room and went directly to the withdrawing room on the second floor, where close friends and family members were received.

His grace was already there, saying loudly, "I demand to see my brother . . . and my sister. At once."

A scared maid almost knocked Lord Abshire down in her haste to do his grace's bidding. "Slow down," Lord Abshire said to the swishing black bombazine, "the jackanapes won't harm you."

"I must needs get her ladyship," said the maid, and off she went, running toward Lady Talbert's quarters.

Laconically, Lord Abshire strolled into the room. He gave

his brother a half smile, which he knew would infuriate Benford. And then he gave a half bow. "Your grace."

The duke held out his ringed hand to be kissed. Lord Abshire pretended not to notice. "Find yourself a seat, brother. I take it you came for a coze. Or did you come for the party. If that be the case, you're early."

"Coze! Party! The devil! I'm here to see what Lady Talbert is up to, threatening to divorce her husband. Don't she know that is not done in proper society? What's she trying to do, disgrace the family?"

Lord Abshire did not speak for a long moment. His alert brown eyes bored into those of his brother. Each had taken a chair on opposite sides of the fireplace. At last his lordship, in a calm, self-assured voice, said to his grace, "I believe 'twas you who brought disgrace on the family, when you arranged to marry your innocent sister off to a scoundrel such as Fox Talbert. I have reason to believe you knew of his secret business, and most likely you were visiting his den of depravity when the two of you decided on the union of two grand estates. It has never been a marriage. If old Henry VIII were still king, most likely you would be beheaded, a fate you richly deserve."

Lord Abshire stretched his long legs out in front of him, and, crossing them at the ankles, eyed his highly polished boots. He flipped an imaginary bit of fuzz from the sleeve of his superfine coat, and then he gazed at his brother's flushed face. Flush hardly described his already mottled complexion; it was a strained purple as he struggled to respond to his brother's accusation.

"It was the duty of my father to arrange my marriage, and it has been a very successful union, with the exception of producing an heir. That's why I'm anxious for you to marry a Lady of Quality. Lady Talbert can take a lover, but I shall forbid her to petition for a divorce."

"Forbid all you like, brother," said Lady Talbert as she swept into the room. Even before the duke could rise from his chair, she gave the expected curtsy, and then continued, "Your threats do not frighten me. We know enough on Lord Talbert to silence him, and I believe, with a bit of work we can uncover some rather disgraceful things on yourself which your peers in the House of Lords would love to know."

Her ladyship did not have a thought as to what she was saying. His grace had a mistress, but that was acceptable behavior among the *ton.* And poor Hortense had a lover, though, with her looks, he must needs be a loser. The look on her brother's face told her she had struck a raw nerve. She gave a small laugh. "How did you know so soon about my intention to divorce Lord Talbert? I will no longer refer to him as my husband."

"Lord Talbert came yesterday to inform me of your disgraceful proposal. I will not allow it."

"Of course, he went directly to you when he left here like a scared ape. Well, you may tell him that you no longer have jurisdiction over me. And don't threaten me that you will cut me off without a cent. I shall seek employment, and then all of England will know what a tyrant you are."

Having not taken a chair, her ladyship went to pull the bell rope. "I will order a repast. No doubt you are hungry after the long journey. Where's Hortense?"

"Below stairs, waiting for me. I did not want her to hear this unpleasant conversation."

"I'll send for her. Do you plan to stay for our Christmas party? 'Tis costume."

"Absolutely not. I shall separate myself from the carryings on of my siblings. You both have windmills in your head."

Lord Abshire laughed heartily. "You must needs stay, your grace. I will be announcing my engagement to Miss Rachel Storm. Remember, I mentioned this to you earlier on. She's little Frank's nanny."

The purple of his grace's complexion deepened, and the veins in his neck looked to be near bursting as he struggled to speak. "You're not still up to that foolishness. Lord Talbert said you were funning, that the chit is a light skirt."

"That lie got Lord Talbert a busted lip." Lord Abshire stopped and let the full sweep of glorious happiness engulf him. "I'm very much in love with Miss Storm, and she with me. The vows will be read on Christmas day. You and Hortense are most welcome, if you would like to attend."

Twenty-five

At Grammacy Chase, the servants were complaining. "I've polished that same console at least three times," one said, and Nora, hearing her, was laughing.

"The countess is expecting a guest, and until he arrives, just polish away. No matter that the house smells of beeswax, or that there's enough food for three feasts prepared."

" 'Tis worth it to see m'lady so happy," answered the maid. "Who's this mystery guest?"

"Oh, no you don't. She would have my head should I tell. My lips are sealed until he arrives."

On the day Lady Talbert and Mother M. called to pay their condolences for the death of his grace, a caller presented himself, asking for the dowager countess. Later, her ladyship had confided to Nora that 'twas Lord Malvey, Albert Ramey's cousin. He had received a missive from Ramey, saying he would be in England before Christmas. Since then, Grammacy Chase had been at sixes and sevens. There was no controlling the dowager. A whole new wardrobe had been ordered, and Christmas boxes were stacked practically to the high ceiling. More mistletoe had been hung, laurel wreaths made the house look like a field of greenery.

Her ladyship was even dressing her hair differently, changing it at least thrice each time the maid, who considered herself an expert in dressing hair for the nobility, came to her dressing room to perform the task. "She'll be the death of me," the maid complained each time she left the dowager, and Nora would laugh.

Now, Nora sat in the above-stairs withdrawing room, waiting for her ladyship. They were to have tea. A light smile played around her mouth as she mused to herself, "I wonder what she will be wanting done this day."

It was wonderful to see the dowager countess so happy.

"Nora, do you suppose this will be the day he comes," the dowager said when she entered the withdrawing room, dressed to the nines in a rose silk gown that showed much of her youthful white bosom. Three red silk roses were nestled in the strands of her silver hair. Her brown eyes and youthful face glowed with expectation.

Nora rose to her feet and curtsied. Even though she had been told 'twas totally unnecessary, she held to the custom, and she liked it. The nobility should be curtsied to, most especially the dowager countess.

"I pray he will come this day," Nora said. She pulled the bell rope to order tea, and then went to sit in the chair she thought of as hers. The dowager, as usual, sat opposite her, the white-clothed table between them.

"I so wanted my Ramey to accompany me to the party at Talbert Hall, and that is tomorrow." She paused for a moment. "In truth, Nora, I've been thinking that should he not arrive in time to go that I will send a missive and regret my absence. Lady Talbert would surely understand."

"No doubt but that she would, but you've been looking forward to this affair for days, and you really should go. Should Mr. Ramey arrive at Grammacy Chase, he will be sent right on over. 'Tis only two hours away."

The maid came, bringing a silver tray which held a silver pot, steam roiling from its spout, and a plate stacked high with scones and an assortment of jellies. The dowager laughed softly. "I'm afraid the household has become quite boring. The staff knows what to do without being told. Thank you, Peggy."

The maid placed the tray on the table, then bobbed into her

black bombazine. "The place is not boring, m'lady, not with you expecting the mystery man." She gave a little laugh. "The household is abuzz with speculation. 'Twill be a wonderful Christmas should he arrive by then."

The dowager recognized the maid's subtle prying, and she laughed heartily. "I pray that he will, and I promise that all my help will be told the whole of it at that time."

"Oh, m'lady. We all wish you the best." She bobbed again and left, and the two women talked and drank tea, as they did every afternoon. "Nora, should he come to the Talbert costume party, do you suppose he will recognize me? I shall be going as old King Henry's Catherine of Aragon. She never recognized his other wives. Although he had divorced her, she died considering herself as his wife. That is the way I feel about my marriage to Ramey. We are husband and wife, and no one can change that." She sipped her tea and watched Nora's face, knowing there would be a smile forthcoming. "I did tell you that Lord Malvey fetched the marriage license, all legally signed. He'd held it all these years. I begged of him to keep it, to guard it with his life. He's going to ask the Prince Regent that my marriage to Lord Longworth be set aside. Since the marriage was not consummated, and because I was already married to Albert Ramey, there's grounds aplenty. His Majesty, King George, is mad as a hatter, and the old duke is dead. There's no longer anyone to fear."

Nora's smile lit up her face. "Yes, your ladyship, you did tell me, but I know it makes you feel better to repeat it, and I'm here to listen as many times as you wish to tell it. I pray for Lord Malvey's success."

"And I, too." The dowager countess rose from her chair and went to the window to look out. The room was heavy with silence. Her eyes skimmed the road atop the hillock, the road Ramey's coach must needs travel when he came to Grammacy Chase. Hateful doubts trampled her happiness, doubts she would never express to anyone, not even Nora. *Lord Malvey had only said that Ramey was returning to England before*

Christmas; he had not said he was coming to Grammacy Chase.

"But my Ramey will come," she said aloud. Tears pushed at her eyes, and as she turned from the window, she saw the questioning look on Nora's face.

Then came the faithful companion's words of assurance: "Of course he will come, your ladyship. You must needs not doubt, and I do encourage you to go to Talbert Hall. I know the party will be a grand affair."

Twenty-six

"I won't be staying to enjoy the party," Benford said to Lord Abshire. "I shall be staying to prevent this misalliance of which you speak so eloquently, and to talk some sense into Lady Talbert's head about divorcing Lord Talbert. It does not bear thinking on. For sure she would lose custody of the Talbert heir. A man has his rights."

His grace spoke as if she were not there, noted Lady Talbert, thinking it typical of her brother, who had no regard for a woman's feelings. She slipped from the room, went to recoup her son from the nursery, and then went to her own quarters. She had no notion of letting her brother within talking proximity. If he talked with her, he must needs talk through the walls.

Holding little Frank to her breast, she sang to him, while rocking in the hard-backed chair she'd had moved into her room for that purpose. Her thoughts went to Rachel, who had been instrumental in making her aware of how a mother was supposed to feel for her child. Before Rachel, she had thought her only responsibility toward her son was to see that he had a proper nanny. She hugged him tighter to her, to make up for that time when she hadn't hugged him, and he squirmed against the restrictive embrace. Laughing, she released him. His little hands came up to pat her cheeks. His gurgling laughter made alive and warm the room where she had spent so many lonely hours. Silently, she thanked God for Rachel's having come to Talbert Hall, and for the Dowager Countess Longworth, who had made her aware of how wonderful love could be.

"I must needs warn Rachel about Benford's presence at Talbert Hall, and of his intent to disrupt the marriage plans," she said aloud. Pushing herself up and carrying Frankie on her hip, she went to pull the bell rope. When a maid appeared, she sent for Rachel. "And have Hannah come for the baby," she added.

The maid bobbed and left, and in a very short time reappeared with Rachel and Hannah.

Lady Talbert kissed the baby. "Take good care of him and don't let anyone near him," she told Hannah, who was looking askance, her big head moving from side to side in puzzlement. She was mumbling to herself when the door closed behind her.

Lady Talbert turned to Rachel. "Brother Benford has arrived at Talbert Hall. He is threatening to disallow your marriage to Trenton."

"Can he do that?" asked Rachel wide-eyed.

"With anyone, besides Trenton, he might be able to stop a marriage. Being a duke gives a man power. But with Trenton, he will only fuel the fire of determination. My purpose in summoning you here is to protect you from Benford's hateful tongue."

She stopped to invite Rachel to sit. Before taking a chair herself, she lit a candle on a nearby table, casting the room into gentle darkness. "When his grace can't convince Trenton marriage between the two of you will be a misalliance, most likely he will try to convince you you're not worthy of the nobility."

"Because I don't have a real name?"

"Because you're of the lower orders," answered Lady Talbert, and she quickly added, "That does not matter a whit to Trenton. Or to me."

"Then why does his brother care?"

Rachel's incredible blue eyes were teary. Lady Talbert, a

lump in her throat, reached to pat her hand. "That is the way of the upper orders. Love does not matter."

"But it does matter," protested Rachel. "I would never marry a man I did not love."

"All that truly matters is that you and Trenton love each other. My wont is to keep you from Benford until the announcement of your engagement is made at the party on the morrow."

"How can you manage that, with his grace here at Talbert Hall?"

Lady Talbert gave a little laugh. "By hiding you in my rooms. I'll let Trenton know, lest he tear down the place looking for you, and I'll caution Hannah to keep her lips sealed."

"And we must needs tell Napoleon and Mother M. For sure they will keep the secret," said Rachel.

And so the planning went. Later, Lady Talbert passed the word to Lord Abshire that Rachel was hiding in her rooms, and he told Napoleon and Mother M. The three of them were to meet his grace at the supper table, and when he enquired of Miss Storm's whereabouts, they were to profess innocence.

It soon became a wonderful game to outsmart a noble duke.

Rachel hid behind a door when a huge meal for one was being delivered, and while Lady Talbert explained to the quizzical maid that, having not eaten the scones served with the afternoon tea, she was famished and could eat everything on the tray. When the maid had left, Rachel and Lady Talbert laughed and congratulated themselves, and shared the food.

In the dining room, with his wife Hortense seated to his right, his grace sat at the head of the beautifully decorated table and stared at the door through which other diners would enter. Lord Abshire was already there, for he would not miss one delicious moment of the fun.

Napoleon, dressed to the nines in yellow pantaloons, silk stockings, and half-boots, and Mother M., dressed in her black-and-white wool gown, nonchalantly entered the room, as if nothing was awry. Lord Abshire made proper introductions and then signaled the footman to begin serving.

His grace bellowed like a male cow. "Where is this Miss Storm? I mean to have a word with her."

"I think not," said Lord Abshire, and Napoleon interrupted to say that Miss Storm had suddenly disappeared, that she often did so on a whim, especially at night, and returning at first light.

"Where does she go? No doubt out to find a lover in her own class," said his grace, and it seemed to Lord Abshire that his duchess shivered and shrank deeper into the high-back chair she occupied.

Mother M. raised an inch off her chair and glared down her long, sharp nose at his grace, clearly ready to rip him to shreds. Lord Abshire signaled to her with his eyes, and she gained her seat with alacrity. But that did not keep her from staring his grace down.

" 'Tis her right . . . to go where she wishes . . . until we are married," his lordship said to his grace, tongue-in-cheek. "Miss Storm is not leg-shackled to me, not until Christmas day."

"And she won't be leg-shackled to you. Not to a member of the Abshire family, I can promise you that," said his grace, looking stern and baleful, then becoming quiet when a plate of boiled beef and cabbage was placed in front of him. Bending his head over the plate, he began shoveling food into his mouth, as if he had not eaten in a fortnight.

It was obvious that food took precedence over his grace's objection to a lower order defaming his noble family tree, thought Lord Abshire, who was not fooled by his brother's sudden silence. For sure more would be heard from his grace, if not before the costume party on the morrow, then when he, Lord Abshire, announced his and Rachel Storm's intent to be married on Christmas day.

* * *

It was not easy to keep Rachel hidden all through the next day. The duke was everywhere in the manor house. He knocked on Lady Talbert's door more than once, only to meet silence, and in case he forced entry, when Lady Talbert left her quarters, Rachel locked herself in the dressing room.

When time to dress for the costume ball neared, Lord Abshire asked his brother to ride with him over the estate. This left Rachel free to return to her own quarters without being seen.

Adaline and an assistant maid came to help her and Mother M. dress. Mother M.'s costume was rather simple; she would wear a black habit, the new one Rachel had purchased for her, and a mask of a very young girl.

But Rachel's ballgown was very grand. Made of silver-shot gold silk, it had a panniered skirt, held out from her body by a padded hoop. A small bustle made her small hips appear larger, and elegant long sleeves reached her small wrists. A gold lace cap covered her black hair.

With Rachel's mask, which showed the face of an older woman, with long black eye lashes, it would be impossible to recognize her, thought Mother M. With deliberate steps, the old woman walked around the only daughter she would ever have, surveyed the drastic change the gown made, and then, lifting her quizzing glass and staring through it for closer scrutiny, she nodded a final approval. "Are you excited, love?" she asked, smiling broadly.

Rachel laughed. "As if you can't tell."

"I'm so glad I stayed on at Talbert Hall," said Mother M., and then, with her face screwed up as if she might cry, she added, "If only for this moment."

"I'm glad you're here, Mother M.," Rachel said, going to the old woman and hugging her. "And you've been a tremendous help."

Then Rachel hushed, lest she tell the maids her reason for coming to Talbert Hall, and for Mother M.'s reason for following her. It was all so complicated, and besides, the help would know soon enough. Lord Abshire had said he would tell the whole of it after the engagement was announced.

A tremendous knock sounded at the door, and Rachel knew immediately it was Lord Abshire. His grace's roaring voice was absent. She went to answer the knock and was, without preliminaries, grabbed up by her future husband's strong arms and swung around. He said, "When his grace sees you, all his objections will vanish, mark my word. He'll be so overcome by your beauty, he will want to marry you himself."

Rachel was laughing, as was Mother M., and the maids clapped their hands as if it were entertainment just for them. "Here, let's put your mask on," one of them said, and when she did so, Lord Abshire pretended terrible disappointment, smiling his wry smile. "Your beauty is hidden with that thing. I can't see your beautiful blue eyes." Stepping closer, he gave a leg and asked to stand for a dance, addressing her as Countess Tashia of Russia.

They danced, while the others gleefully watched, and Adaline said, "No touching, your lordship. Remember the rules."

"A pox on the rules," Lord Abshire said. He knew what the maid was dying to see, so he deftly removed the mask and pulled Rachel to him and kissed her on a blushing cheek, then watched as the pink turned a flaming red, making the giddy maids laugh and clap some more.

Mother M., joining in the laughter, mumbled to herself, "That pink of the *ton* thinks rules are made to be broken, and propriety doesn't mean a fig to him." But she approved of this free-spirited man for her Rachel, and she was happy to at last see Rachel happy. Not once, Mother M. mused, when they were dressing, did Rachel allude to finding her dear papa, not even when the maids could not hear.

Earlier, when she had come from hiding in Lady Talbert's quarters, she had whispered, "Mother M., I pray Lord Talbert is not my dear papa. Trenton told me everything. I fear I could not keep from being judgmental, should he turn out to be the one. Lady Talbert says he has sired several children, but never nurtured one. Not even little Frankie."

Rachel dismissed the maids and then turned to her soon-to-be husband and asked, "Should you not be dressing? May I go with you and see your costume?"

"And give his grace a chance at you. He has a vile tongue, and I will not have you badgered by him. Just when I've convinced you that you are worthy, with the name Storm, of marrying nobility, I would not have him undoing my good work. I might have to call him out. So 'tis much better to protect you by keeping you from his presence."

Bowing from the waist, Lord Abshire left and went to his own quarters, where his valet was pacing the floor and grumbling about a certain person always being late. "Your bath water is ready, m'lord. Most likely it is cold by now." His voice was scolding.

Lord Abshire slapped him on the shoulder and gave his wry grin. "Cheer up, Lawrence, I will not have you spoil this wonderful night by being fussy. Remember, I'm announcing my engagement to Miss Storm this night."

"Are you afraid your brother, the duke, will make a scene? He's a mean-spirited man."

"Only to his family. In front of his peers, he follows propriety as if it were an exact science. Appearance means everything to him. That's why he's so against my marriage to a lower order." His lordship laughed heartily. "He's terrified of what the *ton* will say."

They went to his lordship's dressing room and he began undressing. The room was warm and cozy from a fire that burned brightly in the grate. For his convenience, a bottle of brandy was on a table beside the deep porcelain tub. When he was naked, he crawled into the lukewarm water and poured himself a glass, and then he sang bawdy songs about his tyrannical brother.

The valet, laughing, laid out his costume.

Twenty-seven

From an above-stairs window, Rachel and Mother M. watched as carriages, some pulled by as many as eight sleek horses, wound their way up the lane from the main road. Inside the carriages, the yellow glow of lighted lanterns showed splendidly dressed women and men with tall hats bouncing on the squabs. All were masked.

Bewigged coachmen, splendidly dressed in many-layered coats and wearing three-cornered hats and French gloves, sat on the boxes, occasionally cracking a whip over the horses's backs. It had stopped snowing, but the countryside was white under the rising moon, giving the impression of an incandescent whitewashed nimbus, through which the carriages were eerily moving.

Below, grooms waited to tend the horses, and powdered footman in gorgeous liveries waited to help passengers alight and up the steps, where they would be handed over to the butler, dressed more outrageously gorgeous than all the rest who were waiting to pay homage to the nobility.

"What a spectacle," Mother M. exclaimed.

" 'Tis so exciting, Mother M. Who would have ever dreamed when we were at the Home that we would be standing here like this, waiting to go to a grand ball?"

" 'Tis God's will," the old woman answered, her countenance solemn and thoughtful. "Not that we go to a grand ball, He could care less about that, but 'tis His way of bringing soulmeets together."

"Oh, Mother M., do you really believe Trenton and I to be soulmeets?"

"If I didn't believe that, love, I would not be standing here waiting to go to hear the announcement of your coming marriage."

Rachel knew this to be true. The good sister was here for one purpose only, to see that no harm came to her Rachel. She gave the old woman a warm smile.

They were waiting for a crowd to gather in the great hall before they made an unobtrusive entry via the front door. This had been Lord Abshire's idea, so that his brother Benford would not know which of the costumed women was Rachel. "I don't want him to single you out and lecture you about marrying above your station," he had said, frowning worriedly. "He might even try to bribe you."

Rachel, giggling, had teased, "Are you afraid I will accept his bribe, Trenton?"

Without answering, he kissed Rachel soundly, until she went limp in his arms. "Now, about that bribe," he teased.

He had left then, to go dress for the ball, saying his valet was most likely having a spell of the vapors, like some old woman, because he, Lord Abshire, had stolen away to come to Rachel.

The kiss was still warm on Rachel's lips as she stood and watched the arriving carriages.

"When there's a break, we must needs go down the back stairs and circle the house to the front," said Mother M. "That way no one will see that we are not from a carriage."

The time seemed interminable to Rachel, but she knew in reality it was only a short while before Mother M. said, "I think now," and they were off, moving slowing so as to not tear Rachel's gown. Just as they arrived at the corner of the house, a high-perched phaeton pulled away, and they made a dash to enter behind the new arrivals.

Rachel handed the butler a card with their pretend names

printed on it, and he announced them in: "Countess Tashia of Russia and Sister Mary."

"I wish I could have thought of a more mysterious name," the old woman whispered to Rachel.

"Every one will be wondering why a woman of the church is attending such a sinful affair," Rachel whispered back in the lightest of moods.

"This is a costume; they won't know I'm really a member of an Order. They might even think I'm a courtesan," the old woman said in jest and laughing.

Because everyone's identity was secret, there was no host or hostess to receive them. Rachel's gaze immediately searched the sea of humanity for her future husband, only to find that, hidden behind a mask and an elaborate costume, he looked like every other gentleman in her view. And then two strong arms swept her onto the dance floor. She heard his joyful laugh and felt the pressure with which he held her hand, and she knew it was her beloved, dressed as Sir Lancelot.

Which fitted him perfectly, she thought, smiling under her mask. She wanted to dance with him forever.

So she pretended they were on the dance floor alone. There were no bejeweled women, dressed like former queens and princesses, no gentlemen living out their fantasies of being warriors and rulers of a former time. The huge room, with a fire burning in the fireplace, candles burning in gargantuan chandeliers hanging from the high ceilings, making shadows on the crimson walls, was this night theirs. They danced the country dance, the quadrille, and the waltz. When a gentleman attempted to interrupt the dances by offering to dance with the Russian countess, he was rebuffed by Sir Lancelot.

"When a gentleman dances three dances in one evening with the same lady, he is announcing his intention of paying his addresses," he whispered when he and Rachel came together.

"And most likely they are saying Sir Lancelot is hogging the countess from Russia," Rachel retorted, laughing and loving every minute she was with him. How could she have thought to refuse his proposal just because she did not know her real name?, she mused.

"I love you," she said, and he shushed her, saying, "Don't let the *ton* hear you say that. They think it scandalous for a wife to love her husband."

"I'm not your wife yet."

"You will be, and soon. Ours will be a love match made in heaven, not one to the please the *ton* . . . or my brother."

"Mother M. says its God's will that we be together, that He joins soulmeets."

"I believe that, my beloved Rachel. We'll have our vows blessed by the vicar."

Rachel knew the extreme happiness had to end. She could not dance the night with this dashing man who had claimed her heart for all eternity. A gentleman, dressed as King Henry VIII, claimed her, and she danced with him. "Who is the uncouth gentleman who tried to claim you for the evening?" he asked.

"Sir Lancelot, your majesty," she replied, and old Henry VIII laughed with her.

Rachel looked around for Mother M. and saw her dancing with Lord Abshire. They made a comical sight, the sister's tall, black headdress fighting with Sir Lancelot's chin, and she lifting a lively leg to the lively music, showing a trim ankle and white stocking.

Another partner claimed Rachel, and then another, and another, many stepping lively. She knew immediately when she was face-to-face with her nemesis, her future husband's brother. She could only imagine the scowl hidden behind the mask, but she could smell his anger, and he wasted no time in stating the purpose for his presence at the ball. "Some unworthy chit of the lower orders is trying to snare my brother into wedlock, and I'm here to circumvent the announcement . . . if I can find her under all these foolish masks."

"How do you know she is unworthy? Just because she's of the lower orders does not make her unworthy."

"It makes her unworthy of the nobility, most especially the son of a duke. When the first duke died, I inherited the dukedom, and 'tis my duty to see that my siblings do not make fools of themselves. Why, he could have her without marriage."

Rachel started to slap his masked face, but knowing the commotion it would cause, instead, she kicked his shin, making sure it was the heel of her slipper that made contact with bone. When he squawked loud and clear and grabbed at his leg, she said in a loud voice, so that all who had stopped dancing could hear. "I'm so sorry to have stepped on your booted foot, your grace, and I pray there's not permanent damage."

With that, she left his presence, and Sir Lancelot was immediately at her side. "Did he say insulting things to you, my darling? I'll call him out—"

"You'll do no such thing. I'm sure the pain in his shinbone will keep him awake this night. But I'm afraid I revealed to him that it is I who is the unworthy chit trying to snare his brother into wedlock."

Since it was a costume ball, there was no dowager circle; everyone was expected to participate until the masks were removed. Dowager Countess Longworth had danced every dance, but she could not keep her mind on what she was doing. Her gaze kept wandering to the great room's entry door, and her ears were tuned for the sound of the butler's voice, who, at any moment, would announce the arrival of her beloved Ramey. He would not be in costume, having come straight from Grammacy Chase after Nora had told him of her whereabouts.

"May I stand for this dance," a voice said, and she looked around to see the gentleman give a leg. His build, covered by a costume of a Viking warrior, was that of Ramey's, and his voice . . . no, this man was too young to be him. She smiled under her mask and let the gentleman lead her onto the dance floor, where, embarrassingly, she missed a step. And then another.

"I beg your forgiveness," she said, trying again. "I'm a dowager, and it has been a long time since I've danced."

"Nothing to forgive," he said. "But I don't think 'tis lack of practice that falters your steps. Your thoughts are many miles away."

She laughed softly. "You're very kind." She thought *That's the trouble. I don't know how many miles away, or in which direction. I can only hope.*

Just then the music ceased, and a battle roll came from the orchestra. The dowager countess saw a man dressed as Sir Lancelot and a woman in a beautiful gold gown, the one announced in by the butler as Countess Tashia from Russia, climbing the stairs. A thundering silence fell over the dance floor as every dancer stopped dancing and turned to watch.

On the landing, Sir Lancelot and Countess Tashia turned to look down on the hushed, expectant crowd. It seemed to the dowager that everyone was holding their breath, including herself. And then Lancelot was saying, "I am happy to announce that Miss Storm and I will be married on Christmas day."

"You? Who are you?" a strong male voice shouted above the din of shocked voices. And then it was quiet again as the man on the stair landing removed his mask, "I am Trenton Abshire." He bowed from the waist. "My I present Miss Rachel Storm. I feel that I'm the luckiest man alive that she has consented to marry me. Miss Storm is my nephew's nanny."

Gasps went up from the women in the crowd, and the dowager heard more than one say, unbelievably, "He's marrying a lower order."

Slowly, so it seemed to the dowager countess, Lord Abshire removed his future bride's mask, looking at her lovingly, smiling down into her face, as if they were alone, not only in this huge room with people staring up at them, but alone in the world.

Tears brimmed the dowager's eyes. She knew the look; she knew how it felt to be in love. She thought the girl—she called her a girl because she appeared so young—very pretty.

The dowager, her heart pounding in her throat, pushed her way through the crowd to get a closer look. Did the girl have a smile she knew? She scolded herself. It was her imagination; the girl did not look like Ramey. Was she losing control? she asked herself.

And then Lord Abshire removed the gold lace cap that held captive his future bride's midnight-black hair. The dowager tried not to cry out and was not sure that she was successful, for the room began to spin, and she felt herself in a vortex of whirling voices; a dark and still world began whirling around her until she slipped silently to the floor, and into the darkness.

The dowager did not know how long she lay there, or what transpired while the world whirled around her. When she opened her eyes, Lady Talbert was bent over her and saying in a kind voice. "What is it, Countess Marcella? You've been out a long time." She held a soothing, cold cloth to the dowager's face with one hand while swinging a bottle of vinaigrette under her nose with the other. The dowager noted they were alone, in a room with elegant furnishing. She was on a fainting bench. Wall sconces held burning candles.

"How did I get here?" she asked.

"A gentleman carried you in."

The dowager tried to pull herself up. She said quickly, "Did I draw attention away from the happy couple on the landing?"

Lady Talbert gave a little laugh. "No. You swooned very quietly. I just happened to be nearby, and I asked the nearest male—at least he was dressed as a male and was big and tall—to carry you to this small receiving room on the first floor. I did not recognize you until I removed your mask. Are you feeling better?"

"Yes, I think so. I don't know what came over me."

She did know, and she acknowledged that she did, but she was not ready to share her thinking with anyone. What if she were wrong? Many a man and many a woman had midnight-black hair.

Mayhap it was a mirage she had seen.

"I think I should put you to bed for the night," said Lady Talbert.

"I must needs return to Grammacy Chase." She pushed herself up and leaned against the back of the fainting bench.

Lady Talbert looked askance. "But Countess, you've always spent the night at Talbert Hall after a social gathering."

"But this night is different. I'm expecting Ramey."

The dowager was glad that Lady Talbert did not argue about her leaving. She had to get away, to wait for Ramey. She must needs tell him about their child. Ramey would know how to handle the delicate situation.

Still, she could not forget the resemblance. If only she'd been close enough to look into Miss Storm's eyes . . . Ramey had such incredible blue eyes. "This Miss Storm your brother is going to marry, where did she come from? Did he not say she's your son's nanny?"

"Yes, and she loves little Frank very much."

The dowager asked again, "Where did she live . . . where did you find her? Good nannies are scarce."

"She was reared in Saint Cecilia's Home for Abandoned Children, near the hamlet of Bolventor. When she was nearing her eighteenth birthday, she ran away and came to Talbert Hall, thinking my husband was her dear papa, and that he would surely recognize her should they come face-to-face."

Twenty-eight

Five days passed and still the dowager countess's beloved had not arrived at Grammacy Chase. Christmas was less than a week away, and Lord Malvey had said Ramey would be in England by Christmas. The house was in sixes and sevens, the servants preparing each day for the stranger's arrival, and Nora trying in vain to calm her.

She told Nora about the girl who had been raised in an orphanage and was anxious to know her parentage.

"Did this Miss Storm favor your Ramey?" Nora asked.

"She had black hair, the blackest I've ever seen, just like his, but I was not close enough to see her eyes. I foolishly swooned, and then I ran away, thinking to wait for Ramey to come before I faced this girl who might be our daughter. I realize now I was frightened she would not be my baby." When the dowager next spoke, her voice was low and strained. "I had waited so long for the time I would see her, and then I was too frightened to make inquiries."

She started to cry, then stopped herself by sheer determination. She had often said that she had cried all the tears God had given her all those years ago. "Order tea, Nora. I have to plan what to do. I cannot live another day without knowing."

The answer came in the middle of the night. She would return to Talbert Hall and invite Lord Abshire and Rachel Storm to be married in the small chapel at Grammacy Chase on Christmas day. If necessary, she would play for sympathy, saying the old house was lonely. She would invite Lady Talbert and her son, anyone who wanted to come, and there would be dancing and merriment after the wedding. A great feast would be served.

"And I pray Ramey will have arrived by then," she said aloud to the emptiness that filled the room and engulfed her. What could be keeping him? She retrieved the age-yellowed handkerchief from the chiffonnier and held it to her breast. She could see beyond the windows it was snowing. Raising her lorgnette, she stared at the falling white flakes. The candle in the window—she burned one each night, to guide Ramey should he come—flickered in the darkness. When she realized she was cold, she stirred the dying embers in the fireplace and added more coal. Then, covering herself with a wool shawl, she waited for morning, at which time Nora argued, "You are not going out in this snowstorm."

But Nora's words were wasted. "I'll be all right. Snow doesn't stop the mail," said the dowager countess.

"You're not a mail carrier," Nora retorted, but she quickly realized that nothing she could say would stop the dowager from this day returning to Talbert Hall. Her chin was set in that familiar stubborn line. "I'll come with you," Nora said.

"You must needs stay here and watch for Ramey. He'll be here any day now."

Nora, shaking her head, wondered if the dowager had not developed windmills in her head. No sane person would go out into snow that was falling in sheets. A typical England Christmas, she mused, usually welcome, but now a hindrance, and there was nothing typical about what was going on at Grammacy Chase. She went to Cook and ordered nourishing food and hot coffee be prepared for the dowager countess to take with her, and then she went to ask the boy who would prepare the carriage to see that the bricks were exceptionally warm. "But not hot enough to burn the wraps, which should be thicker than usual."

"I don't know what I would do without you, Nora," the dowager said.

"If this keeps up, you will have to learn. I don't know how much anxiety I can take. 'Tis killing me. I'll be worried sick until you return."

The countess donned a huge Gypsy hat, made of bright red felt with a purple plume, and tied it under her chin. Her black cloak came to her boot tops and was fur-lined, as were the boots.

"If we find it too dangerous to travel, we'll stop at the posting inn until the snow lets up."

"We? Who's we?" Nora wanted to know, torn between anger at the dowager and worry for her.

"My driver and I. If he complains, we'll stop."

Nora gave a big sigh and shook her head and watched her leave, her back straight and her head held at that determined angle. The carriage was soon out of sight, with nothing but snow between it and the house.

The tall wheels sank into the deep snow as the six horses plunged into the thick whiteness. Settling herself into the deep squabs, the dowager immediately felt calmer. But one always did when one took action on whatever was the worry, she told herself. She was glad she had decided to go to Talbert Hall. Most likely her invitation would be well taken. On the night of the ball, after she had swooned and was alone with Lady Talbert, her ladyship had spoken of her plans to petition for a divorce from her husband. "A respite from home just might be well-taken," the dowager said aloud, and then her thoughts went to Rachel Storm. Could Miss Storm's resemblance to Albert Ramey be in her imagination?

Well, she would soon know. Surely she would know her own daughter should she touch her, or hear her speak. Would a mother not know? "A hurting heart reaches out for answers which are not there," she said aloud, wiping away a tear. She thought about Ramey, when he would come to Grammacy

Chase. In her mind's eye, she could see his wonderful smile; her heart listened for his wonderful laughter.

When Ramey comes . . .

So deep in thought was the dowager that she did not notice the approaching carriage until it was upon them, coming dangerously close to her own carriage in passing. A fleeting glimpse of the man sitting tall and straight, and wearing a high-crowned beaver, was all time allowed, and moments passed before she could let down the window and shout to her driver to stop. Which he did with a lurch, and before the driver could climb down from the box and help her, she practically tumbled out of the carriage and started running. Snow hit her face, and it was so deep on the ground it hindered her running. She fell, but quickly got up.

And then the carriage carrying the man stopped and then he was running to her.

The wind took his beaver, and his greatcoat flapped at his legs, but still he came, his arms outstretched.

"Ramey, Ramey," she said, as she ran into his arms. Even in the cold, with the snow covering their faces, and covering them as if they were statues, she felt the warmth of his body when he held her. The tears on his cheeks warmed her face.

She heard a sob and realized it came from her. Words would not come. All the things she had dreamed of saying at this moment would not, could not, escape her throat. He planted dozens of kisses on her upturned face, and she kissed him back, and every cell in her body thrummed with inexorable desire as he held her against his own hardness.

He whispered, "Oh, my love, my love," and then he released her and stepped back, looking at her and straightening her eschewed Gypsy hat. "It's been a long time," he finally said, his voice choked.

"But you're here now."

"And I have wonderful news. My cousin was successful in getting our marriage declared legal and your marriage to Lord Longworth set aside. He left a missive with his butler, then, not knowing just when I would arrive, he took himself off to a hunting lodge with the Prince Regent."

"I've always been your wife, and I hated being called a dowager," she said, smiling.

He laughed.

Oh, that wonderful laugh.

"We can't stand here all day in this snow. Where were you going? Shall we return to your home?"

"No" she said quickly. "I'm on my way to Talbert Hall, and I desperately need your presence. But we can stop at the posting inn for a repast, and to talk. I have so much to tell you."

"And I you. But first, I must needs send my driver on. Let me put you in your carriage before speaking with him."

He let down the step and gently handed her in. She tried to remember piling out of the carriage and could not, and for a moment she studied his face, now that he was not kissing her. Although older, he was still heart-stopping handsome. Gray hair showed at his temples, and his hair was no longer midnight black, but more like salt and pepper. His eyes were still incredibly blue.

"You're as pretty as ever," he told her, leaning into the carriage to gently stroke the tender curve of her jaw with his big hand. "I'll be back shortly."

"Would you please ask your driver to personally assure Nora that I'm wonderfully fine, that she can stop her worrying."

"At your service, my darling," he said, smiling at her and giving a snappy salute before turning to retrace his steps.

"Please call me Marcella . . . Marcella Ramey. Isn't that the most wonderful name. I can't hear it enough," she called after him, and he looked back and laughed and mouthed, "Lady Marcella Ramey."

Lady Marcella laughed. Because she was the daughter of a titled man, in truth, a duke, she was entitled to the courtesy title of "Lady." She watched as he retrieved his beaver and then went to speak to his driver, who handed out a small bag before cracking the whip over the horses' backs and tooling away, the wheels throwing snow behind them. She pinched herself and felt the pain.

Of course she was not dreaming, she scolded, laughing at herself as anxiously she watched her beloved's every move, drinking in the wondrous sight of his broad shoulders, his purposeful steps as, his head bent to the wind, he made his way back to her. The snow was still coming down in sheets.

At the posting inn, snow was banked high against the door. The place appeared deserted. Ramey quickly alighted from the carriage and pounded on the door with a brass knocker. "Someone has to be here," he said worriedly, giving several more loud knocks.

By then the driver had crawled down from the box and, going to speak with her ladyship, told her he feared the weather would not permit their traveling farther. " 'Tis getting where I can't tell the road from the ditch," he said, and she assured him that a comfortable place would be afforded him and the horses. A little giddy, she added, "I can only hope for the same for myself and my husband."

Looking askance, he proffered a hand and helped her from the carriage. "Yer husband? Yer ladyship, no disrespect meant, but I thought him dead. Has someone been funning yer workers?"

"No. 'Tis a strange story, but true. I fear I've been living the life of an impostor. Albert Ramey is my husband."

When the driver's eyebrows shot up to almost touch his three-cornered hat, she added, "I'll explain later. Now, we must needs worry about someone answering the door."

The inn door was opened by a man holding high above his white shaggy head a branch of lighted candles. His hair grew to touch his collarless shirt, which looked as if he might have slept in it. His wrinkled breeches had fared no better, her ladyship noticed.

"Are you crazy, traveling in weather like this?" he asked, but not harshly. Before Ramey could say indeed they were not crazy, the man stepped back, introduced himself as Nicolas. "Come in, come in," he said, "if you can wade the snow."

Trying to appear the model of decorum, Marcella was quickly swept off her feet by Ramey's two strong arms and carried inside the inn. They were laughing, and he kissed her soundly before he sat her down. Pitching the inn keeper a sovereign, he said, "Would you see to the horses and driver. Give them plenty of food and a warm place for the night."

Nicolas sauntered toward the door, took a heavy coat and fur cap from a coat tree by the door and put them on, then turned back to say, "Makes me no difference who you are, but you must needs register before you spend the night. As man and wife. Guard the inn's reputation, I do."

Left alone, Ramey whirled Lady Marcella about, then brought her back, to hug her to him. To her, it seemed utterly natural to have his arms around her, his warm breath stirring the tendrils of her hair. His laughter was light and caressing, and his every move exuded animal magnetism, that of a sleek leopard in a mating dance. She was glad he had not changed. She could not resist him in London, nor could she now. "Ramey, I'm glad you are home," she said, wanting to say more, wanting him with every cell of her thrumming body.

But there was so much she wanted to tell him, so much she wanted him to tell her. As they traveled in the carriage, he had told her about his escape from prison in Australia; his cousin had sent three men to manhandle guards and to get him on a ship to America, under one condition, that he not return to England, until the old Duke of Marcel was dead and buried under six feet of dirt. "I've never known Malvey to be afraid of anyone, except the old duke."

"My father was a formidable foe for anyone," she said. She did not tell Ramey about the baby, their daughter, or that she might be as close as Talbert Hall. That would come later.

Deftly removing her cloak and the big Gypsy hat, he looked

at her with his probing, iridescent blue eyes. "My eyes hungered for the sight of you, and now you are here, and I can see you, and hold you."

She was glad she had worn a new gown of red wool. For a fleeting second, she remembered the red gown she had worn to the old duke's deathbed.

Slowly he unwound the big coil of silvery hair that lay on her nape, combing it with his long fingers and letting it fall down her back. "It used to be brown," he said.

"The brown turned to silver the first year you were gone."

"Had I not been taken prisoner, I would have killed him," he said, and she shushed him, saying that was in the past. "We must needs live for today, and for tomorrow." He kissed her, and tears brimmed those wonderful blue eyes.

"For more than eighteen years, I've dreamed of this moment, and now I'm at a loss to know what to say. 'Tis like being a schoolboy again." His hands began moving over her, and then, feverishly, he buried his head in the scented cleft between her round breasts. She knew he was going to take her . . . there in the entry foyer of the posting inn. If she did not stop him.

"Ramey, there's so much I want to tell you," she said, and he countered with, "I've waited so long, my darling. Let's go upstairs. There must be plenty of empty beds."

She could not deny him, for she wanted him as much as he wanted her. They turned toward the stairs, only to have Nicolas open the door and say, "Oh, no yer don't. Yer ain't registered yet."

He was carrying their bags and the satchel of food Nora had prepared for the journey. "Smells like food in this satchel. I suggest yer find a table in the dining room and eat while I go upstairs and build a fire in the room I save for the nobility. Sure none of m'lords and m'ladies will be out on a day like this. Have more sense. I take it yer on your honeymoon and can't think straight."

Laughing, Ramey whispered to his wife, "A capital idea.

Mayhap he is the only sane one among us. I know I'm so full of longing, I can't remember my name."

In the dining room, a huge fire blazed orange and green and purple, and candles burned in wall sconces, and in chandeliers hanging from the ceiling. They chose a table near the fire, where, looking through the window, they could see that the snow had not abated. The sky was dark with heavy clouds.

"I think the problem, love," Ramey said, "is that there is so much to say that we don't know where to begin. And then there's this other thing; 'tis only natural for a man to want to make love to his wife. Which comes first?"

"Let's talk, Ramey," she said. "I have something very important to tell you. We have a child."

Twenty-nine

Amid the confusion of Christmas morning calls, balls, and soirees at first one country house and then another, and plans for her brother's marriage to Rachel Storm, Lady Talbert was negotiating with her husband's solicitor the terms of the divorce. He had suddenly appeared one day with the proposal that Lord Talbert would petition his peers in Parliament for the divorce; therefore, she would not make an appearance. Her ladyship was well aware of her husband's intent. He did not want her telling them what she knew of his underworld life.

After hours of consideration, she had decided that she did not object to his scheming. Should she file, it would most likely take years for the decree to be granted, and mayhap not be granted at all. The world of the nobility was a man's world, and the women could live in it as long as they produced heirs to the respective titles. The financial settlement, rather where she would live with the Talbert heir, was another question. It was Lord Talbert's desire that she remain at Talbert Hall. It was Lady Talbert's desire to move into town and take up the cause of begging children, thus preventing men of Lord Talbert's bent from using children for their pleasure.

Her ladyship had been surprised to discover this subconscious desire to make herself useful in the world. Although she loved little Frank with all her heart, she needed more. When she told the solicitor of her intent, he had shouted at her, "And be a bluestocking?"

She had laughed and said, "Mayhaps."

It was finally agreed that she would maintain Talbert Hall for when little Frank reached majority. It would be their country home, but a town house would be provided for them, well endowed with Talbert blunt. The solicitor had left, promising that the legal part of the divorce would be over rather quickly, no more than six months. Upon his departure, he had warned, "A woman who is divorced by her husband is cut by the *ton*." and her answer had been a smile.

There had been no mention of what would happen should Lady Talbert marry again, and that was exactly what she intended to do, just as soon as she fell in love. She felt sure that she could be a good wife, a good mother, and still contribute to society, and that did not mean the *ton*.

"This time brother Benford will have no say about whom I marry," she said, as she spun around the room, her heart as light as a feather in the wind. She could feel her brother's anger when he learned that she'd had the temerity to negotiate the terms of her divorce with the solicitor. His grace thought women were chattel owned by men.

Benford and his homely wife had departed Talbert Hall soon after Lord Abshire announced his engagement to Miss Storm. Admitting she was a prime article but berating his brother for choosing his wife from the lower orders, he stormed from the Hall with curse words for his siblings on his lips. If the marriage didn't disgrace the family, Lady Talbert's divorce from Lord Talbert would.

The spectacle made good fun for the other guests at the ball. The gentlemen spent the rest of the evening drinking, sniffing from elaborate snuff boxes, and slapping Abshire on the back and congratulating him on landing such a beauty, a diamond of the first water. No mention was made of the beauty being of the lower orders. This night it did not seem to matter, Lord Abshire noted. It would never matter to him.

The ladies, though envious, hovered around Rachel, wishing her the best of everything, while fluttering their fans and pretending to swoon when Lord Abshire's name was mentioned.

Rachel had laughed and told them she felt the same way, that she practically swooned every time he came in proximity. It was said in jest, but for her it was the truth. The sight of her future husband sent her into a spasm of wanting to be with him every moment of the day, and most especially every moment of the night. Oh, to lie in his arms and feel his body against hers, as if they were one. She found herself blushing. Could she be the same person who, only a short time back, had not known what it was like to be titillated by a man's touch? The same woman who had berated his lordship for ogling her bosom? Now, when she and Lord Abshire kissed, the kind of kiss that was so against propriety, she melted against him and never wanted him to stop.

"Oh, Mother M., I have to pinch myself to know that it is real. I fear that any moment I will wake up and find I've been dreaming. 'Tis wonderful to be in love." She turned and once again traversed the floor of the room she shared with the old woman. She wore a blue wool day dress. The fire in the fireplace crackled in its battle against the cold seeping in around the windows.

Mother M.'s turkey gobble shook as she spoke. "I feel the same way, love, that it's all a big wonderful dream. But 'tis really true. Two days hence, you will be Lord Abshire's bride."

"Can you stand my modeling my wedding gown just one more time?" Rachel asked, and the old woman laughed and told her she could model it as many times as she liked, as long as she did not let the bridegroom-to-be see her in it. "That would be bad luck," she added in all seriousness.

The wedding gown had been delivered only yesterday, by Madame deMoss, who had made it in such a hurry that she, sighing deeply, doubted every stitch was caught. "I so wanted to see the Russian countess, so I braved the weather to deliver the gown myself," the modiste crowed.

"I'm not a Russian countess," Rachel had quickly said. "I was reared in a home for abandoned children on the Bodmin

Moor. The Russian countess ruse was for the costume party only."

"In . . . in a home for abandoned children? I don't get your meaning . . . how could you be marrying nobility? It does not bear thinking on."

The modiste only had time to cluck twice before Mother M. gently, but firmly, pushed her to the side door through which she had entered, saying in a terse tone, "If the gown doesn't fit, I will make the necessary alterations. I sewed for Miss Storm when she was but a wee girl."

But the gown did fit, perfectly. Rachel stood before the looking glass admiring the white silk and lace creation, with short puff sleeves, a bodice that fit snugly under her round breasts, and a short train that swept her tracks. She turned, smiled, and hugged herself. She heard Mother M. suck in her breath, then say, " 'Tis the most beautiful wedding gown I've ever seen, Rachel. It makes your black hair even blacker."

Rachel realized the old woman was crying. Her voice went inaudible. "What are you saying, Mother M.? Is something wrong?"

"I was muttering to myself . . . I'm just so happy you've given up on trying to find your mama and papa. Just being Lord Abshire's wife will make you happy enough."

"That is very true Mother M., I shall be happy married to Trenton, but knowing who I am would make that happiness more complete. There's a corner of my heart which no one but a mama or a papa can fill. If I can't have both, and I'm certain my dear mama is dead, then I would gladly settle for my papa. But I truly hope 'tis not Lord Talbert, after all I've learned about him."

Under a glaring sun, the Longworth crested carriage plowed through the melting snow. After spending two days at the posting inn, while it snowed relentlessly, Lady Marcella Ramey and her husband Albert Ramey were now approaching Talbert

Hall. She looked at the towering edifice and wondered if her long-lost daughter truly worked there as a nanny to the nobility, when in truth, she was the granddaughter of a duke. But that did not signify. All she wanted was to find the child that was ripped from her breast those years ago. The baby's wail came to her, as if it were yesterday, and her chin quivered in expectation as she snuggled closer to her husband for comfort and reassurance.

After she had told him about the birth of their child, and about all that followed, her years of searching, not knowing whether the baby had been a girl or a boy until the valet had called her a she, Ramey had held her and, speaking in a tear-thickened voice, promised they would find their precious child. Bow Street Runners would be hired; he, himself, would participate in the search. No stone would be left unturned.

He took a locket that held a tiny picture of his mother from his waistcoat pocket. "Did this Rachel Storm look like her?" he asked, and Lady Marcella had despairingly said she did not know.

"There was something about her that reminded me of you. Later I thought it must needs have been her black hair. I'm so sorry I swooned and then left Talbert Hall as fast as I could, like a scared rabbit."

"We'll know soon," he said, and he repeated the words this day as Talbert Hall, in all its stately splendor, grew nearer. Lifting her gloved hand, he kissed the palm. "We'll know soon, my darling."

His touch sent a quicksilver thrill through her ladyship's body, and the warmth of his body, his voice, speaking with such confidence, warmed her and filled her spiritually. She was one with him. If doubts had momentarily occurred, the two days at the posting inn had proved her wrong. She smiled now, remembering. Their coming together had been as if those eighteen years plus of forced separation had never happened. For a man of forty summers, his virility was amazingly intact, and she had responded as she had in the gatekeeper's cottage on the Malvey estate, spiraling to the stars, climaxing time and time again, while he cried out in his own pleasure, calling her name. And then he had held her until their sated bodies stopped their trembling and sleep claimed them. She was his bride all over again. Now, thinking about it, she was almost sorry it had stopped snowing.

The thought brought a happy smile to her face, and then her thoughts turned back to what Ramey had said about where they would live. His cousin, Lord Malvey, the fifth earl of Morventor, had asked him to return to his estate in Lincolnshire as manager. His lordship would be living in France; his health was not the best and he thought the climate in the south of France better for it. And, too, upon his demise, Ramey would become the sixth earl of Moventor and would inherit the entailed property, as well as all of Lord Malvey's personal wealth.

She had thought much about Castle Mackinaw and had decided she wanted her and Ramey's daughter, when she was located, to have the old duke's last home. And she hoped the old duke was where he could watch the ultimate result of his mean manipulation of his daughter's life. "Then, things will have gone full circle," she said under her breath.

The carriage lurched to a stop in front of Talbert Hall. To the west, the sun was bidding the day goodbye, leaving behind streaks of brilliant orange, purple, and gold. As Ramey helped her from the carriage, she sucked the cold, sweet air into her lungs. For a moment he held her to him, to give her warmth from his body. Because of the cold, there was no groom waiting, and Ramey told the driver to take the carriage to the stables.

They had decided to seek Lord Abshire's advice on how and when to approach Miss Storm. When the butler opened to the knock on the huge door, Ramey told him who they were and that they wished to see Lord Abshire on important business.

The butler bowed and left, and when he returned, Lord Abshire was with him. Looking puzzled, he said, "I did not know it was you calling, Lady Longworth. The butler said—"

Ramey interrupted with a little laugh. " 'Tis a long story, your lordship. May we indulge your time and tell it to you?"

Stepping back, Lord Abshire invited them to come in out of the cold, and after the butler had taken their coats, with a sweep of his arm, his lordship waved them into the crimson receiving room. Silently they walked toward the welcoming fire at the far end of the room. He offered tea and they refused.

Her ladyship felt awkward, and she was extremely glad Ramey was there to tell the incredible story to Lord Abshire. She looked at her husband. If he felt any awkwardness, he did not show it. He stood tall and straight, his right arm resting on the mantel. Lord Abshire sat in a wing-back chair, and she sat in its mate.

Without preliminaries, Albert Ramey began: "Marcella's marriage to Longworth has been set aside . . ."

Lord Abshire sat forward in his chair and exclaimed, "I don't take your meaning. Our laws are very strict about setting aside a marriage."

"It was never a marriage, because she was legally married to me at the time her father forced her into a union with Lord Longworth. The old duke had all records of our marriage destroyed, with the exception of a duly signed marriage license, which held the stamp of the sovereign. My cousin, Lord Malvey, the fifth earl of Morventor, held that, and when he learned I was to return to England, he sought help from the Prince Regent."

Lord Abshire, looking stunned, sat back in his chair and listened intently while Ramey talked.

Lady Marcella marveled at how well her husband remembered every detail she had told him. He did not dwell on his life in the Australian prison, or his years in America, only that he was forced to live there until the Duke of Marcel's death.

His voice breaking more than once, he told of his dear wife suffering at the hands of the old duke, the forced marriage to

Lord Longworth, and at last he spoke of the child. "A child was born to our union, but the old duke snatched her away at birth. As Longworth's dowager countess, Marcella has spent years and all her blunt looking for our daughter. Now we have reason to believe Rachel Storm is our long-lost child, that the old duke placed her in the home for abandoned children when she was born, then claimed to his valet that she had died."

Ramey wiped tears from his eyes before continuing, "The night of the costume ball here at Talbert Hall, Lady Talbert told my wife of Miss Storm's search for her dear papa . . ."

There, it was out, thought Lady Marcella, the whole incredible story, and Lord Abshire muttered, "The devil take me. 'Tis incredulous, but, if true, my Rachel will be the happiest girl in the Kingdom."

"We thought to speak with you first," said Marcella. "We'll accept your guidance. Your wedding day is two days away, and we would not want to take from that."

"I pray 'tis true," said Lord Abshire, his brown eyes shiny with tears.

Albert Ramey stepped forward and handed the locket with his mother's picture in it to his lordship. "This is a picture of my mother."

"Do you see a resemblance, Lord Abshire?" her ladyship asked anxiously. "I did not see Rachel Storm up close . . . her black hair and smile reminded me of Ramey. That is when I foolishly swooned."

Lord Abshire studied the portrait for a long moment. "This could be Rachel. There's that same widow's peak, and the same bottomless blue eyes." His voice was unsteady when he said, "I'll go fetch her."

After gingerly handing the locket back to Albert Ramey, he turned and hurried up the winding stairs. Marcella went to stand by her Ramey. He placed his arm around her shoulders and held her to him. She felt his uneven breathing, which matched her own. And then she saw them coming, Rachel Storm and Trenton Abshire. His arm was around her protectively as they hurriedly descended the stairs, the sound of their boots hitting the polished wood steps and resounding out into the large room.

Her ladyship wanted to run to them, but she stayed by the fire with her husband, pulling strength from his muscle-hard body. "Hold steady, sweetheart," he said, and his arm tightened around her shoulders as, with trembling hands she reached out to take Rachel's hands in her own. Lord Abshire's voice seemed far away when he said, "Rachel, may I present Lady Marcella and Mr. Albert Ramey."

Sitting on a sopha beside Lord Abshire, Rachel listened intently as the story was told by Lady Marcella Ramey, who had moved to sit in the huge wing-backed chair, her hands demurely in her lap. Her ladyship's voice was low, sometimes not much more than a whisper. Her husband stood behind her, his hand touching her shoulder, and sometimes, when his wife's voice choked and she could not go on, he talked for her.

He left her once, to hand the locket with his mother's portrait to Rachel, who looked at it in unbelievable wonderment. She could be looking at her own portrait, she thought. Even the set of their chins were the same. And there was that slight widow's peak. With trembling hands, she held it to her breast.

Then, the room became loudly quiet. Rachel wanted to shout and cry and dance. She hugged Lord Abshire without restraint, and then, rising from the sopha, rushed to kneel in front of the woman who had given her life, to feel, for the first time, a mother's hands touch her face, the hot tears of a mother's love drop onto her hands, heard the whispered words, "My baby . . . my lovely daughter."

She pushed Rachel's black hair back from her face and kissed her cheek. Rachel hugged her and felt her trembling, heaving shoulders, heard her heart-wrenching, silent sobs.

Through tears streaming from her eyes, Rachel smiled up

at Albert Ramey, who was smiling broadly and beaming his love. In a quiet, choked voice, she said to both of them, "What a wonderful Christmas present, to at last have a mama and a papa . . . and to have a real name. In wonder and awe, she said slowly, "Rachel Ramey"

Outside, in the pearlescent semidarkness, a gentle wind moved through the snow-laden trees, and the moon was rising on the distant white hillocks.

Thirty

The black-and-gold barouche, its snow wheels making it as high as a first-floor window, ponderously plowed through the snow on its way to London. Inside the handsome carriage was George Augustus, the Prince Regent, and Lord Malvey, the fifth earl of Morventor. It was Christmas day, and London was two days travel away. "Fustian, Morventor," said the Prince Regent, "Mayhap we should have stayed at the lodge. At least we would've had a roasted goose for Christmas dinner."

Lord Malvey laughed. "Is your belly all you think about, Augustus?" They had been friends since they were in leading strings, and Lord Malvey felt comfortable using the Regent's given name. Few people did. In truth, he thought, few people approved of the Prince Regent. Many called him Prinny, but not to his face. "I'm sure the posting inn will have a goose, a duck, or something for weary travelers."

"Most likely mutton, which I detest," the Prince Regent countered, and then they were quiet.

Having been snowbound at the hunting lodge for nigh a week, it seemed uncanny to Lord Malvey that now warm sunshine bounced off the banked snow, and off the carriage windows. He was comfortable enough, with the exception of his feet, which had become quite cold. The bricks had long since lost their warmth. Both wore long greatcoats, top boots over heavy breeches, and fur-lined gloves. Black beavers kept their heads warm.

"We are near Grammacy Chase," Lord Malvey said. "Do

you suppose they'd have a Christmas goose cooked." The words were said in jest, but suddenly the idea appealed enormously to him. He was anxious to see if his cousin had arrived from America.

"Isn't that the Longworth estate?" asked the Prince Regent.

"Lord Longworth is dead. 'Tis his dowager who lives at Grammacy Chase. She's the late Duke of Marcel's daughter—the one you helped get her marriage to Longworth set aside because she was already married to my cousin Albert Ramey."

"The devil take me. I do believe that's the most tragic love story I've ever heard. I was only too glad to undo the damage the old king brought upon those people. One can only think he was in a spell of madness when the act took place." He shook his head. "Imagine sending a man to prison on some trumped-up charge. No proof whatsoever, except what the old duke furnished. Fabricated, of course."

"All's well that ends well," said Lord Malvey, feeling in high spirits. "What say, we drop by and see if my cousin has made it from America. He wrote that he'd be in England before Christmas, but you know how crossing the ocean is, ship's sometimes late, sometimes early."

The Prince Regent pushed himself forward on the squab. "A capital idea, Morventor. I'd like to see her ladyship's face if her husband has returned to her. Even if he isn't there, as you say, there'll surely be a Christmas goose."

Lord Malvey chuckled. The Prince Regent was known for his love of food, and for being a romantic. When he loved, he loved desperately, often shedding tears when expressing his affection for his new, or old, love. Letting the window down, Lord Malvey called to the driver to turn on the next road south. It was not his carriage, but when one was with the Regent, one, in the absence of a servant, performed such tasks as directing the driver.

Silence ensued, and it was not long before they were on the ridge above Grammacy Chase. Below, in the flatland, sat the magnificent, but not ostentatious, manor house, smoke curling up from its chimney pots. The place looked warm and inviting, and Lord Malvey could picture himself sitting in front of a huge fire, his cold feet stretched out, mayhap a glass of port in his hand to warm his insides.

"May we see Dowager Countess Longworth?" he asked the powdered, gold-laced footman who answered the knock on the door. Before Lord Malvey could stop himself, he blurted out, "Where's the butler?"

"Her ladyship's husband has returned from America, sir. So she is no longer Dowager Countess Longworth, and if she were, she would not be receiving," said the footman, looking smug. "And the butler is below stairs, in the chapel. There's a wedding taking place."

The Prince Regent stepped forward. "Mayhap if you told her ladyship the Prince Regent is calling, she would all at once be receiving."

Lord Malvey, elated to learn his cousin had reached England by Christmas, as he had said that he would, spoke quickly. "Do not disturb her. No doubt she and my cousin are renewing their vows, and I doubt if she knew the king himself was calling, she'd stop the ceremony. Tell us where the wedding is taking place. I promise we won't disturb the ceremony."

The footman offered to take their greatcoats and beavers, but Lord Malvey refused, saying, "We're still quite cold. We'll remove them later."

"Then follow me," said the footman.

They followed him to a door that opened to stairs leading downward, and then through a long hall to two huge double doors.

The hallway was semidark, lighted only by globed lanterns, but when the doors opened, they were suddenly awash in warm sunlight coming through tall stained-glass windows. It took Lord Malvey's eyes a moment to adjust to the light, and then he saw that the pews were filled, and that servants in black bombazine and high livery lined the walls.

Little wonder the house seemed so quiet when they entered,

the servants were all here, he thought. Looking at the pew holders's backs, he could not distinguish his cousin. A woman in the black habit of a nun sat at the pianoforte, playing an old-time, favorite hymn: "Because Thou Has't Said," written in 1748 by Charles Wesley. In a clear, strong voice, she began singing the words, the look of pure happiness on her face.

Before the altar stood a lovely young woman with long black hair and dressed in a white wedding gown. Standing beside her was a man dressed in long black tails and a white shirt with high collar points. His shoulders were broad and square to his body, and he held the young lady's hand, while looking into her eyes.

The music stopped.

"Oh, isn't this lovely," whispered the Prince Regent.

Unobtrusively the two hunters stepped inside the chapel and closed the doors behind them.

"Will you take this woman to be your lawfully wedded wife . . ." the black-frocked vicar was saying, and in no time at all, so it seemed to Lord Malvey, the vows had been read and answered appropriately, and the groom was kissing his bride.

The only trouble was, Lord Malvey thought, it was not Albert Ramey and Lady Marcella.

He heard clapping of hands, laughter, voices calling out for a life of happiness. Behind him, the doors opened, and once again music poured from the pianoforte, filling the little chapel with another joyful hymn about God's love. The bride and groom rushed down the middle aisle and out into the hall, and then out of sight.

Lord Malvey and the Prince Regent stepped far to the side to allow the wedding guests to depart the chapel. Still wearing their greatcoats and holding their beavers in their hands, no one seemed to notice the pair of interlopers. A young boy, with spiked red hair and about eight, and dressed to the nines in royal blue breeches, an embroidered waistcoat, and a splendidly tailored coat of lighter blue superfine, passed by.

"That's Napoleon," a voice from behind Lord Malvey said. Turning, he saw his cousin Albert Ramey, and standing beside him was the woman who had waited all these years for his return to England. Lord Malvey was struck again by her lovely face and her youthful figure. Clinging to Ramey's arm, she smiled up at Lord Malvey and asked, "How can we ever thank you?"

"Be happy, that will be thanks enough. As you know, Ramey is my heir. So you see my help was not altogether magnanimous. I inherited the earldom from my father, and I would hate to see it go to some stranger." Affectionately, he clapped Ramey on the shoulder. "This man is like a brother to me, or better yet, like my son. I'm only sorry that you were kept apart and cannot give me grandchildren."

He then turned and introduced the Prince Regent, who clearly felt out of place in his hunting attire. "Who was the lovely lady getting married?" he asked after the introductions had been acknowledged.

Albert Ramey and Lady Marcella spoke in unison: "Our daughter Rachel. The bridegroom is Lord Trenton Abshire."

Lord Malvey looked askance, and a frown formed between his dark eyes. He was a man past his prime, with an autocratic nose and hair that was more gray than its original brown. He had lost his young wife in childbirth and had never remarried. It was believed by those who knew him that this accounted for his devotion to his cousin Albert Ramey. "Your daughter? The devil take me!" he exclaimed. "I . . . I don't get your meaning."

"You will," said Albert Ramey. He took his cousin's arm. "Come along. My wife and I will tell you the whole of it."

They walked up the stairs and went to a small sitting room used only by the family. The Prince Regent offered to excuse himself from this family matter, but Albert Ramey would not hear of his going elsewhere while they talked, saying that, according to Lord Malvey's note, he, the Prince Regent, had been helpful in getting the Longworth marriage set aside.

Lord Malvey removed his coat and then took the Regent's

from him, hanging them on a coat rack near the door. "You've been in on this matter for sometime now, Augustus, and you've been a tremendous help. Why should you not hear the rest of the story?"

A fire burned in the cozy room while the story of Rachel's existence was being told, even the part about her coming to Talbert Hall posing as a nanny and how Lord Abshire had fallen instantly in love with her. When it was over, tears were streaming from the Prince Regent's eyes, and Lord Malvey, dumbfounded upon learning about the child, said, "I have a feeling there will be many heirs to the earldom that Ramey will be inheriting upon my demise."

"I hope your demise is not for a long while," Ramey said, meaning it. Talk then turned to Lord Talbert. The Prince Regent was well aware of the man's unsavory life which Talbert attempted, without much success, to keep hidden from his constituents and his peers. When the subject of Lady Talbert's divorce from her husband came up, the Prince Regent promised, "I will see she's not cut by society."

Lady Marcella thanked him profusely. "Lady Talbert is a kind, deserving woman. Her wont is to prove herself useful in some way, as well as to eventually fall in love and remarry."

"A brave step, seeking a divorce from an MP," Lord Malvey said.

After that, the Prince sat for a long while, his thoughts inward while the others chatted about how life had its twists and turns. He thought about his own life, how he had been forced into a marriage with Caroline of Brunswick, his revulsion of her, and how his petition for a divorce would most likely be denied. It hurt, the way people had turned against him, even booing him when he went out. They didn't understand, he thought, what the princess was about. Having gone through so much, he had been eager to help when Lord Malvey had come to him regarding his cousin's plight.

Thinking on it, a pleasant feeling came over the Prince Regent, and he smiled to himself. He felt proud that in a small way he had contributed to someone's happiness. Suddenly a warm feeling engulfed him. From somewhere in the house, Christmas music was bouncing off the rafters and floating in and dancing around his heart. And he wasn't sure, but he thought he smelled food.

"Oh, Ramey, I'm filled with the most exquisite joy," said Lady Marcella Ramey. She held her husband's arm as they looked out over the dance floor. Their darling Rachel and Lord Abshire were dancing the waltz, their eyes locked, both smiling, and when they came together his lips mouthed, "I love you." And then the couple would laugh.

"We have much to be thankful for," Ramey answered in a thoughtful way. For a moment his mind went back to those black days in prison, how hope and his faith in a Higher Power had kept him alive. Someday he would tell his Marcella the whole of it, but not now. He wanted nothing to mar these precious moments of happiness. He, too, looked at their daughter dancing with her husband, and tears filled his eyes. "My cup runneth over," he said under his breath. To Marcella, "My love, 'tis a perfect Christmas," and she agreed.

Soon others were dancing, Lady Talbert with Lord Malvey, even Hannah, Frank's wet nurse, was dancing with the butler, and Napoleon with Nora. The Prince Regent was cutting the light fantastic with Mother M.

Marcella was glad she had hired a full orchestra for the occasion. It had not been easy finding capable musicians on such short notice, but she had promised a huge bonus.

She thought back over the day. At first light, she had exchanged presents with the servants, saying Father Christmas had come to Grammacy Chase, and then two carriages had arrived with the retinue from Talbert Hall. A huge breakfast had been served, after which, in private, she gave Rachel the gifts she had, for eighteen years, bought for her. They had cried and hugged and talked for what seemed like hours. The gifts Marcella had bought for a son, when she did not know the gender of her child, were put aside. "We'll save these for your first son," she told Rachel.

"And my daughter will wear these tiny pink booties you made for my first Christmas."

Ramey's words brought her to the present. "What are you thinking of, love?" He looked at her with devouring eyes.

Eyes as blue as the morning sky, Lady Marcella thought. She said to him, "I was thinking that I'd like for you to dance me over to the mistletoe, and then I would like for you to kiss me."

He laughed. "That's a capital idea, but first we must needs dance with our children, I with our daughter, and you with her husband."

With his arm around her tiny waist, they moved gracefully out onto the dance floor, the hem of her rose-colored silk gown trailing behind her. Tilting her head back, she smiled up at him, and he said to her, "No queen has ever been more regal than you, nor has one ever been as strong. I love you, Marcella Ramey, with all my heart."

She could not speak, so great was her happiness, and when they were beside Rachel and Lord Abshire, they exchanged partners, and the dance went on, in their hearts as well as on the highly polished dance floor.

Then everybody danced with everybody; servants were pulled onto the dance floor, laughter fought with the music for dominance. Mother M., crossing herself and crying with joy, thanked God for the many blessings he had bestowed upon this wonderful family, who had adopted her as one of their own. She found Napoleon and advised him to tell the Prince Regent that someday he would be available to be his architect, which Napoleon did. The Prince Regent laughed and spoke encouraging words, making the former London thief strut with pride.

Later, much later, a huge dinner was served, with a big brown goose gracing the long, heavily laden table.

A touch of merry had truly come to Grammacy Chase,

thought Lady Marcella Ramey as she lifted her glass and wished everyone a very, very Merry Christmas.

They all responded in kind, holding their own glasses high, saying in unison, "Merry Christmas to you, your ladyship."

Thirty-one

"I suppose your brother will approve of your marriage since I'm the granddaughter of a duke," Rachel said.

"And don't forget the dowry. Castle Mackinaw and two thousand acres is no small consideration, and wealth speaks to his grace's heart." Lord Abshire laughed and pulled her down onto his lap. Underneath a blue satin robe, he was naked. "I don't give a fig what my brother approves or disapproves of. You're my wife, and I would have been just as happy to marry you with your name Storm." He kissed her soundly. "I'm just ever so thankful you won't be running around the countryside flailing a false resume in someone's face, looking to be some child's nanny."

"Oh, Trenton, was I so awful?"

"No. That ingenious idea brought you to me."

"And Napoleon to Eton. Trenton, do you suppose we can adopt him?"

"Why not? He can be the first of the great number of children we will have, given time." He gave his wry grin. "It will take a considerable number to fill a castle." His hand gently squeezed her firm breast.

"Oh that reminds me of something else I had planned to ask you. I'm not inclined to living in such a large place. I think it a capital idea to make Castle Mackinaw a home for abandoned children, and Mother M. can live there. If we lived nearby, I would be only too happy to establish a school in one of the many rooms. Lady Marcella . . . my mama . . . says the place is huge beyond one's imagination. And beautiful, sitting on a hill, like a crowned jewel."

Lord Abshire's laughter filled the room. They were in the bridal chamber Countess Marcella had had hastily prepared. A fire smoldered in the fireplace, a single candle burned dimly in a sconce on the wall, and a swatch of moonlight cut across the high bed. Lord Abshire eyed the bed. "My dear Rachel, do I detect hesitancy on your part to take care of the business at hand, like my doing what I've desperately wanted to do from the moment I first laid eyes on you?"

"Why Trenton Abshire, I have no idea what you are talking about." She was laughing.

"I think you do," he said, and he kissed the white flesh that pushed above the low neckline of her white nightdress.

Rachel thought that she would swoon. His lordship's lips felt wonderfully good on her bosom and delicious heat began to suffuse her body. She managed to say in a teasing way, "You couldn't have wanted to kiss me there. My bodice was buttoned to my neck."

"A man worth his salt uses his imagination," said his lordship as his lips moved to kiss her face, her incredible blue eyes, and her lips, which were open and willing. His arms strained to pull her closer to him. He felt her heartbeat pounding against his own. "Oh, dear God," he murmured in a guttural voice.

He carried her to the bed and lay her down, and, after quickly removing his robe and flinging it onto a chair, he joined her in the folds of the satin-covered feather mattress. "Merry Christmas, my darling wife. I promise to love you more next Christmas than now, and each Christmas after that for as long as we live."

"And I will love you just as much," she whispered, her arms opening to him. Tears of happiness pushed at her eyes.

And then the love dance began.